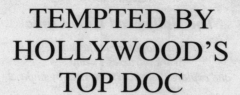

TEMPTED BY HOLLYWOOD'S TOP DOC

BY
LOUISA GEORGE

PERFECT RIVALS...

BY
AMY RUTTAN

MILLS

Welcome to…

The Hollywood Hills Clinic

*Where doctors to the stars
work miracles by day—
and explore their hearts' desires by night…*

When hotshot doc James Rothsberg started
the clinic six years ago he dreamed of a
world-class facility, catering to Hollywood's biggest
celebrities, and his team are unrivalled in their fields.
Now, as the glare of the media spotlight grows, the
Hollywood Hills Clinic is teaming up with the pro bono
Bright Hope Clinic, and James is reunited
with Dr Mila Brightman…the woman he jilted at the altar!

When it comes to juggling the care of Hollywood A-listers
with care for the underprivileged kids of LA *anything* can
happen…and sizzling passions run high in the shadow of
the red carpet. With everything at stake for James, Mila
and the Hollywood Hills Clinic medical team their biggest
challenges have only just begun!

Find out what happens in the dazzling

The Hollywood Hills Clinic miniseries:

Seduced by the Heart Surgeon
by Carol Marinelli

Falling for the Single Dad
by Emily Forbes

Tempted by Hollywood's Top Doc
by Louisa George

Perfect Rivals…
by Amy Ruttan

Look out for another four titles from
The Hollywood Hills Clinic over the next couple of months!

TEMPTED BY HOLLYWOOD'S TOP DOC

BY
LOUISA GEORGE

MILLS &
BOON

Published in Great Britain 2016
By Mills & Boon, an imprint of HarperCollins*Publishers*
1 London Bridge Street, London, SE1 9GF

© 2016 Harlequin Books S.A.

*Special thanks and acknowledgement are given to Louisa George
for her contribution to* The Hollywood Hills Clinic *series.*

ISBN: 978-0-263-25446-4

Dear Reader,

I have to admit I'm fascinated by celebrities and all things Hollywood, so when I was invited to take part in the Hollywood Hills Clinic continuity I was thrilled! Having a screenwriter heroine was a dream, and I was able to indulge my interest in films and Los Angeles and the quirkiness of a place where things are rarely what they seem.

Of course having a grumpy doctor hero who just doesn't understand the whole 'celebrity thing' was a perfect foil for a heroine who lives and breathes it. But sparks fly as neurosurgeon Jake has to learn how to navigate in a very foreign world. Both totally work-focused and ambitious, neither Lola nor Jake is looking for a relationship, so they fight the sparks all along the way!

I do hope you enjoy Jake and Lola's story—and all the other books in the Hollywood Hills Clinic continuity.

I love to hear from readers, so do look me up on louisageorge.com. While you're there sign up for my newsletter to get all my book news and release dates.

Happy reading!

Louisa x

To my Zumba buddies Jackie, Sue,
Roisel, Yenny and Avril.

I can't think of a better way to start the day
than dancing and having fun with friends.

I'm very lucky to have you guys in my life.
Thank you xx

Having tried a variety of careers in retail, marketing and
nursing, **Louisa George** is thrilled that her dream job of writing
for Mills & Boon means she gets to go to work in her pyjamas.
Louisa lives in Auckland, New Zealand, with her husband, two
sons and two male cats. When not writing or reading Louisa
loves to spend time with her family, enjoys traveling, and adores
eating great food.

Books by Louisa George

Mills & Boon Medical Romance

Midwives On-Call at Christmas
Her Doctor's Christmas Proposal

One Month to Become a Mum
Waking Up With His Runaway Bride
The War Hero's Locked-Away Heart
The Last Doctor She Should Ever Date
How to Resist a Heartbreaker
200 Harley Street: The Shameless Maverick
A Baby on Her Christmas List
Tempted by Her Italian Surgeon

Visit the Author Profile page
at millsandboon.co.uk for more titles.

Praise for
Louisa George

'*The Last Doctor She Should Ever Date* is a sweet, fun, yet
deeply moving romance. This book just begs to be read, and
I would definitely recommend this book and any other ones
written by Louisa George to all contemporary romance fans.'
—*Harlequin Junkie*

CHAPTER ONE

'LOLA! WHERE ARE YOU? Lola!' The sing-song screech came from inside the trailer.

Outside the trailer, Lola Bennett came to a halt and took a long calming breath. When that ran out she took another one. And…

So, it seemed calm would be eluding her today.

Behind her she heard muttered grumbles between the director, the assistant producer and the leading man. Irrational though it was, she felt guilty that the woman who employed her was ramping up the film budget and delaying filming because of mild stomach cramps, no doubt brought on by an overdose of her large kale and wheatgrass breakfast smoothie.

Lucky, Lola told herself. *Dream job. Steps to the stars. Foot in the door…*

Phooey. Being personal assistant to A-lister Cameron Fontaine was probably some poor misguided soul's dream job, but for Lola the constant demands were fast turning into a nightmare. Sometimes she thought the waitressing job had been preferable…but then all she had to do was look around her and breathe in the hallowed Hollywood air, see the actors going over their scripts—scripts like the one she was working on—and feel the shiver of excitement course through her. And she knew she was exactly where she wanted to be: Los Angeles. She was here, finally here. The only place on earth where she could achieve her crazy, wild dreams. The City of Angels.

All would be well, if only Cameron Fontaine could be remotely angelic. Once? Too much to ask?

'Lola!' Clearly there was nothing wrong with Miss Fontaine's vocal cords.

'Yes, Miss Fontaine?' Lola swung open the trailer door, letting the heavily perfumed air—a perfect blend of cedarwood, frankincense, sandalwood and lemon balm aromatherapy for clarity and focus today—disperse enough for her to enter without risk of asphyxiation. Then she took a risk and stepped in, with her usual fixed smile. It would all work out well. *Smile and work. Smile and work.* 'Hello! I hope you're feeling better? Here's the paracetamol you asked me to get. And your single-shot decaf latte with cashew milk.'

'You are such a honey.' The leading lady lay on the white leather couch, a hand at her brow, and gave a *brave me* smile. Lola had seen her working on that particular grimace in her large gilt bathroom mirror more than once. 'Tell me, sweetie, what's the gossip from the set? Are they panicking yet? I'll bet that old maid of a director is sweating. Tell them I'll be out soon. I just need to get my strength back.'

'Maybe you should eat something solid, rather than just juicing?'

'You're joking, right? I have to get into this teeny costume every day for the next few weeks.' Cameron mopped at her forehead with the back of her hand. 'And get hold of that doctor…what's his name? Kim? Get him on the phone. Tell him I need to see him again.'

'Oh?' Maybe Cameron really was sick, instead of acting or just plain attention-seeking? Before taking this job,

Lola had seemingly been the only person in the whole world who had had trouble trying to work out the difference between her boss's award-winning talent and her award-winning time-wasting. She'd stopped short of calling her a diva, but that didn't stop the glossies naming her as one. Having got to know her a little more, Lola was reframing Cameron as a hard-working actress with high standards, who wasn't afraid of asking for what she wanted. She could learn something from that. Although the diva did sometimes take centre stage. 'Of course. Yes. I'll get him right away.'

First, she cracked the seal on a fresh bottle of mineral water and poured it into a glass tumbler.

'Lola, what are you waiting for? Phone him.'

'I'm getting you a drink so you can take your tablets. Let's get them into your system and starting to work.' It was going to be a very long day, and Lola would be very glad when she fell into bed later with a good book to whisk her away from the reality of her life. Which hadn't turned out exactly how she'd hoped. No studio had optioned her script, no director had even read it so far. More than once she'd thought about returning home to London...but she needed to give herself a fair chance here, not risk the humiliation of going home and admitting she'd not just failed, but lied to her family too. And, God knew, even though some days she hated it, she needed to keep this job to pay the exorbitant rent on her shabby apartment. And eat. 'Would you like me to get the studio nurse? She's here and available, and I'm sure she wouldn't mind—'

'A *nurse*? A nurse? Honey, I'm award-winning. I need a *doctor*. I need that Kim doctor.' And with that Cameron closed her eyes. Conversation over.

Lola observed her for a few seconds. It didn't need

any kind of medic to see that the actress was in fine health. Her blonde hair shone, she was beautifully pink, breathing normally with a small secretive smile on those camera-ready lips. But Lola was nothing if not dutiful. She pulled out her phone and dialled.

'Hello!' She'd been briefed by Cameron to always converse with a smile in her voice. 'Is this The Hollywood Hills Clinic? Yes? Great! I have Cameron Fontaine here and she needs to see the doctor. Wait, I'll just ask.' Lola cradled the phone to her shoulder and whispered, 'Is it an emergency, Miss Fontaine?'

A perfectly plucked eyebrow rose on a serene, pain-free face. 'It depends what they mean by emergency. *I* would like to see a doctor—so, yes, they should act quickly.'

'But is it a matter of life or death?'

'I suppose…' A reluctant pout. A dramatic pause. 'Not really.'

'Are you dying, Miss Fontaine?'

'Oh. No. No. Of course I'm not *dying*. But don't tell them that, obviously.' Cameron sat up elegantly and straightened her space desert warrior costume, putting little strain on the perfectly honed abdominal muscles that had been on the front of every magazine last month as she'd *frolicked* in the waves in Hawaii—while Lola had been left in LA to supervise a spring clean of Cameron's Bel Air home, take the dogs for grooming, organise a lunch for fifty for Cameron's return…*yada, yada*…

Lola sighed—inwardly, of course—and spoke to the receptionist. 'Please ask him to come as soon as you can. Thank you…I will, yes.' Lola passed along the message. 'The doctor will be here soon. He's in the middle of a surgery, but will pop over when he's finished.'

'Pop over. You're such a sweetie. Say it again…' Cameron gave a real smile now. 'Say it again.'

'Pop over.'

'Pop! Oh, my, I do love your English accent. Just heavenly. Teach me?'

'Yes! Of course!' Clearly, whatever ailed Miss Fontaine would have to wait. But Lola had no doubt that the pain would resurface at exactly the same time as the doctor.

'Excuse me, Dr Lewis, there's another call for you.'

'Another one? Not now,' Jake Lewis barked across the OR at his surgical assistant. 'I told you, I don't want to know until I've finished here.'

'But it's the studio. They won't—'

'Not now.' Jake sucked in the antiseptic air and steadied himself. Refocused on his patient, a nineteen-year-old quarterback with a diagnosis of type-two neurofibromatosis: an incessant ringing in his ears, increasing left-arm numbness and a sudden penchant for falling over. All pointing to a large tumour on his vestibular nerve, which had been confirmed by scans.

With enough luck and Jake's skill, the boy might well be able to catch and pass a ball after this surgery. He would, hopefully, also be able to hear again—although, he might not. He would also probably never fulfil his lifelong dream of playing at a high level in the NFL. The disease process was slow, but there wasn't always a great prognosis long term. This kid's future was on the line and someone wanted Jake to see an actor about, what— an irritating cough?

And, yeah, maybe he was being an assumptive ass, but in his experience there hadn't ever been a need for a neurosurgeon on a film set during the normal day-today scheduling. Emergencies—yes. But this wasn't an emergency, they'd said so already. The first time they'd called. And the second…

The assistant hesitated, the phone still in his out-stretched hand. 'But…they…you…'

'Didn't you tell them last time? If it's an emergency they need to call 911 and I'll meet them in the ER, other-wise I will be there as soon as I've finished this complex neurofibroma surgery. If they don't understand what that is, explain, in words of less than two syllables, that I'm a brain surgeon, and ask them to guess what I'm busy with right now.'

When James Rothsberg had head-hunted him for his Hollywood Hills Clinic it had been the biggest boost to Jake's career, the opportunity to work with the very best California had to offer. And it had promised a de-cent living with money to spare to pay back his parents every cent and more for the sacrifices they'd made for him. Money, too, to pay for healthcare for his father's failing health.

That they wouldn't accept a dime from him was another issue altogether, along with the fact that even though Jake worked in one of the best hospitals in the state, his father refused to set foot through the door. Not that it stopped Jake from trying. Again. And again.

But the job came with the proviso that he'd fill in when necessary on the clinic's film studio roster. In extremis. And Dr Kim's sudden and necessary absence due to fam-ily problems meant they were in extremis. He'd have to live with it, along with all the tender egos who demanded nothing less than a qualified doctor to apply a plaster.

'Okay, everyone. Back to work, concentrate, this is the tricky bit. We have to…' he manipulated the probes

'...isolate and expose the tumour... There it is... Pretty tough guy, this one, will take some clever dissecting...'

Three hours later, after a distressing conversation with his patient's parents, when he'd tried to be as honest and hopeful as he could about the boy's future, Jake pulled into the film studio, showed his security pass and was directed to the set.

Seriously? His whole life he'd been working towards neurosurgery and now, just because one of his colleagues was away, he was here. In... The spool of annoyance on repeat in his head jerked to a stop. He looked around. Stared. *What the hell?* Outer space? The set was a mock-up of a crashed spacecraft on a sandy planet. All around him were creatures with three eyes or two heads and, strangely, holding very Earth-like guns... Plus a lot of cables that could easily trip someone up, and a few worried-looking humans huddled around a large film camera, watching something on a screen.

'Hey?' He stopped a man carrying a ladder as he walked by. 'Cameron Fontaine? Where can I find her? I'm the doctor. She rang, more than once, to request my assistance.'

'In her trailer. *Again*. Out there, take a left.' The man pointed wearily across the set and beyond. 'Biggest trailer, you won't miss it. Do us a favour and wave a wand, bring her back? They're all going nuts here.'

Jake wandered through the set and out into a car lot where there were around a dozen trailers. One, in the far corner, was very definitely, pointedly, larger than the others.

'Excuse me? Can I help you?' A very cross English voice, out of place in...outer space...had him spinning round. The owner was another angry-looking human with wild fiery red hair that appeared to match her bad humour, and a smattering of freckles in a pale complexion. It was the frown that stood out most, though.

'I'm looking for Cameron Fontaine. She called for me. I'm Dr Lewis.'

'You're the doctor? But you're not Kim. She usually sees Kim.'

Believe me, lady, I don't want me to be here either. 'Dr Kim is away at the moment. I'm the fill-in. For the duration of filming.' But he'd be having words with James when he eventually got back to the clinic. Surely someone else could do this? Someone less busy, less qualified, someone who actually cared about all these Hollywood theatrics?

The woman in front of him shook her head and the mass of red curls bobbed around her shoulders. Man, her hair was shiny, and she had dark chocolate eyes that were huge and…condemning. She was wearing a top that was a similar colour to her eyes. And why he even noticed that he had no idea. Standard issue black skinny jeans clung to… No, he wasn't going there. He was not going to look at her and assess her attractiveness like everyone else in this city where looks were king. No doubt she was just the same kind of blinded-by-the-lights airhead wannabe actress. She was pretty enough. Not like the tall willowy brunettes that breezed in and out of his life, but there was something about her that set her apart. A fragile beauty.

So, okay, he had a quick peek and she had a damned fine body. Curves. Something you didn't see often around here. Nice curves.

And a disappointed glint in her eyes that made him feel as if he'd let her down. 'Well, that's just perfect. Brilliant. We've been waiting for you for hours and everyone's starting to get very grumpy and for some reason it's all my fault and you're not even the right guy.'

'Whoa.' It was fine for him to feel bummed out about this, but no way was it okay for her to join in. 'I can leave right now, if you prefer. I have plenty of real patients to keep me occupied.'

'No. No. No. Stay right there. You'll have to do. The director's getting on my back, Cameron won't go outside, and we all need her seen as soon as possible. Please.' Her eyes narrowed for a moment. Then she seemed to pull herself together. Smacking her lips, she clasped her hands in front of her as if steeling her nerve. She found him a smile. It wasn't terribly convincing, but it was there. 'Sorry. I'm Lola Bennett, Miss Fontaine's PA.' He could have sworn she also uttered the word 'dogsbody' under her breath, but he couldn't be certain.

'Jake Lewis. Neurosurgeon to the stars. Apparently.' He stuck out his hand.

Which she took in hers and gave a short firm shake. Her hand was warm and petite and just touching it gave him a weird jolt through his skin. She looked down at where their hands touched, then back at him with a question in her eyes. Then she blinked. 'Okay! Well! Let's do our best, shall we? Miss Fontaine's trailer is right here. Be warned, though, she may not be exactly chuffed to see you.'

'Chuffed?'

'Sorry, I mean pleased. Delighted. English, you see. As in I'm from England… Obviously you speak English too…just a different sort…' And then she smiled for real, the chocolate eyes blazed and her mouth curled into a pretty curve. Which had a very strange but real effect on his cardiac rhythm as he followed her into the trailer.

He put it down to the whole bizarre scenario, the extra-terrestrial vibe, the raised blood pressure caused by harassment during complex surgery. The drive through relentless traffic. It was nothing to do with the very talkative Lola Bennett, of that he was sure.

'Hello!' There was a forced joy to her voice that was just a little panicked as they stepped into the trailer, and for a fleeting moment Jake felt sorry for her. 'Miss Fontaine? The doctor's here!'

'About time too. Kim? Oh, Kim, I'm so glad—' The beautiful blonde actress Jake had seen on billboards around town and on movie screens countless times sat up and glared. 'You're not Kim.'

Lola was by her side in a second, talking as if to a small child, eagerly soothing and endlessly optimistic. 'No, Miss Fontaine, this is Dr Lewis. *Jake*. He's here to see you. Dr Kim is away at the moment.'

'Well, bring him back. I can't see...' she waved her hand at Jake as if shooing away an irritating dog '... Jack here.'

'It's Jake,' Lola said smoothly, as she offered a silent apology to Jake in the form of a shrug and a roll of the eyes. 'He's from the clinic, so he's bound to be good. Excellent, I'll bet.'

Unable to take this fawning any longer, Jake stepped forward. 'Miss Fontaine, I'm Dr Kim's stand-in. There is no question of bringing him back. What's the problem?'

'I can't discuss it with you. Kim knows everything.'

'Oka-a-ay. It'll be in your notes then? I'll remote-access them from here.' He put his laptop bag on the table next to her and unzipped it. Pulled out his computer and fired it up. 'Please be assured that I am bound by the same confidentiality as Dr Kim. I am as capable as he is.' *If not more so. And more highly qualified.* 'If you can just tell me what's wrong, then we can try to fix it.' *Soon.* And, yes, he realised his tone was just a little annoyed. But he had very sick patients, a young man with his whole future in doubt—his whole life—and instead of being where he was needed, he was here. Doing this.

The actress began to shake and blink quickly. 'What's wrong? What's wrong? I need health advice and I have the wrong doctor in my trailer, that's what's wrong. Please go. Now. I won't see anyone but Kim.'

What the hell? 'I can assure you—'

'It's Kim or no one.'

'Then it'll be no one. He's not going to be back for months—'

'So go.'

Jake bit back a curse. 'I came all this way and you won't even let me talk to you? Just like that?'

'Just like that. Now go.' And with a final flourish she flung herself back against the cushions and closed her eyes. He presumed this meant that the consultation was over.

'Sorry to have wasted your time,' he growled, not sorry at all as he slammed down the laptop lid, snatched up his bag and stalked out of the door. Wasting *her* time? Wasting her time? His fist curled around the bag handle as he strode back towards the set. What a joke. He was definitely going to talk to James about this.

'Dr Lewis? Jake? Wait, please.' That English accent again. He swivelled on his heel. Lola was standing at the bottom of the trailer steps, wringing her hands. 'How about I find you a cup of tea? Would that help?'

'I doubt it. It certainly won't get me the last hour of my life back.'

'But it might help to sit for a while. Calm down before you head back into the traffic.' She looked at her watch. 'It's almost rush hour, it'll be a nightmare.'

'I think I've just had one already. Tell me I'm going to wake up soon.'

Lola raised her shoulders. 'She has a habit of changing her mind.'

'So do I. From right this minute. I'm not coming back. I'm not surgeon to the stars.'

'She may ask to see you again. Soon. Like in five minutes.'

'I'll be busy. With patients who actually want my input and expertise. I have better things to do with my time than pander to hypochondriacal celebrities.'

But for some reason he couldn't really understand, he followed Lola towards a truck dispensing snacks and drinks and waited until she'd ordered two English breakfast teas. Tea—the great soother of tempers, according to the Brits. No serial or costume drama was ever made where the mention of tea didn't happen at least twice. He hated it.

Then, taking the tray of drinks, he let her lead the way to a marquee and a plastic table and chair set-up. Lola looked dejected while desperately trying not to appear so. 'I'm so sorry, Jake. Can I call you Jake? Or do you prefer Dr Jake? Dr Lewis?'

'Jake's fine.'

'She's a bit temperamental, she's spent her life telling people what to do. And they do it. Just like that.' She clicked her fingers. 'I'm guilty of doing it too—but, then, I get paid to. She'll come round, you just have to let her calm down and think logically.' She bit her bottom lip, gave a conciliatory smile that lit up her eyes and whispered, 'She will, eventually.'

'Whatever she pays you isn't enough. Leave. Get another job.' So it was curt, but damn…how could Lola let her boss talk to her like that?

The smile and the light vanished. 'I'm sorry?'

'It's not healthy to be around self-obsessives. Actually,

it's really not *worth* it. Just because you want to be noticed, a career in Tinsel Town, right? She's your ticket?
Actress, right? Like all the others who come here because they want the bright lights. It's not worth it, Lola.
Find another job. That kind of person will suck you dry,
drive you mad.'

Now Lola frowned, eyes wide. 'And this is your business because…?'

Good question.

He didn't usually make assumptions and feel the
need to sort someone else's life out. In fact, he usually
steered as far away as possible from involving himself
in anyone's life. Particularly women's. The only thing in-
terfering had ever achieved was a damned headache, and
sent out a message that he cared…or was interested…or
wanted to commit. He wasn't. He didn't. 'I'm just saying, there are better careers than being someone's assistant or a Z-list actress. Most don't get very far anyway,
it's only the top tiny percentage who can make a living
at it. If you want my opinion—'

'Actually, I don't. But thanks for making my day a
whole lot worse.' She stared at the steam rising from
her tea, then stirred two packets of sugar into her cup.
Which was refreshing, because most women he knew
in this city would rather have eaten dust than sugar. It
was the new axis of evil…or something. She looked dejected, and there was a simmering behind her eyes that
signalled danger.

There was also a cloud of coiled anger hanging over
them and, if he was honest, it was probably due to him.
He'd started off this whole debacle in a lousy mood
and things had got worse from there. If she was right
and Cameron did ask him to return, it would help if he
smoothed things between them. Plus, he didn't want word

of this to get back to James, who was insistent that all patients be treated with kid gloves…and that was usually Jake's mojo. The patient came first—always. But also… and this was the weirdest thing…he felt bad at adding to Lola's troubles. He'd seen a glimpse of her smile and, strangely, he wanted it back again.

'Lola—'

'Oh? There's more? Which part of me do you want to pick apart now? You've done my job and my pathetic-sounding future—how about you move on to my face or my body?' The joy in her voice had been replaced with irritation. The happy bounce that had seemed to live in her bones—gone. Yes, she was pissed at him. Very. No one ever spoke to him in that tone, and there were flashes of gold sparking in her eyes now. It was…well, it was all very interesting. She leaned forward, waving her tea-spoon at him. 'You don't know the first thing about me but somehow think you can storm in here and give me life advice?'

'Er…' He began to explain. 'It's—'

But she jumped right on in. 'Well, seeing as we're handing advice out so liberally today, let me give you some, Dr High and Mighty. I don't care who you are or what qualifications you've got, you don't get to conde-scend me as if I am worthless. And you don't get to make assumptions about anything I do or who I am. Okay? I was trying to be nice to you because she can be a bit of a B-I-T-C-H. And I totally understand how you can be angry with her for being a diva too—and now I've said it and I promised myself I never would—because she is a very good actress and she can be thoughtful sometimes. Rarely, but it does happen.

'I thought a cup of tea and a chat would help because in my experience they usually do, but you know what?

Forget it. There are plenty of doctors in Los Angeles who would give their right arm to be here in this privileged position, doctors who care. Who want to help. Who are actually nice. So I'll go phone one of them, shall I? I think we're done here.'

And with that she scraped her chair in the gravel and stood. Her previously pale face was now a bright beetroot red. The sunny smile a mere figment of his memory. And to his chagrin, he realised Lola Bennett had done what no woman had ever done to Jake Lewis—she'd brought him to a point where he had to chase after her and grovel.

CHAPTER TWO

'LOLA.'

God give me strength. Some days she really, *really* wanted to change her name. She hesitated on her path back to the trailer, slowed and then stopped, wishing her burning cheeks would cool down. The doctor may well be dashing and delicious to look at with his cropped dark hair and startling blue eyes, and so what if he had a body that the leading man on set would die for? Jake Lewis was a pompous jerk in a suit and she didn't want him to think he'd got the upper hand.

But he was the only doctor here so she needed to be nice to him because finding another one might take another couple of hours. And she was pretty sure Cameron would change her mind, *again*, and insist on seeing a doctor before the day was out. So Lola was stuck between the two of them trying to find a happy place. 'Yes? What now?'

Dr Lewis's lips twitched at the corners, but he kept his distance. 'You didn't finish your tea.'

'I don't want it any more, thank you.' She tried to keep the irritation out of her voice, she really did, but it shone through regardless.

He stepped forward and beckoned to her. 'But I'm told on good authority that it might help. And it's going cold.'

'So?' She stuck her hands on her hips and waited for his apology.

'So, they're going to clear it away if we don't go back.' The jerk jerked his head towards the canteen seating area. Two forlorn cups sat on the empty table. And, God, she was parched. With all this running around she hadn't had a chance for a drink in ages. Dr Lewis just carried on as if an apology was the furthest thing from his mind and that he hadn't just insulted her every which way he liked. 'Come on, come back and finish it before they take it away.'

But no way would she sit with him again until— 'No, Jake, I'm waiting for an explanation.'

'I see.' The twitch at the mouth turned into a thin line as he pondered her words. He really was very lovely to look at—but, then, so was everyone in LA, even the set carpenters were beautiful and always screen-ready. It was like living in a magazine or on an episode of Entertainment Daily.

This guy, though, he had an arrogance that shot through the better-than-good looks, a haughty jaw and a manner she didn't particularly understand—it was as if he really didn't want to be here. Who wouldn't want to be surrounded by all this wonderful Hollywood chaos?

She tapped her foot. 'Still waiting…'

'Ah. Well, I haven't ever waited tables, Lola, but I think it generally works like this: when customers leave a table—or rather *stomp* away—it indicates that they've finished and it's okay to clear their used cups away.'

'Too clever for your own good.' She couldn't help the smile. 'And I didn't stomp.'

His gaze ran from her face, down over her body and lingered a little at her backside. Which made her face heat even more. Her stomach suddenly started with a strange fluttery feeling and she wondered if she was coming down with the same thing as Cameron.

He nodded. 'You so did. Little angry stomps.'

'Condescending too? Great.' He'd been watching her that closely? 'Well, it's hardly surprising given the circumstances. And I meant I'm waiting for an explanation of why you were so rude.'

'Oh.' He gave a small shrug. 'That.'

'Yes. That. An apology would be nice.'

He actually looked surprised, as if saying sorry was something he'd never ever thought about, let alone done. But he walked back towards the table and she felt intrigued enough to follow him. She just about caught his words, more of a mumble really. 'I apologise if my words upset you.'

'Not sorry you said them. Not sorry you jumped to conclusions. You're just sorry I was upset? Where did you learn the art of apologising?'

'You're supposed to learn it? Is that what they teach in British schools? The art of apology?' He stood at the table while she sat down—no doubt a play for power. 'Figures.'

'By which you mean?'

He lifted his cup to his mouth and took a sip. Grimaced. Put it back down again. 'Look, things got a little heated back there. I think we need to start over.'

Hallelujah. Because she didn't dare face Cameron and admit she'd scared the doctor away. Even if he did deserve it. 'Yes, yes, we do.'

'Excellent. First things first.' He turned and walked over to the café truck, chatted briefly with the chef—even laughed! Laughed. The man had a sense of humour...but clearly had no intention of sharing much of it with her. Then he returned with a steaming cup of coffee. He sat, sipped and smiled. 'Great. Now, where were we?'

'You don't like tea?'

'No.'

'So why didn't you say anything before?'

'You ordered and assumed I'd want it. I was being polite. It is possible.' He leaned back in his chair and smirked. 'I admit, I was an idiot.'

Still no *I'm sorry.* Interesting. 'To be honest, Cameron can be difficult. I have to bite my lip an awful lot.' She didn't tell him about how she screamed into her pillow when she was so frustrated and utterly exhausted by her demands, or had fantasised about a jellyfish attack on that Hawaiian beach, while she had been knee deep in doggy-do with three over-excited, totally over-pampered Chihuahuas at the grooming salon.

An eyebrow peaked. 'So why do you stay?'

'Have you tried to get a job here, with everyone else all vying for something in the industry? She pays reasonably well—although it's long hours. And because she's the closest I've got to a film director since I arrived here. That's my target, really. The longer I'm with Cameron the more I'll meet the right people. I need her. I need this job. I know that sounds mercenary, like I'm using her, but I really need the contacts and exposure. Does that make me a bad person?'

He looked at her for a moment or two, and again she felt a strange rising sensation in her stomach, a need to look away but a compulsion to keep staring into those bluest of blue eyes. 'Lola, I don't know you, but from what I've seen so far I couldn't imagine you're a bad person. A little full on, maybe—'

'My dad says I'm a chatterbox.'

'I'm not commenting on the grounds that I may incriminate myself further.' But he gave a wry smile in agreement. 'Basically, you're just doing what everyone else does—feathering your own nest. Making things work for you. It's the way of the world. It's why I'm here instead of back at the clinic, or back in Van Nuys, where I grew up. Networking, making connections. How are you going to get on in life if you don't use your contacts?'

Well, that certainly made her feel a little better. Although he'd clearly given it a lot of thought and justified it all down the line. Was he one of those true workaholic types? Or was he just completely self-focused?

She'd met a lot of people like that here—really, she'd thought she was highly ambitious, but her over-achieving tendencies paled into insignificance compared to those of some of the men she'd met. The ones who had stood her up because of a last-minute audition and hadn't bothered to call her and had left her sitting in a bar, like a lemon. Or who had used their in-between-jobs actor badges to repeatedly make her pay for everything on dates. Or— the very worst—the one who had slept with her as a way of getting to meet Cameron. That one had really stung. She'd fallen heavily for that guy and all he'd wanted had been an introduction to her boss.

Her love life had taken a serious dive since she'd moved here, and now she was totally off dating anyone. Definitely. It was going to be just her and her scripts and, she thought with a sigh, Cameron and her three little Chihuahua babies.

Having drained his coffee, Jake gave her a small smile. 'So you're an actress, then?'

'No. God, no. Although I did study drama from being about three years old and did my time on stage at university, but I fell in love with words, creating characters. Making things up. I'm a writer. Screenplays.' What a buzz to say that out loud. Finally...*finally*! She'd escaped the endless expectations and was chasing her own dream, instead of being forced to live someone else's. Although, she realised, freedom did come at a price—guilt, mostly.

He sat upright. 'And you came all the way from England just for that?'

'*Just?* People have done things that are far more rash. I wanted to be part of the scene here. This is where screenplays get made into movies. This is where someone can take my work, my idea, and make it a reality. Besides, my dad's from LA and he always talked it up.'

'So if he liked it, why did he leave? I presume he left?'

'He met my mum and married her and they moved back to her home, which is London. Basically, he gave up his career here for love.' He'd taken second best for a job, moved countries, given up dreams. She was not going to follow in his footsteps—she was going to mould her own. Chase her *own* dreams. Hard.

She wasn't going to give anything up for love—when she was ready she was going to have it all. She just wasn't sure if she would ever be ready—how did you know? Her plan was to achieve all those things her father hadn't. To be a success. Because when he'd watched his daughter performing on stage all she'd seen in his eyes had been the light of regret. Lola never wanted to have any regrets. Or to walk on a stage ever again.

Jake looked startled. Shocked. As if the whole idea of love was alien and somehow absurd. 'Why would anyone would do that? Why take a chance on something that could just as easily fall apart? What does he do now?'

'He teaches drama, which he loves. And I'm sure he's happy where he is. I know he adores his family. Too much at times. But he used to tell such amazing stories about living here and the films he was in. Did you see *Big City Drive*? No? It was about life in LA in the eighties. He said it was really accurate. The whole city vibe. I think

I fell in love with this city just from that film. Although it does help that my dad was in it.'

Jake gave her a look that made her think he didn't much like it at all. 'And how's it working out for you?'

She couldn't look him in the eye and lie, so she spoke to the air around them. 'It's going just fine. Great! Look around you—isn't this brilliant? Over there is Alfredo Petrocelli, the best director in the world, as far as I'm concerned. And I'm breathing the same air as Matt Ringwood and Cameron Fontaine—although her air is usually infused with some weird aromatherapy combinations depending on her mood, and they change—a lot. But, all things considered, it couldn't be better.'

'And yet your body language says the opposite.' Those blue eyes narrowed a little. 'Tell me the truth, Lola. It's not all glitz and glamour, is it?'

Why did this man make her feel simultaneously nervous and yet eager to talk? How did he read her so well in the space of…what? Half an hour? She wanted to brush everything off with a big happy shrug but, well, she was a little sick of lying about how much fun it all was and how wonderfully exciting it was, when really sometimes she felt so despondent she wanted to cry. She was lonely. She was poor. She wasn't making the right connections quickly enough. She was running out of money. She couldn't bring herself to show her script to anyone. It was bad enough that she had to lie every time her father phoned.

But, then, she didn't know Jake from a bar of soap, so why should she spill her guts to him? 'It's fabulous, actually. You should see Cameron's house in Bel Air. It's amazing. And she has great parties.' Which Lola organised completely but had to keep a 'low profile' for. No partying for the assistant, just background work creating the illusion that Cameron had done it all on her own. 'Really. Fabulous. Now, I think I should probably be going.'

Jake frowned. 'Where? Back to Cameron? Won't she yell if she needs you? That seems to work.'

'Yes, she will. But I do have other things I should be doing. Besides, she needs me to go over her lines.'

But he didn't seem to want to move, so she was kind of stuck here, being polite. Although that wasn't too much of a hardship. After the initial bad beginning, things had started to smooth out a little—largely, she mused, due to her never-ending search for the positive in things, which was starting to falter a little.

He leaned back and crossed his legs. From what she could see of them they were toned, strong, clothed in expensive fabric. A dark suit, very professional. In fact, from this angle she could see the stretch of linen across his chest, the bunched muscles in his arms. He clearly did more working out than lifting a scalpel. And that was so none of her business. She looked away—only this time it was at his face.

His eyes met hers again and she felt a shiver of something strange as he said, 'So, what's it about, then, your screenplay?'

Wow. The first person to actually ask.

She'd prepared her elevator pitch, she knew exactly how to sell it to a director or producer in one sentence. Perhaps she could try it out on him?

'Lola! Lola!'

No such luck.

She gave him a little nod. 'See. I have to go. But, please, don't disappear on me, she's probably—'

'Lola!' The pitch was high, the voice wobbly.

'Oh, she really does sound upset. Maybe you should come too?'

'Okay. Sure. Once more unto the breach and all that…'
He closed his eyes for a second and then breathed in
deeply, as if summoning up courage. 'Do we need hard
hats?'

For a moment Lola felt as if she had an ally. Everyone
else took Cameron so seriously it was nice to share a confidence. She laughed. 'Only if she throws something at
you.' At his worried grimace she laughed again. Harder.
'She has terrible aim. She hasn't actually hit me yet.'

Jake watched as Lola again clothed herself in her positive jolly guise and entered the trailer. For a few seconds
she'd let him see past that façade to the real woman—
she was an interesting character. Clearly driven, if not a
little spirited. Still, there was nothing wrong in chasing
a dream. She was articulate and had a self-deprecating
sense of humour, which was infectious.

She almost ran over to Cameron and Jake had a suspicion that there was some affection there for her boss
despite what she said. 'Hey, are you okay? What's the
problem?'

The actress wiped tears from her cheeks. 'I don't
know. I feel…well, I don't feel right. I'm so…out of sorts.'

Jake stepped in. 'Are you in pain anywhere, Miss Fontaine?'

'No. Not pain exactly.'

Great. Not helpful. 'Can you describe what this *out of
sorts* feeling is? Is it anywhere in particular? An ache?
A stabbing pain? Nausea? Headache? Dizziness?' It was
like playing lucky dip.

'No.' Tears fell faster.

'She was nauseous earlier.' Lola looked from one to
the other as if that was the complete answer.

'It's gone now, I'm just a little upset. Something I ate,

no doubt.' Cameron sighed. 'But I don't think I'll be able to do much today. Lola, honey, can you tell them I won't be out for the rest of the day?'

Lola frowned, but quickly wiped it from her face. Her voice was soothing, soft and positive. 'Maybe you're just a little over-tired? You've been working very hard recently with only one little break in Hawaii. That wasn't enough—you need to make sure you book in a longer break between shoots next time. I'll put it in your diary.' While she talked she brushed Cameron's hair back from her face and held a glass of water out for her to drink. 'I think they're on their break now, anyway. They've been doing some stunt rehearsing to fill in—Matt's big fight scene, you know what a perfectionist he is, so don't worry, everyone's fine about it. How about we see how you feel in a few minutes? Perhaps Jake could give you a tonic or something?'

A tonic? Did people still have those? He was all clued up on brains and, after his stint in ER as an intern, could manage most emergencies. But general non-specific malaise? He wasn't sure about that. He knelt in front of Cameron.

'Perhaps Lola could excuse us while I examine you?' He shot a hopeful look at Lola and she nodded.

'Great idea. Let's make sure we're not missing anything.'

'No. No. That won't do at all. Please, just give me a tonic. Something…something non-toxic. Oh, I don't know, maybe just water? Would more water help?' Cameron put a protective hand to her stomach, although Jake thought it was an odd subconscious action.

Then his mind began to join the dots. General malaise. Nausea disguised as a stomach upset. Hand on abdomen. Tears. *Non-toxic.*

She's pregnant. She's pregnant and she doesn't want anyone to know. 'I'd really like to talk to you in private, Cameron. Just talk. I won't examine you if you don't want that.'

The actress looked at him for a good long beat. She gave a minute shake of her head, her eyes wide and a little scared. Clearly, anyone finding out about this, even her assistant, was a big deal. But didn't she know she needed to take care? To eat the right things? Did she know for sure or just suspect? Did she have an OB/GYN?

Miss Fontaine sat up and patted her cheeks with a tissue. 'You know what? I'm actually starting to feel a bit better. Perhaps a little more water, then I'll go back outside. Get some air. Maybe we could do some sitting-down scenes to conserve my energy.'

Jake wasn't convinced. 'Cameron, are you sure you don't want me to look you over? Or I can arrange for someone else to come see you? This evening? To your home if you want?' *An OB/GYN? Midwife?* He gave her a studied look, hoping she could read through his words. Trying to maintain confidentiality with someone else in the room was difficult. 'I could call someone.'

'No. Thank you. You've been very attentive. But I'm fine. Absolutely. You can go.'

He fished into his bag and drew out a card, which he gave to her. 'Here's my personal cell number. Call me any time.'

For the first time since he'd met her, Cameron smiled. 'Thank you. You're very kind.'

Just concerned. 'Any time. Okay?'

Then he nodded to Lola to come outside with him. Thankfully she followed until they were out of hearing distance.

'Thank you, Jake. I think all she needs is a bit of reassurance. You know what these people are like—they get very anxious about their bodies—it's so important to them to be perfect. Obviously.'

Yes, well, he still wasn't happy about the situation. He was on a set with a presumably pregnant actress who was at all kinds of risk. However, he also had to remember that pregnancy was a perfectly natural and normal state. 'I think she needs to rest when she's feeling tired. If there's no pain or…anything else, she can continue to work. I've got to go back to the clinic and check on my patient from this morning, but I'll come back later. Just to double-check she's feeling okay.' And to convince her to seek further advice. Somehow.

'Thank you, that's very kind.'

'It's not, it's just routine.'

'But you could have just walked away. Thanks for putting up with us. I'll see you later. If they're filming when you get here, just pop on over to the trailer. That's where I'll be, no doubt. That is…well…you know. If you want. We could wait…in there. Or…sorry, I'm rambling. Bye.'

As Lola smiled he felt momentarily as if his breath had been sucked out of his lungs. She turned and walked back towards the trailer and he realised he was waiting for the angry little stomps. He kind of missed them.

She was all kinds of confusing. She didn't take any rubbish from him, but she took it from her boss. She stood up for herself in some situations, but not in others. She was hard working and committed. And she was, surprisingly and refreshingly, genuinely nice. Lola was the only real thing here—the rest was fabrication and fairy tale.

And he realised, as he climbed back into his car, that he wasn't thinking about coming back to see Cameron at all. It was her assistant that had him looking in the rear-view mirror for one final glimpse.

That was a danger sign if ever he knew one.

CHAPTER THREE

THE HOLLYWOOD HILLS CLINIC was bustling as usual, regardless of the time of day or night. After checking on his patient, Jake took the lift to the management suite and walked along the bright corridor, his footsteps tapping on the marble tiling. It was a far cry from the well-intentioned but underfunded public hospital he'd worked at prior to the phone call from James that had promised to change his life.

It had. And, he hoped, working here had made his parents' lives easier. For too long they'd scrimped and saved and sacrificed for their only son to achieve dreams way beyond any they'd dared to have for themselves. And every once in a while he took a breath and appreciated how very different things could have been for a relatively poor kid from Van Nuys; at least now with his handsome salary he could make up for all of their sacrifices. Even if he couldn't make up for the effect those sacrifices had had on his father's health.

He rapped on the door and opened it. 'James, I need a word, if you have time?'

James Rothsberg smiled as he placed his phone into the holder on the desk. 'Jake, I was just talking about you. Ears burning?'

'No. Not at all.'

'How's it going over at the studio? Not taxing you too much?' James leaned back in his chair and indicated for Jake to sit too. 'Pretty cool job, right?'

Jake took a seat opposite him. 'That's what I want to discuss. It's entirely inappropriate that I'm there, to be honest. I'm wasting my time, and theirs. There are less qualified people who could do the work; it's not difficult, just time-consuming. Very time-consuming.'

James gave an uncharacteristic frown. 'But it's a roster. We all do our share. It's part of your contract.'

'Yes, I know. But now I'm doing Kim's stint too.'

'So we'll rearrange it so you don't get to do it again in a hurry. Fine?'

Not fine. Jake did not want to go back there and exchange heated looks with a redheaded English rose who only had one speed: hyperdrive. He wanted to stay here and work his heart out making people better, the way he knew how. He wanted to focus on his job. This job, here, the one he'd worked so hard to get, and the one he wanted to keep. And not think about pretty little angry stomps or waste his time on non-emergencies and actresses who wanted to keep secrets. 'I'd prefer it if someone else could go.'

'And I'd prefer it if you go. I'm just off the phone with Alfredo. He's very impressed after hearing the rave review Cameron Fontaine gave you this afternoon. He's requested that you accompany them on a location shoot. To keep her happy, mainly. In fact, she's insisting on it.'

Jake felt frustration well up in his gut. 'What? A location shoot? No way. That's out of the question. What about my patients? You know, the brain-injured ones?'

His boss's palm rose. 'Jake, I'm not arguing about this. We can rearrange your schedule. It's only for a few days—mainly over the weekend, so it won't take you away from your patients here. I can give you time off in lieu. It's in the Bahamas. That should appeal, right?'

The Bahamas? What the hell…? What did that have to do with a desiccated space-odyssey landscape? The world had gone mad.

Sun. Sea. And…well, at least the fiery redhead wouldn't be there. Surely? That wasn't the kind of thing assistants did, was it? Accompany their bosses on location shoots? 'I don't know, James. I don't see how I'm the best fit for this. Send someone else.'

'You don't have any surgery booked until Tuesday. I can't see a problem,' James said, as he tapped on his laptop and looked at what Jake imagined was the OR schedule. The atmosphere became charged a little as his boss sat forward, suddenly serious. 'See, the way it works is this: the studio heads contract to the clinic. We're the best in California and everyone knows it, so they want to be associated with us. And it's very lucrative, very prestigious. My point is, Alfredo plays golf with some of the studio guys…we don't want word getting out that we renege on our contracts, do we? That our staff are unhelpful? Way too negative for us. We need you to keep them sweet.'

'When you put it like that…' It was clear this was a battle he couldn't fight. James was right, he could rearrange his outpatient clinics, he didn't have any scheduled surgery for a few days. Jake had made his feelings clear, but was big enough to accept that sometimes there were things he couldn't change.

'Plus, this kind of exposure to celebrities really helps with promoting the Bright Hope Clinic and the work Mila does there. Celebs love being involved with charities, and having our staff involved at all levels helps bring in donations. It's great leverage.'

There was a strange mist in James's eyes as he spoke of the Bright Hope Clinic. But Jake doubted whether it had as much to do with the pro bono work they were all going to do there with underprivileged kids as it had to do with the charity head, Mila Brightman. Every time James and Mila were in the same room there was a strange buzz in the air. It bordered on animosity—but there was something else there too. Fireworks, mainly.

Jake gave his friend a quick smile to show his agreement. He would not put his own needs first when kids' futures were on the line. And, yeah, he was also big enough to admit that, despite what he thought about the airhead celebrity culture, they had big hearts and deep pockets and did a lot of good…and now he was starting to go soft. 'Okay, okay, I'm packing already.'

'Great. See? Not too hard, was it? A free trip to the Bahamas? I wouldn't grumble. So, how's everything else going? How's the wonderful Cameron? Alfredo said she's had a few issues. I've heard she can be a huge pain in the—' James was interrupted by a soft tap at the door. 'Yes? Come in.'

It was Mila. As she walked in Jake saw her cheeks flush a little. She focused solely on the man in front of her. 'Hi, James. I'm so sorry to interrupt you.'

'Mila, no problem, not at all.' His boss stood immediately, suddenly looking like a lost boy rather than the accomplished professional he was. Jake hadn't been working here very long, so he didn't know what, if any, past these two had, but he smiled to himself. Whatever the hell was going on was so damned obvious to everyone—if not to them. The air had become charged in a completely different way, and Jake figured now was a good time to leave. Three was a crowd after all…

He stood to go. 'Hi, Mila. Bye, Mila. Sorry, just leaving.'

'Oh.' She whirled round, her voice a little more high-pitched than he remembered it to be. 'I didn't see you there. Hi, Jake. How's things?'

James cut in. 'Poor guy's got a difficult weekend coming up. A few days in Nassau with Cameron Fontaine.'

'Oh? Exciting.' Mila smiled, her long brown ponytail swishing as she turned her head. 'Must be hard, being you.'

'Tough job, right?' And for a split second he found himself looking forward to the break, imagining a beach at sunset, the last dying rays of sun shimmering on a mass of red curls... Damn it... He needed to get out more. What the hell was wrong with him? Thirty minutes. That's all he'd spent with Lola Bennett. Why she kept stomping into his head he didn't know. But he wished she would stop it. 'Look, I've got to get back to the studio. I'll see you two later.'

But, already lost in their own tense conversation, he doubted they'd heard him. As he ambled to the door he caught snippets, James sounding a little stilted. 'Sure, Mila, I've got the number right here.'

Mila's breathy response was, 'Great. I was just passing, and thought it'd be easier to ask in person than phone. I need a number and a quick chat about her work, character, commitment, really, whether you think she'd be a good fit for Bright Hope. But I can't stay long, I've got to meet someone in an hour.'

'Oh? Tyler?' James's voice was more of a growl at the mention of Mila's boyfriend. Jake wished he could hear this out but he didn't do gossip, no matter how tempting. And yet he still couldn't bring himself to leave just yet. He paused to fasten his bag.

Mila shook her head. 'No. It's with the cleaning com-

pany manager. We have a couple of issues with their contract.' There was a pause. 'Actually, Tyler and I split.'

'Oh? I'm sorry to hear that.' Was that interest in
James's voice? No. It couldn't be. Really?

She gave a bitter laugh. 'I'm not. Now…the number
for that paediatric cardiologist?'

'Yes. Right here. You don't seem too cut up about it.'

And as Jake tried to close the door without disturbing them, he heard her voice harden. 'It wasn't working,
and I'd prefer not to talk about it. I don't like to get my
personal life embroiled in my professional. And I'm certainly not going to discuss it with you.'

'Yes. No. Of course.' James sounded wrong-footed.
Surprised by her reaction. And so was Jake, a little. Normally she was a warm-hearted woman, professional, capable and very caring. Devoted to her patients. But she
did sound a little bitter right now.

And Jake really did need to go. Eavesdropping was
definitely not part of his contract. Plus, he was running
late for a date with a very demanding leading lady…and
her very jolly English assistant.

Lola sat in the trailer, trying to focus on editing her script,
but failing, badly. Usually she welcomed moments like
this where she could spend some time on herself and her
own work, but she was feeling restless, fidgety. Kept
looking towards the door and wishing it would open.

That damned doctor. He'd been the first person to pay
attention to her—to Lola Bennett—rather than her employer or her contacts, or her usefulness. Plus he'd been
quite amiable in the end—once she'd set him straight
on manners.

Really.

He needn't have been so nice to her. She was growing used to being in the background, which was a far cry from being a big fish in the small sea at Oxford University. But it was nothing more than she'd expected. LA was a big city after all, and everyone wanted a piece of the action.

And, well, she needed to focus on her work and the less she thought about Jake's body the better.

But it was so…so hot. Never in her wildest dreams had she thought she'd find a stroppy neurosurgeon attractive. She'd always imagined she'd get embroiled with the creative, arty type. But her cheeks burned just thinking about him.

Which was stupid.

And, besides, he'd shown no interest in her…in *that* way. She was just a little bit lonely. And therefore vulnerable.

No. She would never be vulnerable. She was hardworking, focused and intent. Most of the time.

A knock on the door had her heart racing. 'Come in!'

'Hey, Lola Bennett.' Jake stepped into the trailer and gave her a smile. A little uncomfortable, wary maybe, but there it was. 'I've come back to check on Cameron. But I didn't see her on set and she's not here?'

'She's gone home. They're working on a different scene now—after you'd gone she did very well and they managed to catch up, but she was tired so she's gone for an early night. I called the clinic and told them she was okay and not to worry you, but you'd already set off. Don't you have your cell phone? They said they'd text you.' What was it about him that made her ramble on so much?

'I keep it on silent because it keeps ringing and disturbing me.' He dragged it from his suit jacket pocket and showed her. The strange and yet nice thing about Dr

Lewis was that he wasn't the least bit affected. He was straight up. Honest. Had no pretensions or cocky swagger. And yet he was so damned hot to look at he could have been in any one of her boss's recent movies, or on the cover of a magazine. He just didn't seem to realise it. 'Oh, yes. There is a message.'

'So you've wasted your time. I'm sorry.' *Liar.* She was actually a bit pleased that he was here. Well, she would have been had her heart not started a funny little rhythm that felt like she was being kicked in the chest every few minutes. She was pleased, but judging by his frown he wasn't. 'I waited here in case you turned up. I didn't want you to think we'd all abandoned you.' The added bonus was that she could use the electricity here for free and snack on the leftover food in Cameron's refrigerator. Plus, the thought of going home to her empty, shabby apartment left her cold.

'Well, at least someone cares whether my time's wasted.' He nodded at the pile of paper on the table. 'That your script? You never got round to telling me what it's about. Please don't tell me it's another space disaster movie. I think the world has more than enough of them.'

She laughed. 'How can you say that? The world can never have enough space desert warrior princesses. With AK47s. And very bad dialogue. Make more, I say. Lots of them. With terrible sequels.'

'No. Not sequels too. Please don't encourage them.' The irritation broken, he finally laughed, his eyes shining in the dim light of the trailer lamps. When he relaxed he was pretty damned gorgeous. 'So what kind of movies do you like, Lola?'

'Anything with a good story, really. I love characters I can identify with, with guts and emotions. I'm not big on action thrillers and definitely not horrors—unless there's a real character growth arc… Sorry, am I getting too technical? I'm doing an online course on writing screenplays and learning so much about story development. But the trouble with dissecting movies is that now I can't see one without analysing it. I'm spoilt for ever.'

'That sucks.' He picked up the front sheet of her script. 'Can I see?'

'No. Please, no.' She snatched it back, trying hard not to sound too crazy. Her screenplay was her baby and she wasn't sure it was good enough yet. 'I just don't think it's ready. My eyes only, and all that.'

'Sure, I understand.' At her wary frown he sat down on the sofa opposite. 'I'm a perfectionist too. I hate doing anything less than stellar.'

'That's why you're so good at your job.'

His eyebrows rose. 'You wouldn't know. You've hardly seen me at my best.'

'Well, you were very good with Cameron.'

'Not at first. You'd have been more impressed if you'd seen me manipulating a probe in her motor cortex…that's part of the brain…while she was still awake.' He waved his fingers in the air like a conductor and it was so out of character that she laughed.

'Believe me, I wouldn't. I wouldn't even be in the same room as you. Good God, that sounds hideous.' Although she imagined him all scrubbed up, those strong arms working on a patient. Sweat beading his furrowed brow, his gaze catching hers across a crowded operating theatre… And now she was thinking like a bad romance novel. 'Do you really do operations while your patients are still awake?'

'Sometimes it works better that way as we can assess the patient as we go, see how they're reacting to what we're doing. It's important to make sure we're not af-

fecting certain processes—like speech and movement. It
doesn't hurt—the brain doesn't have any pain receptors.'

'*Eugh.*' Even so, how could he do that? 'I wonder if I
could put that in my movie?'

'Why not? Although if it's a kids' film, you might
have a few complaints. You'd have to have a rider: Do
not do this at home.'

And he had a sense of humour that was refreshing.
'Surely it's not too hard? A few chopsticks and a handy
pocket knife?'

'Sure, that's all there is to it. Easy. Plus fifteen years'
training, one or two pesky exams. Oh, and a steady hand
is a must. Otherwise…well…' He made a slicing motion
at his throat.

'Hmm. Good job you have steady hands, then.' She
reached out and took his hands in hers and held them
straight out to see if they shook. It was just a joke. A
funny little gesture, that was all. It didn't mean anything.

But the strangest thing happened when she touched
him. It was like a force, a shock or a shudder shivering
through her. Her stomach began to fizz in an odd way
and heat spread through her, from her core to the tips of
her fingers and toes.

She looked up at him to see if he'd felt the same thing
and he was looking at her in a funny way. Kind of surprised, yet irritated and bemused. And his eyes were still
shining, but now in a really, really good way; the blue
was dark with intent and she had an urge to lean forward
across the table and kiss him. Right there. As if it was
the most natural thing in the world to do.

But her throat was dry and her heart was hammering,
and he still had a frown and, yet, a small smile. And she
couldn't kiss him. How could she kiss him? He'd think
she was completely mad. And he'd be right. She was

completely mad to want to kiss him. She hardly knew him. And he might not want to kiss her back.

She dragged her eyes away from his heated face and saw her script next to his arm. That was why she was here. Not for a man. Not for a kiss with a strange doctor. Who wasn't strange at all and was actually very sexy. But too distracting. She was here for her career. Just as he was. And she was a perfectionist, just like him. But he was a lot further down the track than she was. He was already hugely successful and she was just a fledgling wannabe. She had a lot of work to do.

So she let his hands go and stood up, even though her legs were wobbly, because there was something about him that made her feel off balance. 'I…er…I think I'm going to call it a day now. No doubt Cameron will be buzzing me early in the morning. It's a five a.m. call.'

'Okay. Great idea.' He stood too, and they both tried to get out of the booth at the same time and brushed against each other. His chest was hard and strong, his breath whispered over her neck, and for a few seconds she didn't know what to do. If she moved forward she'd be in his arms. Which suddenly didn't seem such a bad idea…except…it was.

He stepped back and gestured for her to go first. 'Sorry. After you.'

'Thanks.' She winced in embarrassment as she stepped out of the trailer and down the steps, wrapped her arms around her chest and started to walk towards the car lot.

He was next to her all the way. No talking. No… anything. Just walking in a strange awkward silence while her heart thump-thump-thumped and she clenched her fists tight. And she knew that nothing happening was a good thing. A very good thing. But a small part of her still clung to the fizz that bubbled in her stomach and the jerky heartbeat that made her cough a little.

When she reached her car she stopped. 'Okay, well, thanks again, Jake. I'll see you…? Actually, I'm not sure when that'll be because Cameron's going on location in a couple of days so…'

'I don't suppose you're hungry?' He'd lost that perplexed look and was back to being completely in control again. If that banquette blunder had affected him at all he didn't show it. Which made her feel as if she was going slightly mad. He gave her smile. 'I need to eat and I guess you do too. I know a great Thai place that does amazing noodles. You want to eat?'

Yes! 'No. I don't think—I…er…' *Yes. Yes. Yes. Absolutely not.*

He shook his head quite vehemently. 'I don't mean… not a date or anything. I can't do that.'

His words made her step back. 'Why? Are you married or something?' That would be a good thing. A very good thing. A very good out-of-bounds, hands-off and definitely-no-kissing kind of good thing.

But he kept on shaking his head. 'No. God, *me* married? No way. Really, no. But I'm always open to making new friends and would like some company for dinner. I can apologise again for being an idiot earlier. You can tell me about your story. Then I can show you how to manipulate chopsticks for awake brain surgery research. And you can B-I-T-C-H about your boss in safety, because I'm absolutely bound by confidentiality, and if you told me anything you'd have to kill me or sue me.'

'Oh… I wouldn't do that. Kill you, I mean. Well, not immediately. And everyone needs a friend, right?' And it was all in the name of research and nothing else, so why not? 'That's an offer I definitely can't refuse. To be honest, I'm starving. Lead on.'

So she got into her car and followed the lights of his expensive-looking sedan. Followed him from the dark studio warehouses back to the bright lights of the city, then through a maze of back streets that she knew she would never find her way out of on her own. And for the first time in a long time she felt as if things were looking up. It would be good to have a new friend in this strange but wonderful place.

If only she could stop thinking about kissing him.

CHAPTER FOUR

THE RESTAURANT WAS nothing like she'd imagined. It had basic melamine tables, white plastic chairs that she'd seen in her local two-dollar shop, and a fog of steam fragranced with seriously delicious smells of garlic and sesame oil and fish sauce.

Multicoloured paper lanterns hung from the ceiling, giving off a rosy red-orange glow, and squished in at each table were crowds of people Lola thought must be Thai nationals all chattering and laughing away in a language she didn't understand. An oddly incongruous but perfectly quirky soundtrack of heavy rock pierced the air. Who'd have imagined a place like this? It was like being back in Bangkok.

'Like it? This place is like a second home to me now,' Jake said, as he squashed in next to her at a shared table. There was no room for embarrassment here, it was a case of either sitting close or closer. And she wasn't sure if it was the cloying heat in the room or just being next to him, but she needed a cooling drink. Fast. He ran a finger down the pictures on the menu. 'I recommend the Pad Thai or the house cashew chicken. Perfection. The best Thai food on the West Coast. Fancy a beer? Wine?' He beckoned to a male server who came over, smiled and welcomed him like an old friend.

'Mr Jake. Nice to see you again. Your usual?'

'Hi, Panit, yes, please. And some…?' He looked over at Lola.

Her mouth watering, she scoured the menu for her favourite. 'Oh, yes. A beer, pork larb and a green papaya salad, please.'

Jake leaned back and looked at her, laughing. 'There was me thinking I was going to wow you with unusual flavours and yet you know more about it than me.'

'I travelled around Asia in my uni holidays…vacations. Vietnam, Laos and Thailand.' It had taken her days to convince her parents to let her take time off. They'd had jobs lined up for her, but she didn't do them. Her first strike for freedom. 'It was brilliant. Madly busy but brilliant. And I learnt so much about the food. We even had cooking lessons over there. I came back ten pounds heavier.' She patted her hips where the noodles and rice still clung in lumps and bumps. Her dad had gone mad about that too. *You can never be too thin*, he always said.

'You look great to me.' Jake's eyes wandered to her hands, then slowly up her body until blood rushed to her cheeks just at the moment his gaze hit hers, and there it lingered for just long enough that she felt unsettled. There was something happening—and she knew it wasn't the magical lighting or the steamy atmosphere, and it certainly wasn't the beer because she hadn't had any yet—but there was definitely something scary and weird happening inside her. And if it was just happening to her then she was going to feel like an idiot if it continued.

Jake took a slug of the beer that Panit brought over and broke the connection. 'I'd love to travel more. I just haven't gotten round to anywhere that far away.'

'You've been focusing on work?'

'You bet. My plan is to get to the top of my field and

then take a little time to smell the roses… But, first, no rest for the wicked, right? You've got to push, push, push. I get the feeling you've got the same kind of drive.' Confidence oozed from him, particularly in his smile. She wondered how it would be if this were a real date rather than a non-date. How it would feel to have those hands touch her… And suddenly she wanted them on her.

Was this chemistry real?

No. It couldn't be. She shoved such fanciful ideas to the back of her mind. He'd made his intentions very clear and she was perfectly fine with that. She didn't have time in her life for anything more intimate than this sort of dinner.

The food arrived so quickly she was surprised when the server returned with steaming plates of mains and bowls of rice. Jake picked up his two chopsticks, and one of hers, and held them aloft in front of him. 'So, here we go…brain surgery one-oh-one. Basically you need one head, three probes…'

'You're not really going to…?' She squeezed her eyes half-shut and shuddered.

'And a drill…' He made a drilling sound. Then stopped as she screwed her eyes up even tighter. 'You okay? You've gone a bit green.'

'Please. No. That is so gross.'

'And I thought you had guts, Lola Bennett.'

Did he? How? Why? 'Well, you're going to see them in a minute if you don't stop.' But she was laughing and not really grossed out at all. Although she wouldn't be queueing up to see him in action for real.

He winked. 'Another day, then. Seriously, if you decide to incorporate some medical scenes into your story I'll be happy to help with the technical details.'

'Who knows? I may just take you up on that. I do have

a few medical scenes in there. Perhaps you could write them for me and I can just edit them peering from behind my fingers?'

He smiled. 'The trick, I imagine, is to just give a few spare details and not a lot of gore—unless you're writing a horror movie, in which case the more gore, the better. Everywhere.'

'Especially in the scene where it's night-time and someone hears a noise in the cellar. But no one has a torch...and they go down anyway...while we're all screaming, "No, don't do it!"'

'Aw, no? Lola, I never realised they did that—but now you mention it...every horror movie. Ever. Now you're analysing it and spoiling it for me too.' Laughing, he tucked into the food and she followed suit. It was delicious, totally authentic and quite spicy. The cold beer washed everything down well. They ate in companiable silence until he put his chopsticks down and looked at her. 'So, give me a synopsis of your story.'

'Oh. Okay. Right. Well, I've been practising my elevator pitch—basically that's for when I'm caught in an elevator with a famous director and I have two minutes to tell them about my script before they get out.'

'You get caught in elevators with directors often?'

'Not often enough. Well, never...but I'm prepared anyway in case I do. So...listen up...' No point being nervous. He wasn't going to poke fun at her. He wouldn't criticise it. He was a...friend. She tested how that felt, and it felt good. He was funny and attentive and knew great authentic places to eat and was... Did it matter whether friends were gorgeous to look at? Just looking at him was putting her off her stride, never mind about the scary fluttery thing happening inside her. 'Right... Oh, this is too hard.'

'Come on, Lola. You can do this.'

I can? He believed in her, so why didn't she?

Because so far things hadn't worked out according to her plan, and before she knew it she'd be back on the plane, the second one in her family to give up on Los Angeles hopes and dreams. And she'd have to admit the truth to her parents and she didn't want to do that until she was successful. 'Okay. Here goes: Jane Forrest is thirty, brilliant, and…dying. Her father is missing, estranged and may hold the key to her survival. How far does she need to go to find him before time runs out? How strong are the ties that bind them together after years apart, and what will it take to convince him to help?'

'Wow.' Jake nodded, not looking as if he was overly impressed. 'Great, Lola. Yeah.'

'You're not convinced?'

'Good to hear there are no outer space desert warrior princesses.' He took a mouthful of noodles. Swallowed, licked his lips and grinned. 'Sounds pretty intense.'

'It's actually very funny in parts. I'm told it's uplifting…and sad too. I cried buckets when I wrote it and my tutor said it was one of the best scripts he'd read. It's about a woman trying to find her long-lost father, as she needs a bone-marrow transplant. Her investigation takes her all over the world to all the places he'd visited, and she learns about the great man he'd become. But she eventually comes almost full circle and finds him in the town next to where she grew up. And she gets to wondering, if he was so great, why didn't he look for her too? But also he's dying, so he can't help her. It's… I guess it's about their relationship, forgiveness and healing—even when healing isn't always possible.'

Elbows on the table, he steepled his fingers. 'Sounds brilliant. So why haven't you sold it yet?'

'It's not that easy—you don't just advertise online and get it optioned. I'm tweaking it. It needs work.'

'You need someone else to look it over...a script assessor? Your dad?' Jake's startling blue eyes lit up. 'He's been an actor and a teacher, so what's the harm?'

The harm was that no one in her family knew she was writing. There'd be too many questions—too much she'd have to tell them. And then there'd be the letdown, the disappointment, the betrayal. And, after all that, even if her dad was still interested in reading her screenplay, what if it was rubbish? She'd never live it down. 'I don't know. It's like...it's like handing over your heart and giving someone carte blanche to stomp over it.'

'Stomping runs in the family?'

'We're champion stompers actually. Won awards for it... We are stomping elite.'

'But he wouldn't do that. Surely not?' Jake studied her for a moment. His eyes really were stunning and she didn't want to stop looking at them. Her stomach felt a swooping sensation every time their gazes connected. Knowing she was on a highway to nowhere, she looked away as he spoke. 'You miss them?'

'Of course, every day.' So much. But she had to strike out on her own. She was going to be a success on her terms, then she would go home and celebrate with them. If they were still speaking to her. She turned back to him, wanting to put the focus on him for a while. 'Don't you miss your family too? Where are they? Didn't you say they were north somewhere?'

'Van Nuys. Just parents. I'm an only child.'

'Not far at all, then. Do you see them a lot?'

'They'd probably say not enough, but...you know how it is.' He shrugged, a little closed suddenly, and she wondered why.

'You're busy living your life, right?'

'Sounds selfish when you put it like that.' Eyebrows rising, he huffed out a breath. 'Which is a huge guilt trip for me, seeing as they fought hard for me to do that. Too damned hard at times.' Then he looked away and breathed out heavily.

She felt as if she'd put a big dollop of down on the conversation and thought briefly about putting her hand on his shoulder to show him solidarity, but thought better of it. She couldn't work out why she had this sudden urge to touch the man. Or to make him feel better. 'Go and see them, then.'

He turned back to her. 'That easy, right?'

'Look, I don't know the circumstances, but I'd say some communication is better than none.' She was giving family relationship advice? Go figure.

He finished his beer and stared at the empty glass, clearly not wanting to elaborate. Then he turned to her and smiled. 'You know what? I just might go up there and see them—although I'm going to Nassau this weekend.'

'You too, eh? Lucky duck. I'll be stuck here with the pooches. Cameron has three dogs she adores. And I don't particularly. They're very spoilt,' she finished in a whisper. She would have to play mama while everyone else swanned off to the Bahamas. She refused to allow images of Jake sunbathing into her head. But they came and hung around for a few moments anyway, making her blush. It seemed her mind was in conflict over Jake Lewis. On the one hand, it understood and respected the whole friends thing…and on the other it wanted sneaky, semi-naked thoughts. Actually, it wanted full-blown, butt-naked thoughts. Clearly she was going mad. It was time for bed. Alone. 'Actually, talking of work…it's getting late, I really should be getting home.'

He glanced at his watch and nodded. 'I suppose so.'

He got the bill and refused to discuss her paying a share. Which was another big fat tick for the doctor—because even though she tried to pay it was nice to have someone looking out for her for a change. 'I'll get it next time,' she promised.

'Next time?' There was a smile in his voice and a question. As they walked towards her car she wondered what to do or say now. Would there be a next time? Had she said something inappropriate? Should she kiss him on his cheek, both cheeks, shake hands? Or just walk away? 'Next time sounds good, Lola. It'll have to be after Nassau, though. But, before you go, I have something to ask you...'

'Oh? Yes?' Her voice rose a little as her heart began to hammer.

'Strange question, I know, but is Cameron seeing anyone at the moment?'

Oh, God. Her stomach tumbled. *Here we go again.* Stupid. Stupid. She'd read the signs all wrong. He wasn't remotely interested in her, he was interested in Cameron. She should have known. History repeating itself over and over. That was why he'd insisted it wasn't a date. Stupid fool. When would she learn? No one was interested in her. Plenty of interest in her boss, though.

Hoping he hadn't heard the pathetic *hope* in her voice, she tried to keep her answer in friend territory. 'Not at the moment. That I'm aware of. She was dating Marc Jason a few months ago but that fizzled. It's always the same—busy schedules that never coincide and no one wanting to put their relationships first, because that's the kiss of death to a career-minded person.' And, okay, she was just adding that last bit on to remind him that he was a career-minded person too, and that a relationship with Cameron would never work. It was for his own good. Plus, putting a negative spin on it made her feel a teensy bit better.

'Oh. Okay.' He frowned again, as if he was thinking about something serious—weirdly, he didn't have that dog panting tongue thing going on like most of Cameron's admirers. Maybe he was working out a strategy for when they were in Nassau. A sensible and driven man was Jake, and very goal oriented. Maybe bedding an A-list actress was on that list of goals. Along with shaming the personal assistant. Well, he could tick that one off his list already.

'Do you want me to put a word in for you? Is that what this is all about? Is that what dinner was about? The nondate? You're interested in Cameron because, let's face it, why wouldn't you be? So you thought you'd pay for dinner and buy her secrets from me? Or worse—if you can't have her, you'd try to have me as consolation prize? Second best, right? Here we go again.' Fighting back bitter tears, Lola stomped—yes, she stomped perfectly—towards her car.

But Jake caught her up and pulled her to a complete halt. 'What…? You think…? Me? With Cameron? Are you for real?'

'It wouldn't be the first time that has happened to me.'

'Hell, no. You've totally got this upside down. Not at all. Not at all. I was asking…' again the serious frown and a pause '…to see who would be on the private plane, who to expect generally. How many people I have to look after.' He gave an embarrassed wince because clearly he wasn't convincing anyone with that line. 'But really? Has that happened before? A guy has taken you out so you could introduce him to Cameron?'

'Yep. One too many times.' Lola closed her eyes

briefly at the memory, the sharp sting of betrayal. How gullible she'd been…and was continuing to be. Would she never learn? 'But she is very beautiful and rich and famous and on another level. Why wouldn't anyone be attracted to her?'

Conversely, then, why would anyone be interested in her?

Jake's jaw stiffened, his eyes blazing in the streetlight, his grip on her arm firm. 'I am not attracted to Cameron Fontaine.'

'Then you must be blind.'

Strangely, out of nowhere a smile formed on his lips. 'Oh, no, my vision is perfect.'

'Then you must be gay.' *Please, for the love of all women, including Cameron Fontaine if absolutely necessary, do not be gay.*

'No way.' He stepped closer, so she could see his chest rising and falling, could feel the warmth of his breath on her skin. Could smell the most exquisite scent of man and medicine and spice.

'Then what…?'

'Then this.' And he was suddenly too close. Not close enough. He pulled her to face him and his fingertips lifted her chin. '*This*, Lola.'

His mouth pressed against hers, gently at first, and her body responded in a flush of heat that pooled deep in her core. Every part of her craved him, craved to touch him, to kiss him, to feel him against her.

Initial instinct told her that she shouldn't kiss him back, but something deeper, something intense had her opening her mouth and tasting him. And he tasted good. So good. She felt as inquisitive as the doomed teenagers stepping into the dark basement, and as filled with adrenalin. Knowing, like them, she was headed to disaster but doing it anyway.

She wound her arms around his neck and pulled him closer as his tongue slid past her lips, stoking the furnace that had lit inside her. She moaned at the pleasure of him filling her mouth, of the curling clench in her gut, at the sensations that ran up and down her spine, just being in his arms.

Leaning her against her car door, his hands cupped her face and he pressed harder against her, kissing her open-mouthed, and wet and hungry. She could feel how much he wanted her. How much he wanted something from her.

And like listening to an old-fashioned vinyl record scratching to a stop, she felt a visceral catch as her body stiffened. She put her hands on his chest and pushed a little away from him. 'Stop. No. This…this isn't…'

'What is it? What's wrong?' But he didn't let her go as he hauled in deep ragged breaths, kissed the top of her head and stayed close.

'I can't stop thinking about Cameron and there are too many questions racing in my head. Too many reasons not to do this. Please, I think you should just go.'

'Lola, believe me, this is not about Cameron. She is the furthest thing from my mind. I don't want to go. I want to stay right here, doing this.'

Damn it. Jake's hands dropped from her face as he struggled to control his breathing. God, she was hot. He couldn't describe the way he felt with her pressing against him, kissing him. The fun she found in her life despite everything, the positive spin, the humility. She was a bundle of energy that he wanted to capture, to slow down, to have in his bed. And he'd blown it by saying the wrong thing at the wrong time. Each time he thought he knew what he was doing, things took a very unexpected turn.

Error number one: inviting Lola out for dinner in the first place, when he should have gone home and packed for the break he clearly needed. Because, no matter what he might have said about it being a non-date, the words and the reality were on two very opposing sides.

Error number two: mentioning Cameron at such a defining moment. He'd been thinking about trying to convince Lola's boss to seek medical help, and had wondered whether he should suggest Cameron confide in the baby's father too. He couldn't tell Lola that Cameron was pregnant. That would betray a professional confidence and was something he would never do.

But he did want to keep kissing Lola. 'I was stupid to mention her. I'm sorry I've ruined the moment.'

'I'm sorry? So you can actually say it? Now, there's a revelation.' Lola gazed up at him and he could see the hesitation and the desire still there, and that she was fighting it. Resigned to it being over. 'It was already heading in the wrong direction, right? It wasn't a date, you said openly that you didn't want that, and things have just gotten a little out of control.'

He huffed out a long breath. 'I wanted to kiss you.'

'And I wanted to kiss you back.' She gave him a small smile that was at once coy and sexy.

That gave him some hope, as he wasn't finished with the kissing. Although everything she was saying made absolute sense, his body had other things on its mind. 'So we could have a re-run?'

The red hair swung as she shook her head. 'No, Jake. It was an itch that we had to scratch. But it's done now and I don't think we should do it again. I get the feeling we want very different things.'

'I don't know what I want, Lola. At least I did yesterday. I did this morning. Now I'm not sure, but I think it definitely involves you and a lot more kissing.'

'See? Now I'm messing things up for you.' She turned away from him and unlocked her car. Climbed in. Wound down the window. All in the quick-paced way that she did everything. 'I think it'd be a good idea if I'm not around when you come over to see Cameron. Don't worry, I'll make myself scarce.'

Then she gunned the engine and was gone.

She was right. Kissing was messing with his head. A few days on location with a demanding celebrity would see him back to his normal self—one who didn't do random kissing in the street with a woman he'd only just met.

Although he had a feeling that getting back to normal might take a little time, and that a certain Lola Bennett would be stomping through his dreams tonight.

CHAPTER FIVE

JAKE HAD TO admit that flying by private jet was going to be pretty damned cool. He wasn't easily impressed, but he was looking forward to this part of the potentially mind-numbing trip more than anything else. Somehow he'd managed to score a flight with Cameron, and he needed to find time to talk to her about his suspicions of her pregnancy and what antenatal care she should be having.

Thankfully he could concentrate on that, and then try to get some shut-eye after failing to get a decent night's sleep for the first time in his life. Medical school then interning—being woken up at any time of day and night and expected to respond immediately with both a ready smile and a correct diagnosis—had taught him to be able to sleep anywhere he needed, any time. He could power up and down on demand as easily as his trusty laptop.

Except for the last few nights—when he hadn't been able to get the taste and smell of Lola, along with memories of her easy laugh and mesmerising smile, out of his head. All the more reason he needed this break—mind-numbing or not—to reaffirm his work focus and equilibrium. He would approach it as he did everything else, with single-minded determination to do it to the highest standard.

It was, after all, what he'd promised his father he would do—and the only thought going through his brain right now, other than Lola, were the words he'd used at his father's bedside in the hospital. *'I'll pay you back, double, triple what you've given me. Just get well and come home.'* His dad had paid too high a price for Jake to lose focus.

After ditching his car at valet parking, he strode into the private airfield departure lounge, which was more like a converted hangar than anything particularly luxurious, and was immediately greeted by a cacophony of shouts, hysterical screaming and wild yapping.

'Get her, quick, grab her, hurry!' Cameron was screaming, as a small brown dog wearing a studded diamanté collar, head down and teeth bared, scampered faster than Jake imagined a dog that size could go towards an open door that led to the tarmac. Dropping his bags, Jake set off in hot pursuit, dodging air crew, ground crew, piles of luggage, a refuelling lorry and, thankfully, but only just, a catering trolley heading straight for him.

The dog, seemingly enjoying this game of one hundred metre dash, bounded towards the steps of a private Cessna.

'Peanut! Sit. Sit!' From behind Jake a stern but breathless English voice bellowed through the hangar and, unbelievably, the dog came to an abrupt halt at the foot of the steps. 'Naughty girl! Now, come here.'

Lola?

Jake took the opportunity to creep forward and grab the dazed puppy, securing it under his arm. *I did not sign up for this.*

Then he turned to see the cause of his insomnia, who was doubled over, trying to haul in air while simultaneously juggling two other bejewelled, yapping dogs close to her breasts. *Lucky damned pooches.*

And there he was again—losing himself.

It hadn't occurred to him that she'd be here, but maybe she'd come to wave the Nassau-bound party off? Making sure her boss actually left the ground? Not such a bad idea. Shame she'd be stuck with those dogs, though. Nightmare. 'Peanut? That's a name? I thought it was something you had with beer.'

'Sorry, it's chaos as always. Can we do a swap? Please take Butter for a second while I secure Peanut. Yes, we have Peanut, Butter and this is Jelly. I know.' Lola straightened up, offered one of the other dogs to Jake. He couldn't tell whether she was glaring at him or the dogs. Either way there was no smile, and he felt guilty by association. 'Not my choices, by the way. So, Peanut is the devil incarnate—you need to keep a special eye on her or she'll be AWOL in five seconds flat. Butter is the glutton and Jelly is the sweetie. Take my advice, never, ever get three puppies at the same time.'

'It never crossed my mind to get even one. Ever.' He swapped one wriggling jiggling dog for another, which leaned in close and sniffed his face. Its breath smelt like rank dog biscuits and its claws were sharp. Then it stuck out its pink tongue. For a second he thought it was going to take a bite, but instead it began to lick his cheek with unhindered gusto. 'Ugh. No. Er… Butter. Stop.'

He held it at arm's length, looked over at Lola, who was now grinning at his discomfort, and then wished he hadn't as he noticed the smooth curve of her mouth and her clipped-back hair, the soft cotton flowered top and loose skirt that blew a little round her legs in the light wind. That flight couldn't come soon enough.

With a rise of her eyebrows Lola nodded. 'She likes you. That's her way of kissing.'

'Yuck. Personally, I prefer the human way.' The words tumbled out of his mouth before he could stop them, and the memories of the other night tumbled too, making him feel hot and unsatisfied all over again. It was obvious that Lola was thinking the same, as she bit down on her bottom lip and looked away red-cheeked, leaving him wondering exactly where things would have ended up if he hadn't uttered those kiss-of-death—or rather, death-of-kiss—words: *Cameron Fontaine.*

'Yes. Well…' Lola attached a lead to Peanut's collar, took Butter from his outstretched hands and put all three dogs on the ground. 'Unfortunately she hasn't mastered the art of tact yet.'

'Like her owner.' *And me.* Jake threw Lola a smile, not sure if it was reassuring or what the hell it was. He didn't know the required etiquette for talking to someone who really didn't want to share the same air as him, and had told him as much.

Lola looked up at him through dark, thick eyelashes, solemn and serious. 'Er…about the other day—'

'No need…really.'

'It's just, you know, bad timing.'

'It's fine, I understand.' Although he didn't. Seriously, he was a surgeon, dealing with science and facts and black and white. All this chaos and acting and kissing was way beyond his comprehension.

But he did understand her reluctance to want to do it again. She'd been taking up far too much of his head space. He preferred his liaisons to be brief, satisfactory and forgettable. That way he could focus entirely on his work and paying back his dad. Just the thought of the debt he owed gave Jake a jolt in his chest.

'Lola! Do hurry up! And you too, Dr Lewis.' Ms Fontaine was waving and indicating that it was time to leave. 'Don't make us late. Lola, where are your bags?'

'Sorry! Coming!' Lola started towards her boss, encouraging the three yapping stooges to follow on their leads. 'Come on, sweeties. Hurry up. This way.'

But Jake held back, suddenly off balance all over again. 'What? Your bags?'

'Oh. Yes.' Lola threw the comment over her shoulder, like scraps to a hungry bird. 'Apparently Mommy doesn't want to leave her babies—for some reason she's come over more broody than usual and can't bear to be parted from them. So we're all coming too. Normally I would be thrilled at the idea of going to Nassau for the weekend, but—'

He never got to hear the *but,* although he imagined what it was, as the jet engines powered into life, the noise sending thoughts and words into the wind, and that much of the *but* had to do with him and that kiss. Or maybe he was reading too much into it. Though the blush on Lola's cheeks wasn't due to make-up, and the tone in her voice hadn't been wistful and hopeful. It had been as wary as he felt, a warning almost.

Out on the tarmac a fierce draught blew Lola's red curls round her face, and the dogs' mouths opened and closed with apparent indignation at the racket, but Jake couldn't hear anything over the engine din. He was beginning to realise that whatever plans he'd made were about to crash into oblivion. He was not going to get private time to discuss Cameron's pregnancy. The attraction to her assistant was not abating any time soon. And a decent night's sleep was clearly going to become a thing of the past.

In truth, Lola coming on this trip was the worst possible outcome he could imagine.

Cameron had fallen asleep in one of the sumptuous red and cream leather sofas on board, and Jake was doing a good impression of the same thing. However, as he'd been seated next to her, Lola could see that even though his eyes were closed, his breathing wasn't rhythmic and slow. He was just pretending to be asleep.

He was pretending? Just so he didn't have to talk to her? Charming.

And the problem was, even on a plane like this where seating was plentiful and generous, he was still too close for any kind of comfort. Worse, that ridiculous urge to reach out and touch him hovered around—to just lay her hand against his chest or his arm, or something. The other night had been a close-run thing, and she'd felt mortified when Cameron had demanded she accompany them on this trip when she'd have far preferred not to see Jake again. Somehow she would have to keep her distance. The man was no good for her plans.

After five and a half uncomfortable hours of dark silence, followed by awkward conversation whilst trying to contain three excitable puppies, they landed in Nassau. So much for private flying—not one sip of champagne had passed her lips; Miss Fontaine was on a *clean* diet so that meant everyone else was too.

The lunch had been delicious, though—a decent serving of fresh raw taco shells with spicy vegetables, salsa and cashew cheese. Slightly strange, but far better than any economy class, ever, even if just for the real knives and forks instead of plastic ones, and real linen napkins.

'Well, that was very acceptable. I think I'm spoiled for flying ever again,' she whispered to Jake, just for something to say as they stood shoulder to shoulder at the top of the steps, waiting to disembark. Cameron had insisted on going first, making a grand entrance for the waiting local paparazzi, while the staff hung around in her slipstream. 'I don't suppose you could convince the boss that drinking buckets and buckets of French champagne is very good for you? She's got it into her head that alcohol is very bad, but I'd love a glass.'

He shook his head and frowned. 'A cold beer would have been great, but…not for Cameron. She shouldn't be drinking.'

'Why not?'

He looked pensive. 'Er… I suppose she has to maintain her figure for continuity reasons for the film. No alcohol for the foreseeable future.'

'Spoilsport. I thought you might be on my side.' But, then, she supposed, she'd pushed him away the other day so why should he do anything to please her? 'Here goes. Down the steps… Now, don't say anything as you walk by the cameras, just keep looking ahead. Oh, and could you take one of these, please? Peanut's very wriggly again. I don't think she likes flying.'

'She's definitely not one for cattle class, that's for sure.' Jake didn't look enamoured about carrying a Chihuahua, and she had to admit that a beautiful, tall, toned man carrying a tiny dog did look funny. But he took it anyway, in one hand, and with the other he steadied her down the steps, a gentle touch on her elbow. For a second Lola felt as if she were the star, but the thrumming of her heart and the hot flush to her cheeks just highlighted the shy teenager inside her. Sometimes she didn't know how Cameron dredged up all that confidence every day, every hour. It was exhausting.

The limo journey from the airport, under a cloudless

bright blue sky, took them west past candy-coloured high-rise apartments and along palm-tree-lined roads, through a maze of canals towards Old Fort Bay and the many private residences dotted along the coastline. Beyond the fancy gates and majestic buildings Lola got a glimpse of white sandy beaches and a turquoise sea. Only the rich and famous bought homes here.

One day, she thought.

Wait… Oh, wow. Actually, today… The car turned right into a long gravel driveway, meandered through lush, verdant bushes and eventually came to a stop outside a large white colonial villa clothed in bright pink creeping bougainvillea. 'Oh, my God. It's gorgeous.'

Stunned, Lola bundled the dogs out of the car and gave instructions to the driver as Cameron disappeared into the house. This was way beyond anything she'd imagined.

'I wasn't expecting this. I thought we'd be at a resort or something with the others.' Jake looked equally impressed as he carried luggage from the car boot to the door. He peered up at the magnificent building, then at the manicured front lawn and frowned. 'Before we go in, Lola, can I ask you something?'

Uh-oh. If it was about the other night she'd just about die.

If it was about kissing again she would do that first, and then just about die. 'Sure. What is it?' It was as nonchalant as she could get, in between palpitations.

He pointed to the house. 'What the hell has this all got to do with a space warrior odyssey?'

She breathed out, a flicker of disappointment subsumed by good old common sense. Then she laughed, because she was a damned fool to even think… He wasn't the kind of guy to try again after rejection. 'Oh. Well, it's a flashback scene or a dream sequence, going back to pre-apocalyptic Earth, or something. But between you and me I think it's just a good excuse for a jolly.'

He gave her a funny look. 'A jolly what?'

'A jolly. It means…it means a work thing that's really just all about play.'

'You Brits say the strangest things.' But he was laughing and for a moment the air between them seemed less strained. Maybe, if they kept their conversations superficial, and maintained a decent distance, they could reach some sort of friendly equilibrium after all. Maybe he could be in one wing and she'd isolate herself in the opposite one. The place was certainly big enough. Yes, distance was the solution.

A young woman appeared at the door and explained in a melodic Bahamian accent that she was Tina, the housekeeper, and to please leave everything to her. 'Miss Fontaine has requested sole use of the house. I have put you and the… Dr Jake…' The woman peered up at Jake and smiled. For a moment Lola thought the housekeeper was going to curtsy or kiss him, or just old-fashioned swoon. 'Good afternoon, Dr Jake. Welcome to The Haven. I hope you'll be happy here.'

He shook her outstretched hand. 'I'm sure I will. Thank you, Tina.'

'Anything you want, just go right ahead and ask,' Tina sighed.

Lola sighed too, but hers was more through irritation. *That's right, lady, keep right on looking. I've kissed that mouth.*

A strange and breath-sapping spike of something lodged underneath Lola's ribcage. Must have been the raw taco shells not agreeing with her, she decided, and nothing at all to do with a fierce possessive streak that scuttled through her. Jake was not her property and she would not be jealous of women looking at him like that. Yes, he was gorgeous. Yes, he was dashing and charming. So what? No big deal.

She'd switched off momentarily and hadn't heard what the housekeeper had been saying, but as she tapped behind her across the marble floors through the palatial house, then out past a huge infinity pool, Lola realised that they were being taken to a different building.

'In here, please, Miss Bennett.' They'd stopped outside a smaller, single-storey villa, cream and white with another deep red bush growing up the side, a small picket-fenced garden and a wrought-iron outside table for two on a deck overlooking the ocean. It was more private and secluded than the grand villa. It was, in fact, like a cosy honeymoon retreat.

No. No flipping way. Blood rushed to her cheeks. She couldn't…wouldn't…shouldn't be here with him. She should be in the big house, tending to her boss's every need. Even that was preferable to being in a honeymoon hideaway with Jake. 'I…er…there's been a mistake…'

'No. No mistake.' Oblivious to Lola's growing panic, the housekeeper was still chattering away. 'The Lodge is for you and the doctor to share at Miss Fontaine's insistence. Two bedrooms, two bathrooms. There are interconnecting phones to the main house in the kitchen, the lounge and each bedroom. But Miss Fontaine said, please, to let her rest for a few hours. She will call if she needs anything.'

'Okay.' Lola blew out a big breath. This was so not what she'd had in mind for superficial and distant. But if there was one thing she knew about her boss it was that she wouldn't change her mind once it was made up. She and Jake would be sharing. Period. 'Well, first, I need to

get the dogs some water and some shade. It's too hot for
them. I could take them for a walk around the grounds.
I saw a lovely little shaded area they could play in back
near the big house.' Anything to distract her from the
fact that she would be sharing living quarters with a god.

Tina smiled as she bent to give the dogs a stroke.
'Aren't they adorable? The beach out front is private, so
they can run around there under the trees. I have a little
dog of my own over in the staff annexe, they can come
play any time. I can take them now, give you a break?'

'Thanks, but the walk will do us good after being
cooped up on a plane.' Truthfully, it was just an excuse
for some Jake-free time.

But the traitorous puppies pattered quietly into the
cool lodge, obviously exhausted from their first-class
travelling ordeal, found a plump cushion each on a white
rattan sofa and fell asleep.

The housekeeper fussed around the light, bright house,
showing them the modern kitchen facilities, the menu—
because, yes, The Haven had its own chef—and the well-
stocked pantry and fridge. Then she left, leaving them
to decide who had which bedroom, and what the hell to
do next.

And then there were two.

Lola glanced over at Jake, who was staring at the
beach out of a huge picture window in the lounge. 'Er…
how shall I put this? Do you want to have a look at the
bedrooms and decide where you want to sleep?'

Eyebrows rising, Jake grinned. 'Now you're talking.'

'I didn't mean… No. I meant—'

'I was joking, Lola. Don't look so worried. Take
whichever room you want and I'll have the other.' He
bent and unzipped his bag, grabbed something from it.
'I'm going for a swim while I have the chance. Coming?'

She imagined him in board shorts. A naked chest. Bare skin. Soaking wet. And swallowed through a dry throat. 'Er… No. I don't want to leave these little guys on their own and I really do need to unpack. And Cameron might call…and I'm thirsty…' And…she was rambling again.

'Hey.' He stepped closer. 'Don't worry, Lola. It's all under control. How about I have a swim, then take over childcare while you go and cool off? A roster system?'

'Oh, okay, that sounds great. Thanks. It is very hot. And I could do with a swim. Later, when you get back.'

The smile slipped. 'Sure. And that way we need never be in the same room for longer than a few moments. Just at cross-over. That's what you want? Right?'

Her heart began to hammer—he was very forthright when he wanted to be. Direct and to the point. She supposed he had to be in his line of work—couldn't pussy-foot around a bad diagnosis. But it left her feeling exposed and vulnerable. She wasn't used to people speaking their minds quite so openly. Besides, she didn't know what she wanted in relation to their living arrangements. 'I just think…in light of the other night…it would be better if our paths didn't cross so much.'

'Understood.' He took a step away, then turned. 'It was only a kiss, Lola. We can move on.'

'Of course. Yes! Only a kiss! I've already moved on. No problem!' As if she kissed people she'd just met all the time.

Only a kiss, yes. But a very nice one at that. And she didn't kiss strangers. Ever. She didn't kiss random men. She didn't kiss men she thought were just okay. She kissed men she liked. And she liked Jake. That was a massive part of the problem. She liked him. Too much, it seemed. 'You'd better go get changed then.'

While she wandered into the open-plan kitchen, he

disappeared into a bathroom, returning moments later with a white towel looped round his shoulders, beach shorts slung low over slender hips. She tried very hard not to look, she really did, but she couldn't help it. He was there, walking across the room, larger than life. Her gaze travelled upwards from his hips, past a smattering of dark hair, tanned washboard abs, a broad chest, to a smirking mouth.

For a few seconds she remembered the taste of him. The heat. And she clung to the kitchen countertop as the same heat shimmered through her. How the hell would she be able to stay here with that kind of reaction going on?

And when her eyes settled on his she knew that it was going to be almost impossible. There was humour there in his eyes, and teasing, and it fired an unwanted need in her core.

She dragged her eyes away, found a voice, albeit fractured. 'Enjoy.'

'You look like you just did.' He winked. 'See you later.'

CHAPTER SIX

LOLA WAS PROUD of herself. She'd managed to spend the rest of the day in avoidance mode. Had eaten dinner with Jake and Cameron, which had passed pleasantly enough with small talk and chit-chat about movies and brain surgery—although, Lola noticed, he hadn't offered to show Cameron how to do wide-awake surgery with chopsticks, and he was just a little more reserved around the actress.

Then Lola had taken the dogs for a late-night walk on her own, and had returned to find a quiet lodge. Jake had gone to bed and there'd been no further awkward conversation. She'd fallen asleep after only a couple of hours lying in bed wondering what the hell tomorrow would bring.

And thinking about his mouth. That body. That smile.

In the next damned room.

And how she was going to survive being stuck in close proximity to him?

After her morning puppy walk she returned to find the interconnecting phone ringing and no Jake in sight. Thank God. 'Hello!'

'Lola, honey, it's me.'

'Hi, Cameron! Beautiful day.'

'Sure is. Listen, Alfredo wants to take me on a boat

trip to one of the private islands this morning, meet some of his friends. Take care of the babies, will you? They wouldn't be safe on a boat. I'll be back after lunch, then we can all go to the set.'

'Of course. Have fun. See you later.'

'Was that Cameron?' Jake's voice behind her made her heart bounce to a jerky beat.

She steadied it before turning to find him dressed in workout gear and slightly out of breath. After yesterday's staring faux pas she'd promised herself not to look too closely, so settled on trying to get the swanky coffee machine to work. She fiddled with the little shiny plastic capsules, chose a silver one, popped it in. 'Coffee?'

'Yes, thanks.'

'Been for a run?'

'Working out. There's a gym in the basement up at the house. I thought I might see Cameron there, but she didn't appear. What's the plan?' He wandered to the cabinet, pulled out a cup. Back in her line of vision. He looked sweaty, arm muscles pumped. Hair dishevelled. All kinds of hot. *No. Not looking.*

'Cameron probably worked out last night—she prefers to do it in the evenings. She's going out, back around noon, then we're to accompany her to the set.'

Jake was staring at her with a strange look on his face, which he wiped as soon as he realised she was watching him. 'So we have a free morning?'

'Just Cameron-free. Three hours or so.' Lola added skimmed milk to her coffee and started making his. Trying not to make eye contact. It felt as if she'd said something wrong, but couldn't put her finger on anything relevant. Or maybe it was just the kiss hovering between them again. She needed to get out. 'I have a ton of stuff to do. Actually, I'll go and make a start.'

His hand on her wrist stopped her, his heat seeping into her skin and through her body. 'You haven't had your coffee, Lola.'

'Thanks. No. Well… I can take it with…' She couldn't take her eyes off his hand, long fingers, neat nails. Skilled and powerful, whether holding chopsticks, a scalpel or probes. Hands that had cupped her face so intensely.

Yes, that kiss was definitely there, the huge elephant in the room. She swallowed deeply.

He looked down and hurriedly drew his hand away from her wrist. And she wanted to grab his hand and put it right back, but he pulled out some croissants from the bread bin. 'I'm never going to survive on a skinny actress's rabbit food. I asked the chef to get something decent for us to eat. You want some? I won't tell anyone, it'll be our secret?'

'No, thanks.'

He watched her. 'You don't like them or don't want them? Two different things.'

'I'm trying to be healthy. There's some fruit in the fridge, I'll have that.' There was also champagne, she'd noted, and wondered if he'd requested that too. She watched as flaky crumbs dropped from his lip onto the plate and her stomach rumbled. God, she wanted a bite. And not just of the croissant.

As if he could read her mind, he held it out to her. 'Believe me, if you eat with Cameron every day you'll be more than healthy but not very happy. Or full. And definitely not satisfied. Besides, the brain is made up of sixty per cent fat—we need it to think, work, be. So come on, just a mouthful. This is delicious. All that butter. So good.' He bent and rummaged in the bread bin again, pulled out another pastry. 'Oh, look, here's one with chocolate. Chocolate for breakfast—sinful. In the

Bahamas…in the sunshine. Just a small piece. Come on…
I promise not to tell a soul.'

'Oh, go on, then, just a little bit. I have zero willpower.' She laughed, taking the *pain au chocolat* and
tearing off a piece, which she unashamedly popped into
her mouth. It was indeed delicious. 'So you're being my
enabler now? The chocolate is the gateway drug, then
the croissant is the road to hell.'

He dipped his head to look her directly in the eyes.
'I'm just trying to be friendly. The way I see it, we have
to get along here. We have a small house and we're going
to be spending a lot of time together. Either we try to put
the kiss behind us and make a fresh start, or one of us
will have to explain to Cameron our predicament and ask
to bunk in with her. I can't see that going down well. But
I can't live with tension and awkwardness here either.'

Again the direct approach. It was confronting, but
also refreshing. She studied him for a moment. Those
dark blue eyes weren't playing her, but actually genuinely trying to reach a solution. She could do this. 'Okay.
Fresh start.'

'Great. Eat. Good?'

Was it rude to tear it apart with her teeth? 'Oh, God,
yes. Brain food? Just think how much more clever I'll
be after eating it.'

'I didn't say it would make you more clever. But what
the hell…if it makes you eat, genius. Now, if only I had
something to drink too…'

'Oh, your coffee… I forgot.' She put the pastry down
for a moment while she found him a purple plastic cap-
sule and set the machine. In a few moments the sounds
of gurgling filled the silence.

Once he'd finished eating he gave her a satisfied
smile. 'I was just talking to Tina up at the house. She

says there's some excellent snorkelling over near Lyford Cay. If we had time we could charter a boat and go further offshore, but we only have a couple hours—there's still some interesting fish just off the beach. You fancy heading off and having a look? We can take a couple of motor scooters.'

'What? Now?' Up close and personal with a semi-naked Jake? No way. Once was bad enough. Or, rather, good enough. Too good. That wasn't her idea of a fresh start. 'What about Cameron?'

'Well, we're here to work, but we can't work if the boss isn't around, now, can we?' He shook his head. 'Have you ever snorkelled in the Bahamas before? Ridden a motor scooter?'

Sharing a standing-up breakfast was one thing, sharing a half-naked adventure was something altogether different. 'Snorkelling? Motor scooters? My job isn't the same as yours, Jake, waiting around until someone gets sick. I have other things to do. Lots of things.'

'Can they wait?'

'Says the self-confessed workaholic.'

'Yes, I am… But Tina said if we do nothing else while we're here we must do some snorkelling. She has all the gear. And I'm hardly extending my surgical skills sitting around here, am I? What will I do…? Practise my injection technique on an orange?'

He picked up an orange from the fruit bowl and threw it into the air and caught it. Then picked up another and juggled the two. Then three. His arms flexed as he threw and caught in effortless yet hypnotising fluid movements. She could see his back muscles tighten and release, his shoulders working, the wry smile as he concentrated, almost meditative. God, he was…well, her gut prickled with heat. She became acutely aware that there was just the two of them here. That kiss may have been put aside, but the way it made it her feel hadn't been. Her fingers shook as she started to fill the dishwasher just to do something other than watch him. He caught the oranges in one hand and smiled again.

'You did that?' Her voice was thick with need. She coughed, tried not to think about his body, lowered her voice an octave. 'You injected oranges?'

'Yes, to get the angle right. And practised my suturing on pigskin…then on humans…my classmates, myself…' He put the oranges back, serious again. 'Okay, you're right. I hear you on the work issue. I have to catch up on some reading and there's research I'm assisting with…'

For just a few minutes he'd been carefree and fun, and she didn't want to lose that Jake to a serious Jake. But how could she go with him when she felt like this? 'It sounds lovely…maybe another time. Tomorrow, if we get a chance. There's a list of errands I need to do today. I can't take off and play. Besides, we have the dogs to think about.'

'Tina could have the dogs. I could help you with the errands when we get back.'

Lola lifted her smartphone from the countertop and scrolled through her task list. 'Because finding a decent manicurist on Nassau who can drop everything and come over as Cameron requires is the kind of thing you do every day.'

'Whoa. I didn't realise it would be that kind of difficult.' He looked horrified, eyes wide and panicked. 'That sounds way out of my comfort zone. Give me something easier to do, I don't know…negotiate world peace? But first snorkel?'

What could she say? *I'd like to, but if there was ever a possibility of drowning in lust I'd be victim number one.* 'I just…'

'You just what?' He was scrutinising her face, his jaw taut, eyes narrowed. Then his whole body stilled. 'Ah. I get it, now. You just…don't want to snorkel with *me*, that right? Sorry I took so long to catch on.' Grabbing his half-finished coffee, he started to walk outside to the deck and the mood turned decidedly dark. 'I hear ya, loud and clear, Lola. I won't bother you again.'

He'd gone way past serious Jake and was somewhere on the edge of angry Jake. She followed him outside, feeling hollowed out. 'Jake, I do want to go snorkelling. It sounds fun. I'll come. I was trying to be dedicated to my work… You of all people know how that is.' Did he believe her?

'Yeah, I do. But, you know, for one second there I thought, Let's stuff work for a while. But don't worry, I'll go on my own.'

'No. No, I'll come. I want to, really. I'm sorry. Please.'

He looked at her, weighing up her words. She wasn't sure what he was thinking and her stomach knotted. But eventually he nodded, his enthusiasm around twenty per cent of what it had been. 'Okay. Let's think time management, then. How about one-hour blocks? One hour to snorkel. One hour to travel there and back, shower… One hour for work?'

'Okay. I'll get my things ready.'

He nodded, but the oomph had leached out of him. 'I'll take the pups up to Tina, then meet you at the garages—apparently there's every kind of vehicle we might need in there.'

Looked like she didn't have a choice.

This was the worst damned idea he'd had in years.

Jake watched as Lola discarded her T-shirt and shorts and stood a little away from him on the sand, with a towel tightly wrapped around herself. Underneath, he knew, she was wearing a black bikini that covered her curves well enough, but did nothing to hide her great figure. He swallowed, trying not to look too closely...but in the end it didn't really matter, as his body was hell-bent on reacting anyway. His mouth watered at the thought of her perfect mouth, and his fingers craved to smooth down her wind-wild hair. Never mind the tight clutch low down in his belly that had him turning away from her. Thank God there was cold water close by.

Working would have been a much better idea but here he was, instead, with a reluctant accomplice and a serious case of hot lust. Why he'd even bothered to invite her he didn't know. Playing hooky for once in his thirty-three years had seemed like a good idea when talking to Tina. Harmless.

In truth, he should have stayed back at the house and tried to catch Cameron for that conversation he still hadn't had with her. It had been such a temptation to talk to Lola about the pregnancy—obviously confidentiality meant he never could—but he got the feeling Cameron needed more than him looking out for her.

'Have you got a wetsuit? Rash guard? The sun's fierce, you don't want to get burnt,' he growled at Lola, taking a step away from her. He didn't want to have to rub sunscreen on to that gorgeous body, or they'd never actually get into the ocean.

And what he needed more than anything was a dose of cold seawater to sluice away the physical ache he had for her—especially seeing her right now; lush red curls against creamy pale skin, breasts that threatened to break free from flimsy string masquerading as a bikini, and a waist that looked the perfect size for his hands to grip.

'Yes, boss. Here.' She turned and held up a pink neoprene jacket and put it on, zipping up the front. *Thank God.*

He couldn't get his head around the fact that the kiss had seemed real and wanted on both sides, and yet now she wanted to be anywhere other than with him. But he'd got the message, and she was right. There were too many reasons to prevent him getting involved with anyone, let alone a woman who had such a serious effect on his equilibrium.

'Tina said that over by the rocks was the best place to start. There's some coral there, so take care not to stand on it, we don't want to damage it.' And with that he turned and made his way down towards the water, fins and mask in hand.

But she was with him in two strides.

'So, isn't this the best look ever?' Laughing, Lola dragged her mask over her face and made piggy eyes at him as she pulled the mouth tube into her mouth.

Actually, it was a pretty damned sexy look, and he was shocked by how much he wanted to haul her to him, even with a plastic mask on. So he dived deep into the clear, cool water and got on with fish-spotting.

Jake was always surprised at the serenity of the ocean; all that busy activity down there, yet little sound save for the ebb and flow of waves and the echo of his heartbeat in his ears. The sun warmed his back as a whole new world opened up below him. The little underwater gardens were teeming with life and there was enough interest to grab his attention away from the hunger Lola had started in his gut.

They followed the curve of the bay out west, floating and bobbing with the tide, popping up for air as and when they needed it, agreeing on a course to follow, then swimming and watching and pointing at the sea life. Lola was an excellent snorkeller, easily excited by the large black manta ray gliding along the seabed and the schools of pretty purple and electric-blue fish that darted back and forth in front of them.

Then she kicked away to follow a shoal of bright yellow spotted ones, and for a few moments he was alone—just skimming along the top of the water looking down into the rhythmic swaying of the seaweed on the coral.

His heart rate slowed, and for the first time since he'd set foot in the Caribbean he began to relax. The cool water washed over him and with it his sense of equilibrium and purpose was renewed. It was only a few days in the Bahamas, they could rub along together for that, fill their days with activities and surround themselves with other people. Soon enough they'd be back to LA and their normal lives. After that, the filming would swiftly wrap up and he'd have no reason to see her again. With time, he hoped, this ache would die and she'd just be a quaint memory. Like the other women who'd flitted in and out of his life.

It would all work out fine.

He didn't know how long they'd been there, but suddenly the water turned choppy. Expecting the wave wash of a boat or a jet ski, he lifted his head out of the water and came face-to-face with a grinning Lola. She ripped the mouth tube from her lips and pointed out to sea. 'Look! Look! Dolphins.'

Sure enough, a pod of bottlenose dolphins was diving and playing in the deeper reef. 'Oh, yeah. Pretty cool.'

As she trod water she gripped his shoulder. 'Cool? It's flipping amazing. Look at them, showing off, playing together. Do you think we could swim with them? D'you think?'

'You'll have to be quick.' And before he could argue she'd grabbed his hand and was half swimming and half dragging him through the waves, trying to catch them up. For little more than a few minutes the dolphins gave them a magical show of their skills, corkscrewing over and over, darting underneath their legs and popping up behind them. One of them took a liking to Lola and pushed his nose at her. She reached out and touched him before he darted away. He returned twice and played the same teasing game—pushing his nose at her, waiting for her to reach and then disappearing into the foam. Then, just as quickly as they'd appeared, they were all off in a display of enthusiasm, swimming faster than humanly possible and disappearing into the distance.

'Wow... I can't... This is so...' Lola stopped and grasped his hand again, coughing as she took off her mask. The outlines of the rubber seal had marked her pretty face, but she was grinning widely, tears shimmering in her eyes. She looked so damned beautiful it made his chest constrict. 'I don't know what to say. That was... Oh, my God! Dolphins. That was so amazing.'

'Yeah. Very cool.' He took off his mask too and affected an English accent. 'Pretty flipping amazing, actually.' Like she was, with bright golden flashes in her dark brown eyes, her hair slicked back, droplets of water falling from her eyelashes. A mouth that he ached to taste all over again.

'Yes, it is. All of it. Everything...' Her voice cracked. She looked at him as she held onto his shoulder, her legs working beneath the surface to keep her upright, while something passed between them. Something electric, something real and hot. Everything felt as it had when they'd kissed, the charge in the air was the same—an almost tangible shimmer between them.

But that couldn't be right, because she'd said… What had she said? That she was messing things up for him. But here she wasn't messing up anything, here she was making the trip a whole lot more bearable. But he was useless at reading signals, especially in ten feet of water when words and actions didn't gel. 'Lola, we should probably go now.'

'But—'

'We need to get back. An hour for each, we agreed.' He made a start for the shore, leaving the cooler depths behind and entering the warmer water where it was almost shallow enough to stand up, had it not been for the coral gardens beneath their feet.

'Wait. Stop a minute.' Panting, she caught up with him, grasped his arm. 'Thank you for bringing me here. I'm sorry I was so hard to convince. I don't want to get in the way of your work. I know how important that is to you.'

'Yeah, but you can't work all the time. People keep telling me.' He reached and wiped some water from her cheek. It was cold out here but heat exploded through him. All the more reason to get the hell out. 'But we can't put it off forever either. We'd better make a start back.'

'Stop.' She reached for his jaw and ran her palm over his cheek. 'Do we need to think about work right now?'

Her legs made little swirling kicks around him. He could feel the rhythmic movement, and a need to have her wrap those legs around his hips almost overwhelmed him.

He should have turned and swam away then. He should have listened to the voice in his head reminding him of what she'd said. But he did neither. Instead, he put his hand on her waist and pulled her closer. And, yes—it was a perfect fit for his palm. 'What do you want to think about?'

'Actually, I don't feel much like thinking at all.' She looked up from beneath long eyelashes adorned with droplets like a hundred tiny diamonds highlighting the flashes of colour in her eyes and the intensity of need.

His heart was raging a wild tattoo in his chest. Because even though he was lame at reading signals, he was pretty sure he knew what this one was saying. And, for the record, Lola was nothing like the others. She was special. Unique. 'What do you feel like doing?'

'I want to kiss you again.' She wriggled closer into his open arms and slanted her wet mouth against his, and all thoughts of work and conflicting signals, and all the reasons to stop fled from his brain. He dragged her hard against him and kissed her back.

She tasted of salt and the sea, she tasted fresh and hot and hungry. As she entwined her legs with his he pushed his fingers into her hair, cradled her head and relished the press of her glorious curves against him. Her hand ran down his back as she moaned into his mouth, fingernails grasping at his skin.

Slowly he nipped along her bottom lip then kissed along her collarbone to the soft hollow at her throat, and she tilted her head back and laughed.

'God, Jake, I've been dreaming about this.'

'You too?' He tugged the zip on her neoprene and slowly freed her breasts, slid his palm over one as he took her mouth again. Beneath his fingers her nipples contracted to tight buds and he coaxed them, first gently stroking then—reluctantly leaving her mouth—he was licking them against the rise and fall of the ocean.

It *was* like a crazy dream—a beautiful woman, a deserted beach, the reach and grasp of a delicious need that spiralled through him.

'Oh, yes.' She pulled his mouth from her nipple and cupped his face, anchoring him to her, deepening the kiss, hard and wet, pulsing in time with the waves. The kiss became urgent, the need for her almost frantic. He was so hard. So hard for her and she knew it as she wriggled against him and groaned with pleasure.

Laughing, she wrapped her legs around his hips, and as she did so, something wrapped tight around his heart and tugged. The light sound of her carefree laughter, the sway of the ocean waves, the rush of adrenalin and heat filled him with more than desire. He wanted her, too much.

It would have been so easy to slide back her bikini bottoms and thrust into her there, but reality began to seep into his brain. There was no future in this, and Lola was the kind of woman who would want the fairy-tale future in the end. Regardless of what she may say or do now, he couldn't promise her anything apart from a good time and a goodbye.

She was fresh and untainted, she was something new and good. And, when it came down to it, he wasn't. Not where women were concerned. He didn't want them to cloud his vision, to distract him. He had a lot to achieve— a debt to repay. He didn't want to have to consider another person.

Lola deserved to be considered.

He pulled away and held her wrists. 'Lola, we need to stop this.'

'Yes, God, my legs are killing me, treading water. Let's get to dry land…and then…you know…there's not a soul on the beach and I see a secluded place…'

He shook his head. 'Let's talk once we get to the beach.'

'Talk?' She almost flinched, the hit to her gut was visible, but she slowly absorbed it. Her smile slipped as she realised what he was saying. For a second he thought she was going to agree with him, but she hit her open palm hard on the top of the water so spray arced over him. 'You know what, Jake? You are so damned annoying.'

Then she started to swim hard towards the shore.

After a minute or so she stopped and turned to him, breathless, angry, legs kicking beneath the surface. 'I don't get it. I don't get why you do all that and then listen to whatever it was in your head telling you to stop. Because I know you want to kiss me, Jake. I know you want to fool around and I do too. So why the hell—? Ow! Oh. Wow.' She gasped sharply, then again as her face contorted in pain and she started to thrash under the water. 'Go. To. Hell—Ow! *Ow!*'

'Lola? What's wrong?'

'I—? Leave. Me. Alone.' She bobbed under the water, grasping at her leg. When she resurfaced she was blinking back tears, pressing her hand to her mouth and trying to stay afloat.

Jake's heart hammered. 'What's wrong? Lola, what's happened?'

'Something stung me. Bit me? Ow…' Her face was pinched and he could see she was fighting pain. 'Oh, what the hell do you care anyway?'

'Quite a damned lot, actually.' The reality of that gave him a powerful thump to his solar plexus. This was not the time for arguing or playing stupid games.

CHAPTER SEVEN

'CALM DOWN. TAKE A deep breath. Breathe, Lola. And again. That's it. Good. It's okay. I've got you.' Jake's arms wrapped round her as he kicked hard towards the beach. Her leg felt as if someone was holding a hot poker against it, the burn ripped through the flesh to the bone. She clung on to his shoulders as he powered through the waves.

She just wanted the pain to stop. *I will not cry.* 'Jellyfish? D'you think it's a jellyfish? Are there more? Don't get stung too.' She had to shout over the roar of waves and the rush of white noise in her head, though it came out like a panicked, high-pitched squeal.

'I didn't see anything swimming around… But, then, I was distracted…' He hauled in oxygen, breathing hard as he bore the weight of the two of them. 'Could be anything. Lola, keep still.'

'It hurts.'

'I know it does.' And he was there for her, holding her, saving her. Regardless of what he'd said about the kissing. He was there, she'd remember that—once she'd got over the pain and the humiliation of being rejected. *Again.*

In no time at all they reached the beach and he laid her on the sand at the water's edge and bathed her leg with cooling seawater. His eyes had lost the heat she'd seen before, but there was something else there—concern, hesitation. 'How's it feeling now?'

'Okay. And stop being so bloody nice to me.' It made things a million times worse, and made her like him even more.

'First time anyone's ever complained about me being considerate.' His tone was kind and patient, in contrast to hers.

'That's because you're showing me your nice side, but I know you have a bad side. And, no, it's not okay any more. Every time you stop bathing it hurts even more. I think I'll keep the water on it.' She bit her lip and shuffled deeper into the water, scanning first for any rogue jellyfish that might have followed them. 'My heart's racing really fast.'

'It's probably just adrenalin from the shock—you'll be fine. Just sit a while. Try more deep breaths. In…slowly… and now out…that's it.' Calmly he took her hand, pressed two fingers just below her thumb and focused. After way longer than a minute he was still holding her wrist, his palm stroking her skin. Now her heart was beating erratically for an altogether different reason. Again in that considerate tone he said, 'Here, lean against me. Keep your foot in the water until you feel you can stand. Then I'll take you to a clinic.'

'Clinic? I don't have time… We've got to get back. Cameron needs us.'

'Cameron will have to wait.'

'Seriously? Have you tried telling her to do anything she doesn't…?' But the searing burn was turning now into an aggravating itch. She wanted to tear at her skin. When she looked down she saw huge red welts and blisters starting to appear. So she leaned against him anyway, taking strength from his heat, her fist coiled into his. 'It's starting to itch like crazy. Don't suppose you have jellyfish antidotes back at the lodge?'

'Sure, I have something for every kind of emergency; polar-bear bait, black widow spider anti-venin. Zombie-killer stakes.' He pushed her matted hair away from her face with his free hand and pressed a kiss on to the top of her head—as he would to a child. 'No, oddly, I don't have jellyfish antidote, even if there is such a thing, but usually you just need cold water and something acidic. Seriously, we've got to get it seen by someone. If it was a jellyfish—and it may have been something else—we need to get the right treatment. Some of them are deadly.'

'And now you're making me feel so much better about this. But apart from wanting to rip my skin off, I think I'll take a chance on walking.' She let him haul her up from the sand and watched while he gathered their things together, then she let him half carry her as she hopped towards the motor scooters. 'Maybe the cool rush of air as I'm scooting along will help.'

'You are not driving that scooter on your own, Lola. You're shaking; you won't be able to steer. Climb on the front of mine. I'll send someone to pick yours up later.' Then he made a quick phone call, flicked his cell phone back into his bag and indicated for her to sit in front of him, old-fashioned side-saddle style.

'I... Oh, okay.' She didn't want to, but she did any-way, sliding her arms around his waist, pressing her head against the solid wall of his chest, breathing in the scent of man and elements and some flowery fragrance from the beautiful blooms all around them, but she didn't care about that. All she could think of was the pain and the itch and the kiss and the way he'd felt, so hard, so hun-gry for her. The way he'd turned away from her, denying what he'd so obviously wanted.

And the way he'd looked at her when she'd been hurt, as if he'd do everything in his power to help her. If he hadn't been so nice she'd have bawled him out all the more for stopping the kissing. Because here she was, with a guy who was the hottest thing on two legs and who also had a damned conscience.

'That's fire coral rash, pretty sure, Dr Jake.' Tina was standing over the couch, hands on her ample hips, peering at Lola's leg. Thankfully the painkillers were kicking in and the intense burning was subsiding, but the itch was driving her mad and there were still angry red welts on her ankle. Not to mention swelling.

And outright humiliation. Typical. Only she would be in the middle of paradise and get attacked by a man-eating plant.

'Fire coral?' Jake frowned. 'What's that?'

'Looks like coral, but has venom,' Tina explained. 'She'll live. Vinegar to kill the barbs. Then you can tweezer them out.'

'Great. I saw some vinegar in the kitchen and I'll go grab my medical kit.' Jake nodded. He'd been nothing but focused on her comfort since the second she'd screamed at him in the sea. 'She needs a hot drink for the shock. If you can get that sorted for me, please.'

'Sure. She looks mighty pale.' Tina shook her head and frowned.

He frowned too. 'She'll be okay with rest and something to raise her blood sugar.'

'Hey. I am here.' Tired of being talked over, Lola managed a smile. 'You can talk *to* me if you like. Tina, yes, I'd love a drink if you have time to make me one. And, no, Jake, you're not going anywhere near me with vinegar and tweezers. I can do it myself.'

'Really? You can twist your body at that kind of an angle and rip nematocysts out like a pro? This I've got to see. Wait right there.'

He dashed out of the room as Lola leaned back on the sofa, closed her eyes and groaned. She did not want to be beholden to him and she did not want him touching her again with all that kind consideration. Really, they needed to talk, not touch. Touching brought about way too many hot thoughts and not enough searing reality.

She didn't need reminding that her particular searing reality was that she was here to work and not mess about with a doctor, no matter how much her body had other ideas. And now, accompanying Cameron to the location shoot was looking pretty touch and go. 'Oh…why me?'

'Because, Miss Bennett, you didn't have a full wet-suit on.'

Lola had forgotten the housekeeper was still there. 'Oh, sorry, Tina, I was thinking about how I was going to manage to work this afternoon.'

'You won't, no arguing.' It was Jake again, back with them and holding his large black medical bag, which he set down on the floor. 'Tina, it's okay, we can manage here, thanks. I don't want to take up any more of your time…except I'd be grateful if you could take the dogs for a while. Lola, you're going to stay there and rest.'

Lola sat up. 'I can't do that. There's too much—'

'Shh. I'm the doctor and you'll do what I say. I'll go with Cameron. Once we've got the barbs out you can get some rest. You've had a bad shock.' Not as shocking as necking in an ocean, to be honest, but there it was. He lifted her swollen leg onto a footstool, on which he'd laid out a dressing pack and drape, then he crouched down. 'Now, this is going to sting so I'll go slowly.'

'It won't sting if I do it.' She reached for the tweezers,

bent her legs and shuffled so she could see the barbs. She didn't want him to see her frustrated tears or her weakest moments. She just wanted him to go and leave her to recover in peace.

He watched, eyebrows peaked. 'And pray tell me how you'll stop the sting if I can't?'

'I don't know. Just let me do it and stop asking questions.'

'Okay. Go right ahead.' He rocked back on his heels and smirked as she tried to reach, couldn't quite, and twisted some more. She got a deep ache low in her back. And still the barbs were stuck in her leg. 'Go on, Lola, I'm waiting.'

'Okay, clever clogs, you do it then.' She all but threw the tweezers at him.

He rocked forward and grabbed them. 'Stop me any time, there's no hurry.'

'No problem.' She wasn't sure where this big brave act was coming from, but in truth she didn't want to owe him anything or to let him see how upset she felt. She was a grown-up, smart adult woman—she could deal with this. 'I'll be fine.'

His eyes were gentle and warm as he smiled. 'Sure you will. You can handle anything, Lola.'

'Yep.' At least one of them had some faith in her. She sucked in a breath as he touched her leg, sending shivers of pain through her calf. She would not shout. She would not cry.

He paused, tweezers in mid-air, and it was worse to see compassion mixed with teasing in his eyes. 'It is okay to scream. I have ear plugs somewhere.'

'Get on with it, man. The suspense is killing me more than the damned venom ever will.'

The next few minutes passed in a blur of angry stinging, fierce tensing of muscles she hadn't known she had and almost ripping the stuffing from the chair arm. When Jake felt satisfied he'd removed every barb, he smoothed cream over the now very puce ankle and calf and gave her another dose of painkiller. 'You did well. Lie back and get some rest. I'm going up to the house to talk Cameron into letting you stay here.'

'Good luck with that. I doubt she'll be happy. It's okay. Give me a few minutes for the pain to calm down and I'll come with you.'

'You'll stay right there, missy.'

'Or what?'

'Or you'll get a spanking.' His hand was on the door but instead of leaving he looked at her and shook his head. 'I shouldn't have said that.'

She smiled on a sigh. 'Promises…promises.'

'Lola…' There was a warning in his voice but a glint in his eyes.

'I know, I know. Timing. Work. Stuff. Life. I get it. If you look for excuses you'll find them.'

'They're everywhere, Lola. I don't need to look. Now, I'm going to tell Cameron that you have to stay here.'

'My money's on an immediate departure to the set for all of us, dogs included.'

But Cameron, it seemed, had other ideas. Very surprising.

Apparently she insisted that her assistant stay at the lodge and that Jake stay with her. A situation they both found irritating. More Jake, it seemed.

He slumped down in the chair opposite Lola, grumbling, 'She was surrounded by Alfredo's guests and just wafted her hand and told me to stay with you as if it was no big deal that a top neurosurgeon was wasting his time here—and I couldn't get to talk to her privately. She demanded I come all this way, cancel my clinics and rearrange my schedule, and now she doesn't even need me to go with her, and won't let me talk to her.'

Lola lifted her head from the couch then laid it back again when the room started to spin a little. 'I think you're just her insurance policy. She hasn't been feeling great over the last few months on that stupid diet. She probably just needs to know you're close by in case of emergency. You're here, filming's only a few miles away, she can call if she needs you.'

'Which was exactly what she said to me.'

'Why do you want to go anyway? Seems to me you don't want to be here in the first place, so an afternoon off would suit you just fine.'

'It's my job.' He shrugged, pulling out his laptop. 'Right, if you're okay with it I'll log into the clinic intranet and get some work done. I can't sit around doing nothing.'

'Me neither.' Lola swung her legs from the stool and tried to stand. It was relatively easy to bear weight, but the pain knocked the wind out of her lungs. 'Oof.'

'What do you think you're doing?' He glared at her over the top of his computer screen.

'Going to get my phone. I'll do some ringing around, sort out a dress for Cameron for the after-shoot dinner tomorrow night.'

'All that luggage and she didn't bring a dress?'

'Of course she did. I packed more than enough clothes for a whole month. But there are some fabulous Bahamian designers and she wants to try their clothes. I call, they send. She wears. Or not. It's routine. She could make them a lot of money being seen in one of their creations. Top one on my list is Evelyn Rice—some of her dresses were worn at awards ceremonies earlier in the year and—'

'Okay.' Jake came over to her and made her sit back down, his hand slipping around her waist. He was comfortable around her body when there wasn't the immediate threat of a kiss, it seemed. His voice was soothing. 'I'll get your phone. You can make one call. One. Then you need to do something that isn't work. Solitaire? Knitting? Your script? Yes. Your script. This is legitimate sick time, which means no work—just relaxation.'

'You know, you can be quite bossy when you try.' But she had to agree it would be nice to sit and do something for herself. The extra-strong painkillers had started to make her head feel woozy and her limbs like melting honey—limpid and weak. She felt as if she was sinking and flying at the same time, which was doubly weird. 'My phone's in my beach bag and my script's on my dresser in the bedroom.'

'By the look of you, those meds are kicking in. Very soon you won't want to do anything, you'll be asleep in five minutes.'

When he came back she was still trying to find a comfortable position on the sofa. 'The cushion doesn't feel right.' And she was indeed very tired. Very tired indeed.

'Hold on.' Jake put her phone and her script on the arm of the sofa and sat down next to her to plump up the cushion. 'Better?'

'Not really. But thank you for trying and for talking to Cameron. I know she doesn't mean to be difficult, she's just learnt to be like that. She can be really nice—she gave me a dress once, just because I liked it. But I get how everyone sees the bad in her when she gets so demanding. If I could just sell my screenplay then I wouldn't have to stay… Where did you put it?' Why was she only hearing her own voice? Was she talking too much? She probably was, but she couldn't stop even though it was getting harder to control her mouth movements. She had to concentrate to say the words. 'Ah, there it is. Thank you.'

'Have you sent it to him to read yet?'

'My dad?' Her heart thumped once at the thought of what she'd done but then...she didn't feel so bad right now... 'No. I can't. I haven't... I should. But, oh, Jake, there's too much... It's hard...to explain... I will, though. I will send it to him...' How to start that conversation? *I know you think I'm in LA making the most of Cameron's connections, but I lied and I keep on lying...* 'I'll send it tomorrow. Maybe... I might have to...'

Jake ran his finger over her cheek. 'Now I understand why he calls you a chatterbox. One tiny relaxant and you're in full throttle. Let me know when you need me to reply, because the gaps you're leaving aren't big enough for me to get a word in.'

'Oops, sorry.'

'No need to apologise. Now read.' Smiling, Jake lifted her leg and she kind of swung sideways and landed against his arm. Without thinking twice, she snuggled under and into his armpit. He was so warm and strong. Comfortable... And he smelt delicious. Her eyes started to close, her heart slowed a little and it was so tempting just to lie against him and... She should really look at her script, but she didn't have the energy...

He gave her a little nudge. 'Lola. Lola...don't go to sleep here.'

'Hmm?'

His voice was by her ear, warm and soft. 'Maybe you should go to bed. You'll be more comfortable.'

'Hmm? No. I'm fine.' There was an opportunity for more innuendo there, but she couldn't move her mouth enough to say anything much. It was as if her brain was on a go-slow. She just wanted to lie here in his arms and let the pain drift away. 'Can't walk... Stay right here?'

When he didn't answer she let herself fall further down into the black hole. When he nuzzled the top of her head she spiralled further and further... He was very close. Nice and close and warm. Her body started to tingle, starting first in her gut but then spreading through her, to her breasts and down low, deep inside. Half asleep and half turned on. No—all turned on, in a drowsy, calm, warm kind of way. Sex would be delicious right now. Sex with Jake would be more than delicious.

She managed to twist herself so she was facing him. His mouth was only inches from hers. His eyes glittered with concern and desire, his Adam's apple bobbed as he swallowed. 'Lola—'

Again a warning. She knew exactly what she wanted to do right now, and wondered if he thought the same thing. 'Jake. I know you said—'

'Hush.' He placed a finger over her mouth. 'You need some rest.'

She curled her hand around his finger and drew it away. Then she leaned close and pressed her mouth against his, because she couldn't not. Because she knew it was what they both wanted. And for a brief moment she felt his hesitation, heard his low groan before his free hand cupped her cheek and he kissed her back, soft and gentle. She reached for his face, for the soft touch of his skin; she wanted to be sheathed in his scent, to taste him over and over and over.

This time the kiss went deeper than passion, to somewhere beyond the rabid desperation she felt inside. It stoked something fierce, something rare and beautiful. Something precious.

She didn't want this to stop; she curled the back of her hand against his cheek and melted into the press of his lips against hers, into the dance of his tongue, the tight clutch of her stomach. This was something. He was something. Something important. Something good. For the first time ever she felt soul-deep that this was right.

When he drew away Jake was shaking and there were deep lines across his forehead. He looked unsettled, spooked.

Worse, she felt as if someone had taken her lifeline away. 'I'm not going crazy, am I? There is something here? You do want this, right?' She knew her words were coming out a little slurred, as if her mouth was full of cotton-wool. But she wanted to know…needed to know. He'd said they'd talk, well, now she was going to say a few things… 'Because I want to kiss you. And maybe more. Some more…yes, more.' She laid her hand on his chest, felt the reassuring beat of his heart under her fingers. There was something about Jake that was different from any other man she'd ever known. There was a quiet strength to him—one that irritated her slightly as he fought the attraction. There was a calmness there. He was funny and beautiful to look at. He made her feel good about herself. He made her think that anything was possible.

He made her lose track of her thinking—and that wasn't always such a good thing. Because she had to keep her mind focused on her goals. She didn't want to fall for him—but maybe it was already too late. Right now she was so laconic she didn't care.

There was a long pause while he looked at her. Sin flashed across his gaze. 'Yes. Yes, I do want to kiss you again, Lola, and more. But wanting and doing are different things. You're hurting now, and pretty much flying high on meds, you don't know what you're doing—and, to be brutally honest, neither do I. You need to sleep it all off. Things will look different when you wake up.'

His rejection should have hurt, but it didn't touch her. Because she knew. Knew he wanted her. Knew this was right. She couldn't stop looking at his mouth. She wanted to feel his mouth on her skin, on her body. Everywhere. 'Why do you keep pushing me away?'

'Because I wouldn't be good for you.'

Oh, you would. So damned good. But she had to admit that her vision had started to blur at the edges and she was feeling quite strange. 'I think I can decide what's good for me. I think sex with you would be amazing—'

His growl was low and almost feral as he edged away from her. 'So do I, Lola. Which is exactly why we're not going to do it.'

CHAPTER EIGHT

THE AIR WAS cooler when she woke, alone on the sofa, her body contorted, her limbs still limp, her head aching just a little. Her mouth was dry. And she was sure she was supposed to be doing something important, but all she could remember was lying in Jake's heat and how safe she'd felt.

It was going dark too. Almost six o'clock.

She'd been asleep for hours, way too long.

Whoa, shoot. She was supposed to have phoned Evelyn Rice's office and organised some clothes. And the beauty therapist…damn, damn, damn.

Her head was clearing now, very quickly. Unfortunately. There was no soft-focus buzz to make the neglect of her duties appear in any way warm and fuzzy. She reached for her phone.

But it was gone. As was her script. She jumped to her feet. Wobbled a little on her bad leg. Righted herself. What in hell had she been thinking, sleeping for so long as if she hadn't a care in the world? What had he given her for the pain that had wiped her brain of any sense? 'Jake? Jake?'

He wasn't in the kitchen, bedrooms…the bathrooms were empty. She started to wander outside, but met him and the dogs in the hallway. He'd changed out of beach clothes and wore a navy collared T-shirt that clung interestingly to his biceps, and tan shorts that made a perfect gift of his backside. And he gripped three leads tightly in his fist. 'Hey, you're awake. Get down, Butter or Jelly, or whoever you are. Stop fussing. We've been for a walk. I think Tina was getting just a little tired of them. Cameron's still on set.'

Lola was still a little drowsy, but her head was no longer filled with mush. She bent to stroke the dogs, gave them all the kisses they needed, then stood. Wobbled a little. 'Why did you let me sleep so long?'

Jake held her arms at her sides and looked her up and down, steadied her. 'You needed it. Your body told you what it needed. You've been working hard, you were in shock…'

'I was drugged.'

He laughed. 'Lightweight. Seriously, they weren't even strong. How're you feeling? You seem to be walking okay.'

She peered down at her leg. It was still red and swollen, but not as raw as it had been. The pain had definitely subsided and whatever cream he'd put on had helped reduce the itch. Reduce, not obliterate. 'Better. But I haven't time to think about that. I need to phone Evelyn Rice and arrange some clothes for tomorrow. But, damn, she's probably left already, and I only have the workshop number.'

'No need.' He walked her back through to the kitchen and let the dogs off their leads, and after they'd scoffed some biscuits they scampered through the open-plan space to the lounge area, climbed onto their favourite rattan sofa and began preening. Just like their 'mother'.

Talking of which… 'But—I have to—Cameron asked me—'

'Wait.' Jake opened the fridge, lifted out a bottle and

filled a glass with iced water then handed it to Lola. 'Drink this. Okay, I've already phoned Miss Rice. It's all sorted.'

'You called her? Oh, my God, what on earth did you say?' This was it. She was fired. Gone. Back to London. Regretting everything…except the part where she'd kissed Jake. Twice.

Whatever, she was doomed.

He grinned, obviously pleased with himself. 'I explained what the issue was, and that I hadn't a clue what I was doing. She took pity on me. She was delighted Cameron wanted to sample her clothes and we guessed her size. She's sending an assortment of this season's garments over tonight, different sizes just in case.'

Lola tiptoed to kiss his cheek, but thought better of it. The last time she'd kissed him things had gone downhill pretty quickly. 'Great, thanks. That's brilliant. You are brilliant.'

'I know.'

'And very modest too. So the only other major thing I need to do today is arrange a beautician for tomorrow evening for before the dinner.'

This time he gave her a very satisfied look. 'Done.'

'What?' He was a revelation.

'Evelyn recommended someone. I called, she's fitting Cameron in. In fact, she's rearranged her whole day for *that divine woman*. Her words, not mine.'

This time she did give him a quick peck on the cheek and neither of them seemed to mind. 'Double brilliant. Thank you. You're a lifesaver.'

'I know.'

'But what I don't understand is why.' To think that only a few days ago she'd never even met the man, and now he was doing her job for her, tending to her leg. And not trying to sleep with her… Maybe he was just an altogether good guy.

Apart from not trying to sleep with her…

'To save your ass. The last thing you needed was to make a drug-slurred call to a top designer. Not a great look. Now…' He took her hand and walked her out to the deck. In the distance someone was playing soca music, light and lyrical. 'Sit down. Chef is sending dinner over in ten minutes. Watch the sunset…or something. I'll just check on the dogs.'

'Oh. Wow. Yes.' She gazed out and wondered whether the drugs were having an effect on her vision—because the view was breathtaking. It looked like someone had taken a paintbrush and daubed the brightest colours they could find right across the horizon.

The sky met the ocean in a deep molten orange that reflected across the water. A bright yellow globe dipped into the sea and shimmered almost golden. To her left, palm trees swayed in silhouette, black against the ombre haze. And there, just in front of her, were two large torches, flames flickering in the gentle breeze, and a table set for two with candles and white linen.

Her phone was there, too, next to her script. The pages were held down with pebbles at the place where he'd stopped reading. The End.

All this had happened while she'd been asleep?

'The more time I spend here the more impressed I am.' He pulled out a chair and indicated for her to sit. 'The dogs are fine. Asleep. Cameron's busy. Sit down.'

'You read my script?' She sat. Heat burnt her cheeks. She might as well have been naked in front of him. Worse. What could be worse than laying open her naked self to him?

Ah, yes. Laying open her heart. That was something

she didn't want to do. Flirting and fun were one thing, but she didn't need him to know about the clutch of her heart when she'd kissed him. She didn't want him to know how much she admired him. Some things she had to keep to herself to protect her heart from the fallout.

He sat opposite her and was about to speak when the chef arrived with a tray of food. Lobster, crab, potatoes, fruit. An amazing array of delicious local delicacies. She turned down wine and stuck to water, not wanting to mix the painkillers with alcohol and befuddle her head even more.

After a couple of mouthfuls and uninhibited groans of delight at the fresh flavours, he put his knife and fork down.

'So, yes, I did read your script.' He was unabashed, as if reading her words hadn't been like peering into her soul.

'And?'

'It's excellent. Really, I think you should do something with it.' He drank some rosé wine, took up his cutlery again. 'But what do I know? I'm a doctor. You need an expert opinion, not mine. Show it to Cameron, she's an expert on tap.'

Lola almost choked on her lobster. 'I couldn't do that. I'd rather die than press it on her and beg her to read it. Believe me, she wouldn't anyway, she has far too much to do. She doesn't even know I write.'

'Well, she should. That story deserves a home. You're right, it is surprisingly funny. Although I shouldn't be surprised—it's just an extension of you. With all the things you are—funny, smart, witty, brave.'

'Wow. Thank you. Thank you so much.' She felt a surge of confidence. 'I don't think I'll ever believe it's ready to go out into the big wide world.'

'Email it to your dad.'

This time she felt the thuds in her heart go on and on at the mention of her dad. But she wasn't going to have that conversation with Jake. 'Yeah…maybe.'

'Tomorrow?'

'Pushy.'

His tone got serious. 'What are you waiting for? You want a career in this? Yes? You've given up everything to come out here for *this*?' He stabbed his finger at the paper on the table. 'But you're still at first base. You won't get on if you don't *do* things. You know the old saying—if you want something to work for you, you have to *make* it work. Right?'

'Right.' She was almost carried along with his enthusiasm. Sure, she was dedicated, ambitious, hard-working… but putting herself out there? There was too much at stake for her right now. He was talking about things he had no knowledge of. 'Are you this demanding on everyone?'

'Usually just myself.'

'Why?'

He looked down at his food. 'We work hard… Look, my parents didn't have much, but they taught me that you can achieve anything if you're prepared to put the hours in. Now, about that script…'

It didn't escape her notice that he'd changed the subject back to her as soon as he could. Talking about his family clearly wasn't a favourite thing of his. Well, snap to that. 'Yes. Okay. I'll get it out there as soon as I can.'

'Send a copy to me too so I can take another look at the medical scenes. Soup them up a bit. You're in a prime position to change your life, Lola.'

'Yes, yes, I am.' He was good at this—voicing the feelings she'd arrived with in LA. 'Have you always been this in control of your own life? Planning world domination?'

He grinned. 'Like I said, my career's fine, thanks. Going right according to plan. No need to analyse that any further.'

'So what do you do when you're *not* working?'

'Like that happens.'

'You must do something. You can't work all the time.' At his shrug she realised he really, truly, probably did. 'You don't have hobbies?'

'I work out. Hike. Surf, if I get a chance. Haven't done that for a while. I've been building my practice—these things don't just happen. I—well, I work, Lola. Although sometimes to the detriment of other things—I understand that. You have to make sacrifices.' It was almost as if he'd just realised that he didn't do anything else— as if the realisation was finally seeping into his brain, and what exactly that meant for his life. Then he smiled. 'Oh, and I juggle, but that's more for relaxation. Well, I used to—it's been a while. Years, actually. Probably a decade, if I'm honest. So, okay, I admit I'm a sad case of a workaholic—I do all the things I tell my juniors not to do. But I have to work, no one's going to carry me the rest of my life. Where I end up is up to me. No one else.'

And she wondered what he meant by that—but sensed he was reluctant to talk about it, so she tried to keep things light. 'So you juggle, like with the oranges earlier? That's a strange thing to do.'

His eyebrows rose. 'Unusual, yes. Strange—not so. It's very therapeutic, especially if your brain's stuck in one thing and you want to move on. I was part of a study when I was at med school. We were testing whether learning a new skill could promote white and grey matter growth in the brain. It does, by the way. It also helps you focus and relax, helps posture and co-ordination…and usually makes people smile.'

'I might have known it would have some connection to work.'

'Of course. Plus, it's a great babe magnet.'

She laughed. 'Why? How?'

'That's my secret.'

'Tell me?'

'No.'

'Okay, then, teach me?'

'Sure. Why not?' Standing, he took hold of her arm and they went inside to the kitchen. He picked up two oranges from the fruit bowl, one in each hand, and threw them up in the air. She was mesmerised by the fluidity of his movements, the flex of his hands, the primed, yet relaxed stance. His smile. She was mesmerised by him.

He caught the oranges in one hand, held one out to her. 'Start like this. Just up and down. That's right. Now, try two. Throw from one hand to the other in an arc shape. Copy me.'

She did as she was told and copied him as he threw first one orange, then added in another so they crossed in mid throw. 'Easy!'

'Okay… Now try using your non-dominant hand. That's the tricky bit.'

'Oops.' One orange landed on the floor in a splat.

He laughed. 'Not quite ready for flames yet…'

'You juggle with fire?'

'I have. I can. Try it like this.' He stood behind her and captured her between his arms, his hands cupping hers as they threw the oranges into the air. She leaned against him and he held her weight, his breath coming easily against her neck. She could feel the hard wall of his chest against her back, could smell his scent, and she suddenly felt more alive and more clear-headed than she had all day.

Arousal snaked up her spine, through her veins. Her heart began to beat faster. She wanted to turn around and press herself against him, to feel him naked against her. Her hands shook as she held the oranges. His words were in her ear, on her neck, in her hair. 'Lola…your turn now, on your own. I'll stay here ready to catch them if you drop them.'

'I think I'm getting the hang…' She didn't finish. Couldn't finish because his hands were in no place to catch any falling citrus fruit. They had circled her waist and he was turning her round.

As she completed the turn she stared straight into those black pupils glittering with need. The air stilled around them, heavy with intent, like his eyes. '*God*, Lola…'

'Yes?' But she didn't hear his answer, if indeed he answered at all, because his mouth was on hers, hard and hungry. This wasn't the kind of kiss they'd shared before. This wasn't gentle or coaxing; this was pure, raw need. And she kissed him back just as hard, the oranges spinning across the floor as she dropped them to spike her fingers into his hair, to pull him closer, and ever closer.

There was only so much a guy could resist.

He'd thought earlier he was a damned saint for walking away from her—*twice*. But now he was going to hell and he outright didn't care.

Because having Lola Bennett was the only thing he'd had on his mind all damned day. All damned week, if he was honest, and if he didn't act on this he was going to implode. A mist clouded his brain as he pulled her harder to him. All he could see was Lola, all he could breathe, smell, taste was her. Nothing else mattered. Just this. And her. She mattered.

He felt her curves beneath his hands, spoke against her lips. 'Forget what I said earlier. I was an idiot. I want you, Lola. I want you, right here.'

'Finally. You know, I was starting to get a complex. One minute you wanted me, the next…not so much.'

'I always wanted you. I was trying to protect you.'

He felt her body stiffen. She took a step back. 'Whoa, mister, I don't need protecting. I'm very grateful for everything you've done for me today, but I can manage my life just fine on my own.'

'Hmm—I know, but you can't kiss on your own.' He licked behind her ear, felt her soften a little. 'Can't do this on your own. Right?'

'Good point.' She giggled—a throaty, dirty sound that stoked even more fury through his veins. Her hands were on his T-shirt, dragging it up over his head. 'Your bedroom? Or mine?'

'Not sure we'll make it that far. Next time maybe. Beds are overrated.' Right now the kitchen table looked enticing. So did the floor. He was tearing at her clothes, nipping along her throat, en route to tasting those exquisite breasts again. Luckily she still had the bikini on underneath her T-shirt and shorts—two quick tugs and she'd be naked.

Her hand stilled on his. 'Are you sure about this, Jake. I mean, really sure?'

'Do you have to ask?'

'Ya think? With your track record? I'm not going to start something if you're just going to stop and leave me frustrated. I'm over that.'

'Come with me. Now.' There weren't words enough to tell her how sure he was. He slipped his hands under her legs and picked her up, carried her to the closest soft horizontal surface he could find. One of the couches in the lounge. The flickering torchlight filtered through the blinds, illuminating her full beauty. God, she was more beautiful than a hundred Hollywood actresses. More real. Just more. So much more.

Careful of her leg, he straddled her and slammed his mouth over hers, drank her in, fed on her kisses like a starving man. Her skin was soft, her kisses hot, her moans like licks of heat piercing him. There was nothing he could do to stop this. Nothing he wanted to do more.

She raked her hands across his chest, ran her fingers over his belly towards his belt. He grabbed her hand. 'Not so fast. I want to taste you first…'

She started to undo the buckle. 'But—'

His grip tightened. 'Look here, Miss Independent… relax. Let me do something for you.'

'You've done that all day, looked after me. Now it's your turn. I want to show you my gratitude.'

'Lola,' he growled in her ear. 'I get that you want to be your own woman—but this? This is about the two of us. I want to make you feel so damned good. You first…'

She pouted and pretended to think about that option for all of a nanosecond. Then she laughed. 'Oh, okay… if you insist.'

'I do.' His mouth was on her throat, making a soft trail to her breasts. He flicked off her bikini and sucked a nipple into his mouth. Underneath him she bucked against his hardness, a soft purr coming from her throat. Her hands fisted his hair, yanking with every lick on her nipple. 'You taste so good.'

Then things got serious as he made a slow trail down her belly, slipped off her shorts and bikini bottom. 'You have no idea how you make me feel, Lola.'

'Oh, I can guess. I feel it too.' Her palm covered him

over his pants and he gasped, desperate for her to free him from the restrictive fabric. But he'd have to wait.

She gave him a slow sexy smile that glittered in her eyes, the connection deepening, the connection very real. Tangible. A fist round his heart. Damn, but he'd never felt like this about a woman before—as if there'd been something he hadn't known he'd been looking for, and now he'd found it. Like finding the last piece in a jigsaw puzzle. Complete.

And it should have scared him. Hell, it did, more than anything. He'd been fine before he'd met her—he'd already felt complete, goddammit. He didn't need a woman to make him more whole…but it also spurred him on.

He nudged her thighs apart and dipped his head, tasting the hot slickness of her as she rocked against him, her moan intensifying, urging him on. She was so wet as he stroked his tongue across that tight nub of flesh, as he gripped her backside and trapped her in place. He could sense her orgasm mounting with the tightened grasp, the sob of delight. Each moan of hers elicited a groan from him. God, he needed to be inside her.

When she shuddered he thought he might explode. When she called out his name he thought he'd die.

But she was pulling him up, reaching for his zip, pushing down his shorts, finally freeing him from all constraints. He had to be inside her. To feel her around him, to feel her climax against him. 'Condom…'

'Yes. Yes. Yes.'

He reached down to his shorts, pulled out the packet, sheathed in record time. And then she was taking control, wrapping her hand around his thickness, making him gasp.

He looked down the length of her, saw the redness of her leg… 'Wait… I don't want to hurt you.'

She gave him a smile that almost broke his heart in two. 'It's okay. You won't hurt me. I promise. Jake... I want you so much. I want you.'

He reached and bent her leg slowly so there'd be no danger of hurting her. Then she was pulling him into her, deep into her core, the silky softness wrapping around him, her muscles gripping him in a sweet tightness. His mouth covered hers in a desperate kiss, his gaze never leaving hers—the truth spinning between them, faster, mesmerising, intoxicating. If there was a heaven, this was it.

She rocked with his rhythm, urging him harder, faster, calling his name until he could take no more. Pleasure, need and hunger slammed into him, and he groaned out her name, caught the first shudders of her release. Felt the thin ethereal threads that connected them tighten. Then and only then did he finally let go.

CHAPTER NINE

WHAT THE HELL had just happened?

Lola wasn't just thinking about the sex—she was thinking about the sharp tug on her heart as she'd kissed him, eyes open, and had seen deep into his gaze. The way he'd encouraged her to be herself—to let go, to let him show her the way. Mirrored in his eyes were the emotions she'd felt, heart full, overwhelming. This wasn't just about her, this was about the two of them. Together.

Tears pricked her eyes but she blinked them away. She was surely just being silly. She couldn't feel so much for Jake after such a short time. It was dangerous, and bordering on absurd.

But she did feel something…something new.

He twisted to the side and wrapped her close in his arms, spooning behind her. And it felt right. Two hearts catching the same rhythm, breaths gradually slowing after exercise, his warmth. And he fitted around her as if he was meant to be there. So right, so crazy. Her head was spinning while he was whispering in her ear, 'See… babe magnet.'

'Believe me, this has got nothing to do with juggling oranges.'

'That's what you think.'

'I know so…' She turned and prodded his tummy as

he laughed, thinking how easy it could be to relax into this and be happy. *Happy*. Now, there was a thought.

He kissed behind her ear and growled, 'It's just animal magnetism, then.'

'Yes. Probably.' And a whole lot more she didn't want to put a name to. However, it was fine to get all romantic here when neither of them had much to do. But back at work, back in Los Angeles it would be different. Busy lives. Plans. Not plans that blended easily, if at all.

Suddenly there was a warm, wet raspy feeling on her toe. 'Ugh. What the hell—? *Butter?* Oh, my God, I'd forgotten about the dogs. Look at us here, like this. Naked!' She threw back her head and laughed, because, yes, it was absurd. 'They're going to need therapy after this. We might have scarred them for life.'

Jake grabbed a throw and wrapped it around her, while he found a cushion and covered himself. And laughed, heartily. 'Shoo. Go away. No harm done. Just teaching them a thing or two. Birds and bees…or whatever it is in puppy language.'

'Thank God they can't talk.'

Butter stopped licking and twitched to the right, nose in the air, ears back. Then she began to bark. Just as the doorbell rang. A creeping panic built in Lola's chest. 'Oh…oh, could it be Cameron? Oh, hell. Quick. Clothes. On.'

'Damn. Damn. Damn.' Cushion still firmly in place, Jake jumped back then started to drag on his shorts. In her mind-melted state she did manage to sneak a look at his perfect body one last time and remember how good it had been to have the weight of him over her.

And then she gave in to her panic. The doorbell rang again. Jake offered her his hand and pulled her from the sofa, tightened the throw around her. 'Go put something on, I'll get the door. Thank God for blinds is all I can say.' He gave her the gentlest smile she'd seen in years. 'Come on, Lola. Laugh.'

She tried to smile, tried to find this the funniest thing she'd experienced in years, she did. Taking time out of work for great sex in the dining room of her boss's rented house, while looking after three dogs and nursing a sore foot. But how could she? None of this was funny. Not any more. She hissed, 'It's my job at risk. Okay? And yours possibly. But mostly mine.'

'Go. Disappear. I'll fix this.' And he wafted his hand towards her bedroom.

While in there she heard voices, one female, some thumping, a groan. It didn't sound like Cameron's vapid loud, crisp voice or Tina's laconic, lyrical tones. Then the door closed. Silence.

She thought about going out to see what was going on, but with her luck there'd be a troop of paparazzi there, waiting to ambush her. She could just imagine the headline: *'PA to the stars caught having sofa sex with a canine audience'*. Just great.

Within seconds Jake stood in her doorway, looking very pleased with himself. 'Hey, it was just Evelyn Rice, dropping off the clothes. I told her I'd just been to the beach and to excuse the clothing. She was fine. A little nosy perhaps…she wanted to come in and meet Cameron…but just fine. She's gone, the coast is clear. Although, as we are renting this place, you have every right to be naked or otherwise.'

Having managed to shrug on a bathrobe, she followed him into the lounge and to a rack of exquisite tailored clothes in jewel colours. 'Good. Thanks. Wow, she'll love these. You arranged for her to bring them here rather than to the house?'

'I wasn't sure what to do. I thought if she brought them here I'd save face if I'd got the wrong things, Cameron need never know.'

Lola ran her hand along the rack and picked out a vivid aquamarine dress that she just knew would fit her perfectly. 'Oh, these are gorgeous. You did well. I should thank you again for arranging it all.' Yet another reminder that she was failing somewhat in her duties. Jake had taken her mind off her job, snorkelling had taken her finger off the pulse… What had she been thinking, letting him convince her to take time off? And now…sex. Sex when she was supposed to be working. 'Seems I'm all about thanking you today.'

'Hey! What's with the mood slip? Everything's fine— no one knows what we were doing. Peanut, Butter and Jelly don't speak human, so you don't have to worry about them. Come here.' He slipped his arms around her waist and nuzzled her neck. Punctuating his words with kisses, he said, 'Stop. Worrying. It's. Going. To. Be. Fine.'

Only a few moments ago she'd thought about being happy, but now that was fading fast. She whirled round to face him, regretting having to do this but doing it anyway. There. The first regret. 'How can you be so sure everything's going to be okay?'

'Go with it, Lola. We have two more nights here— look around you, it's amazing. It's a gift.'

'We took our foot off the pedal. It could have been Cameron, Alfredo…Tina. We could have got the sack.'

'I doubt anything that dramatic would have happened. Anyway, I don't care what anyone thinks.'

'I do.' She drew away from him, her mind reeling with questions and reasons, but her body craving his touch regardless. 'Look, I don't know what to say…to think…'

She cast her eyes towards the sofa where it had all happened. 'But we can't do this here.'

'No, you're right—too uncomfortable. We have two bedrooms to choose from…'

'No. I mean we can't do this. This…' In an attempt to make things clearer she wafted her hand between the two of them. Her heart had started to ache just a little at what she was about to let go. *'This.'*

Taking her wrist, he pulled her to him. 'Lola, we can do anything we damned well like.'

'Not if it means losing my job.'

His jovial smile faltered. 'Hell, you're as bad as me, work obsessed.'

Irritation started to prickle up her spine. 'Maybe, but I am also food obsessed. Rent obsessed. Paying the bills obsessed… I need this job, it was hard to come by. You try finding a job that pays enough to let you live in LA and brings you a step closer to the life you want to live.' She pushed a finger into his chest, ignoring the heat, ignoring the fading light in his eyes. 'This is my life. We don't get to jeopardise that just for a bit of sex.'

It was more than that, so much more…but how could she do this with him and keep all the promises to herself? She was here to work, to achieve her potential. Losing sight of that would be costly on so many levels.

'Okay, then how about a *lot* of sex? No?'

'You don't get it, Jake. There's too much at stake.'

'What? Exactly? Other than a job you're not fond of?'

Me. My life. My dreams. Everything I'm working for. My parents' hearts. Before she could stop him his lips melded with hers in a long slow, bone-melting kiss. She wanted to push away, to run, to shout, to make him listen to all the objections she had on her list. But he anchored her there, to him, making her feel dizzy with desire. Heat slammed into her and despite everything she wrapped her arms around his neck, not listening to the little voice in her head telling her to stop.

He was still shirtless and his naked chest was a delight to her senses—smooth skin, the solid planes of his body, the strong beat of his heart. He kissed her and kissed her some more, long and slow as if they had all the time in the world. He explored her mouth, her neck, her throat all over again. Then feasted some more on her mouth until she was weak with need, until there was nothing more she could ever want than to be here, with him.

When he finally pulled away, his smile was confident and sure—very unlike how she was feeling. 'That seems to work. Good.'

A little dizzy at the heady rush of his touch she made a bit of space between them. 'Charming.'

'I try my best.' His fingers ran down her cheek. 'I like you, Lola. In fact, to be truthful, I've never met anyone like you before. You're unique, beautiful, sexy and smart. I like who you are and what you're trying to do with your life—I totally respect that and I'm not going to get in the way of anything you want to do. A few hours ago you wanted this as much as I do. Look, I promise not to interfere with your work tomorrow or any day after that. I will be professional to the core and when we get back to LA I promise I'll dip out of your life just as you want. But right now we have something good going, and I don't see anyone holding a gun to your head and making you fill in a time sheet.'

'But—I don't know…' What the hell could she say to that? She was discombobulated by him. His kisses made her feel dizzy and stopped any kind of rational thought process—but he was only suggesting a little play. She could do that. Hell, Cameron spent most of her life playing…

His hand smoothed across the nape of her neck. 'There's not much of today left. Tomorrow we're booked up all day at the set and then the wrap dinner. That leaves us a few hours now…private and personal hours where we can do what the hell we like. I've seen plenty of Nassau, but nowhere near enough of your bedroom. Now, you can either give me a sightseeing tour or I can go to bed on my own. Personally, I think that would be a big mistake.'

Lola didn't like making mistakes. Plus, he was the sexiest man she'd ever seen. What a waste if she walked away from that, from crazy commitment-free fun in paradise.

As he drew her closer Lola decided not to think any more. She wasn't going to ruin it by worrying, she was going to go with her gut. So she let him lead her into the bedroom and lay her down, relished the press of his heat and the safety of living in the moment with no regard for what tomorrow would bring.

'Hey, Jake! Dr Jake, come talk to Alfredo. He's got a problem with his gall bladder. Needs advice.' Cameron Fontaine was nothing but enthusiastic about using all Jake's talents when she wanted to; she just also dodged any direct questioning or personal one-to-one conversations.

The day had started with her personally checking up on Lola and insisting on hearing a rundown of the jellyfish barb removal all over again, in full detail. Then interspersing scene takes with chatter about healthy eating—he'd guessed that was for her own benefit, though. She'd asked pointed questions without referring to herself or a pregnancy or maternal diet. And damn if she kept herself surrounded by people.

The crowded tapas bar overlooked a marina and some of the cast and crew spilled out dockside, a few of them sitting out on one of the launches. Alfredo and Cameron were waving and shouting to them. He sauntered over. 'Alfredo, Cameron.'

'Honey, I'm going to join those reprobates over there for a little cruise around the harbour. Alfredo needs you for one second, then he's coming with me.' Cameron gave him an air kiss. 'Tell Lola I'll need a call at five. Be good, you two. Sleep well.'

Not so fast. He followed her a step or two and tried to get her attention. 'Cameron, I need to talk with you, privately. Now.'

He doubted anyone had spoken to her like that before. Her smile faltered as she pressed her palm on her belly over her floaty dress, her voice low. 'Yes, honey, I know you know… But not here, or now—too many spies. Later, tomorrow… No, we're travelling. Wednesday? I'm back on set on Wednesday. Yes, Wednesday in my trailer.'

'Now works better for me.'

'No can do. Got to keep on top of things here. I have a boat to catch. It's worked out just fine, though? Yes? Our little secret?' With a grand flourish she gave him a second chaste air kiss. 'Ciao.'

Jake really preferred it when he had his patients safely in the clinic environment, they were a lot less likely to run out on him—and he could at least get a word in.

Oblivious to the celebrity gossip story of the year playing out under his nose, Alfredo caught him up and shook his hand. 'Jake, I do not want to spoil your night with my medical issues—besides, business is finished for the day. But I would like to say how impressed I've been with you. An inside view on how anti-gravity affects the brain was terrific for us to play up the confusion, ramp up the effects and the emotion today. Just great. And the way you dealt with that arm injury was very impressive. Who'd have thought you could make a splint out of a rolled-up pair of trousers? Tell James I'll be sure to recommend the clinic, and specifically you, to anyone who needs a medic.'

'Thank you. James will be pleased.' Jake wasn't sure he was. If he'd been in any doubt at all, he was now convinced he didn't want to be a film medic or a secret obstetrician. He wanted to be a neurosurgeon and left in peace to get on with it. Although he had to admit he'd enjoyed today, interspersed as it had been with minor emergencies anyone with a small amount of first-aid knowledge could have dealt with. And at least Alfredo and the rest of the crew were normal human beings, even if Cameron was in a league of her own.

Mostly, he'd enjoyed last night and this morning… waking up with Lola. That had been a revelation.

The aging director gave a weary sigh. 'I'd better go join our leading lady… Wish me luck.'

'You're going to need it. Oh—and if you do need a decent gastro surgeon, just ask. I can make a few calls.'

And now what? Jake turned to see Lola sitting at a table with the location production assistant and a couple from Set Dec. They were laughing at something she was saying, her russet hair highlighted in the subdued lighting, her creamy skin illuminated and clear.

But for him nothing was clear at all—his head was awash with fresh memories of her curves, her kisses, her soft moans. Cameron had given her the pick of the Evelyn Rice dresses and she'd chosen a silk blue one that elevated her to the star of tonight's dinner. Hell, he was surrounded by Hollywood royalty and he didn't care. In fact, he was supposed to be working and his mind was not on his job. Which was, what? First time ever?

So he was in trouble and he didn't know what the hell to do about it.

He waited a few beats as the storm inside him died down, then strolled over. 'Hey.'

'Hi, Doc. We were just about to leave. Early flight and all that…' Lola smiled and stood, her eyes fixing on his. Memories of last night, of her body and what was underneath that dress intensified and reverberated between them, and he wished the rest of the crew would just disappear and leave them alone.

'Cameron's gone on a harbour cruise, she won't be back for a while. Fancy a walk back to the lodge? We could go along the beach.'

'Okay, yes. Why not?' She said her goodbyes to the team and they headed outside. The rhythmic lapping of waves soothed them into a silence as they made their way down the wooden steps to the beach.

He steadied her as she took her shoes off. 'Be careful with that ankle.'

'I'm fine, really. The hydrocortisone ointment helped a lot. I haven't felt like I wanted to scratch the whole limb off for a good few hours now.'

'That's good. I'm not sure how you'd manage walking three tearaway dogs with one leg.'

'Oh, I'd manage.'

'Sure you would.' He slipped an arm around her shoulder and they walked along slowly, sinking into the soft white sand with every step. 'Good day?'

'Oh, yes. I caught up on everything I needed to do. Thank goodness.' Her hand snaked round his waist and she slid it into the back pocket of his shorts, then rested her head against his shoulder. The air was fresh and clean and it felt good to just be out in the elements, talking about something and nothing with Lola. He couldn't remember the last time he'd done that with a woman. He couldn't remember the last woman to enthral him so much—but there was something he was missing. A piece of that jigsaw that had come unstuck. Judging by her extreme reaction to almost being caught having sex, there was more to Lola's story, but she was keeping tight-lipped about it.

She smiled up at him. 'So, Cameron did just fine with the dream scenes, don't you think?'

'Sure.' He hadn't noticed. 'How much filming is left?'

'Once we get back there're some night shoots, then it moves into post-production and we move on. Cameron's got a month or so before she starts rehearsals for her next film, which is a big cowboy saga.'

'Involving horse-riding, I imagine?' Jake huffed out a breath. At some point the woman was going to have to embrace it and announce her pregnancy, and then the correct safety measures could be put in place for her. Again, no issues with horse-riding in pregnancy, but that kind of activity carried a risk and she needed to know what it was. And so did her co-stars and director.

Lola smiled. 'Yes. Why?'

'No reason. Just wondering. One day it's space, the next it's the Wild West... I don't know how you do it.'

'It's exciting. No two days are the same.' Lola's smile distracted him from his work thoughts. 'Glad you're leaving all this madness soon?'

'Yes. And no. I have a full clinic the day after we get back and surgery booked the day after that, and I have to fit visits to the set in between times. Night shoots will work well and shouldn't disrupt anything at the clinic. Who needs sleep?'

'See? You're getting into the swing of this life.' She gave him a little nudge in the ribs with her elbow, her voice soft. 'But tomorrow we're back to reality.'

'We always knew it would happen.'

'Yes. I just didn't expect…' She came to a stop and gazed out at the ocean. A bright moon lit up the surface and he remembered swimming with the dolphins. The ocean kiss. The way he'd tried, and failed, to keep away from her—for what? Looking back, being with her had been inevitable. She sounded wistful. 'I didn't expect for so much to happen here.'

His chest suddenly tightened. 'You could always come back some time.'

'It wouldn't be the same.' She turned and gave him a knowing look—and, yes, he was expert at avoiding intimate conversation, but they both knew what this was, and what it wasn't. Neither of them needed a complication in their real lives. 'These things never are, are they? A good rule is to never go back to a place if you've had the best fun there—you're just chasing a dream and it's never as good the second time round. Having said that, my mum would love it here. It's exactly what she needs. City life is all very well, but this is so peaceful everyone should come here once in their lives. I'm going to email her about it. Maybe she could bring my sister and I could meet them here. Family vacation.'

'You're close? You and your sister? You've never mentioned her.'

'Oh, you know, as close as you can be when you live thousands of miles apart. She's three years older than me, a teacher, like my dad. We're just a regular two-point-four family.'

He wondered what that felt like. There'd been so much pressure on him as an only child. He'd been everything in his parents' lives. At times it had been too much and he'd become so frustrated that they'd poured all their hopes and dreams into him.

The guilt started to bite.

'Yeah. Dad would love it here too.' He tried not to give in to the familiar spiral of bleakness at the thought of his father. The tight clench of his gut was visceral and instinctive. He breathed in deeply again… It seemed tonight was all about the sharp clutch in his chest and the sinking feeling in his belly whichever way he turned.

Lola linked her arm through his with a breezy smile. 'Then make it happen. Bring them. We could have a family reunion. Actually, no. Forget I said that. It would be weird. But bring them. A holiday of a lifetime.'

'It wouldn't be the same.' He kissed her neck, hoping she understood what he meant without putting his heart on his sleeve. If she hadn't been here it would have been a very dull…what had she called it? A very dull *jolly*. 'Dad's not great at going on vacation.'

'Like his son?'

'This is hardly a vacation. And…'

She nudged him to continue. 'And what?'

'Ah, nothing.' This was private stuff…something he didn't usually share with other people.

'Something, I think, or you wouldn't have gone all quiet and moody. Talk to me, Jake. It's our last night here.'

'And spoil it with my stuff? I don't think so.'

She stared out at the ocean again. 'All that out there, so vast and wide… And all this in here…' She prodded his chest. 'All caught up in a tight ball of hurt. Whatever it is, let it go.'

'Are those drugs still affecting your brain?' He tried to laugh, but it didn't come out right. And she was here and, well, hell…*she was here*, and something about that made it easier for him to think and to speak. He followed her gaze out to sea. 'He's sick, Lola. Very. He can't travel far, he needs oxygen to help him breathe. It's hard to travel with a tank by your side, and wheelchair access is terrible everywhere—his excuse, not mine. I keep telling him nothing's impossible, but he doesn't listen. That's half his problem. He's a stubborn old coot.'

'That's where you get it from, then.' Holding his hand tightly, she tugged him to sit down on the sand with her. 'I'm sorry he's sick, Jake.'

And the guilt rolled and rolled through him. 'I'm trying to get him the best treatment, arranged plenty of appointments, but he won't come to the city—says he has everything he needs in Van Nuys. He's used to the doctors there and likes his home comforts. I know he could do better with my colleagues. He just won't listen.' He was going to die and everything Jake had been trying to do would be futile.

She stroked down his back. 'What's wrong with him?'

'COPD. Chronic obstructive pulmonary disease. He's a chronic asthmatic, and a few years ago he got a serious lung infection too. He was really sick, but the stubborn old goat didn't get help until it was almost too late.'

'That must have been scary for you all.'

Jake's chest was sore as he remembered the phone call at med school. His mother's shaking voice. The plummeting of his gut. His father on life support. *He was like that because of me.*

'He'd been working two jobs to pay my college fees. Said a good father wouldn't see his son facing huge bills, so instead of going to the doctor he carried on working. My mom worked shifts back then, so she didn't see him much and didn't realise how sick he was getting. He nearly didn't make it. Since then things haven't improved much. His lungs are fragile and vulnerable to infection. He had to give up those two jobs, now he's housebound, depressed and cantankerous with not much left to look forward to. Mom gave up work to care for him.'

'And you think it's your fault?'

'He did all that for me, pressed on for me, worked himself too hard for me. There's a common denominator there and it's got my name on it. Wouldn't you feel guilty?'

'Oh, yes.' She leaned her head on his shoulder. 'I know why you would, believe me.'

'Why?'

She waved her hand, blinking fast. 'Oh… I just imagine I would too. I can see why you'd want to help, to fix it. But he chose to do those things, Jake. He chooses not to get the right help. And sometimes you just can't fix everything.'

Guilt turned into frustration and he edged away from her, wanting some space. She didn't need this stuff in her life. 'I've paid him back, every cent. Doubled. I send them cash every month for bills, for anything they need, but it just accumulates in a bank account they won't touch. He won't accept my help. Says it's a father's work to help out a son and not the other way round. He's too darned proud.'

'And you try to pay him back by working just as hard as he did? Harder? Now I understand why you're so dedicated, so driven. It's not about the job, it's about your dad. About being good enough, about being worth the sacrifice? If you're so fixed on him getting the money back, go and see him and try to convince him to take it, face-to-face.'

The weight of it all hung heavily on his shoulders. 'You think I haven't? Over and over again until I just gave up trying. He won't take it. If he did he'd believe he'd failed as a parent, as a man.'

Her eyes never left his as she shook her head. 'Then just go see him and talk, Jake. Tell him that you love him, that you're grateful for what he did—not angry. No pressure, no money talk. Just see him. That's all he'll want. To know that you've turned out to be a good man—that everything he did was worth it. Put the anger aside and give him your gratitude. Tell him how you feel.'

'He knows how I feel.'

'Are you sure? I'm no expert—really, I don't do family dynamics well. But dig deeper, Jake.'

'It's not as if I haven't tried, Lola. But every damned time I go I get so angry with them we have an argument. I know he could be better cared for, I know he could have a better life and I can't watch him waste away when I can help.' He heard the reactive anger in his voice and tried to dampen it, but failed. And if he looked closely inside himself, Jake knew those visits were difficult because of things *he* said and felt, not necessarily his parents. The sad truth was, it was easier to bury himself in work than it was to try to fix things back at home.

Not wanting to talk about that any more, he turned to her. 'When we go back—'

'No. Don't talk about going back,' Lola interrupted in a whisper, and reached for him. 'Don't talk about what's going to happen.'

'Things will change.'

'Hush. Don't break the spell.' She circled her arms around his neck and pulled him to lie with her. The white sand was soft beneath his body, a warm breeze floated over them and for many moments he just looked at her and marvelled at how one person could soothe away the anger. She had a way of seeing inside him, of looking for the good in him and making that good come out, no problem at all. She made smoothing over things with his family seem possible. Within reach.

She traced her finger over his lips. 'Can you hear the waves? Can you see that sky? A million stars. A billion.' She laughed. 'A billion trillion. Oh, I don't know, I'm no good at maths.

'Let's celebrate that, Jake. Let's not allow anyone or anything to spoil tonight. Reality's for tomorrow. Okay? I want you. Let's make right now perfect.'

The kiss she gave him was more than he deserved, more than he could ever have imagined. Sweet, slow and giving until the frustration and the anger and all thoughts of his father and the differences between Lola and himself drifted away.

It was a long time before she let go, but when she did there was renewed heat in her eyes. She wanted him. Here. The glittering in her eyes was golden, rich and warm. And the current in the air seemed to be supercharged with need. She reached for his shirt buttons and began to slip them open.

And there was no more talking as he bent to kiss her again. He slipped his hand underneath her top and started to explore the curves and dips that he had come to know so well in such a short space of time. They had all night on a deserted beach underneath a canopy of stars in a midnight sky. She wanted perfection, and he aimed to give her exactly that. Before she started talking time sheets again and before he dipped out of her life. Like he'd promised to do.

Sometimes promises came at a cost. He just hadn't expected this one to be so high.

CHAPTER TEN

LOLA WOKE WITH a start. Shards of yellow moonlight filtered through the white wooden slats, casting Jake's room in a warm liquid honey glow. Which was exactly what she'd felt falling asleep in his arms.

Even now he slept with an arm draped over her, possessive, keeping her close. And she liked that—liked that he seemed to crave her touch as much as she craved his. A strange feeling, this. A need like she'd never had before.

His breath whispered along her neck, his lithe, toned body totally relaxed in sleep. His face was inches from hers and she looked at him, committing the enviably long eyelashes, the tiny bump along his nose and his proud jawline to memory.

Because they hadn't discussed the *What next?* step and she was all kinds of confused about what she wanted now. What should she do for the best—for *her* best? If she committed herself to Jake, wouldn't she be doing exactly what she'd sworn not to do—be responsible for someone else's happiness? And yet the thought of a Jake-free life had her stomach spiralling into freefall.

The alarm began its shrill cacophony and as she reached to hit the snooze button the dogs began to bark. She collapsed back onto the pillow, laughing. 'Oh, yes. Wakey-wakey, world. No rest for the wicked.'

'We weren't all that wicked, Lola. Just a little bit. In fact…now I think about it, not nearly wicked enough.' Jake's arm tightened around her waist, preventing her from getting out of bed. 'We've only just closed our eyes. What time is it?'

'Four-thirty.'

'The middle of the night? What the hell?'

She gave him a quick kiss on his mussed-up hair, a lump tight in her throat. 'Someone's grumpy today.'

'Today? It's still yesterday as far as I'm concerned. It's not today until either the sun comes up, or I've had at least five hours' sleep.' Something hard prodded her thigh and she grinned. His voice was husky with sleep and desire. 'Do you know what would make me feel a whole lot better?'

Damn right, it would make her feel better too. So would spending the rest of the day here. But it was impossible—real life was back with a vengeance.

'Nothing would get my day off to a better start, believe me, but we have to get going. We should have packed last night instead of…' Like hell she'd have preferred packing to making love on a beach. Or showering the sand off later, together… Her body thrummed with the soft ache of exercise, and she had an inner glow that would keep her warm for some time to come, but that didn't stop time marching on. Too quickly. 'I'm sorry, Jake. Come on. Time to get up. The fun's over.'

'Why?'

'We're going home. We talked… It's over.'

'Whoa. Wait a minute. What's the hurry?' He sat up. His hand closed over hers and made her pause as her heart began to pump against her ribcage. 'What do you mean?'

'We have a plane to catch.'

'Yes, and we're ahead of schedule. So why are you running?'

'I'm not running.'

'Could have fooled me.' He tugged on her hand. 'Look at me, Lola. Look at me.'

It all suddenly seemed too hard. She didn't want a sad goodbye, she just wanted to leave without pain. She started to throw her clothes into her bag. 'I have too much to do. This isn't the time or place, Jake.'

'You think? I have a few questions for you…so hear me out. What is this rush? Why is pleasing Cameron so important to you? I mean, really? Why? It's like it's the biggest thing in your life. It's not even the job you want.'

'It's not about the job.' She wasn't going to discuss it here. 'Come on, let's get packed or you'll make us late.'

'And that would never do, right?' He grabbed the pillow and pulled it onto his head. 'I'm not moving, Lola. Not until you tell me what the hell is going on.'

'You'd do that? You'd make things worse for me?'

'If it meant I got the truth, yes. If it's not about the job, what is it about?'

She glanced at the clock and her heart beat a little faster. 'And now there's a time restriction on my words. Great.' But he did deserve some kind of explanation, because she had to admit her obsession with making everything work for her probably did seem a little extreme. 'Okay…well. This is the situation… And don't judge me, okay?' She twisted the sheet in her fist, screwing it tighter and tighter, because admitting this was like exposing a raw nerve. 'My family doesn't know anything about my writing. They think I'm in LA to act. It's all I've ever done since I was a baby. All they've ever wanted me to do. And I hate it. The last thing I want to do is get up on a stage and say someone else's words. I want to write my own.'

'They think you're here to…' He smiled. 'Way to go. That's why you won't send your dad the script.'

'He'd go crazy—you have no idea. They think I have *it*. You know, that little nugget of talent to be great, and they'd think I was throwing a huge opportunity away. Just like Dad did. But it's their dream, Jake, not mine. They won't listen, of course, because they want to live vicariously through me. They trussed me up and pushed me onto stages, into advertisements, pantomimes, TV shows, anything where I could *shine*. Paid for acting lessons, one-on-one tuition, immersion classes, dancing… anything I earned went straight back into my drama education. It was relentless. They pushed and pushed and pushed until I'd had a gut full of learning lines and make-up and playing nice or playing naughty or being Santa's helper or a dead body or bloody Lady Macbeth. I'd had enough, so I left. I needed to come to a place where I could be me. If they knew I wasn't even trying to act here, they'd be devastated. So I have to make this work. My script, my dream. My choice. My life. Do you see? I have to make it work and that takes dedication, time management, studying, practice—a whole lifetime of catching up. And now…look, you're making me late. I can't be late. I can't take a chance on losing this job, because, apart from giving me enough money to just about survive here, working for Cameron helps with the pretence…'

'The lie.'

'Yes.' She tilted her chin. She wasn't proud of it, but she would do anything to get where she wanted to be. Including misleading her family. 'The lie. Oh, it's easy when you have someone who wants you to follow your dreams, altogether another when they won't even let you have one of your own. Now, please. Can we go? I will tell them. I will. When I've sold my script. When I'm ready—and not when you or anyone else decides. Now we have to go. Okay?'

'Okay. Okay.' His palms went up. He was frowning. Now he knew she wasn't who she'd said she was. She was someone who would break her parents' hearts just to be free. Then he stroked the inside of her arm and made her shiver. 'I wouldn't tread on your dreams, Lola. I wouldn't jeopardise them.'

Making me fall for you would do exactly that. This was too damned hard. 'Please, hurry. Cameron will be waiting.'

The catch in her throat as she gave him one final kiss was with her as she threw her clothes into her suitcase, fed the dogs, gave them their anti-nausea medicine, took them for one last walk along that divine beach. It was still there as she wheeled the rack of clothes up to the house for collection later. And when he held the car door open for her and gave her a smile that told her he was thinking of last night, and the earlier hours of this morning, and the things they'd done and the way they'd made each other feel. And not about what she'd told him and how damned selfish she could be.

She tried to ignore the prickle of sadness that had lodged behind her ribcage, and the thickness in her throat. And she dug deep and found the joy she infused into everything—regardless of whatever came next she was happy simply because it had happened.

The flight back was less serene than the one out. Butter had eaten something that upset her and spent the journey being ill, Cameron slept with earmuffs and an eye mask, and Jake stared out of the window.

When they hit the tarmac in Los Angeles, Lola still didn't know what to say to Jake. It was all well and good when you wrote the dialogue, but not when you actually lived the big, dark conflict in the story.

And this time she was tasked with picking up Cameron's suitcases while, for once, the actress took the dogs through customs, looking like a devoted and doting dog-owner and not the rather absent one she'd been in Nassau.

So there was only a quick moment to chat to Jake as he waited for a cab to take him home. No fine limousines here—at least, not for the hired help. Lola turned to him and her heart jittered a little and her cheeks burned. She wanted to touch him, to run her hands over his face, to lay her head against his chest. To kiss him once more. But she did none of those things. She stood a little apart from him and gave him a pathetic wave. 'Okay, well, that was fun! Thanks so much! I guess I'll see you on set? Wednesday?'

'Yes. Wednesday. Lola—' He took a step forward but the cab driver tooted and Cameron was shouting and the dogs were barking again and Lola started to feel as queasy as Butter.

'Okay! I need to go!' She turned to walk away.

'Lola...wait.'

'Yes?' She whizzed round, tangling herself in the trolley wheels as the suitcases swung one way and she the other.

'Watch it!' He gave her a rueful grin. 'Listen. It's been... great.'

She tightened her grip on the trolley handle and fixed her smile. 'Yes, it has. Great.'

'So...let's just see what happens, eh?'

Which could have been Jake-speak for *Don't call*

me, I'll call you. Or could have been a damned offer of marriage or something in between, she didn't know. For someone who was largely direct and open, he was being remarkably tight-lipped. But she didn't have time to ponder any more. Other people needed her. More to the point, she needed some space to think about what had happened and just exactly how she felt about it all. About him.

She reached and gave his hand a tight squeeze, which was Lola-speak for *I have no bloody idea.*

Then started on the rest of her day.

Routine was good. Routine soothed his brain. Routine erased all thoughts except the purity of surgery and healing his patients.

Jake liked routine. He was back in his space and could breathe easily.

Well, easier.

'I don't like the way that artery is leaking.' He spoke to his assistant quietly and calmly, pointing to the ooze coming from around the middle cerebral artery. Jake checked the three-dimensional computer imaging again—the mass had been completely resected and the leak was minimal. There was no desperate urgency. But there was a definite need to stop the damned thing. 'Great. You got it. Excellent.' He raised his voice a little. 'How are you doing, Moira? Won't be long now.'

Their patient's eyelids fluttered open. 'Just fine, thanks.'

'Great, can you sing me something? *Carmen* maybe? Just quietly…'

'"Habanera"?' The famous opera singer smiled as the anaesthesiologist adjusted the oxygen mask so she could inhale deeply and sing. 'Oh, yes. Of course, my favourite.

I'd love to...' And so she began... *"'L'amour est un oi-
seau rebelle. Que nul ne peut apprivoiser...'"*

Her strong melodious voice filled the OR. He'd asked
her to sing quietly, but there was nothing about this
woman that was quiet. She was a joy to watch on stage
and he intended to keep her up there for many more
years, having removed the meningioma. A little recu-
peration and she'd hopefully be free from the headaches
and blurred vision that she'd ignored for the last few
months due to her heavy work schedule. Some people
put work too far up their priority list to the detriment of
everything else.

Listen to yourself.

'Just perfect. Not long now. We've got all of the tumour out and, as you can see, none of your speech or
memory functions have been affected.' They were of
the most concern to her—she wanted to be able to remember the words and the tunes, but mostly she wanted
to remember her children, the little moments, the every-
day. He started to hum the catchy refrain as they began
to close up the incision. 'So, what do the words mean?'

She was sleepy, but in control. 'Love is a rebellious
bird, that none can tame...'

Ain't that the truth?

Whoa. Nobody said anything about love. Three days
in Nassau, that's all it had been. A little before that. Nothing since. Lola's admission had been a surprise, but it
explained a lot about her drive and persistence. He just
wasn't at all sure what it meant for them. Thinking they
both needed space, he'd avoided calling her. He wished
he hadn't, but there it was.

Routine. He stuck to his routine. Nothing in his routine involved seeing a woman for more than a few dates.
'Excellent. Philip is going to finish up while I go talk to

your kids. They've been waiting outside for you. You're very loved.'

She squeezed his hand. 'I know. I'm very blessed. My children are devoted. Go, tell them I'm fine.'

He washed up and wandered out to the family room where he found Moira's son and daughter—both around his age, in their early thirties—pale with worry. He'd been there on the other side a couple of times, waiting for the prognosis on his father. He knew how they felt, the anguish, the pain. Knew how to be honest but to tread lightly. Knew that they wouldn't rest until they saw her. As he approached they both stood, stepped forward, worry smudged across their faces. 'Dr Jake...how is she? Is she okay?'

'She's fine. She's actually been great through the whole procedure. She's sedated a little, and will now be able to rest, but we'll keep a close eye on her.'

The son stepped forward and shook his hand. 'Thank you. Thank you. I don't know what we'd have done without her. She's...well, she's just the best mom.'

She was also the best mezzo-soprano in the world, but they wouldn't care as much about that as having their mother alive. 'No problem at all. I understand. I'll be back later to check up on her.'

As he strode down the corridor he felt a sharp sting in his chest. He'd hated being on the other side, hated being out of control, and had wanted anything for his father to live. He could still remember the pain of waiting, the promises he'd made, the deals he'd forged between himself and some higher being—*if he survives I'll repay him every last cent. If he lives I'll show him it was worth it. Just let him live.* It was still raw, like a hard lump in his ribcage.

But for what? All he had done since had been to be-rate his father for working himself into an early grave, for not listening to his son's advice, for not letting him take on the burden. Something that Lola had said to him about showing gratitude struck a chord. He flicked out his phone and dialled.

Five hours later, with something of a little respite in that heartburn, he arrived at the set for the night shoot. There were two things on his agenda tonight and he was going to achieve them, whatever else happened. Unfortunately they both depended on Cameron being amenable.

Not seeing her on set, he meandered over to the trailers and rapped sharply on the door to Cameron's. The loud yelping of three dogs greeted him as Lola answered. She was wearing that Evelyn Rice blue dress she'd had on the other night, her hair was piled loosely on her head, accentuating her eyes, which were back to being guarded again. He wanted to kiss that away. Actually, he wanted to make love with her again right now. But although there were very strange things happening on the space-desert-warrior-princess set, sex wasn't one of them. Even so, his body reacted to her instinctively, taking in her curves, her soft lips...

Her smile slipped as she looked at him. 'Oh. Jake. Hi.'

He wasn't sure exactly what sort of greeting it was meant to be, but it didn't say, *We had great sex, let's do it again. Soon.* Or... *I missed you.* It didn't even have the hallmarks of Lola's usual happy-go-lucky, semi-forced jolly *Hello!* complete with the requisite unspoken exclamation point. But it wasn't a damning indictment either.

He was at a loss how to navigate this. He could pretend that things hadn't changed, but they had. He knew her now—knew what she was fighting, knew how beautiful she was, knew that she was scared to take any risks that would jeopardise her plans. 'Hey, Lola. How's things?'

'Great. Thanks.'

'The leg? How's it doing?'

'Fine, thank you.' Giving nothing away, she looked down at her ankle and he followed her line of vision. It was still red and slightly swollen but he could see from this angle that things were progressing nicely. 'Oh, get down, Jelly.'

'Hey, dog.' He reached in to pat the pup, who was trying to climb up his leg, and was immediately subsumed by an intense pungent smell. Not Lola's intimate flowery scent, something altogether more pungent coming from inside the trailer. He gave her a questioning smile and whispered, 'What the hell's that smell?'

'Rosemary and geranium. Memory and stress.' There was no congenial smile, no conspiratorial grin. No joke about the strangeness of this world they were in. Instead, she took a step back up into the trailer and let him in. 'Cameron, it's Jake.'

Great, she was here. He'd have to speak to Lola later. Now he would deal with item one on his agenda: he would speak to Cameron about the pregnancy. Now. Tonight. No excuses. Work. Work. Work.

'Dr Jake, honey. Thank you for stopping by.' It was said so casually, as if he was here entirely for his own benefit and not because he was contracted to fulfil her every need. Cameron patted the sofa. 'Sit, please. I have five minutes. Let's talk.'

'Okay. Right…in that case…' Lola looked at them both, then filled the ensuing heavy silence with a scrabble around for dog leads. 'I'll take the dogs out.'

Not so fast. If she was dashing off this was probably his only chance to achieve item two on his agenda, so he had to say something before she left. With no regard for how Cameron might take this exchange he managed to attract Lola's eye and spoke to her. 'Wait, Lola. I need to talk to you too.'

'The dogs need to go out and you're here for Cameron.' With that she was gone.

And he should have been grateful for the chance to see Cameron alone, but he really wanted to chase Lola down, kidnap her and take her back to his apartment. To unwrap that dress for a second time and take her to his bed. The intensity with which he wanted her was alarming. Overwhelming. He wasn't sure at all about how he'd handled their last conversation, but what to say in a cacophony of noise and a time constraint? He stared at the space where she'd been standing and was at a loss as to what to think.

'Dr Jake?'

Work. That was what he did best. Not relationships. The disaster between him and his parents was proof enough of that. 'Cameron. Yes. Sorry. We need to talk.'

'I know we do.' The actress sat, arranged her warrior princess skirts around her and then looked directly at him. 'Yes, I am pregnant. There. I've said it. First time too. Out loud. Although my head's been in a whirl for weeks. I'm pregnant and I'm scared and I have a contract for another film starting in a month's time and I don't know what to do. There it is.'

He wanted to ask if she was happy about it, but she didn't look it. She looked young and vulnerable and terrified, and for once in her life she wasn't acting.

'How far along do you think you are? Do you know?'

'Four months or so, I guess.'

Whoa. Her waist was tiny, so either she was naturally petite or she'd been starving herself. He was concerned it was the latter, having seen how little she'd eaten in Nassau. 'First, there's nothing to be scared about, it's a perfectly natural state, but there are some considerations you could make to ensure you and the baby are in the best possible shape. Firstly, you need an OB/GYN and a midwife who can walk you through the steps. They'll give you information and advice, can book blood tests and scans, and they will put your mind completely at rest. You may have one in mind, but if not, I can refer you to one at The Hills. Gabriella Cain is excellent—'

'No.' Cameron's voice was leading-lady commanding but laced with anxiety. 'I mean, yes. But not until this film wraps, okay? I don't want anyone to know. No one, d'you hear me?'

'I do. But Gabriella's entirely professional and will be completely confidential, and the sooner you book in to see her the better.'

'Next week, Jake. I will see her late next week once we're done here. Now, I don't want to talk about it again. Not a word until this…' she waved her hand at the trailer and nodded as if he'd already agreed and there was no more debate. '…is over. Not a word.'

'But—' The damned woman was refusing to even talk about it?

'Please…' She gave him a genuinely wobbly smile and leaned closer. 'We all have secrets, Jake. Look at you and Lola—don't deny it. It's obvious to everyone. You're not fooling anyone.'

That was none of her business. 'There is no me and Lola.'

'Whatever you say.' Surprisingly, she covered his hand with hers. 'See? Sometimes we need to hug our secrets to ourselves for a little longer until they take root. Yes? I just need to keep this secret mine before the whole world starts speculating about who the father is and what I'm going to do. And asking whether it's the death of my career. I also need to talk with my agent and the director on *Hayley's Way*, do you understand?'

He had to agree he'd wondered all of those things. 'Of course. Of course, but rest assured no one from the clinic will leak the information.'

'Honey, everyone has a price.'

'I don't.'

'No. I don't imagine you do.' Bored or weary or just plain over the conversation, he didn't know, Cameron lay back on the sofa. 'So let me wait a week longer before all hell descends—it'll be chaos and poor Lola will take most of the hits. She answers the phone, she deals with everything…everything. But you've been very kind so if I can do anything for you…anything you need…just ask.'

Instinct told him not to even consider a conversation about his life or what he needed, but his mind started to work through the pros and cons and ramifications. This could be his chance to get item two on his agenda sorted. And as he worked out what to say about that another germ of an idea started to form… This could be brilliant. Lola would probably want to kill him, but it would be brilliant. 'Actually, Cameron, there is something you could do for me…'

CHAPTER ELEVEN

'I SHOULD BE very cross with you.' Lola opened the door of her tiny Inglewood studio apartment, embarrassed that Jake would see the almost-closet she lived in, and simultaneously trying to control her erratic heartbeat. She'd received a strange call from him, asking her to be free on Saturday. No clues about why. And nothing from him since.

Now he was standing in the doorway, hair slightly damp from a recent shower, smelling fresh and clean and appetising. The grey T-shirt accentuated his toned body, the jeans underlining the casual clothes he'd told her to wear. 'You should not have asked Cameron if I could have the day off without my permission.'

'So you said on the phone. Twice. But you'd gone AWOL with the dogs, so I had no choice. In fact, the words I used to her were, "If Lola wanted the day off on Saturday, could she have it?" At that point I didn't know if you'd agree to this. Isn't everyone supposed to have two days a week off anyway?'

'In the real world, yes. In Cameron's world, not so much. Anyway…what's the big surprise?'

'You deserve a day out. I thought we could have a trip down to the beach. Then…' Jake glanced at his shoes then back at her, and she got the distinct impression he was having trouble asking her whatever it was he was asking her. 'My parents are preparing dinner for us.'

'Your what? You want me to go with you to see your parents?' *What the hell?*

Maybe 'Let's see what happens' really had been a marriage proposal? No?

No.

And in a pink polka dot sundress she was hardly dressed for a dinner with his parents.

His eyebrows rose in a question. 'Big deal?'

Yes. Huge damned deal. Especially after everything she'd told him. 'It depends. Why do you want me to go with you?'

He shrugged. 'You said I should go see them. So I'm going. This is all your fault…' When he realised that wasn't going to work he gave her a smile that he must have known would have her saying yes immediately. 'Lola, they're nice people. Besides, I thought you might like the drive out. I can show you around the area, seeing as you're new here and all.'

So basically he was acting on her advice and he wanted her to ride shotgun. 'You want support? Sure. Say the words. Ask me and I'll think about it, but don't use me as an excuse. Dr Direct has suddenly become Dr Coy—and I'm not sure how I feel about that.'

'Dr Direct? Really?'

'Yes, too direct sometimes but, yes. You say what you think. Honesty is a good thing.' She should try it herself once or twice.

'That's my philosophy too. Usually.' Actually, it was funny to see him try to ask for something. In the time she'd known him he'd been very good at giving, at anticipating, at looking after everyone, but he obviously wasn't used to asking for things for himself. That made her heart squeeze a little, but not enough that she was going to take pity on him.

'Okay. Lola, I'd like you to come and see my parents. I think we'd get along better if we had a buffer. You. This was your idea. Please.'

Her eyes narrowed. 'That was almost… Try harder next time. And I'm coming along as a what, exactly? A mysterious friend?'

'Yes. Well, not that mysterious.'

'Your friend.' It was a statement, not a question.

And clearly not a proposal.

She laughed to herself, because there was a tiny part of her that had died a little. *Hope.*

She had no place hoping for something that was so out of reach for her right now.

He came over and took her into his arms. 'Aren't you? A friend?'

'I'm not sure what we are. To be honest, I don't know how to react around you.'

He frowned. 'Why not?'

'Because of what I told you the other day.'

'What I heard was that you're a young woman out living her life. Nothing wrong with that. I'm just not sure where I fit in.'

You and me both. 'Friends, like we just said. That would work.' Maybe that was enough for now. Although she had a feeling that where he was concerned she'd never have enough. That was what frightened her. 'Okay, I'd love a day out. Which beach should we go to?'

'Well, we could detour via Santa Monica. Grab some lunch, take a walk down the pier.'

'I don't know…' She grimaced. 'The last time I was at a beach I got bitten by a man-eating plant.'

'No…the last time you were on a beach something

entirely different happened.' He tipped her chin up and planted a kiss on her mouth. 'Which I seem to remember you enjoyed so much you had me do it all over again in the shower…and in bed…over and over.'

With the memories of their last night on Nassau swirling in her head, she blushed. Blushed, and a hot rush of need swirled with her thoughts. 'Oh, God. Yes.'

'Later maybe?' His lips brushed hers. 'Hmm. Later definitely. But first I promise I'll look after you and protect you from the man-eating plants and aquatic life.'

'Okay, I'll just get my bag.' She turned away from him, realising, too late, that it wasn't the sea life she needed protection from. It was the damage he would do to her heart.

Lola had been to Santa Monica many times before. She loved the shopping and the relaxed beach community atmosphere, particularly down the promenade, but coming here with Jake gave it even more appeal. As usual there were street performers playing music, some dancers and a couple of jugglers wowing the crowds. Having bought the best salted caramel gelato Lola had ever tasted, they stopped for a while to lick the drips from their fingers and watch the entertainment.

As one of the jugglers threw three lit fire sticks into the air she nudged Jake. 'There you go. If ever brains turn out not to be your thing, there's always a place for you here.'

He laughed. 'Well, it would be nice to work outdoors every now and then.'

'And there's balls, sticks *and* hoops—a lot of diversity in the role.'

'Probably wouldn't pay as well as my current job.'

'But look at the smiling faces.'

His eyebrows rose. 'Hey, I make people smile. Sometimes, if I'm not careful it's a wonky smile…but still…' He grabbed her arm. 'Come on, let's hit the pier.'

You make me *smile*, she thought, and then tried not to think and just live in the moment. Because she didn't get many moments like this, when she wasn't worrying or working. Usually both at the same time.

The afternoon flew by in a whirl of laughter. Joining the crowds of tourists, he dragged her onto the Ferris wheel and pointed out important landmarks, they swam in the sea and she pretended all over again to be attacked by a killer plant just so he could rescue her. They ate freshly baked pretzels from a stall and he tried—and failed—to get her onto the roller coaster. She was keen to walk and swim and enjoyed the carousel, but turning her upside down might have made the pretzel reappear. and she wasn't sure he'd be impressed by that.

Just as they were making their way back to the car his phone rang.

'My mom,' he explained, looking at the small screen. 'I'll just take this. Hang on.'

As he stepped away from her Lola watched his whole demeanour change. There was no smile now. His shoulders had started to hunch and his jaw clenched as he gripped the phone. His voice rose. 'No. No, Mom, that's not okay…' He paused to listen. Then, 'I don't care. I want them to take him to The Hills, to my clinic. For God's sake, Mom, he'll be seen immediately, he'll be looked after better. This time I'm not taking no for an answer, okay?'

Lola laid her hand on a taut shoulder and smoothed a palm down his back. Jake turned and gave her a weary shrug, shaking his head at the phone with irritation. 'Mom. Listen to me… Okay, put them on. Hi, it's Dr

Lewis here, yes, I'm his son. Yes, I know his condition. Absolutely not. Take him to The Hollywood Hills Clinic, I can get him seen much quicker. I'll meet you there.'

He slid the phone into his pocket and stood there, taking several deep breaths.

'Your dad?'

'Turns out even the thought of seeing me gets him worked up. His breathing's off, his oxygen sats are down. They're taking him—' He exhaled his irritation as he started to pace up and down. 'Why did I say we'd go for dinner? I know he gets stressed just at the thought of me. I shouldn't have arranged anything.'

Lola knew what a burden it was to be the absolute focus of someone else's hopes; that it felt as if you carried sole responsibility for a parent's happiness—and in Jake's case their health too. She also knew that at some point you had to unshackle yourself from that, to stop taking the blame for their problems. 'This is not your fault, Jake.'

The look he gave her was bleak as they marched towards the car. 'Well, it sure as hell isn't anyone else's.'

'How's he doing?' Jake dashed into the HDU and found his mom, pale and red-eyed, by the side of the large bed. Her fingers absentmindedly worried the handles of her worn-out bag. She was dressed in a shabby beige coat he remembered she'd been excited about buying years ago. Her shoes were scuffed and a little battered. Like her heart. Looking after an obstinate old fool who preferred to eke out a tired life than take a hand-out from his son had worn her away at the edges.

Anger rose in his gut. His dad might have been too proud, but his mother could have had her pick of anything in Macy's. She'd have liked that, he was sure.

And, hell, that was not what was important right now.

'He's a lot better than he was. He got really out of breath and worked up—he's been in a lousy mood all day. He went a little blue and I was…well, let's just say I'm grateful we're here. The nebulisers are definitely working and it's a really nice place. Thank you, Jake… Oh!' His mom looked surprised to see Lola behind him. Why the hell he'd asked his mom to cook them dinner he didn't know. It had seemed like a good idea at the time. He'd never mentioned the word 'date', of course, but his mother's head would be working overtime, trying to join dots that didn't exist. 'Hello, you must be…?'

'Lola.' She stepped forward with a smile and gave his mom's hand a shake. 'I hope it's okay for me to be here? Jake said—'

'It's fine for you to be here.' He grabbed her a chair and had her sit next to his mom. 'This is my mom, Deanna, and my dad, Bill.'

His father lay propped up by pillows, his breath rattling in and out, with an oxygen mask over his face. His cheeks were dark hollows, his eyes scared and piercing. He'd lost more weight, Jake noticed. Constantly fighting for air did that to a man.

Jake laced his voice with as much positivity as he could muster. 'Hey, Dad.'

'Son.' The word was breathed, pained. Oxygen was dragged in. Out. In. Out. A conscious act, desperate. 'Got. Your. Way. In. The. End.'

'Dad, please don't start. I was trying to help. I didn't want you sitting for hours in a cold cubicle struggling to breathe until someone was free to see you. It's so much better here. See, you were admitted straight away. Whatever you want, just ask. I've got this.'

His dad didn't say anything, he didn't have to. He just

turned his head away and closed his eyes. His silent comment: *I don't want anything from you*.

And right now Jake didn't care what his dad thought about being here. It was better than the public hospital and Bill Lewis deserved the best. But Jake understood that being there would put a dent in the old man's pride.

He picked up his dad's admission notes and scanned them. Blood pressure was erratic, blood gases were haywire, his lung function was severely compromised. This visit was just one of many he'd probably have over the next few years. COPD was a long, slow struggle of fighting infection and trying to halt further deterioration.

There was silence as everyone looked at their feet. It was so damned sad that they had nothing to say to each other at a time like this. He went for the mundane, to keep the peace. 'How's the house? Garden?'

His mom's face brightened at the distraction, a bit of normality. 'Oh, you know, same as always. I'd like to spruce the place up a bit, but…well…' She nodded towards his dad. 'You know…'

He did. The wallpaper in the dining room had been exactly the same all Jake's life, the carpet too—too much upheaval, they'd said, to change it all. Too much dust—and no respite for a man with damaged lungs. The dining suite must have been thirty years old, the upholstery fraying on the seats.

Jake nodded. 'Fresh air helps—if it's not too humid. How about trying to get outside? You've got that nice outdoor furniture—sit out a while.'

Mom shook her head. 'The garden's got away from us these days—it's too big to deal with. And things grow so fast. I couldn't sit and look at that mess.'

'Then I'll come round and sort it out.' No excuses. 'You can sit out and feel the sun on your back.' She was too drawn and pale these days, looking after an obstinate man who put pride before any kind of enjoyment.

'That would be lovely, Jakey. Thank you. We were so looking forward to you coming for dinner today. Such a shame...' His mom's voice died away and silence fell again.

Meanwhile, Lola sat to his left, her hands in her lap, knees tight. She looked about as uncomfortable as Jake felt.

He checked the oxygen flow, read the heart monitor. Again. Pulse rate was fast but settling. Blood pressure a little lower than before. Sats still low but rising. 'So, Dad, how're you feeling now? That medicine doing its magic?'

'Can't. Complain. Son.' A shallow breath. Heaving chest. Another breath. But his skin was starting to pink up. 'How's that job?'

'Just fine.'

'Good.'

This was how it was. His father never commented on how he felt and they kept conversation to anything other than personal. He couldn't think of a single thing to say. No. Not right. He could think of a million things to say but they wouldn't listen.

He thought about his old home, the photos that lined the walls. Pictures of him when he was a little boy, high on his dad's shoulders. Of the three of them at a baseball game. Christmases. His birthdays. Of his graduation. In all of them they were smiling. So proud. Even though money had been woefully tight on the salaries of a part-time nurse aide and an untenured teacher, they'd been happy. A fist clamped tight round his heart. At what point had they gone from a unit of three to strangers? Would they ever get it back?

Was it too late?

'So he kicked towards me, grabbed me tight and swam hard to the beach.' Lola's voice brought him back—she was showing them her war wound. 'It was a plant, would you believe it? A plant can do that much harm?'

'There are a few plants you need to avoid in California that you may not have in London. Jake'll tell you all about poison oak. He once—'

'Not necessary to tell Lola all my secrets, Mom. Especially the ones that involve me being naked.' He turned to Lola. 'I was four at the time. We were camping.'

'Sounds painful. But I bet you were super-cute then.' She smiled. Heat flashed across her eyes and she swallowed, the glimmer of a private smile on her lips. Then her gaze caught his and the word 'naked' had stoked his memory. And he was surprised at the heat that flashed through him. Intense. Immediate. She turned back to his mom and dad. 'Well, he won't admit it, but I'd like to say he saved my life.'

His mom looked impressed. 'That's my Jakey.'

Lola nodded and smiled, knowing damned well he hadn't saved her life. He knew what she was doing, trying to make him out to be some kind of hero. It was a kind gesture. Smoothing things over, making light of them, her smile ready for everyone. She had an easy manner that seemed to cut through the tension. It had never occurred to him to bring any of his friends to meet them before. At first it had been due to—he was ashamed to realise now—embarrassment of the lowliness of his origins in comparison to those of the other medical students. Then anger had overshadowed the embarrassment. Then there had seemed little point, because there was nothing to say when he came.

Lola smiled at his mom. 'And you were a nurse, Mrs Lewis? Is that right? Is that why you decided to be a doctor, Jake? Following your mum's footsteps into medicine?'

'Oh, no.' His mom blushed and waved her hand in front of her face. 'Jakey was far too clever to follow me. We knew that from when he was a little boy. He did everything faster, better than the other kids. He was singled out at school. They have a name for it now, gifted and talented. But back then he was just top of the class in everything. His father used to give him extra lessons to keep him from getting bored.'

'That's enough about me, Mom. Thanks. We don't want to bore Lola to death.' But his mother wasn't listening.

'We don't see enough of him now, of course. He's so busy.'

'I know, Mom. I'm sorry.'

'Your…mother…misses…you.' It was the first thing his father had said for what felt like hours. It was a barb. It wasn't warm, like his mom's joking. It was a dart targeted at Jake's heart. And they both knew it. Staying away had been the way to avoid all the arguments, but it had made coming back all that much harder.

The temperature on the unit felt like it had plummeted. Things could go in one of two ways now, depending on how he handled this. He chose compliance. 'I know, I'm sorry, things get busy. I come when I can.'

'Not enough.' His father shook his head. 'You should come home more.'

'When you're better you could come to see me—a trip up to the city? Mom would like that. I could pick you up. It would be easy. You could get out of the house for a while.'

'What's wrong with the house?'

'Jake, I'm fine. It's fine. Bill, leave it. Please.' His mom's lip quivered, and just like that the tension spilled over.

'It's not fine, Deanna.' His father was shaking now, gulping air. 'Not at all.'

'There's nothing wrong with home, Dad. I just think it would be nice for you two to get out a little. We could take a drive. Have lunch out. Go to the ocean. Mom likes the ocean, remember?'

'I'm fine, Jake.' His mom's voice began to shake too. She'd always trod a fine line to keep the peace and made resolutely sure never to take sides. It must have been so hard for her. Every time. 'Please—leave it. Don't go upsetting your father.'

His dad's shoulders heaved up and down. 'Still…not seeing you means we…don't have to listen to all…those damned instructions…you bark at us. *Get a new car. Buy this. Change the kitchen. I'll buy that.* Like we can't manage.'

Lola stared down at her hands. Easy how things could go from hero to zero once he and his dad were in the same room.

'I'm sorry, Mom, Dad. I know I should let you be.' *Show gratitude*, Lola had said. 'I just want the best for you. I want you to know how grateful I am and that's the only way I can think of showing it.'

'Oh, Jakey, we know you're grateful. You don't have to do anything. Nothing at all.' His mom gave him a weary smile, popped her hand over his father's tight fist and waited until he'd relaxed a little. 'We're both so proud of you.'

And so he sat and tried to control the anger that was swirling inside him. And not to focus on the pain in his mom's eyes and the slump of her shoulders and the shabby coat. He tried hard not to notice the old shoes and the fraying handbag. He tried even harder not to listen to the rapid inhalation of his father's broken lungs, and tried not to think about all the things he could do to make their lives easier. If only they would listen.

Keep a lid on it. Gratitude. At the very least, be nice.

As they spent the next ten minutes chatting about nothing he focused on smiling and nodding at the conversation. He listened to Lola's attempts at jokes and he liked her even more for trying. Any other woman would have excused herself by now or thrown him *I want to leave* looks, but not Lola. She just carried on asking questions about his childhood as if there wasn't a thick cloud of doom hanging over them all, as if she didn't notice the dreariness and the atmosphere.

Gradually his father improved enough to take the mask off a little and, feeling reassured about his progress, Lola and his mother disappeared to get coffees. So Jake was left with his dad and the anger and the frustration, and he tried to suppress it. He wanted to try gratitude one more time, but the words wouldn't come because it wasn't their way. It wasn't how they did things.

He should have left it, buttoned his lip, but it was all too much for him to ignore. 'So, I get it that you have too much pride to use my money, Dad, and I know it's all just accumulating in some account somewhere and will all come back to me when you're both gone, just as you want. But look at Mom. Just look at her. She's tired, she's getting old, she needs a break. You both do. When was the last time you went on holiday?'

His father's face sagged with ill-concealed frustration. 'How can I go on holiday like this? Get real, Jake.'

He still tried to keep a lid on his temper, but it was wriggling loose at the edges, out of his grasp. 'It doesn't have to be hard. First class gets you decent help. I could hire a nurse. Two. Somewhere with great fishing. Mom could relax, and while you're away we'll organise some house renovations. Fresh paint, the garden—'

'For heaven's sake, Jake, how many times…?'

A little bit anger more wriggled loose, and he was just grateful Lola wasn't there to witness it. He tried to keep his voice quiet but, goddammit, sometimes it got loud. 'Hear me out, Dad. Please. I don't want you getting worked up. I know you don't want me to help, I know you say that providing all those years is a father's job, but it's a son's job too. How do you think I feel when I see you struggling? When I can help? When I can make things easier—if not on you then on Mom? I could organise a home-care nurse and give her a break…or just some housekeeping help. Doesn't *she* deserve a break?'

They didn't need to be here, doing this. If his dad had better housing he wouldn't get so sick. If he got better treatment, these attacks would be fewer. If he'd sought help at the beginning… *If…if…damned if…*

His dad didn't have much time left and for the most part he could be well enough to travel—a short way, with help. They needed to be ticking things off a bucket list— or at the very least living in a place that wasn't making his condition worse.

'Dad, you remember when we went on vacation to Yosemite? D'you remember what fun we had? How much Mom laughed? You said you loved it when she did that. When was the last time you saw that?' And despite every attempt to keep it locked in, his anger finally wriggled free. He pressed his hand over his dad's, something he'd never done before. His dad's skin was paper thin, his fingers were frail and cold, but inside that man, Jake knew, there was a determined heart—it may have been damaged over the years and fighting to keep going, but it was full and proud. Hell, he'd gotten his grit from his father after all. 'Just stop being so damned stubborn. *Please*. You might not want to enjoy the last few years you have, but she deserves to. She wants to go out. She wants to have nice things. Stop trying to look after me. I don't need it. I'm all grown up now—it's my turn to look after you. I need to do this. You need to listen.'

There was a silence except for the rhythmic whirr of the oxygen cylinder, the irregular intake of breath. His father looked at him with dark sunken eyes, lines of ribs showed under his pyjama top, his thin wrists gripping the sides of his duvet. He looked and he kept on looking.

Jake looked right back. At the man who had taught him how to ride a bike and how to fish, how to change a car tyre and how to put up a shelf straight. And then at what he'd been reduced to—for *him*. And the anger solidified into a hard physical lump in his chest. 'Oh, and just for the record, Dad, you don't get the monopoly on love either, you know. You don't get to make hard sacrifices for me without knowing this one thing; I'm very grateful. Really. I know I could never have got where I am without you, that's why I want to help. Why I *have* to help.' Jake took a wild leap. It was raw and angry but it was said. 'I love you, Dad.'

With that, Jake turned away. There was nothing more he could do or say. His throat was sore. His chest felt as if it was going to explode. He didn't know if it was enough—because how could words be enough after his father had sacrificed his health? But it was all Jake had—that and his repeated offers to be there for them if they needed him. That, after all, had been what he'd been trying to say for the last ten years through the anger and the fights. Just that. *I love you.*

And, damn it, just as Lola and his mom bustled back

into the room, all polite smiles and coffee cups, he could have sworn he heard his father say, 'I know, son.' But he wasn't sure.

He didn't turn round to speak to them, he turned back to look at the man he'd adored with every childish breath. His eyes met his dad's again and they held. The older man's softened as Jake felt his soften. And he felt the strength of this once mighty man emanate from what was left of his broken body and pass to him. From father to son. A handing down, a rite of passage. A gift.

Nothing was said, but something gave. Finally. It wasn't a battle won, it was a war ended. 'Let's make it work, Dad,' he whispered, under the pretence of fixing the oxygen tubing.

And there, for a moment, was his dad's hand on his. A pat. Warmth in those bluish fingers and a fragile smile. The pride, though, his dad still had a good grip on that. *And so he should*, Jake thought. There was nothing wrong with being proud of what he'd achieved. 'Right you are, son. Starting now.'

Lola's hand was on his arm and she gave him a wary smile. He didn't know if she'd heard anything of what had been said between himself and his dad but she gave no indication of her thoughts. 'Jake, I hope you don't mind, but I've had a call. I need to get back to Bel Air.'

His heart was swollen but his mind was immediately on Cameron's pregnancy. 'Sure. Anything serious?'

'Depends on what you mean by serious. In her eyes, yes. She's a perfectionist and wants to get things right first take. She's got an important final shoot tomorrow and she wants to go over her lines,' Lola explained with a shrug. 'I should have said no. But I can't… I just… I'm so sorry. You know how it is. Work comes first.'

'But…' What was the point in arguing? He would take

her to Bel Air and then come back here. End of. Although it was usually him breaking dates for emergencies. It was uncomfortable to feel it from the other side.

'I said I'd be there within the hour if possible.'

'Sure.' He was about to excuse himself from his parents, just for the time it'd take him to get her home.

But, as if she'd read his mind, she interrupted. 'No.'

Her gaze travelled from him to his dad and back. 'You stay here. They need you here. I can make my own way.'

'I'll call you a cab at least. And—well, thank you.' He almost said more, but didn't. How could he? The fantasy he'd had about ending the day together in bed fizzled out. He'd wanted to show her his appreciation of how she'd helped him today—although that fantasy had also included him having a spectacularly great time too. It would have to wait until…until another time when they could both carve space out in their diaries.

One more night shoot and they'd have to work extra-hard at carving out that time because their paths wouldn't cross like they did on set. He'd be back to a full-time clinic and on-call roster. Cameron had already prepared him for the time-suck her pregnancy would be for Lola, at least in the short term. And with that and her work and her stubborn determination to win a battle only she was fighting, it would be hard to carve out anything meaningful.

In fact, if he looked at it rationally, her leaving now was a good thing—it meant they were both committed to the important things, they could sharpen their focus on their careers and consign this, whatever it was that they had, to a happy memory and not a distraction. And yet there was a strange twist in his chest at the thought of this coming to an end.

'Okay, Lola?'

'Yes, thanks. I've had a smashing day.' She gave him a sort of wobbly smile that meant she was sorry *but…* and he understood. Because work always did come first.

CHAPTER TWELVE

As SOON AS she walked into Cameron's house Lola was put on high alert. Her boss was more than a little tetchy as she paced up and down the family room, wringing her hands. Her usually perfect hair was a mess, there were black rings round her eyes, smudged lines of mascara down her cheeks.

'Cameron? Oh, my goodness, what's wrong?'

'Lola.' She didn't stop pacing. 'I thought you said you'd be back soon.'

'I came as quickly as I could. What is it? You look… well, you look dreadful.'

'It's this.' Cameron picked up her desert warrior dress from the sofa and threw it to Lola. Strange, because all costumes were meant to stay in the wardrobe trailer, not come home. Ever. Everyone knew the rules.

'Your dress? What's wrong with it? I know it's a bit out there, but you've been fine about wearing it for the whole film.'

Cameron shook her head. 'It. Doesn't. Fit.'

'What? Where?'

'Everywhere.' Her boss sat down on the couch and worried her hands. 'I'm too big. All over.'

'That's okay, we'll get Maria to let it out. No big deal. I'll sort it, first thing in the morning.'

'She'll ask questions. I can't…' She ran her hand across her stomach and Lola looked closer. Her boobs were quite a bit bigger than normal. Her tummy was a little rounded. Cameron looked…well, apart from the make-up mess, she was glowing with health.

Holy. Moly. 'You're pregnant.'

'Yes.' Her voice was a tiny squeak. The healthy glow had given way to a little green around the lips. Pregnancy explained a lot—the strange diet, the mood swings, the broodiness. The need for a physician. 'What am I going to do?'

'What do you want to do?' Something twisted in Lola's gut. It wasn't jealousy as such. Or maybe it was. Lola hadn't given a thought to settling down and having a family, at least any time in the near or medium future, so she couldn't fathom why she should suddenly ache for a piece of that. Sympathy hormones, clearly. Get two women in the same room for any amount of time and their hormones fell into sync. She'd clearly been spending way too much time with Cameron.

With this crisis, that would only escalate.

'Keep it, I think. I don't know. The timing's all wrong. But… I didn't want to even think about it. I didn't want to be pregnant and it's taken me a lot of time to get used to the idea. And I have to fit into that dress. I have to wear nineteenth-century corsets and ride a damned horse in a month.' She took a quick breath and carried on, her words coming faster and faster. 'I think I felt it kick an hour ago. I don't know, maybe not, but there was something. A flutter. And now it all feels so real and I've been squishing it into this dress, pretending it wasn't happeni—'

'Stop it. Stop it, right now.' Lola stepped forward and took her boss's hands. She'd started to sound hysterical. 'Getting worked up won't be good for your baby.

You have to be a mum now, responsible. Think about what it needs, not just what you need.' *That was probably going to be the hardest bit*, Lola thought. Then she caught herself—because when Cameron focused on a project she always did it to perfection. 'You'll be a great mum. You will.'

Her boss stared at her open-mouthed. Then nodded, slowly. 'Yes. Yes, of course. And I need to stay calm.'

'Exactly.' Although a little hysteria now would be nothing compared to the media furore when word of this got out. Lola would be on call night and day, and could kiss goodbye to any kind of personal life for a while. There would be journalists to deflect, speculation on the baby's gender, an army of paparazzi whenever Cameron went out. A barrage of baby and maternity wear and gifts that would arrive from companies across the world, wanting Cameron to endorse their brands, and they would need cataloguing and thank-you cards. OB/GYN appointments…tests. A different kind of gym workout. A new menu, probably a new chef who specialised in maternal nutrition. It might even be easier if she moved into Cameron's for a while.

And…who was the father? Wouldn't he want a say, wouldn't she have to co-ordinate diaries? Organise nannies and nurses and research the best diapers— because Cameron always wanted to be seen as eco-conscious because that got more headlines. Not counting private planes and carbon footprints, obviously.

It would be a terrible time for a PA to leave or to demand extra time for herself. Cameron needed her. It would be fine, Lola asserted. It would be okay. Busy, but okay.

'Look, Cameron, we'll work it all out. We'll sit down and make a list and go through it all one thing at a time.

When you're ready. But first off I'll get out my sewing machine and let out your costume tonight—no one will know, we can say you accidentally left it in your trailer. Next thing; let's get you something to eat and drink— you need to feed the baby. Thirdly, you don't have to do *Hayley's Way*. You know, you are in charge of your career.' Lola didn't miss the irony of those words.

'Honey, that was my chance for Cannes. It was going to be my career-affirming film.'

'You're at the top of your field already, you couldn't be more career-affirmed. This has happened and now you just have to deal with it. Enjoy it. Carve out some time in your life… It is possible. You can do this. Now, let me make you a cup of mint tea. That'll help settle you. And a snack. We can talk. Think. Plan.'

This was a very strange end to her day. She couldn't have imagined when Jake had knocked on her door—

Jake.

She had that same twisting in her gut at the thought of him. If she'd thought that there might be time for any kind of fling then, that was now dead in the ground. There wasn't going to be any time for her to focus on herself, never mind him, or a relationship, and what guy would put up with that?

This was her life, this was her job, and it was a doorway to a much better place. She just needed to suck it up and do what Bill Lewis had done: make sacrifices, no matter how much they hurt. She had to step up for Cameron.

Oh, but before she did that there was one thing she would do for herself: she would call her family and confess. She would ask her father's opinion about her script. Then she would put her head down and work in what little spare time she could find. Which meant no Jake.

One day she'd be in a position to put the rest of her life first. To fall in love and have all the trimmings. One day she'd be in control of her timetable enough to have everything. Because that was what she'd have to deny herself to get to that point, everything that other people had—the house, the job, the guy.

One day she'd have time for someone significant. Someone she loved and who loved her right back. It wasn't a lot to ask, no wild or whacky dreams—she didn't want anything extraordinary. Something that Mr and Mrs Lewis had would be great. Better than great. A whole lifetime with one person—a life together, memories, children, a commitment.

With Jake?

She wasn't one hundred per cent sure, but she had a sneaking suspicion that the answer to that question was yes. One day. Just not today.

Or any time soon.

The dress fitted well after Lola's late-night alterations. Cameron was pleased that no one had questioned why the costume had disappeared overnight, and the shoot was almost complete. Just a short break then the final lines would be said and the truly dreadful space-desert-odyssey would be a wrap.

Then they would be navigating uncharted territory: announcing the pregnancy and dealing with the fallout; renegotiating the *Hayley's Way* contract—a meeting with lawyers and Cameron's agent had been scheduled for tomorrow.

Lola just had to get through tonight. Seeing Jake. Telling him about having to refocus on her job…pregnancy talk would be strictly off limits. Cameron had made her swear utter secrecy.

Leaving Jake.

She glanced outside the trailer into the car lot and thought for a second that she could see him strolling towards her. But that was wishful thinking. Relief and dread threaded through her; it was madness to feel like this. To want a man so badly and to have to break things off.

She closed her eyes for a moment as a keen pain fisted in her chest. She'd found a good man. One who wanted her—at least, she thought he did. One who made her laugh, made her sigh, made her want things so out of reach. She had two options. She could do what her father did and commit to a relationship at the risk of everything else in his life. Or she could suggest a clean break, enjoy the memories and survive the heartache.

She knew without a shadow of a doubt that she wasn't her father.

Then she shut off all lines of thought because it was just too hard to keep thinking and rethinking, and seeing Jake's face in her mind's eye and remembering his touch and the way he made her feel.

'So! A great day's work today so far? A cup of tea, Cameron, while we're waiting? A smoothie?'

'Oh, you darling. Peppermint tea, please.'

'Of course!'

A snuffling at her feet had her looking down at the floor. Jelly clearly wanted some attention, so she bent to pat her and as she did so her hand brushed against Cameron's bag. There was a script there. Not unusual—Cameron was always working. But it wasn't the one Cameron was supposed to be reading… Lola's heart almost stopped. Then it started to thump loud and hard against her ribcage. *Her* script? How could Cameron have got hold of it? Had she seen it, *borrowed* it to read? Had she been going through Lola's things?

This was not okay. 'Er…excuse me, Cameron?'

'Yes, honey?' Her boss was propped up by satin cushions, snoozing, feet up on the couch after a hard hour or two's acting. She didn't usually like to be interrupted. But…*what the hell*?

'Sorry, but is that…is that…my script you're reading?' She could hardly say the words, her mouth was suddenly dry and thick.

'Why, yes, it is. Jake gave it to me the other day. He said it was good, but he was wrong…'

'Oh.' *Jake gave it to her? Jake gave it to her? And she hated it.*

The actress's eyes flickered open. She smiled. 'It wasn't good, Lola, it was great. I love it. In fact…' she patted the cushion next to her, inviting Lola to sit '… I'd like to option it.'

'Option it? But you don't have a production company.'

'I'm thinking of starting one after the baby comes. We have to diversify as we age, darling.'

Lola tried to control herself, because…well, Cameron was nothing but astute. She'd made a decent career for herself. She wanted to do something with Lola's script— out of all the scripts she saw month after month.

This was huge.

But Jake! What had he been thinking? Why the hell would he want to step in and take over, when he knew how she felt about being in control of her own life? Had anything she'd said meant anything to him?

'You know, Cameron… I'm not actually all that sure what I'm going to do with it yet. I wasn't going to show it to anyone for a little while. Not until I'd made sure it was finished. But…well… Wow. If you think it might work, that would be…' Lola stood and glanced out the window again. This time she did see Jake striding across the lot, wearing the same guarded expression he'd had last night. 'Sorry…got to go… I won't be long.'

Cameron sighed. 'Take the dogs—?'

Lola didn't have the wherewithal to listen to Cameron's next words. Her ears were burning with a raging white noise. She pulled the door closed, stormed down the steps, ignoring the tug in her heart just at the sight of him, and hissed, 'What on earth did you think you were doing? Showing Cameron my script? How dare you?'

'Good evening, Lola.' He stopped short, clearly understanding how important it was right now to keep his distance. 'You're going to have to help me out here because I was trying to do a good thing.'

'That is my script. That is my work. How dare you interfere? I will fashion my career when I'm ready, not when you think's a good time.'

'Hey, I thought it might give you a hand up. You're not exactly pushing yourself forward. I was trying to help. I believe in that script. And you, Lola. I believe in you.'

'I am sick of people thinking they know what's best for me. Okay? I will do things the way I want, when I want.' He was just like her parents. Would no one listen? 'Besides, I was waiting to hear what my dad said about it.'

His eyebrows rose. 'You told him? Everything?'

She took a deep breath. It would have been nice to share this in better circumstances but there it was. 'Yes. I did. He wasn't thrilled, neither of them were. It was difficult…there were tears…but it's now out in the open. He said they'd only wanted me to be happy, that I should have told them earlier. Most of all they were disappointed I lied. I get that. I know I did the wrong thing, but I doubt they'd have been open to it before.'

'Feels better, right?' Jake reached out and smoothed his hand over her hair. 'Took some guts.'

It had taken great willpower, but she'd done it because she'd seen what a difference being honest had made to Jake and his father. It was a sound platform for them to develop something better. 'You bet it did.'

'I know it did.' He smiled. 'So he read it?'

'He emailed me this morning. He loves it…he's given me a couple of suggestions for changes. I wanted to make them before I showed it to anyone. Like…you know… Cameron? I can't believe you took my property and handed it over without asking my permission. That is unforgivable.'

'We can talk to her.' He seemed to realise his mistake immediately. 'Sorry, *you* can talk to her. Suggest you tweak it a little—ask her if she thinks it needs it. Tell her what you need.'

'To be honest, I'm not sure she'll care what I need right now, she's got other things on her mind.' In the background, underneath the noise in her ears and Jake's voice, Lola could hear barking. Lots of barking. She ignored it, raised her voice. 'Just this once I'm going to let Cameron deal with them.' She tugged him away from the trailer to a more deserted part of the lot. 'While I deal with you.'

He came willingly. *Annoyingly.* Because she wanted him to refuse, she wanted to drag him bodily across the tarmac and cause some serious damage to his lovely leather shoes. Just…well, just because.

She wanted to tell him that she was so damned angry that he'd overstepped the mark. And yet she still wanted him. That he caused too many emotions in her head. That her heart hurt every time she woke up without him. That he'd caused a tsunami of chaos in her life and had made her want so much more. So. Much. More. But she couldn't have it. She couldn't focus on what she needed to do, what she'd fought hard for, and give him what he deserved.

She wanted to tell him that of all the emotions he'd imprinted in her, the one that shone so brightly in the centre of her chest was something she was scared of. Scared because it was so huge, so important. So devastating. She wanted to tell him that…that she loved him.

Because surely that was what this was? She loved him. Needed him in her life. She ached to wake up with him. For him to be the last person she thought of every night. For them to have a future.

She closed her eyes. *Oh, God.* She loved him.

A sharp pain pierced her heart. How had that happened, when she'd tried to convince herself all along that she was in control of her own destiny? Loving Jake wasn't something she could do—not now. Not here. Not when everything was against them.

Which meant it wasn't going to be okay. It wasn't going to be okay at all.

He had the audacity to smile. 'So is this the part where we kiss and make up?'

'No, Jake.' And she started to shake. 'This is the part where it ends.'

Jake looked at her—at the way she was standing, hands on hips, trembling with anger, a flashback to the first day he'd met her, which seemed like a lifetime ago and yet was only a matter of weeks. And yet so much had changed. So much that he'd had to work through. More than one sleepless night. But most noticeably, last night, when he'd gone to bed with a definite plan of ending it. It was too complicated. Too hard in a world when clambering to the top of a career was tough enough.

But he'd woken up with such a need to see her that he

couldn't bring himself to conjure up the words. And the moment he'd laid eyes on her again and felt the lift in his heart he'd known that this wasn't something ordinary. This was the most special thing he'd ever had. And now she was throwing it away because he'd done something lame. To her way of thinking. In his, he'd been doing a darned good thing.

And now here she was, saying the words he'd practised and then dismissed, because he believed in what they had. Believed they had a future if they were prepared to work towards it together.

He looked into the intense brown eyes that were raging with emotions—so many he couldn't keep up. Anger—yes, there was a lot of that. And desire—that was there too. A little bit of humility and embarrassment. And something else. Something that he connected with so profoundly it stripped the breath from his lungs—so he couldn't work out why her words and her eyes didn't match. 'You want to end it?'

'Yes.'

'Because I gave Cameron your script?'

She frowned. 'No. Don't be stupid. That's not a valid reason. Although I am fuming about that. Really bloody angry.'

'Yes. You are. I can see and I'm sorry. But if it's not because of that, then why? Why does it have to end?'

'Because it isn't a great time for me right now. There's too much at stake for me to get distracted by something that may come to an end... I can't risk the rest of my life on you.' Here her voice cracked. 'I'm sorry, Jake. We said in Nassau that it was short term. Just for fun. We've got to...just stick by that.'

'Things can change, Lola. We can change with them. Hell, it's up to us what we do.'

She shook her head vehemently. 'But that's where you're wrong. Your career is established but you still have to do things that interfere with it—like the trip to the Bahamas. Like working here—you didn't want to do it. It was out of your control. But for me, I'm striving here, I have a plan and I need to follow it.'

'And that doesn't include me.'

'No. I'm sorry.' She glanced back towards the trailer, where the barking was continuing, as if to prove her point. Cameron was useless without someone to run her life. He got that. But it didn't have to be all-consuming, did it? Lola shrugged. 'We have too much to do, too much to create for ourselves before we can commit to settling down. There's just too much. I can't do it all—I'm so tired. It's exhausting trying to sleep and think and feel all these things for you. And then keep on working all hours and write and edit…and still keep on feeling these things.'

He tried to cajole her. Made a joke. 'You could take a leaf out of my book and learn how to juggle a bit better—if it's good for the brain, it might work for the heart too.'

'Not right now, Jake. I'm sorry.' The corners of her mouth lifted. 'And Cameron needs me. There's…things happening.'

She knows Cameron's pregnant. She knows but she can't say. And neither could he—because he couldn't take the risk. If he mentioned it first he'd be blowing all confidentiality and that would risk harming the clinic's reputation, his job…her work. Her damned plan.

It seemed everything came down to that.

But it wasn't insurmountable. 'Other people manage to have relationships and work hard. Plenty.'

'And many don't. Relationships suffer or someone has to compromise—like my dad did. Give up a dream. Regret. *God*, I don't want that to happen. I don't want to look at my kids with that in my eyes. That would break my heart...'

He already felt as if his already had. 'Don't I get a say in any of this? What about what I want? What if I think it can work? What if I say I want it to?'

She reached her hand to his chest and laid her palm there. 'One day. One day we'll both be in the right space to do this.'

'What? You'll call me? You'll call and say, *Hey, I'm ready now*? And you think I'll come running? When? A year? Five? Ten? You think this is going to stay in here?' He pointed to his heart and, yes, he knew he'd still feel these things for her in a year, two, a decade. His heart felt blown open, raw. She'd taught him how to live again and now she wanted to cut off his damned oxygen. He wanted to fight, wanted to grab her and talk sense in to her. But this impossibly positive woman didn't think it would work. And if she didn't think it would work—if she couldn't make it work by infusing everything with a zillion of her jolly exclamation points—then they were certainly totally doomed. 'You want to take a chance on that? On us both being in the right space at the right time some time in the future?'

'It's all I've got, Jake.' She had to raise her voice a little, as the barking was louder now. She took two steps away from him. Might well have been a hundred. 'I'm sorry, I really think I'd better go and see what's happening—'

'Go to Cameron. Figures.'

'Jake, I've got to—'

'You want to prioritise a job you don't even want over a relationship? It doesn't add up, Lola. You're not making sense.' She was about to argue back, he could see, but he rattled on. Unable to stop. 'What the hell are you scared of?'

She was defiant, chin in the air. 'Scared? I'm not scared. You just don't understand what it's like to finally start to live a life you want, instead of moulding yourself on someone else's dream.'

'Are you really saying I don't know what it's like to have parents who have poured their whole lives into yours? Really? You saw my father, Lola. I live with that every single day.'

Her hands fisted at her sides. Tears pricked her eyes but she blinked them away. 'I'm saying you don't know what it's like to fight your way out of that. It was suffocating. Too much pressure. Too much living someone else's life. I need to live my own life. I need to know that I can make it. On my own.'

'And that doesn't include compromise? Or falling in love? Or taking a risk? Not a great life, Lola.'

'Right now it's the best I can do. I'm not afraid to make hard choices. I'm sorry, Jake. So sorry.' She turned to leave but he grabbed her wrist, pulled her to him and felt the tight press of her body against his. The way her bones moulded against his, the way her eyes told him of the way she truly felt and the way her mouth said words he didn't want to hear.

So he did the only thing that made sense and he cut the words off. He slammed his mouth over hers and kissed her with everything he had. For a moment she kissed him back with just the same amount of force. But then she pulled away. Her eyes were filled with tears and she put a hand to her mouth as if holding in a cry. Then she swallowed and shook her head. 'Jake, I can't. I want to. But I can't.'

With that she turned and ran back towards the trailer.

Jake shoved his hands into his pockets. Walked back towards the set where Alfredo gave him a warm smile and indicated for him to sit and watch them inch towards the final take of the worst movie in living history. And in his chest a fist of darkness tightened. He'd lost her. Lost her to this crazy life where nothing was real, where nothing made sense—not least his raging emotions. And there was absolutely nothing he could do about it. He felt like a raw exposed nerve. A damned artery, leaking hope, that he couldn't cauterise.

'*A-a-a-nd* action!' Alfredo called, and silence descended across the fake lunarscape. The leading man started to crawl across the floor, maimed and injured after a supposed alien attack. But the set of his jaw told the hushed audience that he would rise again and fight back.

Jake almost laughed. *Go on, man. Fight for all you're worth. Sometimes you just can't win, no matter what you do.*

Then out of the silence rose a terrified cry. Then another. And his heart began to drum. Because it wasn't on set, it was out in the car lot.

It was Lola, screaming his name.

CHAPTER THIRTEEN

HE RAN TO HER, doctor's bag in hand, the echo of his fast-beating heart drumming in his ears. She was standing at the top of the trailer steps, chest heaving as she smothered a sob. And he wanted to scoop her up, to kiss those cheeks pink again. But she held her hand up, keeping him at a distance, as if touching him would break her.

There was blood on her palms.

'What the hell…? Lola, what's happened?'

'Cameron…' She shook her head but motioned for him to come inside. There, on the floor, was the actress lying in a heap. She was moaning, pale. Blood on her forehead.

And her skirt.

The baby.

Head injury and threatened miscarriage. Potential brain bleed. Loss of blood.

The dogs were yelping around her, licking her face, running in circles.

Jake focused. 'Lola, get them out of here. They're going to get in the way. And call the clinic. Now. Get them to send the helicopter. Immediately.'

'Absolutely.' She took the dogs outside and he heard her on her cell phone. Her voice was surprisingly calm, compared to the chalk white panic of her face.

He knelt at Cameron's side and felt her pulse as he

spoke gently. 'Cameron? Cameron. Hey…' Her eyelids flickered open and she opened her mouth to speak, but her face crumpled. 'It's okay…it's okay. Just lie here, it's okay. I'm going to ask you some questions. I'm going to need you to tell me a few things.'

She nodded, then closed her eyes again. Her hand was on her abdomen. But the blood loss appeared worse on her head, so he dealt with that first. He rummaged in his bag for his blood-pressure monitor. 'How did you end up down here?'

'Fell. Dogs.'

'You fell over the dogs?' No surprise there.

She nodded weakly. Her trembling hand went to the bump on her head. At first glance it looked superficial. Just a gash that was bleeding heavily. But that didn't mean there wasn't deeper damage. He cradled her head in his hands, keeping it still, and checked the depth of the wound, the size of the lump. Clearly no neck or spinal damage as she was moving all limbs. 'You took a nasty knock there. What did you hit it on, can you remember?'

'Table.'

'You fell over the dogs and hit your head on the table?' He assumed it had been the corner judging by the jagged edge of the laceration. But she was showing no memory loss. 'Did you black out?'

'No. I don't think so.'

'You know where you are?'

'On the floor, honey, and it's sticky.'

At least her sense of humour was intact. 'In? Location?'

'West LA. Film set.' She sounded groggy, her limbs heavy as he tested her reflexes and her pupil reactions. All normal. He'd do a full concussion check once they were at the clinic. Signs of concussion or something worse might not show for a few hours.

'And now here?' He placed his hand softly against the tiny pregnancy bump. The blood on her skirt didn't appear to be getting any worse. 'How does this feel?'

A single tear edged down her cheek. 'Hurts.'

Lola tiptoed back into the trailer. 'ETA five minutes. They can land over in the far car lot. I've okayed that with security. But you need to know something, Jake… She's…' Lola worried her bottom lip with her teeth, then sighed. 'I'm sorry, Cameron, I'm going to have to tell him—'

'Pregnant.' He held Lola's gaze and she gave him a faint smile of acknowledgement. 'I know. I've known for a while.'

'Of course you have.' She knelt and took her boss's hand. 'Cameron, it's going to be okay. Jake will take care of you.'

Blood pressure low, but not dangerous. Yet. At least that was something, but her pulse was racing. He looked at Lola and they both looked at the spotting on Cameron's white skirt. He needed to assess just how much blood she was losing. 'Cameron, I need to examine your abdomen to check on the baby. Is that okay? And I need to know how much blood loss there is. Do you want to lie on a couch?'

'No. Here.' The actress shuddered on a sob, but nodded. Lola fetched some towels, then held Cameron's hand while he assessed the size of the uterus and checked for tenderness and further blood loss. 'This isn't exactly a great place for doing this. We need to get you to the clinic and get you checked out.'

'But…the film.'

'This is more important. I'll talk to Alfredo.'

Lola nodded. 'I just have. He's fine. He wants me to let him know how you are. Later.' She stroked her employer's hair back away from the cut and then held the gauze Jake gave her over it to stem the bleeding.

He watched her as she chatted away, gently soothing. He imagined if the tables were turned and it were Lola lying on the floor. Cameron would be a mess.

Lola caught his gaze and held it for a few seconds. Underneath the reassuring noises she was pale and spooked, he could see that, but she was strong and holding everything together. As she looked at him her eyes softened and she bit her wobbling lip.

Pain ripped through him. After this he wouldn't see Lola again. He couldn't imagine that. Didn't want to think about it. Didn't want to acknowledge the emotion that was lodged in his throat as he watched her. So he turned away and focused on his patient. 'I'm just going to take your blood pressure again, Cameron.'

Her hand grasped his. 'Please. Don't let me lose this baby. Please. I—I wasn't ready, but I am now. I'm ready for this. Don't let me lose it. So precious…'

'He won't,' Lola whispered to her boss, but she stared right at Jake—her eyes boring into him with such belief and hope that he didn't deserve. 'He won't let you lose this baby.'

Cameron's fingers gripped white on his as she finally realised what she had and what she was at risk of losing. But their faith in him was too damned high. He closed his eyes. Because, really, it was out of his hands. He could monitor her blood pressure and give her IV fluids when the paramedics arrived. He could treat her as best he could in the helicopter, but he couldn't promise anything, not where a baby was concerned. He was a neurosurgeon, not a gynaecologist.

Then the air was filled with the sound of chopper blades and he told Lola to go out and bring the paramedics over. And he tried to keep his patient as reassured as best he possibly could.

When the team had safely got Cameron onto a stretcher with an IV line in situ and she was haemodynamically stable for now, he helped them down the steps and over the tarmac.

Lola stood, arms wrapped around her chest as she watched them load the stretcher into the helicopter. Her face was bleak, haunted. Sad. It took everything he had not to bundle her to him, but she'd drawn a line and he had to respect that. One stolen kiss was probably a step too far already. 'She'll be okay, Lola.'

She looked at him with black-rimmed eyes. 'How can you be sure?'

'She'll be fine. Go with her. In the chopper. Go.'

The trembling from earlier was back. 'No. You go. You're the doctor, you'll know what to do. I'll be useless.'

He took hold of her hands. 'She needs *you*.'

'No, she doesn't.' Her head shook. 'Go, Jake. I'll drop the dogs at home with the housekeeper. I shouldn't have brought them here in the first place but she went on and on about wanting her babies with her. I knew it was a stupid idea. I shouldn't have left her with them.'

'Lola. Stop it. None of this is your fault.'

'How can you say that?'

'Because accidents happen. Don't beat yourself up about this. You did not cause this.' The irony of the words haunted him and for the first time he realised that he was not responsible for his father's illness. There could have been many reasons why he'd got so sick and why he hadn't asked for help in the early stages—and only some of them were about his son. The rest were about his father's stubbornness, about the arbitrary nature of life. How some people could bounce back from infection and others needed adjunct therapy. How some people survived surgery and others didn't. How you met someone who had a profound effect on your life and because... *because* they're made like you, it seemed impossible that either of you could find space to make it work.

Wide eyes peered up at him beneath a frown. 'If we hadn't been outside... If I'd come back in as soon as I heard the dogs... Jake, what if she loses the baby?'

'You can't live your life on ifs, Lola. We'll do everything we can to make sure that doesn't happen. Now, go. Do what you need to do with the dogs and meet me at the clinic.'

'Save her, Jake.'

'I'll try.'

She gave him the first smile he'd seen from her in hours. 'Oh, I have faith in you.'

'Do you?' He couldn't help but feel pain at that laughable statement. 'In my skills, yes. But nothing else.'

'What do you mean? Of course I have faith in your skills. You're an amazing doctor.'

He wanted her. Wanted to hear more than that from her, because she was deluding herself if she thought they could put some kind of halt to the way they felt about each other. Love wasn't something you could put on hold until you decided you wanted it—it burned into you like a brand.

Love.

Yeah. So there it was. He loved her.

At this revelation his heart skipped a couple of beats, and he felt the space in his chest implode, then it thudded back to a sorta, kinda sinus rhythm. The same but different—just like he was, having met Lola. The same guy with the same goals, but changed. Irrevocably.

It was a fine time to realise this as the chopper's blades began to whir and his work called to him—and she was walking away. It was the second time in two days he'd thought about how much he loved someone—and thought about telling them. This time, though, he'd keep it to himself. She didn't need to know how he felt.

He didn't want to admit it, but the thought of loving and losing Lola was just too damned hard. 'And there I was thinking that we make a great team. You know what's better than being on your own? Someone who can work *with* you, like we just did. A champion. Someone who believes in you more than you believe in yourself. Who's there to pick you up when you need it. Like you did with me and my dad. Like I did when you were sick. We make a good team, Lola—we could be brilliant together. I would never stand in the way of your dreams but, hell, I'd cheer you on. Anywhere. Everywhere. I'd support you, I'd carry you when you needed it and I'd stand back to let you shine in your own way too.'

'I know you would.' Her lip began to tremble. 'I know.'

'So here's what I don't get about this—you say you trust me enough to look after the life of your employer and her unborn child. You trust that I will make things right with my parents—that I will strive to look after them, whatever happens. You trust me to keep everyone safe. Except you.' He could see the pain in his heart mirrored on her face, but he didn't have time to make things right with her, or to convince her that he even could. He started to walk towards the chopper, the rush from the rotating blades blasting his words away as he turned around to look at her one last time. 'Why can't you trust me with your heart too?'

* * *

Lola drove way faster than the speed limit—and she didn't really care—along the narrow, winding roads towards The Hollywood Hills Clinic, heaving the car to the side every few minutes to allow yet another tourist bus to scrape past. Hundreds of people trying to catch a glimpse of a celebrity in the big houses flanking the road. No wonder the tarmac was in such a bad condition. She bumped in and out of potholes, each pause adding time to her journey. None of this mattered, of course. Only Cameron and the baby's safety.

And Jake.

His words resonated in her the whole trip. Had she been fooling herself that all this time she had been hiding behind her own dreams, when the real reason she'd held him off had been because she'd just been too scared to trust him?

Did she love him, truly? And what would that mean for her? For him? Could they make it work?

Bill and Deanna Lewis had found time for each other despite a child to care for, conflicting shifts and working all hours. The love between them had been right there, almost tangible. And her father had made a sacrifice for love; even though he'd chosen to move to London, she had no doubt he had made that choice willingly. Because there was a better thing than blindly following a career. A better thing than being totally alone just to prove a point, just to be able to say, *I am an independent person.* There was that thing called love that made everything just that little bit better.

What was the point in carving out a life for yourself if you had no one to share it? She'd be damned lonely in that studio apartment with just a script for company.

What if she lost Jake? That was just too much to contemplate.

She all but threw her car keys at the valet and ran into the impressive white building, and was greeted by soothing music, a water feature in the lobby and a smartly dressed, smiling receptionist at the front desk, with 'Stephanie' on her name badge. They'd bypassed this when she'd come here the other day to see Bill Lewis.

The calm that Jake usually emanated was right here in this place under the Hollywood sign, up in the hills. A far cry from the turbulent darkness in his eyes, the harsh anger as he'd spoken those last words to her. And her heart pounded even more. Not for Cameron this time, but for herself. Was it too late?

'Hi! I'm looking for Dr Lewis. Jake. And…' Lola leant forward so that the conversation would be private. Not that there were many people around, but confidentiality was king for Cameron. 'Cameron Fontaine?'

Stephanie smiled. 'Oh…er… I'll page Dr Lewis. Is he expecting you?'

'Yes. Tell him Lola's here.' She didn't press the point about Cameron…she'd hear soon enough from either the actress herself or Jake. The worse part was waiting, being the one who was excluded. The one who'd have to pick up the pieces. If…

She didn't want to think about it. 'I'm ready…' Cameron had said. She'd taken a huge step and for the first time in her life wanted something more than herself. Cameron knew just how much would change, it would have to—but she was going to do it. She was embracing it—and even though it would be a struggle, Lola hoped that Cameron would successfully manage thinking for two people.

Her boss was a whole lot braver than she herself was.

Because right up until he'd mentioned trust, she hadn't been brave enough to let someone have a piece of her heart, or to allow herself to think about sharing her life.

But now…

It took him less than five minutes to appear in the lobby, but in that time she'd managed to control her heart-beat and take in some of the beautiful artworks on the wall, tried to allow the sound of the tinkling water to calm her nerves. She couldn't gauge his emotion as he walked towards her.

She couldn't gauge her own. Because, damn it, despite the words she'd said to him she was still not feeling the sentiment of them. Every part of her body ached to touch him, to feel his touch. She couldn't walk away. It made no sense. Being with Jake was the only thing that was clear.

But would he still want her after everything she had said?

He was wearing a white coat with the requisite stetho-scope around his neck, and looked every inch like the dashing doctor in a starring role. 'Lola.'

'Hey, Jake.' And she felt like the villain. She didn't want to be anything other than herself, and right now she didn't feel the bright optimistic front she usually wore. She felt sad. Deflated. Anxious. Lost. Beaten. 'How's Cameron doing?'

He reached a hand to her arm and squeezed. His heat rushed through her and she saw kindness in his eyes. And…she dared to hope…something else. 'Cameron's being assessed by our obstetric team. She's in good hands.'

'And her head?'

'In the scheme of things it's not serious. Head wounds bleed. A lot. But she doesn't appear to have done any major damage. She's going to have a headache for a few

days, but we'll keep an eye on all that along with the
baby. One good thing, they were scanning as I left and I
heard a heartbeat...'

'Thank God for that.' Lola closed her eyes and
breathed out heavily, her hand on her chest. When she
opened her eyes he was still there, his expression still
unreadable. 'No, actually, thank you. Thank you.'

He shrugged. 'So. I'll take you to the family room and
you can wait there. I have things to do.'

'Actually, wait. Can I talk to you? Maybe outside?
I need some air.' She had no idea what she was going
to say, or how to say it. Or even if he'd listen. But she
wanted to tell him that she wanted to try. To be two. To
be together.

'Sure. Whatever you want, Lola.' He started to lead
her through the automatic doors and into the afternoon
sunshine. 'If it's about your script again, I'm still sorry.
I shouldn't have done it. I've learnt my lesson, I won't
be looking to help again. You're on your own from now
on. That's what you want, right?'

No. She wanted him. 'I don't know what Cameron will
want to do with the script now. I have to bide my time,
but she'll do right by me, I'm sure.'

'Good. It needs a home. It'll make a damn fine movie.'
His eyebrows rose. 'So, what do you want to talk about?'

'Us.'

He came to halt. 'You made it very clear that—'

'I love you.' It wasn't exactly finessed, but it got the
point over. It certainly shut him up.

'Oh.' He blinked, looking momentarily as lost as she
was. 'I see.'

'And I want to share my life with you. At least, commit
to each other. Something. Something important. Some-

thing mind-blowingly amazing. I don't know why I was so determined not to make a go of things, why I ended it so quickly. I think… You were right. I was scared by how much you mean to me. You grew on me pretty quickly and I was rattled by that. I didn't expect that it could feel so good…so, yes, I'm scared. Scared of throwing away everything I've worked so hard for. Scared that part of me would get lost a little in the concept of us, but scared even more about what I'll miss out on if I don't take that chance. I didn't mean to hurt you, Jake. I just couldn't figure out how we could love each other and keep that love alive in the midst of two very busy careers.'

'As I said before, lots of people do it. They make it work. We could have.'

'We still could. Make each other a priority. Really. I couldn't think of anything I'd like more than to see you in every spare moment I have. And I'll make more. Loads more. I'll speak to Cameron and ensure we stick strictly to the contract. If everything works out with the baby, I'll make her hire a nanny, two. Three. One each for the dogs… If everything works out with the screenplay I won't have to work for her at all…'

'Lola.' He paced in front of her, his logical brain clearly dealing with how to say no, gently. His directness was lost. She loved that about him. That he was clear-headed about everything but her. 'You made it clear that things were over. And now you come back here and hit me with this? What am I supposed to think now? Or to feel? It's crazy. You're crazy. I don't want to hear any of this.'

'Oh.' Her throat stung. It was too late. She didn't know what to do now. She'd been so sure he wanted her. That her love for him would convince him. That they'd make it work. She'd been so sure. She stood for a moment and let the reality seep into her bones, into her heart. She'd lost him. Had been too cautious and had treated him badly. She allowed herself one last look at his deep blue eyes and his impossibly beautiful mouth. Then she hauled up every bit of strength she had, dug deep for the optimistic Lola he seemed to like. 'Okay! That's okay! It's fine! Really! I'll just go and find Cameron, see if she needs anything…' She turned and began to walk away.

She would not cry. She fought against the pain and a rising sob. Pressed a hand to her mouth. She would not cry.

'I mean, Lola, I don't want to hear another word because…' He pulled her close and kissed her hard on the mouth. Kissed her until her bones began to melt and her legs turned a little to jelly—or Jell-O, or whatever. They were wobbly, and her heart began to race. In a good way. A very good way. He kissed her until she was in no doubt as to how he felt. When he pulled away he was as breathless as her. 'I love you, Lola Bennett. And—strangely—I love your weird world of doggy danger and space-desert odysseys. And wildly demanding actresses and private planes and personal chefs. Of passion and dreams so beyond reach, and yet within grasp if you believe. Anything's possible. It's beyond bizarre. But I love it.'

'Things may get worse… I have a wild idea for my next screenplay. You may not like it, but I want to diversify. Cameron says we all should.'

He frowned. 'What could be worse than the princess-space-desert odyssey I've just lived through?'

'Zombie apocalypse?'

'Of course. That makes perfect sense.' He tipped his head back and laughed. 'Man, this is a crazy city. Bring it on. I love you, Lola Bennett, and your crazy life, and I

want to share it. But mine might be a little dull in comparison.'

'There is nothing dull about your life at all—look at all
those people you save, with just chopsticks.' She smiled,
wondering how she'd ever thought she would have a complete life without him in it. 'And the passion with which
you love people—so much it hurts—but you try to hide
it. I love the things you do for me. You give me hope, you
give me love, you give me wings. I love you right back.'

He kissed the tip of her nose and looked up at the Hollywood sign way up on the hill. 'Is this where we cue the
soppy romantic music or the waves crashing on a beach?'

'No.' She took hold of the lapels of his white coat and
tiptoed up to him. 'This is where you kiss me all over
again.'

'Oh, I can do that. My pleasure. Over and over
and over again.' He lowered his voice and his mouth,
'*A-a-a-nd* action!'

* * * * *

Look out for the next great story in
THE HOLLYWOOD HILLS CLINIC *8 book series*
PERFECT RIVALS... by Amy Ruttan

And if you missed where it all started, check out
SEDUCED BY THE HEART SURGEON
by Carol Marinelli
FALLING FOR THE SINGLE DAD
by Emily Forbes

All available now!
And there are four more fabulous stories to come...

PERFECT RIVALS…

BY
AMY RUTTAN

Published in Great Britain 2016
By Mills & Boon, an imprint of HarperCollins*Publishers*
1 London Bridge Street, London, SE1 9GF

© 2016 Harlequin Books S.A.

*Special thanks and acknowledgement are given to Amy Ruttan
for her contribution to* The Hollywood Hills Clinic *series.*

ISBN: 978-0-263-25446-4

Our policy is to use papers that are natural, renewable and recyclable
products and made from wood grown in sustainable forests.
The logging and manufacturing processes conform to the legal
environmental regulations of the country of origin.

Printed and bound in Spain
by CPI, Barcelona

Dear Reader,

Thank you for picking up a copy of *Perfect Rivals*…! I can't believe this is my tenth book for Mills & Boon Medical Romance. It seems like only yesterday I sold my first book.

I was absolutely thrilled when the Medical team approached me about joining this continuity series—a series that is full of my favourite authors. I was excited and nervous at the same time.

Dr Florence Chiu is a character I instantly connected with. Her character absolutely gutted me repeatedly over the course of writing her story. I haven't had much experience in transplant surgery, but I know what an amazing gift donor organs can be, and for my heroine it means a second chance at life.

My hero is no stranger to Dr Chiu's world. He's lost someone very dear to him, and because of that he's guarded his heart and devoted his life to medicine. Having a fake relationship is the riskiest thing he's done in a long time.

I hope you enjoy Flo and Nate's story.

I love hearing from readers, so please drop by my website, amyruttan.com, or give me a shout on Twitter @ruttanamy.

With warmest wishes,

Amy Ruttan

This book is dedicated to my agent, Scott, for telling me to take this chance and write this continuity story.

Thank you to Elisa, who patiently answered my questions while I was researching this book.
Thank you so much for all your help!

And a huge thank you to the Medical team for assigning me Flo and Nate's story. They were an amazing hero and heroine and I loved every second in their world.

Born and raised just outside Toronto, Canada, **Amy Ruttan** fled the big city to settle down with the country boy of her dreams. After the birth of her second child, Amy was lucky enough to realise her lifelong dream of becoming a romance author. When she's not furiously typing away at her computer, she's mum to three wonderful children who use her as a personal taxi and chef.

Books by Amy Ruttan

Mills & Boon Medical Romance

Sealed by a Valentine's Kiss
His Shock Valentine's Proposal
Craving Her Ex-Army Doc

New York City Docs
One Night in New York

Safe in His Hands
Melting the Ice Queen's Heart
Pregnant with the Soldier's Son
Dare She Date Again?
It Happened in Vegas
Taming Her Navy Doc

Visit the Author Profile page at
millsandboon.co.uk for more titles.

Praise for
Amy Ruttan

'Amy Ruttan delivers an entertaining read that transports readers into a world of blissful romance set amidst the backdrop of the medical field. Sharp, witty and descriptive, *One Night in New York* is sure to keep readers turning the pages!'
—*Contemporary Romance Reviews*

CHAPTER ONE

THIS TAKES ME BACK.

Dr. Flo Chiu remembered all the times she'd been raced to the hospital as a young girl. The familiar whir of a chopper coming in for a landing. Followed by the bump as the chopper landed, causing her to become nauseous. Even now, watching the helicopter, her stomach did a little flip. Everything reminded her of that moment. Something she hadn't thought about in a long time. The gray haze tinting the sky, as if it was promising rain, but this was Los Angeles. The haze was just smog. In Seattle, it would mean rain, and the day she'd flown in her own helicopter to a hospital helipad it had been raining.

Hard.

And that was all she remembered of her emergent helicopter ride over Seattle. That, and her father screaming out orders in Mandarin to a helicopter pilot who only spoke English, but, then, when her dad was frightened he often put aside his second language of English for his native tongue. And when her dad was mad, the beautiful language she loved to listen to was quick and hard to follow. It had frightened her to hear him talk like that.

She took a deep breath and wrapped her arms around herself, trying to shake the thought away. Usually she wasn't this nervous about another surgeon coming in to

The Hollywood Hills Clinic, but this was not just any other surgeon. This surgeon was her competition. This surgeon had been brought in specially from New York at the request of her patient. And her patient happened to be the world-famous, award-winning actor Kyle Francis. An actor she'd always admired and had had a bit of a crush on when she'd been fourteen.

She'd watched a lot of movies when she'd been younger. Of course, there hadn't been much else to do when you were confined to a hospital bed. And Kyle Francis had been the perfect twenty-something rising star and heartthrob of her youth.

On the outside Kyle had aged well. His heart and lungs, on the other hand, hadn't. Which was why he was now a patient.

He'd collapsed at a press conference in Los Angeles and had been brought straight to The Hollywood Hills Clinic, where it had quickly been established that Kyle Francis was dying.

And that's where Flo had stepped in.

She was, after all, a world-renowned transplant surgeon, and that's just what Kyle Francis needed. Actually, what he specifically needed was a heart and lung transplant.

It was right up Flo's alley. She'd done many, and on worse cases than Kyle, but if they let it go much longer, Kyle would be a worst-case scenario and it would make the job harder.

She had been wheeling Kyle into the operating room to help stabilize him until she had been stopped.

That was when Freya had dropped the bombshell on her that another surgeon was coming.

"Another surgeon? Why was another surgeon called,

Freya? I'm a damn good surgeon. I can do this surgery on my own. You've seen me do one."

"I know, but this is out of my hands, Flo. Mr. Francis's management team has called in Dr. King from Manhattan. Dr. King's the one who has been treating his failing heart and lungs for some time. There's no negotiation. You'll have to work with Dr. King."

Flo couldn't really argue with that.

So that's why she was here, huddled in the elevator, waiting for the helicopter to land and deposit this Dr. King in her lap. He was probably some old-money type of surgeon, and she only hoped that he would be willing to work with her. Some of these big-city surgeons were a pain in the rump to deal with. They didn't think someone who was only thirty had the skill to be an excellent or extraordinary surgeon and a transplant specialist to boot.

The chopper landed and Flo ducked down, holding back the wisps of black hair that were escaping from her long braid as she headed out onto the helipad to greet this new doctor.

Please, don't be a jerk. Please, don't be a jerk.

She could deal with almost anyone but a jerk. Other surgeons tended to look down on her because of her size and her gender. That, and she looked a lot younger than her age. Even though she hoped this surgeon wasn't a jerk, she'd been warned about his arrogance so she braced herself for it.

The door of the chopper opened and her mouth almost dropped open in surprise. Dr. King was not at all what she had expected. He wasn't old at all. Probably in his mid-thirties. Tall, tanned and muscular. His blond hair was tousled and short. His face was chiseled, and the well-tailored gray suit molded his broad chest and thick muscular thighs almost perfectly. He was an all-

American high-school hottie. The kind of man who had probably got through med school on a football scholarship. The kind of man who would have ignored a perpetually sick, geeky wallflower like her at school dances. The kind of man she'd always secretly wished would look her way.

Johnny had been good looking, but not like this, and look how that had turned out. Flo shook her ex from her thoughts. He'd been gone for a long time and there was no place for him in her mind today.

Heat rushed to her cheeks when he turned to look at her. Light blue, almost ice-blue eyes fixed their hard gaze on her, as if assessing her and sizing her up in a matter of moments. It unnerved her, but also excited her. She almost wondered what it would be like steal a kiss from a man like this. And then she kicked herself mentally for thinking about the competition this way.

No matter how attractive she thought he was, he was still the competition.

All-American athletes like him were the kind of guy she'd always wanted to date. At least once in her life, because it wasn't the type of guy her father or mother would like if she brought him home. They hadn't been thrilled with Johnny either and he was a lawyer.

Focus. He's staring at you.

It was then she realized the chopper had already left the helipad and was headed away from the clinic toward LAX.

"Are you all right?" he asked.

"Fine. Dr. King, I'm—"

"I don't have time for pleasantries. You need to take me to my patient."

Great. He's a pompous jerk.

Well, an arrogant surgeon she could deal with. Her

father was an arrogant businessman in Beijing and Seattle. Flo's mother, who was American, was the only one who could get him to toe the line, and she'd taught Flo well. She'd taught her not to cower to arrogant men and to stand up for herself. Especially in light of the fact that Flo had been sick her whole life and people tried to walk all over her.

"As I was saying, I'm Dr. Chiu and I'm head of transplant surgery here at The Hollywood Hills Clinic. I've been treating Mr. Francis since his collapse last night."

Dr. King's eyes widened in shock. "Is that so?"

"Yes. Now, if you will follow me, Dr. King, I will take you to *our* patient." She got into the elevator and when he also entered, she pushed the button for the wing that housed Kyle Francis. It was the wing that had the most security to guarantee privacy for high-profile patients.

"Did you say 'our' patient, Dr. Chiu?"

"I did."

"I have to say I'm a bit confused. Kyle Francis has been my patient for a couple of years now. I'm the one who put him on the transplant list. He's my patient."

She grinned at him sardonically. "Oh, no. He's *our* patient. Mr. Francis's management team may have flown you in here, but the transplant wing is my wing. I'm granting you surgical privileges here, buster, and don't you forget it."

He grinned at her, amused, or at least she hoped so as those ice-blue eyes were twinkling. "Buster? I've never heard that one before."

Flo rolled her eyes, but smiled. "Sorry. Something I picked up from my mother."

The elevator doors opened up and Flo swiped her security card to open the doors to allow them entry to the high-security wing. Kyle's large suite was at the end of the hall.

"So, when he arrived he was bradycardic. We got his breathing and rhythm stabilized, but it's apparent to me that his heart is failing and his time is running out. He needs to be put on a left ventricular assist device."

"An LVAD?" Dr. King nodded. "I can see why you would think that, but let's not jump to conclusions. We don't know what caused the collapse. He was stable when he left New York last week. And putting him on a left ventricular assist device complicates his transplant further."

"I am aware of that. I'm not jumping to conclusions. I've performed a heart and lung transplant before, Dr. King. I know what I'm doing. I know what I'm seeing."

"Then if you know what it is, why isn't he on a left ventricular assist device?"

Really?

"I was about to have him prepped for the OR when his management team put a stop to the procedure and insisted on flying you out here, Dr. King."

"Nate."

"Pardon?" Flo said as she picked up a tablet to bring up Kyle's chart.

"My name is Nathaniel, but you can call me Nate. And what can I call you, Dr. Chiu?"

"You can call me Dr. Chiu." She tried to step past him, but he blocked her path.

"If you knew my patient, you would know that he likes everything to be informal. It puts him at ease. So I think it's in the best interests of the patient that we address each other by our given names."

"My name is Florence, but everyone calls me Flo." She handed him the tablet with Kyle's chart.

He grinned. "Thank you, Flo. Let's see *our* patient, shall we?"

Flo gritted her teeth. This was going to be a trying ordeal and it had nothing to do with the complicated surgery that awaited Kyle Francis. Someone was going to die and it wouldn't be the patient if Dr. Nate King kept being a thorn in her side.

Nate didn't particularly want to be back in California, even though he'd grown up here and his parents now lived up in San Francisco. He hadn't been back to California since he'd started medical school, and that had been years ago.

He hadn't been in California since the accident. Since Serena had died when they'd been rock climbing on El Capitan in Yosemite National Park. He just couldn't be in the place where they'd fallen in love, the place where they'd lived for the rush, whether it had been surfing breakers in the Pacific Ocean, skiing at Mammoth Mountain or rock climbing.

Serena had been an adrenaline junkie, just like him.

And then, on a climb they'd done a hundred times before, a rope had given way and Serena had fallen.

His guilt still ate at him. He was so certain he'd checked all those clips, tightened the rope, but he couldn't recall actually doing it and her death weighed on him.

He'd realized then how recklessly he'd been living. So he'd taken the scholarship at Harvard and thrown himself into schooling. Nate had sworn over Serena's coffin that he would become the best damn transplant surgeon, focusing a lot of his research on regeneration and the means to sustain life longer when there were no viable donors.

People died every day while they waited on the transplant list.

Serena had died while she'd waited.

Don't think about her now.

Nate stared at the chart, at the scans they'd done on Kyle when he'd been admitted to The Hollywood Hills Clinic.

Dang. She was right.

Kyle needed a left ventricular assist device and he needed one right away. She was watching him as he scanned Kyle's chart. He snuck a glance, just a brief glance, at her and he tried not to smile. He didn't want to give her an inch.

She was feisty. There was a certain passion hidden deep in that petite frame. Her skin was almost flawless and her long black hair shone in the tight braid down her back, except for the few stray wisps that floated around her perfect oval face. Her eyes were dark brown, like chocolate, and they glinted as she watched him. Her full ruby lips were pressed together firmly, as if she was waiting for the moment to smirk at him when he announced that she'd been right.

Dr. Florence Chiu was intelligent, gorgeous and full of life. She didn't back down from him, even though he towered over her five-foot-five frame at six feet.

If he hadn't sworn off the idea of women in general, he would pursue a woman just like Dr. Chiu. He liked a bit of wildness as well as the fact she was a transplant surgeon. It was as if she was the perfect woman for him.

Don't think about her like that.

Just from a quick moment in Flo's presence he realized that she was a danger to his well-being. He was not looking for love.

He'd been hurt before. His heart had shattered when Serena had died, so Flo was off-limits. He was here to work. He was here for his patient and that's all that mattered. Being the foremost transplant surgeon on the east coast afforded him the ability to further his research on finding other means of sustaining organs or life while patients waited for organs.

All that mattered to Nate was his career and he had to remember that. Love was not for him. He didn't deserve it.

He cleared his throat. "You're right, Dr. Chiu. He does need a left ventricular assist device. I assume, since you were prepping for surgery, that you have one ready to go?"

Flo nodded. "Yes. I can prep the OR in about an hour and we can get him in there and hooked up to the equipment. I'm sorry that your trip to California was a waste."

He cocked his head to one side and smiled at her. "Why is it a waste now?"

"Well, clearly I can handle this here. You came here and basically said I was right in the course of my treatment for Mr. Francis, so you can go back to New York."

Such tenacity.

"Oh, Dr. Chiu. I'm not heading anywhere. Mr. Francis is my top priority. There are other surgeons in New York who can run my service while I'm here. I'm staying and I plan to be in that OR with you and assist you in implanting the LVAD."

"You're kidding, right?"

"No. I never kid when it comes to my patients. I have been treating Mr. Francis for a couple of years. I'm the one who put him on the transplant list and I'll be the one performing his transplant, even if that means I'll be spending years in California. I'm not leaving his side."

Her mouth had opened to say something else when alarms went off and a code blue was called in Kyle's suite. They ran into the suite and a nursing team was already working over him.

"He's crashing, Dr. Chiu!" Nurse Olivia Dempsey called out as she lowered the bed and the rest of the team rushed in with an AED and tray of instruments.

Flo jumped into action, rapidly firing off instructions as Kyle Francis flatlined. Nate wasn't leaving his patient.

He wasn't going anywhere. Even if it meant staying in California. Even if it meant being tempted constantly by Dr. Chiu. He was made of strong mettle. He could resist temptation.

Couldn't he?

CHAPTER TWO

DON'T DIE. DON'T DIE.

Flo glanced up at the monitors as she worked on Kyle Francis, and she tried not to think about the fact that Dr. Nate King was standing on the opposite side of the bed, working with her as they tried to stabilize him. If Kyle died, he'd judge her. He seemed like the arrogant type who would put the blame on her when really it was the management team that Kyle employed who would be at fault. They were the ones who'd put a stop to her helping him right away, insisting that Dr. King be flown in.

Making her and Kyle wait.

That wouldn't have happened if she'd been allowed to put in the left ventricular assist device when Kyle had first come in, and she was going to make sure that Freya and James Rothsberg both knew that. Especially if Kyle died.

Come on.

Right now she'd like to throttle that acting management team. Their delay might've cost Kyle his life.

"Come on," she whispered under her breath as she pictured all the thousand ways she'd torture Kyle's managers.

There was a bleep from the monitor as the sensor picked up a faint pulse. Flo gave an inward sigh of relief. Thoughts of murder and disemboweling some Hollywood yuppies dissipating for now.

"Good job, everyone!" She took off her latex gloves as the nursing team stepped in to make sure that Kyle didn't code again. "I need this man prepped and ready for surgery. I'm on my way to get an OR prepped. I want a repeat of his labs drawn."

"Yes, Dr. Chiu," said Olivia.

"Make sure that I'm informed of those labs as well, Nurse," Nate said, not even glancing in the direction of Flo's favorite transplant nurse.

Olivia looked at Flo for confirmation and she nodded.

Flo glanced at Nate, who was scowling as he monitored Kyle's vitals. She thought maybe she could sneak past him. She didn't want to deal with arrogance this minute. Moments like that just brought back the vivid memories of the time she'd collapsed during band practice. When her kidney had failed her at fourteen and she had been rushed to hospital.

They were jumbled memories, but her parents liked to tell that story about how she'd hovered near death. She'd needed a donor then and Kyle needed one now. But a heart and lung transplant match was tricky. The list was long and the United Network of Organ Sharing didn't care who Kyle was. Placement on the list was prioritized on who got on the list first.

There were other people waiting for a heart and lung transplant. Kyle was at the top of two lists, one for the heart and one for the lungs. He had to have both at the same time from the same donor.

At least the left ventricular assist device would stabilize Kyle while they waited. By the time her kidney had failed, dialysis had no longer worked for her. At least kidneys could be donated by a living donor.

You could live with one kidney.

Flo always had.

Her stomach twisted as she thought of that, because her time was so uncertain. She'd had this kidney for fifteen years now. How much longer until she was on her sickbed? On dialysis and waiting for another transplant?

Another precious gift so she could go on living?

Which was why she had to continue to live life to the fullest.

"Going somewhere, Dr. Chiu?"

Drat.

She turned around to see that Nate had followed her out of Kyle's suite. "I'm going to schedule our surgery."

"I'm so glad you said 'our' surgery."

Flo rolled her eyes and he fell into step beside her. "Really, I can handle this surgery on my own."

"I know you can, but what would be the fun in that?" Nate asked, his scowl changing into a teasing smile.

"Trust me. It's fun." She grinned back at him and he chuckled. He had a gorgeous smile, perfect white teeth against that tanned face. There was a faint scar that ran through his eyebrow and another on his chin.

Definitely a jock.

"So where can I get set up with a pager and scrubs? I wouldn't mind an office, either."

"You're not asking for much, are you?" Flo remarked.

"Well, if I'm going to be here a while I would like to continue my research."

"Research? What're you researching or is that a secret?"

"No. It's no secret. I've published several papers on regenerative tissues as well as robotic and mechanical devices to prolong organs and life while waiting for transplants."

Flo was impressed. She'd never read any of Nate's papers, but the premise was interesting.

"Well, if you're looking for a place to set up shop then you would have to talk to Freya Rothsberg, but she's gone home for the evening."

"Okay, I'll talk to her in the morning. I don't have to talk to her about getting a pair of scrubs, do I?"

Flo laughed. She couldn't help it. The jerk was charming. She pointed to the OR charge desk, where a nurse sat behind her desk and was electronically entering patients' details onto a vast surgical board. "No, just speak to that OR nurse and she'll point you in the right direction."

He smiled again, one that made her melt just slightly, before he headed off to get scrubs. She admired his well-defined backside as he strode away.

Don't think about him like that.

Flo had no time for romantic inclinations, because the one time she had and Johnny had found out that she had a chronic kidney disease because of her time in NICU, he'd run in the opposite direction, breaking her heart. He had crushed her completely. It was easier to guard her heart than have it mangled by someone you thought you loved and who loved you back. She'd bared her most intimate side to Johnny, but the moment he'd seen her scar, the game had changed. Attraction had been replaced by disgust and fear. Even pity.

So Flo had given up on the notion of love. Which probably why she was still a virgin at thirty.

She didn't need it. Besides, if she involved someone else in her life they would tell her that her bucket list was crazy and no one was going to dictate to her how she was going to live her life. She'd been given a gift when she'd been given that kidney and she wasn't going to spend the rest of her life like she'd spent her childhood, wrapped up in cotton wool by two well-meaning but overprotective parents.

No, she was going to live her life to the fullest, until her donor kidney failed and she'd go back on the list again. When she was waiting she'd have all these amazing memories to think about and not have any regrets if she died while on the list.

And no man was going to get in her way.

Not even the all-American hottie she had always pined for.

"Suction, please," Flo said.

"With pleasure." Nate suctioned around the area where Flo was working. Usually he was the one giving directions about suctioning or retracting, but instead he was the one on the other side of the table from the lead surgeon and it made him grind his teeth just a bit.

At least Flo had let him into her OR, because she was correct—she had every right to tell him to take off. She was the head of transplant surgery, he was just the patient's doctor from out east. Nate was very aware that he was in Dr. Flo Chiu's territory.

Scrub nurses and residents alike all respected and admired Dr. Chiu. Even though he should be bitter about the fact that she was working on his patient, he couldn't help but admire her surgical skill. Her tiny, delicate hands handled the heart with precision as she carefully sutured in the device. A device that would allow Kyle to live a bit longer.

"It's amazing how this can sustain his life," Nate remarked.

"Yes. It is. Medical research such as yours, Dr. King, is definitely valuable."

"You know, for a long time LVADs couldn't be used on children or women."

"I know, Dr. King."

"I know you do, Dr. Chiu, but maybe some of your residents in this room can tell me why LVADs couldn't be used on women and children in the past."

Flo shot him a look. "There are no residents here. The Hollywood Hills Clinic isn't a teaching hospital. All these surgeons are transplant fellows."

"Well, a fellow still has to learn under a seasoned surgeon." Nate glanced around the room. "Come on, someone has to know the answer."

"Would someone answer Dr. King, please? And maybe after this Dr. King would stop subjecting us to his pub quiz on cardiothoracic surgery."

There was laughter and Nate had to laugh to himself, as well.

Oh, she's feisty.

He liked that in a woman. Strong and not afraid to stand up for herself.

Flo wasn't afraid of much.

"The LVAD device was too large for the chests of women and children, that's why it couldn't be used on them in the past," a surgeon finally said.

"Right, thank you." Nate turned back to Flo. "See, this is why I'm doing my research and maybe this young doctor here would like to assist me while I continue with my research here in Los Angeles."

"Thank you, Dr. King," the surgeon said, stunned.

Flo shot him another look that said, *Are you kidding me?*

"I never questioned why you were doing your research, Dr. King. I admire it, but since Mr. Francis here will be stabilized, albeit bound to this hospital with his LVAD, maybe you could return to New York. I'll let you know when UNOS has a heart and lung ready for Mr. Francis." Flo continued with her work.

"Ah, but that's the thing. They won't be calling you, Dr. Chiu. UNOS will call me. I'm the one who put Mr. Francis on the transplant list."

Her head snapped back up and she fixed him with a stern look over her surgical mask.

That got her attention.

"You are persistent in your need to stay here, aren't you?" she said, with a hint of admiration in her voice.

"When it comes to my patients I am very persistent."

She looked up at him briefly and he knew by the way her eyes crinkled in the corners that she was smiling behind that mask. "Me, too."

"Dr. Chiu, I don't see why we both can't work together on Mr. Francis's care. We don't both have to stay at this hospital twenty-four-seven, waiting for a heart and lungs. Surely you have a life outside this hospital?"

"What're you implying, Dr. King? Are you implying I don't have a life?"

"On the contrary, I'm sure you have a life. Someone special."

"What?" she asked, not looking at him.

"A boyfriend."

There were a few titters in the crowd and Flo quickly shot them all a dirty look, which silenced the laughter.

"Not that it's any of your business, Dr. King, but I don't have a boyfriend. My work is my life."

"Oh, that's a shame."

Flo groaned. "Don't tell me you're one of those kinds of men?"

"What kind of men?"

"Men who think that a woman is worthless if she doesn't have a boyfriend or a significant other."

"No, I'm not. It's just…" Then he trailed off as he thought about Serena. "Life's too short."

She looked up at him, her brown eyes warm and tender as if silently agreeing with him. As if she knew personally how fragile life was, and he couldn't help but wonder what had happened in her life. Had she lost someone she'd cared about?

Nate certainly hoped not. That was a pain he wouldn't wish on his worst enemy.

"You're right," she said. "Life is too short. At least with this operation he won't be one of the ten to fifteen percent who die while waiting. It will give him a chance to beat the odds."

Nate nodded, but didn't say anything further as they worked together to attach Kyle's left ventricular assist device. Kyle was lucky that they'd brought him to Dr. Chiu, in light of the fact that he himself was based in New York.

There was talent here.

There was skill.

Together they could save Kyle's life. There were always variables when it came to heart and lung transplants, but maybe together they could succeed.

No. You can't. Not together.

Flo was the type of woman his old self would have pursued in a heartbeat and that thought scared him. If he had to work closely with her, then he would be tempted.

How could he not be tempted by a woman like Flo?

He had to keep his distance from her. It would be hard, but he had to put a wall between the two of them. It had to be professional. It had to be businesslike. That was all there was to it. Nate couldn't risk his heart again.

Risk was a dangerous thing and he wasn't willing to play around with that.

Look where his life of risk had gotten him.

Don't think about Serena now. You don't deserve to mourn her.

After the surgery was successfully completed, Nate didn't say much. He just scrubbed out and then tried to find his way off the surgical floor. He needed air. It took him a few minutes, but he found his way back up to the roof, to the helipad. Maybe the height would get him out of the LA smog.

It was hot out, different from New York, where the bitter remnants of March still clung to the city. He'd forgotten how much he missed the heat of California. He took a deep breath and tried to calm his jangled nerves.

He couldn't remember the last time he'd felt like this.

Since Serena had died he'd been busy burying his feelings in his work. He didn't usually connect with anyone, but Flo had got under his skin.

Even in the brief time he'd known her.

She made him forget. She made him forget how he had a tight rein on his emotions. Absolute control at all times.

"There you are," Flo said behind him, making him jump slightly.

"Why did you follow me up here?" he snapped.

"Don't get so testy. I followed you because I wanted to give you this temporary pass." She held out the scan card in her delicate fingers. "If you don't have this you can't get access to Mr. Francis or basically get around the hospital."

Nate sighed inwardly and took the scan card from her. "Sorry. Thanks."

"I guess I could've kept it and you would've been trapped up here." A smile played at the corners of her lips. "You would deserve it, too, asking all those personal questions during surgery. My team doesn't need to know about my personal life."

"I was trying to lighten the mood in there."

Since when?

In New York City he was always serious. Residents and interns alike quaked in their boots around him. He wasn't known for lightening the mood, or even chatting in an operating room. He didn't know what had come over him.

She crossed her arms. "There was no need for mood lightening in there. Besides, from what I hear, you're not exactly jovial all the time."

"Who told you that?" he asked.

"Mr. Francis, when he first came in and was stabilized. When he found out his management team had called you he warned me about you. He said you were a bit of an arrogant brute."

"I doubt he said arrogant brute."

"You're right," she said, a twinkle in her eyes. "It was much more colorful."

Nate chuckled to himself. That sounded like something Kyle would do. And when he glanced at Flo he could see a soft side to her. She gave off the appearance of being a tough cookie in the operating room, but there was a softness about her. A warmth.

Something he'd been missing in his life for so long.

"Thanks for helping me in there. I'm so glad he's stabilized. Let's just hope we can keep him that way until UNOS calls *you*." She smiled at him. "I'll leave you to it. If you need anything, just have me paged. I'll be at the hospital for some time still."

She turned to leave, but Nate reached out and took her elbow to stop her. Flo turned, a questioning look on her face.

"Thank you for being here to help my patient," he said. "I'm glad a surgeon of your caliber was here to help him. And I'll get UNOS to add you to the call list."

Her brown eyes widened in surprise and then she smiled, a pink blush tinging her round cheeks as she tucked an errant wisp of hair behind her ear. "Thank you, and of course."

Nate knew that he should let her go, only he couldn't. He felt mesmerized by her and without thinking he pulled her tight against and kissed her.

For one moment, while he tasted her sweet lips, he felt her melt against him, which prompted him to wrap his arms around her, deepening the kiss. Her petite body was pressed against his, his hands in her hair as he bent over to kiss her.

Nate wanted to take this further. If they had been back at his place in New York, he'd be scooping her up in his arms and carrying her off to bed to make love to her, but he was standing with her on a helipad in Los Angeles.

He was tumbling down a dangerous path.

Then he remembered what he was doing.

That this was not keeping his distance from her at all. It was the exact opposite.

He broke off the kiss and took a step away from her, running his hand through his hair, trying to calm the erratic beat of his pulse and the longing in his blood.

Flo stood there, just as shocked as he was, her fingers pressing her lips, her eyes wide.

"I'm sorry. I don't know…" He trailed off. He knew what had come over him and he was angry at himself for letting lust take over his senses, even for just one moment.

"No, it's okay," she said quickly. "The rush of the moment. I get it. We won't talk about it again, Dr. King."

And then, before he had a chance to say anything else, she turned on her heel and jogged away, putting the distance between them that he should've done in the first place.

CHAPTER THREE

FLO WOKE WITH a start and forgot for a moment that she was in an on-call room. Her arm had pins and needles because when she'd crashed, she'd crashed with her arm hanging over the side of the bed, clutching her pager, which was currently vibrating in her hand.

She glanced at it and saw that Freya Rothsberg was looking for her.

Drat.

She hoped it didn't have anything to do with sharing her office with Nate. She wouldn't have really minded or put up a fight before, but after yesterday Flo knew that sharing an office was a *bad* idea.

She'd been so surprised when he'd pulled her into his strong arms and kissed her. A little voice inside her head had told her to push him away, but she'd been unable to because the kiss had been the hottest kiss she'd ever had.

Every other kiss in her life, before Nate's kiss, had been chaste in comparison. The moment his hand had cupped the back of her head, his fingers playing in the wisps of hair at the back of her neck, it had sent a jolt of pure longing and desire through her veins.

And she'd wanted him.

That side of her that lived for the moment had screamed at her to take him. Though the sensible side of her had reminded her that the last time she'd become close to a man, when she'd almost taken the plunge and had had sex, a certain scar had scared Johnny. It spoke to the world that she was ill. That her life was uncertain, and no one wanted to be tied down to a risk. Johnny had made that much clear.

He'd been afraid to touch her again after he'd seen the scar, and she'd told him why she had it hoping that would calm the issue, but it hadn't. It had just made it worse. Besides, what did she really know about sex? She'd never had it before.

It was good that Nate had broken off that kiss, though it was going to be hard to work with him. Especially if Freya insisted that they share an office.

Flo got out of bed, tidied her hair and brushed her teeth in the on-call room, then made her way to her office. Thankfully, her administrative assistant wasn't in yet, because Sally would certainly pepper her with a ton of questions about Kyle Francis and Flo's bedraggled appearance.

You slept in the on-call room again, didn't you?

Flo locked the door to her office and went to the closet to pull out the set of business clothes that she always kept on hand, because this wasn't the first time she'd slept over at The Hollywood Hills Clinic and had needed to make an appearance in front of the bosses the next day.

She tossed her scrubs in the laundry basket and then pulled on a reliable white blouse and pinstripe black pencil skirt. She traded her comfortable running shoes for her black heels and hoped no one would see the dents in her ankles from the elastic in her socks after wearing them all night.

Flo fixed her hair, putting it up in a bun, and then slipped on her white lab coat, attaching her security cards and identification. With one last look she reached down and grabbed a tablet so she could bring up Kyle Francis's file, because she was positive that Freya would want to talk about that.

Once she had everything she quickly made her way through the halls of The Hollywood Hills Clinic to the boardroom, where Freya had asked her to meet her, which also had Flo's nerves on edge. She knocked and then entered the boardroom and tried not to blush when she saw Nate sitting in a chair at the table.

He was chatting to Freya amicably, but the moment Flo walked in those piercing blue eyes trained on her, and it took all her willpower to stop her knees knocking together. She would not let Nate get to her.

They were colleagues. That's it.

Besides, even if something came of it, once he found out she was a transplant patient herself, he'd run, like all the others had. Her uncertain future like kryptonite to men. Which was why she kept it to herself, both in her personal and professional life.

"Sorry for running late, Freya."

"No, it's quite all right, Flo. Please have a seat." Freya motioned to the seat directly across from Nate, on her left side. Flo sat down and tried not to look in Nate's direction.

"I understand Mr. Francis has been stabilized?" Freya said, sitting down at the head of the table and brushing her long hair over her shoulder in that refined way she had.

"He has." Flo pulled up Kyle's file. "The surgical report is here if you need it."

Freya held up her hand. "No, I'm not here to talk about Mr. Francis's surgery. I'm glad to know that he's been stabilized."

"I thought you wanted to talk about Kyle Francis? The page said there was going to be discussion about him."

"Well, it's indirectly about Mr. Francis." Freya brought up an image on the screen behind her with a click of the remote.

Flo almost fell out of her chair when she saw the headline of a local paper and the photograph that was underneath it.

Superstar Kyle Francis's doctors locked in a kiss while actor hovers near death.

"And then there's this one." Freya clicked the remote again and a close-up photograph of Flo in Nate's arms, lips locked, was emblazoned across a more reputable local paper with the caption underneath, *Love match between heart surgeons.*

"We're not heart surgeons," Nate joked, trying to defuse the situation. "We have cardiothoracic training, but we only transplant hearts when it comes to cardio care."

Freya fixed her sternest gaze on him. "Yet the world knows Kyle Francis is waiting for a heart and lung transplant."

"How did they know that?"

Freya sighed, "A paramedic leaked it. Not someone from our clinic thankfully, but still security and privacy measures at our clinic are now being questioned. Especially in light of a paramedic leaking the information about Kyle Francis's surgery and then a paparazzo snapping a picture of two surgeons making out on the roof of our clinic. Our reputation is on the line."

Flo's stomach twisted in a knot and she felt like she was going to be sick.

How could she have been so foolish? She liked to

live for the moment and take risks, but not when it jeop-
ardized her career or the reputation of The Hollywood
Hills Clinic.

"Freya, I'm so sorry…"

"There's no need to apologize, Flo. There's still a
chance to solve this problem." She smiled at them both.
"Which is why I'm so glad both of you are dressed re-
spectably. We're going to hold a press conference in a
few moments."

"A press conference about what?" Nate asked.

"We're going to talk about Kyle's procedure. We have
clearance from his management team. It will be good PR
for him. We're also going to talk about a pro bono case
that both of you will be working on. We'll be working
in conjunction with the Bright Hope Clinic to help Eva
Martinez. She's a child in need of a kidney transplant.
Her mother, a single mom and waitress, is a perfect match
and is donating a kidney to her daughter. It's caught the
attention of the media."

Flo's heart skipped a beat as Freya brought up the
dossier of Eva Martinez. Eva was twelve. Just a couple
of years younger than she herself had been when she'd
needed her kidney transplant. It struck a chord deep in
her heart.

"Of course," Flo said, finally finding her voice. "Of
course I'm willing to work on a pro bono case for a child.
That's no problem."

"Is that all?" Nate asked.

"No," Freya said quietly, crossing her arms and leaning back in the chair. "We have to address the issue of
two prominent transplant surgeons kissing on the roof of
The Hollywood Hills Clinic and being caught doing it."

"There's nothing between us," Flo said quickly. "It
won't happen again."

Nate was eyeing her speculatively, as if she'd slapped him or something. "Of course. It won't happen again. It was an impulse after a long surgery."

"I don't need to know why it happened. I don't care if our surgeons date, but I do care about the fact those two surgeons were caught kissing on the clinic roof when we advertise privacy and security to our VIPs. So, I want you two to pretend you're in a relationship."

Flo blinked, because she couldn't believe what Freya was saying. "Pardon?"

"The Hollywood Hills dream team is going to save the life of Eva Martinez *and* Kyle Francis. The positive PR this will bring to The Hills is too good an opportunity to pass up. We need to restore our reputation. Until that reputation is restored and our clients begin to trust us again, your wagons are officially hitched together."

Nate knew he should refuse, get up and walk away. After all, he wasn't a surgeon at the clinic. He was only here because of his patient and that's why he couldn't leave.

He also didn't want to hurt Flo.

She was a surgeon here at The Hollywood Hills Clinic. Her reputation would be tainted because of this. He really didn't have much of choice. He might not like it, but it was just a prettiness. It wasn't like they had to *do* anything, and he didn't have plans to surf the local single scene in California. It wasn't going to put a damper on his style.

"Okay," Nate said.

"Okay?" Flo asked, shocked, and she fixed him with an *are you crazy* look.

"I'm fine with the pretense and I'm more than happy to help that little girl. The fact that a match has already been found makes it all the easier. I don't mind working on a pro bono case."

Freya smiled. "Good. What about you, Flo?"

Flo was sitting back in her chair, still in shock. "I guess that's okay. I'm fine with the pro bono case and… yeah, I'm fine with the other angle."

"Good," Freya said, and stood. "I'll let the press into the press room and we'll get this conference started in ten minutes."

Nate watched as Freya walked out of the boardroom, leaving Flo and him by themselves. They didn't say anything to each other. There was lots he wanted to say to Flo; he wanted to apologize to her, because it was his fault they were in this situation. He was the one who'd been unable to control his desire for her.

He'd acted impetuously. Something he hadn't done in a long time.

This is why I need to maintain control and keep my distance at all times.

If he didn't maintain that tight control on himself, he acted irrationally and people paid for his indiscretion. Which was why he always tried to remain in control. Control of his life was the most important thing.

"Well, perhaps we should get to the press room."

"What was that?" Flo asked, her arms crossed.

"What was what?" he asked.

"Why did you agree so easily? I thought you would've put up a fight. I mean, you don't work for the clinic. You could just leave, go back to New York."

Nate snorted. "You'd like that, wouldn't you?"

Flo rolled her eyes. "This doesn't have anything to do with Kyle's surgery."

"Doesn't it?" Nate stood and leaned over the board-room table. "You've been trying to get me to go back home since I first arrived. You don't like another surgeon sniffing around your territory."

Flo grinned. "You're right. I don't, but I had resigned myself to the fact you were staying. Honestly, if it were my patient I would probably do the same thing. What I don't understand now is why you're being so accommodating."

"Look, it was my fault what happened up there. I shouldn't have done it. I was an idiot and not thinking clearly. If I could go back in time and change the fact that I kissed you I would. It was a huge mistake."

A faint trace of disappointment crossed her face. "Okay."

"Let's just put on our best professional facades out there and play nice. Besides, I look forward to working on a kidney transplant with you. It should be a simple surgery."

A strange look passed over her face again, one he couldn't recognize as other than pain, but it was just fleeting as she stood up and straightened her lab coat. "Right. A nice pro bono case. Good PR."

There was a hint of bitterness to her tone.

"Are you okay?" Nate asked.

"Now you care how I feel?" Flo asked.

"Well, I am supposed to be your boyfriend. I might as well get into the act."

Flo shook her head and sighed. "Come on, then, Mr. Dreamboat. Let's get this press conference over with."

"That's Dr. Dreamboat to you," Nate teased.

Flo stuck out her tongue and they walked out of the boardroom and headed toward the press conference, with a lot of gazes fixed on them. A few whispers. So word had got out already about the "dream team".

Nate took Flo's hand and she flinched, so he leaned over, the scent of her soap tickling his senses.

"Relax, we're supposed to hold hands. We're a couple."

Flo nodded and then held her head high as they walked hand in hand to the press conference. Though he shouldn't like it, he did. Her delicate hands, the ones that had so expertly stitched in that left ventricular assist device just yesterday, were strong and soft in his.

And it felt right.

Too right.

The moment they stepped into the press conference they were met by a ton of flashes and questions being fired at them. Flo looked a bit shell shocked. Perhaps she wasn't used to press conferences, but Nate was.

He often spoke to the board and at conferences about transplant surgery. This was an old hat for him. The only thing that was a bit new for him, and unwelcome at that, was pretending to be Flo's significant other.

Well, it wasn't totally unwelcome to pretend to be Flo's boyfriend. What bothered him was that he wanted to act on it. He wanted another kiss. All the previous night in his hotel he'd thought about her, to the point he'd been unable to sleep and had spent most of the night in the hotel's swimming pool, swimming laps to burn off energy.

Energy that he'd wanted to spend in a different way.

Don't think about it.

"It's okay," Nate whispered in her ear, reassuringly. "Just smile. This is for The Hollywood Hills Clinic, remember?"

"Right," Flo said through gritted teeth, and she nodded as they made their way to the podium, taking a seat on either side of Freya.

He could do this. Keep his cool.

He could go with this charade.

He was made of strong mettle.

This was just an act. Just a risky, foolish act. One he should be keeping far away from.

CHAPTER FOUR

FLO'S PULSE THUNDERED in her ears. She didn't like crowds too much. Crowds like this just reminded her of junior high school when she'd been a sickly girl sitting off on the sidelines but wanting to be part of the action. Her mom had taught her to be strong, but that was usually in a one-on-one situation. There were a lot of people in this room. People who weren't doctors.

Stand her in front of a bunch of other surgeons, doctors and nurses in a conference setting and she was fine. Press? That was new territory. Especially given the fact that she was on the arm of the hottest man in the room.

And usually good-looking men didn't get to her, either. James Rothsberg was in the room and Flo had always found him attractive, with his golden blond hair, deep blue eyes and athletic frame. So what was it about Dr. Nathaniel King that made her feel so nervous?

Probably because you've never kissed James Rothsberg and have no desire to do so.

Whereas Nate King. Oh, yeah, she'd been fighting that craving since he'd first got off the helicopter.

Get a grip on yourself.

Freya was talking, but Flo really couldn't focus on what she was saying. She was talking about The Hollywood Hills Clinic and initiatives with the Bright Hope

Clinic. Flo glanced over and could see a petite woman with mahogany hair and hazel eyes smiling and nodding at everything that Freya was saying, and Flo recognized her as Mila Brightman, who ran the Bright Hope Clinic, but it was the look that James was shooting at Mila that caught Flo's attention immediately. There was underlying tension there, something Flo recognized as akin to her own feelings regarding Nate and their shared passionate kiss.

Flo couldn't help but wonder if there was something going on between James and Mila. James was usually so reserved in press conferences, so detached and cool, but this was different. Something was bubbling just under the surface of James Rothsberg.

Just like something was threatening to bubble out from her.

You can do this. Just stay focused.

All she had to do was keep reminding herself that as soon as Nate found out about her health condition, about how she had almost died from chronic kidney failure as a child because of complications from her premature birth and spending a month in a NICU, he'd turn tail and run. Like all of them did.

"And as part of the Bright Hope Clinic's collaboration with The Hollywood Hills Clinic, we're pleased to announce that our dream team of Dr. Florence Chiu and Dr. Nathaniel King, two of the best transplant surgeons in the country, will be taking on Eva Martinez's case while they continue to provide care to Kyle Francis." Freya motioned for Flo to get up and approach the microphone.

You can do this.

There was a round of applause and as soon as she got to the microphone she was hammered by a loud din of questions being asked rapid-fire. James stood up and bent over the microphone.

"Please, one question at a time. I'm sure Dr. Chiu would be more than happy to answer all your questions." His tone was such that his word wouldn't be challenged. The din quieted down and he stepped away, leaving Flo up there by herself.

"You, sir. What's your question?" Flo pointed to a balding, pudgy man in the front row.

"Photographs of you and Dr. King have arisen that gives rise to questions about the state of security at The Hollywood Hills Clinic. Patients are wondering if their privacy will be protected and whether their doctors' focus will be on them, or will it be solely on who to hop into bed with next?"

Flo could feel her cheeks burning with a flame of embarrassment. "I can assure you that *my* focus is solely on my patients' care."

Nate stood up. "Dr. Chiu and I are in a committed relationship. We went on the rooftop after a successful surgery involving Mr. Francis and got carried away. Are you telling me that you've never got carried away celebrating with your significant other before?"

Nate then flashed a dazzling smile to the audience, which had them all laughing.

Oh, he was good.

"That still doesn't address the privacy and security concerns," the balding reporter called.

"The picture was snapped by a paparazzo from an office window across from the clinic. We can't control what happens outside our perimeters, but he was not able to get any photographs inside our facility, neither was he able to take photographs of our patients," Freya said.

"What about the paramedic that leaked the information?" another reporter asked.

"My understanding is he's been reprimanded and he will not be allowed back on The Hollywood Hills Clinic property in a capacity where he'll have access to confidential health information," James said brusquely.

Once they were satisfied another reporter stepped forward. "How long have you and Dr. King been in a relationship?"

"For a couple of months. We met to discuss Mr. Francis's care while our patient was in California to shoot a movie."

Nate nodded and touched the small of her back. Just the simple touch made goose pimples break out on her skin. Good thing he couldn't feel them.

"Can you tell us a little bit about Mr. Francis's procedure?"

"Of course. Mr. Francis is in congestive heart failure, but because he's been in heart failure for some time, this has put a strain on his already weak lungs. Mr. Francis had a pre-existing struggle with asthma for many years. Because his lungs are so damaged by the extra strain his heart is causing, he will require a heart and lung transplant. We were hoping to perform a domino procedure, but now that Mr. Francis is on a left ventricular assist device, he is no longer a candidate. We will have to wait for a set of lungs and a heart that matches Mr. Francis's blood type, but the LVAD will prolong his life while he waits."

Nate gave her a thumbs-up and Flo gave an inward sigh of relief. She sat back down next to Nate and he took her hand and held it. It was reassuring and made her feel good, but then she remembered this was all an act.

He'd pretty much said that he wasn't interested in her and that their kiss had been a mistake.

That's what you wanted, wasn't it?

"Now, if there are no more questions we'll conclude this press conference," Freya said. "Please make sure you take the statement with you. If you have any other questions, please don't hesitate to contact me. Thank you all for coming."

Flo took another deep breath.

"See, that wasn't too bad," Nate said, but he didn't let go of her hand as the journalists filtered out of the room slowly.

"No. It wasn't." She let go of his hand and got up to leave, but Freya and James were talking to the side and motioned for her over.

Oh, no. Now what?

"Good job, Flo," Freya said.

James nodded. "Yes. You handled that well."

"Thank you."

"I think that will help salvage the reputation of The Hollywood Hills Clinic and help reinforce our joint effort with the Bright Hope Clinic."

"I think it will," Mila said, joining them and extending a hand to take Flo's. "Dr. Mila Brightman. A pleasure to meet you, Dr. Chiu. I'm so pleased that you and Dr. King will be working on Eva Martinez's case."

"It will be a pleasure to do so," Flo responded.

"All this good publicity for the clinic will put my mind at ease," said Freya.

"A good thing, given your condition—" James cut off abruptly at the sharp stare from his sister and the surprised looks from the rest of the group.

"Well, since *some* people clearly don't know how to keep a secret, I guess the cat's out of the bag—I'm pregnant!" Freya announced.

James smiled sheepishly. "I'm so happy for you, Freya."

Then he turned to Mila and Flo noticed something pass between them. It was as if he wanted to embrace Dr. Brightman but held himself back. She couldn't help but wonder what was going on there, but, then, she liked her privacy, as well. She felt a bit humiliated that that private mistake of a kiss between her and Nate had been caught on camera so it wasn't her place to pry.

"Well, I'll leave you all to it," Flo said. "I'm going to go check on my new patient. I assume that Eva Martinez has been admitted to the transplant floor?"

Freya nodded. "Yes, thank you, Flo."

Flo walked away briskly. She was done with awkward situations. It was bad enough she had to be pretend to be in a relationship with Nate. That was uncomfortable, especially with the way he affected her.

She needed to focus on her new patient.

Eva's case struck close to home for her. Only, for Flo, it hadn't been her mother who had donated a kidney to her. Flo's kidney donation had come from a deceased organ donor. Being of mixed heritage had caused a bit of a cross-match problem for Flo. It didn't happen often, but Flo's case had been a hard one from the moment she'd been born prematurely thirty years ago.

If it hadn't been for that anonymous donor, who, of course, had sadly lost their life, Flo would've lost hers. Of course her *năinai* had always said she'd been a tough cookie from the moment she'd been born. Flo had been fighting her whole life. It's why she fought so hard for others; it's why she wanted to live in the moment.

Even though pretending to be Nate's girlfriend made her feel uncomfortable, because it was a temptation that she was in danger of indulging in, she was going to do what had been asked of her. What could it hurt?

It could hurt your heart.

Flo shook that thought away. This wasn't a serious relationship. It would *never* be a serious relationship. She didn't have serious relationships because of her health issues and she'd made her peace with that a long time ago.

Have you?

She caught sight of Nate in the hallway, talking with a group of doctors and what looked like members of Kyle's management team. Just the sight of Nate standing there made her heart flutter with insatiable need. She turned on her heel and quickly headed in the opposite direction.

Focus, Flo. She had to forget the carnal urges that Nate stirred in her. She had to remind herself that this was all an act. This would be fun. She could do this. What did she have to lose?

Pretending to be his was going to be so difficult. So dangerous. Even if she was a tough cookie, like her *năinai* said.

Nate glanced over his shoulder to see Flo retreating in the other direction, which was unlike her. She had never seemed fazed or frightened by anything before. She hadn't backed down from him when they'd first met.

He admired that about her.

Don't think about her that way.

He tried to turn his attention back the conversation he'd been having, not that he could really remember what he'd been talking about. It hadn't really been that important because all of his focus had been on Flo, and it bothered him that he was so absorbed with her that he'd agreed to play along with The Hills' ridiculous request.

His hospital in New York would never have asked him to do such a thing, but then again the hospital in New York wasn't a private upscale clinic that prided itself on the security of its clients. Neither did he like the fact that Freya had conspired with Kyle's management team about the idea.

Only problem was, he wasn't a good actor.

A few years ago and he might've gone along with it, but now he liked to maintain control in all aspects of his life. One little slip and that reckless man he'd once been started to creep toward the surface.

And he couldn't let that happen. Only when he was around Flo, she made him forget his control. He lost all reason. That's why he'd pulled her into that kiss on the roof and got them into trouble in the first place.

They were in this mess because of him.

"Dr. King?"

Nate turned and saw James Rothsberg standing behind him. Beside James was an attractive redhead.

"Are we interrupting?" James asked sardonically.

"No. Not at all."

James nodded. "This is Dr. Mila Brightman from the Bright Hope Clinic. She wanted to meet you."

Mila stuck out her hand. "It's a pleasure to meet you, Dr. King."

"The pleasure is all mine."

It was then that Nate caught a flash of something in James's eyes, something akin to jealousy or a silent warning maybe to keep his distance, and Nate couldn't help but wonder if there was or had been something between Mila Brightman and James Rothsberg.

Not that it was Nate's concern, but he couldn't miss that underlying tension between them, the same current that ran between him and Flo.

It's all in your head. You're paranoid.

"I want to thank you and Dr. Chiu for working on Eva. She's a special child," Mila said.

"It's no trouble. I'm here and glad to help. If you'll

excuse me, I'm going to check on my patient." Nate extracted himself from that situation. The tension was uncomfortable and when he glanced back briefly he could see the awkwardness between James and Mila. They barely said anything, barely looked at each other before wandering off on their own separate ways.

This was exactly the reason why he didn't want to get involved with anyone. Especially not at work. His focus was surgery.

He should just tell Freya that he wasn't going to play along with this PR stunt, but where would that leave Flo?

Who cares?

Only he did. Just a bit, because it was his fault, his weakness that had got them into this situation. If he had been stronger he wouldn't have been tempted by Flo. He could've kept his distance. He should've kept his distance. He could do this.

Who are you kidding?

He had to get out of the hospital, had to head to his hotel and swim. He had to relieve this tension that was building up inside him, because if he didn't he was liable to crack and do something he would enjoy thoroughly but also deeply regret.

CHAPTER FIVE

WHAT AM I DOING? What am I doing?

The scent of chlorine stung her nose. She'd never really liked the smell of chlorine, probably because it reminded her of the many hours she'd spent poolside, watching her brother and sister swim competitively, something she'd never been able to do because she'd been sick for so long.

Thinking about her siblings swimming made her think about how she'd always wanted to learn how to dive. It was on her bucket list, but she'd never found the time.

And standing poolside at Nate King's hotel, watching said hottie swim countless laps, was not the time to start. She was having a hard time not staring at him, the way he moved through the water.

She'd wanted to talk to him before he'd left the hospital. If they were going to participate in this facade then she was going to get her facts straight. She was nothing if not efficient.

That's why she kept lists. She was organized, and when she did something, she did it right. If she was going to be Dr. Nate King's pretend girlfriend, she was going to do it right.

Except cleaning. She was a bit scatterbrained when it came to cleaning her apartment.

At least her office and workspace were organized.

He finished swimming and pulled himself out of the water at the far end of the pool. Flo tried not to stare at his muscular thighs and tight butt only covered in wet spandex. When he'd wrapped a white cotton towel around his waist, partially obscuring his six pack, only then did she hold her head high and walk toward him.

"Nate," she said.

He spun around in surprise, raking a hand through his dripping-wet beach-blond locks.

"Dr. Chiu."

"It's Flo, remember. We are dating after all." She laughed nervously, but he didn't smile. "I was hoping to talk to you before you left the clinic tonight but I just missed you. So that's why I'm here."

"About what?" he asked, picking up a second towel and drying off his face.

"About our 'relationship'." She used air quotes to emphasize it.

He groaned. "Now?"

"Are you busy? Do you have a prior engagement?" she asked, crossing her arms.

Nate dropped the towel he was wiping his face with and smiled, but that smile wasn't the cheeky one he usually gave her. It was a bit predatory and made her nervous.

"Would you be jealous if I did?" He took a step closer. "If I did, what would you do?"

"No. I'm not jealous, but for the sake of the clinic and our patients it would be bad form to have plans."

He chuckled and then snorted sardonically. "Would it? Don't you think this whole charade is bad form?"

Yes. Only she didn't say that out loud because she didn't understand PR like Freya and Mila did. Both of them thought this charade would be a good idea.

"We're just smoothing over a tricky situation," Flo said.

He arched his eyebrows. "Is that a fact? And have you canceled all your private engagements? Dumped your boyfriends?"

She sighed impatiently. "What is your obsession with my boyfriends?"

"Well, I don't think it would be good form for our charade if you had a couple of boyfriends lingering about."

"As I told you before, I don't have a boyfriend. As for private engagements, surgery is my life."

He grunted again and pushed past her. "How did you know where to find me?"

"Freya told me." She followed him out of the pool toward a bank of elevators.

"Of course she did." He shook his head.

"Well, shouldn't I know where my 'boyfriend' lives? Especially since we've been together for some time?"

"Good point. I never really thought about that. Deception really isn't my forte." The elevator doors opened and he stepped in. "Aren't you coming up?"

"To your room?" She hoped her voice didn't squeak too much because the idea of going up to his room was not on her agenda tonight. She couldn't go up to his room.

That was not part of the plan.

He grinned at her. That predatory grin again. "Yes. Play along, right? Isn't that what you told me?"

"How about I wait for you down here? We can have a drink in the hotel lobby."

"Now, how would that look to the paparazzi milling about at the concierge's desk?"

Flo glance over her shoulder and saw the press.

Hell.

She jumped into the elevator, the door closing just as

a photographer caught sight of them. That would've been bad and their cover would've been blown.

Nate was laughing at her. "Smooth move, Dr. Chiu."

"When did you notice him?"

"A while ago."

"You could've warned me."

"I did. That's why you're in the elevator now instead of waiting for me in the hotel's bar."

"I'd prefer to wait in the lobby bar," she mumbled.

"Why?" he asked.

Because it's safer.

"I don't know you. I don't think it's appropriate to go up to your hotel room."

Nate laughed. The elevator dinged and they stepped off. She followed him down the hall to the end. He swiped the key card and opened the door. Flo followed him inside, just on the off chance the paparazzi followed them up here. She shut the door and was surprised by the large suite. It was like a small apartment. There was a bedroom that Nate had disappeared into, a living room and small kitchenette.

She set her purse down on the counter and wandered to the huge windows, where the Los Angeles skyline lit up the night. It was a gorgeous night. Clear, but it wasn't like you could see the sky, not with all the light pollution from LA. Nate's suite had a large balcony and a hot tub tucked away in the corner.

"There are drinks in the fridge. I'm going to have a quick shower," Nate said from around the door of his bedroom.

"Okay, thanks."

Nate nodded and shut the door to his bedroom. It wasn't too long before Flo heard the shower on through the closed door and she tried not to think about the fact that Nate was naked and in it.

This was a bad idea.

She could've just waited until he came to work the next day and talked to him there, but no. She'd got it in her head that this would be a better idea and now she couldn't remember for the life of her why she'd thought that.

Probably because she hadn't expected to find him half-naked, swimming in a pool, and then be forced to come up to his opulent suite and wait while he showered in the next room. This was an experience that was *not* on her bucket list.

Flo took a seat on the edge of the couch and just waited. She tried to keep her mind occupied on something else. Anything to take her mind off what was going on in the next room and how he'd looked just wrapped in a towel, fresh from a swim. The only men she'd seen built like that were either in the movies or magazines. She'd never seen one up close and personal.

She'd worked on Hollywood's rich and famous at The Hollywood Hills Clinic, but what was on screen versus reality had opened to her eyes to the whole magical mystery of Hollywood's elite. Photo editing was a beautiful thing indeed.

She often wished she could edit herself in real life. Maybe then she could erase the large scar on her abdomen and that way no one would ever need to know that she'd had a kidney transplant. That she'd been sick.

If Johnny hadn't known, he wouldn't have treated her differently.

Maybe they'd still be together. Then she wouldn't have kissed Nate and be in this situation, faking a relationship and being in his hotel room with him naked in the shower. In the next room. Of course, that's not how it had happened at all, because that's not how real life worked. There had been no photo-editing solution and her disease had frightened Johnny away.

He'd made it clear he didn't want to get involved with her, not when there was a possibility that at any time in the near future that donor organ could fail and she might die. No one wanted to get involved with a woman who didn't have the greatest odds of staying alive.

Kidney survival rates were good, but they weren't perfect.

Kidneys could fail.

Especially when you'd had a chronic kidney disease as a child and had suffered kidney failure at fourteen. Following dialysis for a year and a near-death experience, she'd received her new lease on life.

And since that time she'd tried to live her life to the fullest.

Getting married and having a family had always been on her bucket list, until she'd learned the true nature of most men. When Johnny had run scared and left her heartbroken, she'd scratched that secret hope off her list.

A husband, romance and love were not meant to be. She'd made her peace with that, but now, because of a foolish and irrational moment on top of The Hollywood Hills Clinic, she found herself thrust into a situation she'd long given up on.

It's fake, though. It's not real.

Still, the idea made her uncomfortable because she was going to have to be really careful to keep her feelings out of it. She could have fun, but she couldn't let Nate get too close, because once Kyle Francis was on the mend, Dr. Nathaniel King would be returning to New York and she would be alone again.

"Did you want something to drink?"

Flo startled to see a freshly showered and dressed Nate standing in the doorway. He was dressed very much the same as he'd been when she'd first laid eyes on him. When he'd come out of that helicopter looking sexy as hell.

Don't think about it.

"How about we go downstairs?" Flo asked, tearing her gaze away from Nate.

"Well, first I think we should go over some ground rules for this whole charade, and I don't think that those ground rules should be discussed downstairs with paparazzi milling about. They were told we've been going out for some time. You can't be all skittish and embarrassed around me."

"I'm not skittish or embarrassed. I'm professional."

Nate rolled his eyes and shook his head. "You can't be professional with your boyfriend."

"Boyfriend sounds like we're in junior high or something."

"Lover, then?"

Warmth flooded her cheeks and her whole body quivered with the quick burn of arousal as an image of Nate, naked and pressed against her, filled her mind.

Lover.

That was something she was not intimately familiar with, but she wished she was.

She cleared her throat. "Fine. I can be relaxed around you."

Nate grinned, leaning over the polished marble counter in his kitchenette. "Can you?"

"Of course I can."

"Prove it."

"How?" she asked.

"Kiss me again."

* * *

Nate had no idea what had come over him when he'd asked Flo to kiss him. It had just seemed the natural thing to do and he'd be an idiot if he said he didn't want to kiss her again. Who wouldn't want to kiss her again? And he knew by the flush creeping up her long slender neck to her cheeks that she was feeling it, too.

She wanted him, but was holding back.

Like you should be, too.

And that was when it struck him that he'd done something he really shouldn't have, and that no woman since Serena had affected him this way.

He'd been attracted to other women, but he'd always managed to keep them at a distance. Then he'd met Flo. He tried to tell himself over and over again that the kiss on the rooftop had only been his relief at having been able to stabilize Kyle. They'd been able to extend Kyle's life while he waited for his new heart and lungs. That relief had caused him to let his guard down, so what was this?

This wasn't relief.

Even though he really didn't want to play in this charade that Freya Rothsberg had cooked up, he really had no choice, that's why he threw up his walls again. He was determined that even though on the outside, for all intents and purposes, he was Flo's significant other, he wasn't going to let her in.

He wasn't going to let his guard down around her.

At least, that's what he was going to do in theory. Twenty minutes with her and she was in his hotel suite, sitting on his couch only five feet away from him, looking as sinfully sexy as ever. Her long black hair, which she usually wore up, was loose over her shoulders. There was a bit of make-up on her, not much, but the red lipstick on her lips just accentuated the fullness of them. Add the blush to those high, round cheeks and he was a lost man.

He forgot that Flo was off-limits to him, just like every woman had been since Serena. Yet here he was, asking Flo to kiss him again. And he wanted to kiss her. So badly.

"Pardon?" she said, breaking the silence.

"I think you heard me."

"I don't think that's a wise idea, Nate. Do you?"

It's not.

"Why? You want to show the world that we're together. We have to be at ease with each other so we can be believable."

What are you doing?

"Believable, but also professional. So I don't think kissing you is the wisest idea." She tossed her hair over her shoulder. "You certainly like to goad me, don't you?"

Nate's eyes twinkled. "Perhaps, but it's so easy."

She glared at him and then smiled. "I'm highly competitive and I don't like to have my buttons pushed."

"I gathered that, or it wouldn't be so easy to push them."

Flo nodded. "Perhaps we can go downstairs and get that drink? Discuss Eva's case and our plan of attack?"

"Okay, but still I think you should kiss me."

She grinned in a willful way that spelled trouble for him. "I do like to hear you beg."

He rolled his eyes as she walked past him toward the door. On one hand he was extremely relieved that she hadn't kissed him, but he knew that if he kissed her again he would lose himself completely and carry her off to his bed, which wasn't far away.

And taking her to bed would be good, so deliciously good, but only for a short time. He didn't want to hurt her, not when they had possibly months of working together while they waited for Kyle's heart and lung transplant.

That would be awkward and horrible for everyone.

It was better this way.

That's what he had to keep telling himself to get over the smidgen of disappointment he had that she hadn't taken him up on his offer and kissed him.

Instead, as they walked down the hall toward the elevator, he reached down and took her hand in his. That small delicate hand that he'd admired so much during Kyle's LVAD surgery.

"What're you doing?" she asked, surprised.

"The paparazzi could be still downstairs. This way, there won't be any questions."

"Oh…right. Good point."

Nate could tell that she was nervous, and he liked that he had that effect on her. Serena had been the same when they'd first dated, but not for long. Maybe one date, because one date was all it had taken and they'd been in bed together and then heading off on a crazy adventure.

Don't think about Serena.

If he thought about Serena he'd pull away from Flo again and then the press would pick up on the fact that this was all just a charade. He had to remember what it was like to just let things happen and not control every aspect of his life, which was a hard thing for him to do because control allowed him to focus on saving lives.

There was no room in his heart for love or romance. Not again.

"You okay?" Flo asked as they rode down to the lobby in the elevator.

"Yeah, why?"

"I don't know. You just tensed up."

"I'm fine." He tried to give her a reassuring smile.

"I'm really fine, it's just that I don't like this. I don't like deception."

"I know. Neither do I, but it's for the clinic."

"Right. The clinic." The doors dinged and opened and they stepped out into the lobby. He knew that press guy was lingering around somewhere. It felt like there were a million eyes on them as they walked hand in hand toward the hotel's bar. Even when they found a private booth far in the corner of the bar, he still felt like they were under a microscope, and it made him uneasy.

It was only after the waiter had brought them their drinks that Flo said, "I feel like we're being watched."

"We are." He took a sip of his coffee. "Is this your first time working on someone as famous as Kyle Francis?"

"No. I've worked on some others, it's just The Hollywood Hills Clinic's security has never been breached before."

"Sorry about that."

Flo shrugged and took a sip of her water. "It's unfortunate but there's nothing we can do."

Nate chuckled. "Look at us, we've come to a bar and we don't even order alcoholic drinks."

"I don't drink," Flo said, and then she blushed, clearing her throat. "I mean, I have to get up early tomorrow and I don't want to drink tonight."

"Rounds?"

She nodded. "I want to check on Kyle and Eva, our two VIP patients."

"I'm not on rounds. I have privileges, but no regular patients beyond Kyle and Eva."

"You could always round with me." She smiled at him. It was warm, inviting and friendly, and now he could clearly remember why he'd kissed her on the rooftop. He wanted a piece of that. He wanted to feel that warmth.

"Sure. Thanks."

"No problem." She set her water glass down and glanced at the watch on her arm. "Oh, my, is that the time? It's almost ten."

"Ten isn't late."

"It is when you're rounding at five in the morning." Flo sighed. "I have to go."

"I'll walk you out." Nate signed the bill to his suite, the whole couple of bucks for the coffee, and walked her out of the bar to the hotel entrance. "Did you drive yourself?"

"I don't drive. I live close to the clinic. I usually just ride my bike."

"You don't drive?"

"I never learned, but it's on my bucket list." Then she blushed again.

"Bucket list? Usually that's for people who don't have a lot of time left. Unless I'm mistaken, Dr. Chiu, you have many years left."

"Oh, yeah, of course. It's nothing really. Just stuff I want to do before I… Anyway, I'd better go. The doorman can flag down a taxi for me."

"Sure. I'll see you tomorrow." Nate walked her outside and they stood there while the doorman waved down a taxi. When the taxi pulled up Flo turned quickly and pressed a sweet, light kiss against his lips. It caught him off guard and his blood heated. He fought back the urge to take her in his arms and deepen the kiss, make it last.

Which was a dangerous thing indeed.

"See you tomorrow," she said, not looking at him as she climbed into the cab.

As the cab drove away he stood there, his blood burning through his veins at just the simple butterfly kiss that had been brushed against his lips. So innocent, so sweet. It left him wanting more.

So much more.

CHAPTER SIX

FLO DOWNED HER second cup of coffee, which had two shots of espresso in it. She didn't know what had made her reach out and kiss Nate, because she'd had no plans to do that. Especially not after he'd basically dared her to kiss him in his hotel suite.

When he'd asked her that, it had taken all her willpower not to leap into his arms and kiss him again. To experience that heat and heady sensation he'd stirred within her since he'd first kissed her on the rooftop. Nate was incredibly sexy and Flo had never been attracted to a man so strongly before. So much so that she almost forgot herself and the fact that she'd sworn off all romantic entanglements.

Besides, Nate would run as soon as he realized what was going on with her. She tried to tell herself that maybe he would understand as he was a transplant surgeon himself, but then maybe that would make him back off all the more, because he would understand better than anyone what her body had been through.

Still, she'd been a fool and kissed him while waiting for the taxi, even though it had been for the press. She was pretty sure there would be pictures of them kissing and that would make Freya happy.

There was a lot of press camped outside The Hollywood Hills Clinic. She could see them lurking in shadows, waiting for something, anything, to give them juicy details about Kyle Francis and his surgeons who were in love.

Flo snorted. *Love. Sure.*

She didn't believe in love. Well, not for her anyway. Once she'd believed in love, but then love had turned on her. There was love. She'd seen it in her parents. They'd overcome a lot of odds and barriers in their way to be together. They came from different worlds yet that hadn't mattered to them in the end.

For them it worked.

Love couldn't work for her. Not when she couldn't promise any length of time to anyone. It wasn't really fair to someone else.

Flo groaned and crushed the empty coffee cup, tossing it in the garbage. Last week none of this had been an issue. Last week she'd been free of Dr. Nathaniel King. Last week she'd just been a great surgeon, with a stupid bucket list and a job that hadn't let her think about her personal life.

Last week she'd been happy. Now she was miserable.

Are you so sure about that?

"Flo!"

Flo turned to see Freya walking toward her. "Freya, I'm surprised to see you here so early."

"I couldn't sleep and had morning sickness." Freya held out a paper. "I'm glad to see that you and Dr. King are keeping up appearances."

Flo glanced down at the tabloid paper and saw photos of her kiss with Nate. That quick, impulsive kiss that had burned its memory on her lips and taunted her all night, which was the reason why she'd downed two large black coffees with espresso shots, because she hadn't been able to stop thinking about it all night.

And now seeing it plastered over the tabloids reminded her of how hot that moment had been, and how foolish. She was willing to climb a mountain or do some other high-adrenaline sport, but when it came to the possibility of romance, she wasn't willing to let her heart get involved.

It was too dangerous.

"Ah," Flo said nervously. "Yeah, well, I thought I would pay Dr. King a visit to talk about our arrangement."

"Well, keep up the good work. Tomorrow night there's a dinner with some possible investors and they want the dream team to attend. It's business casual and will be at Dan Tana's at eight-thirty."

"Dinner? I...I have a shift tomorrow. Rounds in the evening."

"I have another doctor covering for you, one of your fellows." Freya glanced over her shoulder and waved. "Dr. King, can you come here a moment, please?"

Flo froze and was very aware the moment that Nate walked up behind her. She could smell the clean spicy scent of his body wash. She'd been very aware of it when she'd impulsively kissed him.

"Good morning, ladies." He had already changed into scrubs and had a white lab coat with an identification card. The white of the lab coat accentuated his tan and the blueness of his eyes.

"I was just telling Flo how pleased I was to see you two cooperating." Freya handed Nate the tabloid. Flo watched his expression carefully, but if it affected him she had no clue. He just nodded, smiled charmingly and handed the paper back to Freya.

"Just doing our part," he said.

"I was just telling Flo that there's a dinner tomorrow night at Dan Tana's. Business casual as we'll be meeting with investors." Freya tucked the paper under her arm. "I have to run. I look forward to seeing you both tomorrow."

Flo didn't even have a chance to say no, she didn't want to have dinner with a bunch of investors and pretend to be Nate's girlfriend, but she really had no choice.

Her job was on the line.

If she didn't play her part then people would stop coming to The Hollywood Hills Clinic, investors would stop giving money and the clinic could shut down. Then she couldn't help Eva, and she was very on board with this partnership with the Bright Hope Clinic and providing pro bono surgery to kids like Eva.

To kids who reminded her of herself.

"Dan Tana's is a nice place," Nate remarked. "I used to go there a lot as a kid."

"I thought you were from New York?" Flo said.

"I work in New York, but I'm a native Californian."

Flo snorted. "That doesn't surprise me. You have the look of a beach boy."

Nate fell into step beside her. "Where are you from?"

"Seattle," Flo responded, offhand. "Though my father is from Beijing and my mother is from the Deep South. They felt Seattle was a nice halfway point to raise their family."

Flo smiled as she thought of her family. She hadn't talked to them in a while as she'd been so busy. Actually, she was surprised that her father wasn't calling her cell phone every two minutes to question what was going on and why she was kissing men on rooftops.

Her parents had always been a little overprotective, trying to keep her wrapped up in cotton wool, like she was some kind of fragile piece of crystal that was about to shatter into a million pieces.

Which was why when she'd got her kidney she'd rebelled a bit. Pushed the boundaries and decided to study medicine at Johns Hopkins across the country, almost a world away from her parents. After spending most of her childhood basically in a bubble, her first taste of freedom had been an amazing rush.

It's why she had the bucket list.

So many things she wanted to do. So little time.

"So you mentioned learning to drive is on this bucket list," Nate said casually.

"It is. I just don't have time to take lessons. My work here takes a lot of my time."

"I can teach you."

Flo laughed. "Yeah, right."

"Who better to teach you? I've driven in two of the busiest cities in America—Los Angeles and New York City."

"You have a point, but when? I don't have time."

"How about tonight?"

Flo cocked an eyebrow. "Tonight? You're going to teach me to drive tonight?"

"Sure. I can't take you out on the streets, but I know a place out of the city where there's an abandoned parking lot and plenty of room for you to make mistakes."

"Okay. I get off at three."

"I know." Nate took a step back away from her. "I have to make a phone call to my office in New York. I'll meet you up at Eva's room in twenty."

"Sure, leave all the grunt work to me," she teased.

He just smiled at her and disappeared down a hall, leaving her standing there absolutely perplexed about what had just happened. She told herself she was going to be stronger. When she had to make public appearances with him, she was going to play the part of the girlfriend, but this learning-to-drive date she'd just made with him, that was just them. That wasn't something public.

It was just going be the two of them.

And that thought made her nervous.

Don't think about it.

She put her hands under the sanitary gel dispenser. Right now she couldn't think about that. Right now she had to be a surgeon. She glanced through the window to see Eva, so sick and in bed with an IV and looking so lost. Her mother was next to her, holding her hand.

It tore at Flo's heart. She'd been there.

She'd felt that way and her parents had been there. Only her mother hadn't been the one to give her a kidney, so she couldn't even begin to fathom the kind of strain that Ms. Martinez was going through or the amount of time it would take for both of them to recover, both emotionally, physically and financially.

Right now, this was Flo's focus. This was her passion, saving lives, especially giving a chance to a little girl who reminded her so much of herself that it was almost haunting.

"Good morning, Ms. Martinez and Eva. I'm Dr. Flo Chiu and I'll be one of the surgeons on your case."

The phone call back to New York had taken longer than expected, but by the end of the call he had been assured that all his patients were being taken good care of and that his practice was in safe hands. For so long Kyle had been his main focus, he didn't really have a lot of other patients who needed him as much.

Kyle had been very specific that Nate's sole focus was to be on him, and he paid him well enough that he didn't have to take on too many patients, which meant he wasn't really missed in New York.

Nate didn't have friends in New York City. Colleagues, yes, but not any people he would consider friends. Neither did he have any family in New York. His parents were here in California and he definitely didn't have a significant other.

No one missed him and he didn't mind much.

He might've been chomping at the bit to get back to his practice, but being around Flo and working with her was exciting. It was fun, and that kiss she'd given him had kept him up all night.

So to take his mind off it he'd spent the night going over Eva's case. It had been a year since he'd done a kidney transplant with a live donor. Kyle had been his focus and any other cases he took on were usually complicated. Nate hadn't realized that for a long time he'd been focusing solely on the heart and lung. He'd had to brush up on his reading about kidney transplants. What concerned him most was that Ms. Martinez was a single parent. The sole breadwinner. Donating a kidney would put her out of commission for a long time. Weeks, for sure. Even if they did the retrieval laparoscopically and reduced her recovery time, she'd still be off for a couple of weeks.

Ms. Martinez was a waitress. She would need a month to heal from a laparoscopic procedure. She wouldn't be able to lift heavy objects and would still tire easily.

Even then, Nate wasn't sure that Ms. Martinez was a candidate for a laparoscopic procedure. He would have to do some more tests to be sure. Get some better MRI images.

Ms. Martinez could become destitute while she recovered. Being a waitress was a minimum-wage job, one that probably didn't have medical leave coverage.

Eva was pretty stable, so maybe in the family's best interests they should wait for a deceased donor.

When he got to Eva's room he paused in the hallway. He saw Flo sitting on the end of Eva's bed and she was playing cards with her. Nate smiled. When he'd first met Flo he'd thought she would be a bit uptight, reserved, but seeing her with Eva and playing a game of cards, well, he couldn't help but smile.

She was so warm with Eva.

There were so many layers to Flo; she was so intriguing. At times she was so prudish and then the next moment she was giving him a kiss that made him want her more than anything. Other times she was standoffish, but then could give a good quip that got through his thick-walled exterior. Back in New York City he had a reputation of being hardheaded. Someone you didn't want to mess with.

The moment he'd tried that with her, Flo had been right in his face and giving back as good as he could give her, but there was something Flo was hiding. She'd mentioned a bucket list and had then brushed it off as something silly. Only Nate knew there was something more there, and he shouldn't care what it was because he didn't want to get too close to her. He couldn't get too close to her, but he did care.

He wanted to know all of her, even though nothing could come of it. This relationship wasn't a relationship. It was just a facade. And when Kyle was on the mend and this pro bono case was done, he would pack his bags and head back to New York and his life.

Just like she would go back to hers, because this wasn't real. It was all fake.

And that thought made him sad, because just for one

moment he was wishing it wasn't all fake, that Flo and him were really dating.

Don't think like that.

He shook that thought from his head, disgusted with himself for allowing himself to think like that again. For letting his mind head down that path again. He was here to do work; he was here to save two lives.

This whole situation was temporary. There wouldn't be any permanence. There couldn't be any permanence to it.

He knocked on the door and plastered his best smile on his face. One he knew well and had practiced. A shield to the armor he wore every day to keep people out. "Am I interrupting?"

"Yes," Flo said, smiling and winking at Eva, who giggled. "Eva, this is your other surgeon. This is Dr. Nathaniel King."

Nate stood beside Flo and Eva smiled up at Nate.

"It's nice to meet you, Eva," Nate said.

"Nice to meet you, too, Dr. King." For a twelve-year-old girl she had excellent manners.

"You can call me Nate. I've just come to check your vitals. Is that okay?"

Eva's brow furrowed and she looked at Flo with concern. "Will it hurt?"

"No, this is just a vital check. No needles." Flo set down her cards and got off the bed, moving the swinging table out of the way. "Nate is super nice."

"I promise you it won't hurt at all." Nate pulled out his stethoscope. "I just want to have a listen to your heart first. Is that okay?"

"Sure." Eva sat up the best she could and Nate listened to her chest.

"Deep breaths for me, Eva." He moved his stethoscope and listened. "One more for me."

"Is that it?" Eva asked.

"Just blood pressure now."

Eva winced. "I don't like the squeeze."

"It's just for a second. It's nothing. Trust me, I would know," Flo said reassuringly, squeezing Eva's foot under the blanket. "You need to relax. Nate will get a better reading if you relax."

Eva nodded and Nate put the cuff on her and took her blood pressure. It was as good as it could be for a young girl in renal failure.

"Thank you, Eva. Do you mind if I borrow Flo for a moment?"

"Sure." Eva leaned back and picked up her cards.

"No cheating!" Flo warned, giving her a wink that caused Eva to laugh.

They stepped out of the room and Nate shut the door. Flo frowned and crossed her arms. "Is there something wrong? I checked her when I first arrived and her vitals were fine."

"Her vitals are fine. I was just hoping that Ms. Martinez would be around so that I could talk to her about her side of the donation."

"Ms. Martinez had to make some arrangements. She's going to be out of commission for some time, as well."

"That's what I wanted to talk to her about. Eva is stable, so why don't we wait for a deceased donor?"

Flo's brow furrowed further. "Ms. Martinez is a match. Her cross-match is the best I've seen in a long time. Why would we wait? Waiting just puts Eva in danger."

"Ms. Martinez is a single mother. She could continue working while Eva recovered here."

Flo shook her head. "The cross-match is almost perfect. A cross-match from a deceased donor wouldn't be as good. Ms. Martinez won't wait while her child sits on a list, she's done that. It's in their file. That's why she went to the Bright Hope Clinic, because she is the perfect donor for Eva. Eva is less likely to reject her mother's kidney."

"Less likely, though, Dr. Chiu. There's still a chance. There's always a high chance of rejection."

Flo's spine stiffened, her face unreadable. It was as if he'd slapped her across the face. "I'm *very* well aware of that, Dr. King. You don't have to remind me of that. I'm still head surgeon on this case. Ms. Martinez knows the risks. She doesn't want to wait, she doesn't want her daughter to get worse. It's her gift to give Eva. We're not going to discuss this matter further or try to convince her of anything different."

"I would feel better if I talked to Ms. Martinez all the same."

Flo glared at him. "Fine, but let it be on your head. I doubt you'll convince her. She wants to save her child and what she's doing is an amazing thing."

She tried to turn and storm off, but he grabbed her by her elbow. "What has got into you?"

"Nothing, I'm just annoyed that you're trying to talk a woman, who knows all the facts because her daughter has been fighting renal failure her whole life, out of saving her daughter's life."

Nate sighed. "I'm not trying to talk her out of it. I just don't want to see her lose her job."

"She won't," Flo said, calming down. "Her work is being compliant. Mila Brightman talked to them about the situation."

Nate nodded. "Okay. That's great. I'm glad she knows everything. I wasn't trying to endanger the patient. Please trust me, because if you don't trust me here, you won't trust me in the OR and I need you to trust me in the OR when we work on Eva and Kyle."

Mollified, Flo nodded. "I trust you, Nate. I trust you as a surgeon. It's just…this is a touchy subject for me."

Intrigued, Nate let go of his grip on her. "Why?"

"I knew someone who suffered a long time, waiting for a deceased donor who was a good cross-match. A young girl, like Eva, whose parents would've given their kidneys, but they weren't a match."

Nate nodded. "I understand."

"Do you?"

"Yes," Nate said wearily. "I lost someone I cared for. Someone who was waiting on organs."

Her expression softened. "Then why wait now? It's just putting Eva at risk."

"You're right. We don't want Eva to suffer like your other patient. Like my friend."

"Right, my other patient. Well, I'd better get back to my game of poker. Eva cheats." She paused in the doorway. "I am sorry about your friend."

"Thanks," he said. "Okay, so I'll see you after your shift? Where should I pick you up?"

"The front doors. Though I hope you have space for my bike." She nodded and walked back into Eva's room.

There was a sadness about her. She'd obviously been affected deeply by her other patient to fight so strongly for Eva, to be so personally connected. And he couldn't help but wonder if the patient was someone close to Flo.

It was a close call. Flo didn't mean to let her emotions take control of her when they were talking about Ms. Martinez donating a kidney to Eva. She should've let him talk to her, not thought twice about it. It was Nate's prerogative as a surgeon to talk to his patients and make sure they were informed.

She shouldn't have let it affect her so much, but the problem was, it did. Eva reminded her so much of her own time in the hospital, and if her parents could've given her a kidney they would've. Only her parents, her brother and her sister hadn't been cross-matches. Her *nǎinai* had been, but she had been too elderly, so her kidney hadn't been viable for Flo.

So she'd sat on the list, waiting for some poor soul to die.

It was a great gift that anonymous person had given her, but it also weighed heavily on her. That's why she was trying to live life to the fullest. And Nate had lost a loved one who had been waiting on the list and she couldn't help but wonder who it had been.

It's none of your business.

It may not be, but it gave some connection to Nate that hadn't been there before. It helped her understand him more. He got it. Even just a little bit, he understood the emotions, fear and pain of this whole process. It just made him all the more attractive to her.

She shouldn't be going out with Nate tonight, but even though she was emotionally drained from their spat, she was intrigued.

He was taking her somewhere out of Los Angeles, somewhere she would have a lot of room to drive. She could tick it off her bucket list and, really, what did she have to lose? Seeing Eva chained to her hospital bed had brought back too many painful memories for her, and she'd lashed out, almost telling him that it was she who had been that girl, clinging to life while she'd waited on the transplant list.

And that wasn't anyone's business.

Thankfully, she had been able to convince Nate that it was a former patient of hers.

There was a roar of an engine and Flo glanced over to see a vintage Corvette screech around the corner and pull up in front of the building.

She smiled when she saw Nate get out of the driver's side of the car. "Well, what do you think?"

"Where in the world did you get this?"

"Believe it or not, it's mine. I keep it in storage here. For when I visit. Will it do?"

Flo laughed. "I think so. Will there be room for my bike?"

"Yep. We'll toss it in the trunk, it'll be fine."

Flo wheeled her bike over and Nate took it from her and secured it in the trunk. She noticed he wasn't dressed in his business casual clothes. Instead he was wearing denim jeans, biker boots and a tight, black V-neck shirt. His eyes were obscured by aviator sunglasses. He was a typical Californian bad boy. Or at least how Flo had always pictured them. She didn't have a lot of experience with the bad-boy type of man.

He was too damn sexy for her own good and she had to keep reminding herself that he was off-limits.

She climbed into the passenger side after Nate held open the door for her. Flo had never sat in a sports car before. That was something else she could check off her bucket list. Nate slid into the driver's side and turned the key, revving the engine.

"You ready?" he asked.

"I'm always ready," she said.

He grinned and then took off out of the clinic's loop driveway and out into the streets. Flo's hair, which had still been in a bun, blew out of it and whipped around her face as Nate drove through the streets of Los Angeles like a maniac.

When they stopped at a light Flo put her hair back into a tight ponytail. "I guess this is why women with long hair wear hats in these cars."

Nate chuckled. "Or scarves."

"I'm not wearing a scarf. Try not to drive like a lunatic."

"And what would you know about driving?" He revved the engine as the light turned green and then took off again toward the highway that led east out of LA and toward Vegas.

"You're not taking me to Vegas, are you? That's, like, six hours away!"

"No, it's in Barstow."

"Barstow! That's two hours from here."

"It's only four-thirty p.m. Do you have plans? I know for a fact you don't have an early shift tomorrow. You have a pretty decent one followed by a really nice dinner out."

She glared at him, but honestly she was glad for the car ride. She'd never been to Barstow. Heck, she'd never really been on a road trip. She'd always wanted to drive across the country. That was on her bucket list, as well. She wanted to drive Route 66 and hit every kitschy place she could. She also wanted to drive across the badlands and through Montana, Wyoming and maybe even up into Canada to Alaska.

She also wanted to do the drive in an RV and her family was *not* an RV type of family. Vacations were spent on a tropical beach somewhere, a place where Flo could rest and recuperate. A place of peace and tranquility.

Flo had had enough of peace and tranquility. She wanted to do things, see places. She wanted a collection of goofy postcards from places like the home of the world's biggest ball of string and Mount Rushmore.

Nate turned on the radio and Flo relaxed into the drive. She didn't have to say anything to him, she could just enjoy the sights of driving into the desert, watching the city trickle away into wide open spaces with the wind in her face and the sun at her back.

She forgot everything that had happened today, she forgot about her bucket list and limited time and for the first time in a long time she just relaxed.

"Hey, sleepyhead. Wake up."

Flo woke with a start and realized that she'd drifted off. The car was parked at a deserted drag strip and it was dusk.

And when she glanced at the dashboard she could see it was seven in the evening.

"How long was I sleeping for?"

"A couple of hours. You looked so peaceful I didn't want to disturb you."

"I'm so sorry."

Nate shrugged. "It's okay, but I thought you might want to *try* and drive a bit tonight before we have to turn around and head back to Los Angeles."

"Sorry." Flo got out of the car and stretched. "Where are we?"

"A buddy of my father owns this old drag strip. He's planning on refurbishing it, but he said we could come out here and practice driving around the parking lot. I'm not sure if he actually wants us to drive on the strip, though, so if drag racing is on that bucket list of yours…"

"It's not, meaning I've never really considered it."

Nate climbed out of the driving seat. "You ready to try your hand at driving?"

"Oh, yeah," Flo said, probably a little too eagerly. She

climbed into the driver's seat and did up the seat belt. Nate took her vacated spot in the passenger side. "What do I do first?"

Nate chuckled. "Turn the key in the ignition. That would be a good start."

"Ha-ha. I meant after that." She turned the ignition key.

"Whoa, don't jump the gun. Driving is an art form."

Flo snorted. "I find that hard to believe when any old schmuck can do it."

Nate rolled his eyes then placed her hands on the wheel. "Put your hands at ten and two and be quiet for a moment."

Flo stuck out her tongue. "What next?"

"Have you never been in the front seat of a car? Even fifteen-year-olds know this."

She grabbed the stick and put the car out of park into drive. It rolled forward a bit. "Which one's the gas and which is the brake?"

"Press it and you'll find out. Just gently."

"So no slamming?"

Nate arched an eyebrow. "Only on the brake, if needed."

"Okay." Flo pressed her foot down and the car lurched forward. She immediately jammed her foot down on the other pedal. "Whoa."

"There you go. Try again."

"Okay." Flo stepped down on the gas less and the car moved forward slowly. She smiled as Nate instructed her and she drove around the parking lot. Sometimes slow and sometimes fast, which caused Nate to shout out. But it was exhilarating.

She'd always wanted to drive, but her parents had refused to let her learn, even though by the time she was sixteen she had been two years post-op from her kidney transplant and doing well. She'd begged and pleaded, but her father had not relented.

"Why do you need to drive? We have a driver who will take you wherever you want to go."

Her parents had been so stubborn and then when she'd gone off to college and medical school, she'd never really thought about driving and had just been happy to take public transportation and not have a driver take her around.

Learning to drive was way down the bucket list, though it was something she had to do before she drove across the country. It was nice that Nate had faith in her and was letting her try and drive. No one else had ever suggested that to her.

Not even Johnny.

Don't think about him. This moment was just about friends doing something fun.

It was laid back and easy.

It was fun.

And it was only temporary.

Nate allowed her to drive around until dusk turned to darkness and a smattering of stars spread out across the sky. They grabbed a quick drive-through dinner then parked back at the deserted drag strip, lying out on the hood of Nate's car. Flo couldn't remember the last time she'd seen so many stars.

She had been young and it may have been once or twice when they'd been driving somewhere late at night in the country. The details were foggy, but she remembered the night sky being flooded with brilliant light, and that's what she could see now.

It was beautiful.

She glanced over at Nate. His arm was behind his head and he was staring up at the night sky with the same kind of wonder she was feeling. It made her heart skip a beat and she fought the urge to reach out and kiss him again.

It would be perfect if she did—kissing Nate under a star-filled sky—but she suppressed that urge and turned her gaze away. It was better that she didn't act on her impulse. There was no one else around. They didn't have to put on their act now. They were just friends.

And she wasn't even sure if they were friends, because she doubted she'd hear from him again once he returned to New York, and that realization made her feel sad.

"See, it was worth the drive, wasn't it?" he said, interrupting her thoughts.

"It was. You're right, this is great. I never see the sky like this in LA," she said with a sigh.

"It is. I used to come out this way with my dad. We'd find a campground out in the desert and watch meteor showers."

"Do your parents still live in Los Angeles?"

"No, they live in San Francisco. They love San Francisco and the lifestyle there. Why?"

"Just wondered. I mean, if they were here I'd ask why you're not staying with them."

"Would you stay with your parents if they were in town?"

"I wouldn't have a choice," Flo mumbled.

Nate chuckled. "Oh, really?"

"My dad grew up in Beijing and my mom in the deep south. They're quite overbearing and old-fashioned sometimes. They also drive me crazy."

"See, you wouldn't stay with them, either. Besides, maybe I have a bad relationship with my parents," he teased.

"Do you?"

"No," he said. "I care for them. I've just been so busy

in New York City. I never get to San Francisco. It's been a long time since I've been out this way. I forgot how much I love it out here. How I love the desert. I used to spend a lot of time out in the mountains when I was younger. I did a lot of rock climbing, too." Then his smile disappeared into a frown. "Well, that was a long time ago. I don't have time for that kind of stuff any more."

"I've always wanted to do rock climbing, or climb a mountain. Maybe Everest."

Nate shrugged. "It's hard work and dangerous."

"So?"

"It's on that crazy bucket list of yours, isn't it?"

"And if it is?" she asked.

Nate shook his head. "Why would you want to risk your life?"

"Life is meant to be lived."

"You can live your life without doing crazy things."

"What's the fun in that?" Flo teased.

"There's more to life than fun." There was a sadness to his voice.

"You okay?"

"Perfectly. Why wouldn't I be?"

"You sounded sad there."

"Not sad, just realistic. Well, we'd better get back to LA. Work tomorrow and dinner with potential investors." Nate slid off the hood and climbed back into the driver's seat. The moment was shattered and she blamed herself. Flo reluctantly got into the passenger seat. She didn't want to go back home to her lonely apartment. She wanted to keep driving. She wanted to spend the night on the hood of Nate's car, wrapped in his arms.

No. Not in his arms.

Nate was right. It was getting late and it was time to

head back to reality and LA. It was safer in LA, safer in her apartment far away from Nate.

"Thanks for tonight. It was fun," she said.

He smiled at her, but it wasn't the same easygoing, fun smile she was used to. It was subdued Nate again. "No problem. It was my pleasure."

Flo didn't say anything more to Nate as they headed west, back to the city, back to reality and back to the facade they were both very comfortable with.

CHAPTER SEVEN

"How much longer am I going to be holed up here, Doc? I'm supposed to start my stint on Broadway in five months. I have to prepare."

Nate glanced up from Kyle's chart. Kyle was sitting up in bed and doing better a couple days post-op from his LVAD surgery, but he still had a long way to go and even then he had an uncertain time ahead, hooked up to his machine as he waited for a new heart and lungs.

"I think it's in your best interests to cancel your stint on Broadway."

Kyle snorted and then winced in pain. "Are you crazy? This is a huge opportunity."

"One you'll have to pass up unfortunately." Nate crossed his arms. "You're hooked up to a machine. You can't leave the clinic. That machine is keeping you alive."

"The nurse said it was portable. She was having me walk around yesterday."

"Portable, but you still need to be monitored and you still need to be on oxygen a lot of the time. I don't see you tap dancing your way across a Broadway stage any time in the near future."

Kyle grinned. That famous smile that melted the hearts of many women, but which didn't work on Nate one bit.

He actually found it annoying more than anything else when Kyle tried to use that charm on him.

"There's no dancing. Besides, I could have a new heart and lungs tomorrow."

Nate pinched the bridge of his nose. "You could, but it still doesn't mean that you'll be up on your feet in a couple of weeks. You will be in the intensive care unit for a while, your body will have to heal from a long surgery, we'll have to monitor you for signs of rejection. It will be a long process of healing before you can return to the stage."

Kyle sighed and laid his head back. "I didn't ask for this."

"I know. I'm sorry."

"You paint a pretty bleak picture, Doc. At least that other doctor, at least she can give me some hope."

Nate frowned. "Was she the one who told you you'd be up on your feet in a short time?"

"No, she's just nice to look at." Kyle winked.

Nate laughed. "Thanks."

"Well, I don't have to tell you, right? I mean, I do keep up with gossip. You and her are a thing, right?"

Nate groaned inwardly. "Right."

"It's about time. You're always working; you never seem to have fun. I invite you to all my parties and you never come. Do you know how many beautiful women come to those parties?"

"I'm aware. Now, would you lie back and get some rest and either Dr. Chiu or myself will come in and look on you later."

Kyle grinned. "I hope it's Dr. Chiu. No offense, Dr. King, but I might just steal her out from under you."

"Sure you will. I'll see you later." Nate left Kyle's room and shook his head. Didn't people understand the severity of transplant surgery? They thought that once they had a new organ things would go back to normal. That they'd be able to do all the same things they'd been able to do before, but it was a huge lifestyle change. The chance of rejection in Kyle's case was high. Granted, it was getting better all the time with medical advances, but surgery was still the *practice* of medicine, which meant things weren't perfect.

If only they were.

If only organs could be grown from patients' tissues and blood. If only there wasn't rejection. If only…

Nate scrubbed a hand over his face. He hadn't had a moment to turn to his research since coming to Los Angeles and he was annoyed. When he was in New York his research was his companion at night and that was all he needed.

Since he'd landed back in LA, he hadn't even glanced at it. His nights had been filled with Dr. Florence Chiu and his days had been filled with prepping Eva Martinez and her mother for their kidney transplant surgery, as well as monitoring Kyle Francis, who was his top priority.

The thing was, he didn't really miss his research. He'd enjoyed the last couple of nights with Flo. Maybe because it was just temporary, there was no permanence to it and it made him feel safe. Since there was no permanence there was less chance of heartache.

The only problem was, he wasn't sure if he wanted to go back to the way his life had been before. Empty.

You don't have a choice.

Nate groaned as he noticed the time. He had to grab his suit from the office he shared with Flo and try to make himself presentable for this dinner, which was the last thing he felt like doing today. Especially when this wasn't even his place of employment.

He was just a locum surgeon, just passing through. *It's your own fault. You had to kiss her.*

And he'd wanted to kiss her when they'd been lying out under the stars. Actually, any time he was around her he wanted to kiss her. It was maddening. It was distracting and he wished he could act on it, but he couldn't.

Nate placed the tablet he'd been using back on the charging station and headed toward the office. He'd brought in his suit so that he could make a quick change here and drive Flo to the restaurant in West Hollywood.

He just wanted to get this dinner and schmoozing over with as fast as he could. Then he could come back here and force himself to do some work on his research. His research was his life. There was no room for anything or anyone else.

When he got to the office Flo was already in there and already dressed in a suit, her long hair up and smooth, instead of the usual wisps that framed her face. His gaze was drawn to her long slender neck. She wore a red silk blouse and a tight black pencil skirt, with black heels, the kind that had a red sole.

She was absolutely stunning and he knew that this dinner was going to be a challenge.

Flo glanced up at him. "You're not dressed yet?"

"I was just coming to do that."

"Where were you?"

"Checking on Kyle." Nate peeled off his white lab coat and tossed it on Flo's couch. She frowned, moved past him and hung up his lab coat in the closet. He couldn't help but smile to himself. "You're such a neat freak."

"Actually, I'm not. Just in my office. I like my workplace organized, but at home my decorating style is *There appears to have been a struggle.*"

"Is that a style?" he asked.

"At my apartment it is. I don't have time to tidy it much. And I'm rarely there."

"I would've never pegged you for someone who would live in clutter."

"It's not a sty, it's just not as organized as it is here." Flo crossed her arms. "I can't believe you're not dressed."

"Chill, I brought my suit here. I'll just go into your bathroom and change." He opened the door and saw toothpaste smeared on the porcelain of the sink, scrubs wadded up on the floor and an abandoned hair straightener. There was also some lingerie on the floor. He chuckled and picked up the delicate lace with one hand. "It looks like your office bathroom has the same style as your apartment."

Her cheeks went beet red and she snatched the flimsy garment from him. "Would you get ready, for the love of all that's good and holy?"

Nate didn't argue any further. It wasn't worth it, because the gleam in her eyes brooked no argument. He quickly changed into his suit and cleaned himself up, mostly to get the smell of hospital off himself.

When he opened the door to the bathroom Flo was waiting for him. Her gaze raking him from head to toe and a finger thoughtfully tapped her chin.

"You clean up nice."

"Thank you, Dr. Chiu. You do, too."

She smiled. "Well, let's get this over and done with."

"I think we should swing by Kyle's room. Make him jealous."

Flo arched an eyebrow. "What're you talking about?"

"He's trying to move in on my territory." And then he realized what he'd said. He only hoped that Flo took it as a joke.

"Your territory?" she teased. "Since when have I been your territory?"

"Since the rooftop, or have you forgotten?"

She rolled her eyes and took his proffered arm. They walked out of her office together and he knew, as they walked through the halls of The Hollywood Hills Clinic, that everyone was watching them.

Usually that would make him feel a bit uncomfortable, because he didn't like to be associated with any woman. He didn't want rumors flying about him, but he didn't mind walking through the halls with Dr. Florence Chiu on his arm, and in those heels she was almost as tall as him. He could smell her hair. It was lavender.

There was a limo outside and Freya was standing outside. She waved when they walked over to her.

"I'm afraid I can't go with you tonight," Freya said.

Flo frowned. "Why not?"

"I'm needed somewhere else. I'm sure you and Dr. King can handle this dinner. Besides, it's you two the investors want to meet. They know me." Freya glanced at her cell phone. "I have to run, but the limo is yours and dinner is on the clinic. I've already talked to Dan Tana's. Everything is a go."

And before either of them could protest Freya was walking off in the other direction, texting someone.

"A limo. Wow." Flo walked over to it and the chauffeur opened the door for her. She slid in and as she did so Nate caught a glimpse of her thigh. It made his blood heat and he pulled at the suddenly tight collar of his dress shirt. All he could think about was being alone with her in a limo and how much room and privacy there was for the two of them. "Are you coming, Nate? It's great in here."

"Yeah." He took a calming breath and tried to chase those dirty, bad thoughts from his mind. The last thing he needed was to have an erection during a boring meeting with investors. Also because there was no way he could act on it. He hadn't planned on doing laps tonight at the pool, but now he was.

He had to seriously get a grip, but the more he tried to tell himself that the more his grip lessened.

Flo had never been to Dan Tana's. Actually, even though she'd been living in LA for a couple years, she really hadn't gotten out much. She didn't go to fancy restaurants, hadn't since she was a child, and she certainly didn't like investor meetings.

"You okay?" Nate asked.

"Why wouldn't I be?"

"Well, a moment ago you were pretty excited about riding in a limo and now you're stiff, on edge, like a rod is holding you upright."

Flo rolled her eyes and sighed, her shoulders dropping. "Fine. I don't like talking in front of crowds."

"Who said there will be a crowd?"

"Well, fine, a group of strangers. It makes me uncomfortable."

"You handled that press conference well," Nate said.

"No, I didn't. You did, though. I can speak to a crowd of doctors or nurses, anyone from the medical profession, but throw in people who aren't part of the medical profession and I just want to crumple up in a ball and cry."

Nate frowned. "That doesn't seem like you."

"How would you know?" She regretted the words. "I'm sorry."

He shook his head. "Fair enough. We haven't known each other long, but really it doesn't seem like you to be nervous like this."

"It is. Trust me." Flo began to tap her leg in agitation. "I have no idea what to say beyond 'Give us your money.'"

He reached out and put his hand on her knee to calm the tapping of her leg. It caused a zing of pleasure to race through her, his strong hand on her knee firing her senses. He moved his hand away. Her leg tapping had stopped and she was at ease.

Flo cleared her throat. "So what should I do? Do you have any suggestions?"

"Picture them naked."

Flo gasped and saw that devious twinkle in his eyes. He was joking with her. "You're crazy."

He shrugged. "There's nothing fundamentally different about talking to a press conference or investors. You're strong. You stood up to me the first day we met. Not many people have had the guts to do that."

"Why? You're not scary."

His brow furrowed. "Thanks for that."

"Why are you bothered by that?"

"You weren't scared when you met me?"

"No. Why would I be?"

"You just admitted large crowds make you nervous, but when you met me you weren't nervous?"

Flo felt her heart rate pick up speed. Of course she'd been nervous when she'd met him. He was gorgeous. He was the kind of guy who would never give a girl like her a second glance, so she'd been nervous when he'd stepped off that helicopter, looking so sexy. She just wouldn't admit it.

And she wouldn't admit that he made her nervous now, but in a much different way.

"No, I wasn't nervous. You're a surgeon, though, and only one man."

He frowned. "Most residents and interns are nervous

when they first meet me. They say I'm a bit of a monster. Cold. Detached."

"First, I find that hard to believe, and second, I'm not a resident. I'm a surgeon. I can deal with cold and detached. My father was a businessman, a CEO, and a lot of people feared him. My mom taught me to stand up for myself."

He grinned. "Then it should be easy to deal with a couple of investors. Just channel your inner dad and deal with them."

"You mean curse at them in Mandarin until they do what I want?" Then she laughed as she thought of her father. He'd tried for so long to get her to speak Mandarin, but she'd had no interest in learning it, except for the swear words.

He'd be horrified to know that's what she'd picked up in her endless classes in Mandarin. Of course, now she wished she had a second language under her belt and maybe that was something she could add to her bucket list.

"I think cursing at them will defeat the purpose." They shared a smile and the limo slowed down and stopped in front of the restaurant.

Flo took a deep breath and stared at the front of the restaurant.

You can do this.

"You can do this," Nate said, as if reading her thoughts.

"Maybe it shouldn't be me. Maybe it should be you."

He shook his head. "No, you're The Hollywood Hills Clinic's chief of transplant surgery. This is all you."

"Okay."

He nodded and opened the door, stepping out. Then he offered his hand and helped her out of the limo. As he held her hand he gave it a reassuring squeeze. It was exactly what she needed at that moment. A vote of confidence from someone she admired.

Yeah, she could do this. She had to do this.

They were whisked inside the restaurant, which was decorated in deep, rich colors, and the concierge led them to a large patent-leather booth in the far corner where the investors were waiting. As she walked through the restaurant she felt a hand in the small of her back as Nate gently guided her. It made shivers of anticipation run down her spine. To make matters worse, he looked so darned good in a well-tailored suit.

It was maddening.

"Ah, Dr. King and Dr. Chiu, I am so glad you could join us. I'm Cecil McKenzie."

"A pleasure to meet you, Mr. McKenzie." Flo shook his hand and Nate followed suit.

"This is Ian Brownstone and Travis Fleming," Cecil said, introducing the other two men at the table.

Flo shook their hands and then sat down, Nate and the rest of the men at the table sitting down only after she had.

"I have to say we were quite worried when your story leaked in the press," Ian said. "The Hollywood Hills Clinic prides itself on privacy and protection of their clientele."

"It was an unfortunate incident," Nate said. "Thankfully one that was unfounded as Dr. Chiu and I were in a relationship."

Nate was so smooth with the investors. He was obviously used to this. Flo was, somewhat, but only from watching her father schmooze clients in his business. Schmoozing was not her thing.

"Dr. King wasn't fully aware of the clinic's strict guidelines on privacy," Flo said. "He is from New York."

That got a bit of laughter from the men at the table.

"Well, we're glad to see that it's all been smoothed over and, honestly, it's been spun in such a good way. We're also extremely impressed with the pro bono case you've both taken on with Eva Martinez. Can you tell us a little bit about that?"

"Of course, The Hollywood Hills Clinic is working with the Bright Hope Clinic and Eva is one of hopefully many more children who will benefit from this initiative. You know, of course, that cases like this will bring in more positive press for paying clientele," Nate said.

And he continued to talk to the investors, winning them over.

Flo was trying to pay attention, but again this wasn't her forte and, frankly, bored the socks off her. She was pretty sure that these men didn't want to hear about the science behind the surgery and that's what interested her most.

Also the journey, because she'd lived it.

Only it was better they didn't want to know about the emotions. The struggles one faced when undergoing an organ transplant, because then she would have to tell Nate about hers and that was something she would never do.

That was her scar to bear alone.

As the salads were being taken away her cell phone began to buzz and it was long distance.

"Excuse me, gentlemen. No need to get up." Flo pulled out her phone and slid out of the booth, walking to a secluded, quiet spot by the bathrooms before she answered the call. "Dr. Chiu speaking."

"Dr. Chiu, I'm calling from UNOS regarding your patient Kyle Xavier Francis."

"Please go on."

"We have organs for him. We need you to come to San Francisco and retrieve them."

Flo's pulse thundered through her ears as the words sank in. This was the moment. The magic moment where someone was given a second chance, but also a moment of reverence because it meant the end of a life.

A brave soul who was giving the ultimate gift.

"I'll be there within the hour."

CHAPTER EIGHT

FLO FINISHED HER conversation with UNOS and then promptly called The Hollywood Hills Clinic to ready a chopper to take them to the airport and to have a chartered jet be readied to fly to San Francisco. She also ordered her team and the nurses to stop feeding Kyle and prep him for surgery. It was amazing luck to find a viable heart and lungs so soon. It was a relief. Then she cursed herself for being somewhat optimistic. She didn't know if the organs were viable. Not until she examined them herself.

Focus. Don't rush.

They had a little bit of breathing time as the surgery wasn't scheduled to start for another hour and the heart and lungs would be the last to be taken out, and she was going to be the one to do it. She was very particular about that.

She headed back to the table. Everyone stood up again.

"I'm very sorry to have to do this, gentlemen, but there is a medical emergency and Dr. King and I need to leave right away. I do apologize."

Nate glanced at his phone and she could see the text message there confirming the news she had just received. "Gentlemen, I'm sorry we have to cut this evening short."

"Of course," Mr. McKenzie said. "Don't worry about

us, and you can tell Ms. Rothsberg that we're impressed and indeed interested in furthering our commitment to The Hollywood Hills Clinic."

"Thank you." Flo shook their hands briefly and then turned and walked away as fast as her heels would carry her. The limo was called and it only took five minutes for the car to pull up in front of the restaurant.

Nate told the driver to take them back to The Hollywood Hills Clinic.

"The chopper is waiting for us," Flo said, shaking her leg in impatience. "Mr. Francis is fortunate."

Nate nodded. "He is. I'm glad you had your phone on. I'm annoyed with myself that I put mine on silent."

"I never keep my phone on silent or I'd miss the calls completely. I never know when it's vibrating."

They didn't say much else to each other. There was nothing to say, because as soon as the organs were transplanted and Kyle was stabilized it would be the end of their charade. Which was a shame, because Flo did enjoy being around Nate. She liked working with him, too, but they both knew there was a time limit on this act.

It was good that it would be over and done with. Then she could get back to her normal existence. She could throw herself back into her work and not think about Nate so much, because she did. He also made her realize her loneliness.

And even though she hated to admit it, she was going to miss him.

The limo had barely parked and Flo was out, kicking off her heels so that she could run through the halls toward her office to throw on her scrubs and grab the heart and lung machine that would keep the donor organs alive and cool as they traveled back to Los Angeles. She began to undress, with the door to her office barely shut.

"Whoa," Nate said.

She spun around, just in her red lace thong and bra with her shirt covering her torso. Then she realized what she was doing and covered her scar the best she could with her blouse. What had she been thinking? How could she have been so lax about it? She'd never changed in front of people. Not even when she'd been a surgical resident. She always found an excuse to slip away into a stall and change. She didn't want anyone to see her scar and think that she was weak when she wasn't.

Nate was looking the other way, but he was clearly uncomfortable. And she quickly turned around so her back was to him and slipped on her scrub top, dropping the blouse that had hidden her scar. She prayed he hadn't seen it. She didn't want to get into a discussion about her scar. There was no time for that and she didn't want him to know.

"What?" she asked.

"I wasn't expecting you to strip down."

Flo rolled her eyes. "Don't be immature. We don't have time."

She breathed a sigh of relief that he hadn't noticed her scar, but then she'd had her back to him as fast as she could when he'd walked into the room, plus she'd covered it with her blouse.

Why, though?

She was being chicken. Nate wasn't Johnny and he could handle seeing her scar. Why was she so scared about telling him? He'd said she was strong, and for a moment she'd believed him, but right now she didn't feel so strong. Not when she'd been so afraid of him seeing her so vulnerable.

Part of having her bucket list was being bold and brave. How could she be either if she hid the truth from the one person who might understand? Who wouldn't pity her?

Are you sure about that?

That doubt weasel in her head was stronger than she'd thought. It reminded her why it was better to be alone. To guard her heart like she'd been doing for so long. She couldn't go back to being hurt like that.

Still, she wished she could overcome her fear of people finding out about her illness. Maybe if she shared her experience then people would understand her deep connection and passion to saving those on the waiting list.

Maybe it would make her a better surgeon.

Maybe they would all pity you and question your abilities. Maybe they would think you were too emotionally attached to make a rational decision.

She shook those thoughts out of her head. "Are you going to get changed or what?"

"Fine." Nate shut the door and began to take off his clothes. First the suit jacket, which he tossed on the couch again, then the tie and the button-down blue shirt that brought out the color of his eyes.

Look away.

Only she was having a hard time trying not to look at him as she pulled on her scrubs. She'd seen him half-naked before, in tight swimming trunks, no less, with water running down his hard, tanned body.

Get a grip.

She pulled her hair up into a ponytail and grabbed her ID and jacket with "The Hollywood Hills Clinic" embroidered into it.

"I'm going to get the heart and lung machine. Shall I meet you on the helipad?" Flo asked, not looking at him as he kicked off his shoes and began to unbuckle the tight, tailored pants.

"Yep."

Thank goodness.

She snuck a quick glance at his tight backside and then shut the door, heading back up to her floor. When she got up onto the transplant floor, it was like a madhouse as people were scrambling and getting ready for the big show.

Flo stopped at Kyle's room. There were nurses hovering around him, more than usual. He saw her in the doorway and smiled.

"Do I understand there are organs for me?"

Flo nodded and walked toward him. "Yes, but remember, if they're not viable…" She couldn't even finish that sentence. She'd been over this with Kyle before.

He nodded. "I know. This could be one of those false starts you were talking about."

Flo squeezed his foot under the blanket. "I'm going to retrieve them with Dr. King. As soon as we land at LAX they'll wheel you into surgery. Dr. King will work on you, removing the LVAD, and put you on bypass."

Kyle held up his hand. "I understand. I'm more than ready, Dr. Chiu."

She smiled. "I'll see you in a bit."

A nurse handed Flo Kyle's chart on a tablet that was charged, and the means to transport the organs back. Flo took a deep breath and headed up to the rooftop. Nate was pacing and the helicopter was waiting.

It reminded her of the first moment she'd seen Nate, only this time they were riding off together and together they would save this man's life.

"You ready?" Nate shouted over the roar of the helicopter's blades.

"Ready."

He helped her load the equipment onto the chopper

before they got in. As soon as they were belted in the helicopter rose from the helipad and headed out over Los Angeles towards LAX, where the private jet was on the runway, waiting for them.

They didn't say a word to each other, not that they could've heard much over the noise of the blades. And when they were seated in the plane, they didn't say much either that didn't involve Kyle's surgery and the organ retrieval surgery. Flo would be the lead retrieval surgeon on the heart and lungs. She would hand the organs over to Nate, who would make sure they stayed stable and viable on their trip back.

Flo didn't mind. She didn't feel like talking.

She needed to keep focused on the task at hand and sent up a silent prayer for the lives that were being saved by this one person. It's what she always did even though she wasn't particularly religious, but still something she did.

When the plane landed there was an ambulance ready and waiting to whisk them off to the hospital, where the organ retrieval had started only ten minutes previously. Right now they were doing the laparotomy to make sure the organs were viable. If any organ wasn't viable then they could inform the surgeon who was retrieving the organ and the recipient could go back on the waiting list.

She fidgeted nervously as the ambulance raced through the San Francisco streets. She glanced over at Nate, who was absolutely comfortable. Or at least he appeared that way.

"You're not nervous?" she asked.

"Why would I be nervous? I've done this many times."

"What if the organs aren't viable?"

Nate sighed. "It would be too bad, but nothing I can stop. There's no use worrying about it. Why are you worried?"

"Because he's a big client. I wanted to do the laparotomy myself. I'm a bit controlling that way." That was part of the reason. She couldn't form the words and tell him that every time she went through the process she thought of the one time she'd gotten her hopes up and the organ hadn't been viable. The other kidney, which had gone to another recipient, had been fine, but the one destined for her hadn't.

And she almost hadn't survived her time on the waiting list again.

So she knew first hand what it would be like if she had to go back and tell Kyle that they couldn't retrieve his heart and lungs successfully.

When the doors to the ambulance opened, Flo jumped out and was ushered into the hospital by a resident, who took them straight through the hospital and to the ER. As she walked through the hospital she caught sight of a family.

A family in the waiting room.

A family that was grieving. They were holding each other up, mourning their loved one.

Her heart skipped a beat and for a moment she wasn't even there, because in her mind she was transported back to her own hospital bed, with hazy, tangled memories of her parents weeping and holding each other while she'd clung to life. The walk through the waiting room went in slow motion for Flo, her thoughts immediately going to her own donor.

She would never know who that person was, but if she did know she'd visit wherever they had been laid to rest and thank them.

Thank them for her second chance at life.

"Dr. Chiu?"

Flo shook her head and saw Nate was staring at her

with a concerned look and the resident was holding open the door to the OR floor.

"Sorry." She didn't glance back at the family. She couldn't.

She peeled off her jacket and hung it on a hook and then geared up, putting on a paper scrub cap and then scrubbing her hands. She glanced through the windows into the OR and saw the line of people waiting for organs.

"This will be fine," Nate said, scrubbing beside her.

"I know. It's just I don't like this part too much. I'm a surgeon and…" She couldn't even finish that sentence, because this was a life that wasn't being saved.

It was ending.

She preferred live donors. Like kidney, liver and sometimes lungs, when someone donated one lung to a loved one. There were rarely deaths in those retrievals. Those retrievals were done in love. There was a certain beauty to it.

There was a certain beauty to this moment as well, it was just that it had ended tragically for the donor.

She put on her mask and then headed into the OR, with Nate behind her holding one of the basins to collect the organs. She was gowned and gloved.

All she could do was wait. And she watched as organs were removed and people stepped forward to take them. They would be going off to different parts of the country. Saving countless lives.

"Dr. Chiu, we're ready for you now." The other surgeon moved to the opposite side of the table to assist. Flo stepped up. She closed her eyes and then went to work, but it didn't take her long. The bronchoscopy was done before the retrieval surgery to make sure that there were no signs of infection and the Gram stain came back clear.

It was now time to make sure that externally the lungs

were viable as the bronchoscopy only could see the lungs internally.

And as she carefully clamped and made ready to dissect she saw a dark spot. Her heart dropped to the soles of her shoes and she cursed under her breath as she felt the mass that grew into the pulmonary artery. She checked the heart and could see a minute dark spot beginning to grow.

Cancer.

Her stomach twisted in a knot and she tried not to be sick.

"I need to take a biopsy and I need it stat." If it wasn't cancer, maybe it was something benign and it would still be viable. She handed the specimens to the resident, who ran out of the OR to the lab.

Flo raised her hands, keeping them clean and rested while waiting, and tried not to curse. It couldn't be cancer. It just couldn't.

Nate came up behind her. "Dr. Chiu, what's wrong?"

"Look." She showed him the mass, the dark spots and where it spread.

Nate cursed, too. "Dammit."

Tears stung her eyes. If it had just been the lungs that were damaged, the heart could've gone to someone else. In Flo's case she couldn't take one and not the other, because it had to be one operation. Kyle's cardiopulmonary system couldn't stand the shock of two different surgeries. In his case it wasn't one or the other.

It needed to be both. The surgery had to happen at the same time.

Flo watched the clock, waiting for her answer. The donor couldn't be on bypass much longer. Even if the mass was benign, the organs would be useless if they were kept much longer where they were because the donor was missing other vital organs.

It was a race.

The resident returned. "I'm sorry, Dr. Chiu. It's stage-four lung cancer and the tumor originated from the heart. There's no record of any of it in the patient's file so it's highly likely the donor was unaware he had cancer."

Flo closed her eyes and cursed. "Thank you, Doctor. Would you please take the patient off bypass."

Dammit.

She tried not to cry.

The resident nodded and Flo began to close up the donor.

"I can do that," the resident said.

"No. I want to do it," she said, hoping her voice didn't crack with the emotion threatening to overtake her. She didn't want to explain to the resident why she felt the need to see this through. It was her way of thanking the donor for the ultimate gift.

A way to process the loss.

A way to thank her own donor for her life.

In fact, everything she did to advance transplant surgery was a thank-you, but, then, one could never thank someone enough for the ultimate gift. Except to live life to the fullest. The heart and lungs were not viable. She had been afraid of this, because it had seemed too good to be true. They hadn't seen it on the laparotomy because it had been on the other side and hidden. The mass hadn't infiltrated the lungs yet.

Nate had left the OR. She didn't even know he'd left, but he came back in now. "I called the clinic and told them to cancel Kyle's surgery."

Flo nodded and continued to work. When the monitors flatlined, she sighed.

I'm so sorry.

The apology was for this donor and for Kyle.

"Time of death twenty-two thirty-five." She pulled off her mask, not able to control the tears threatening to escape. "Doctor, can you finish closing for me? I have to get back to Los Angeles and my patient."

"No problem, Dr. Chiu." The resident took over and Flo dragged herself out of the OR, ripping off the paper mask and jamming it in the garbage can. Then she tossed off her gown and scrub cap, angrily throwing them into the receptacle before kicking it.

Dammit. It was so unfair.

"Whoa, what's gotten into you?" Nate asked.

"The organs weren't viable. What do you think has gotten into me?" Flo snapped.

"It happens, Flo. Why are you taking this so personally?"

Flo just rolled her eyes and began to scrub vigorously. "I'm not taking this personally. It's just frustrating."

Liar.

Of course she was taking this personally, because it had happened to her. And when it had happened to her she'd resigned herself at that moment to the thought that she was going to die. She'd been tired of fighting. No fourteen-year-old, no child, should resign themselves to dying.

She only hoped Kyle didn't.

She wanted to give him hope. It was just that right now she didn't know how.

At least the donor had saved countless other lives, just not her patient's. She finished scrubbing and they walked silently back out to the ambulance, the machine empty.

She was not looking forward to disappointing Kyle.

"I'll tell Kyle," Nate whispered, as if reading her mind.

"Thanks." Flo climbed into the ambulance, exhausted and defeated.

"I'm sorry you're taking this so hard," Nate said.

"Thanks."

"Think about all the lives that donor did save, though." She smiled. "I know. I just feel bad for Kyle."

"He'll love it that you feel bad for him. He told me the other day that he's going to make a move on you."

Flo chuckled. "What?"

"That's what he told me. He really likes it when you come to check on him rather than me. He told me he was going to steal you away from me. Not that there would be any stealing on his part."

It was a sting, but it was the truth.

Nate wasn't hers and she wasn't Nate's. Still, it hurt all the same and she didn't know why she let it hurt. Nate couldn't be hers.

It was temporary.

She couldn't let Nate in. She couldn't risk her heart again.

"I'm afraid I'll still be disappointing him when I turn him down," Flo said.

Nate cocked an eyebrow. "Oh, really?"

"I don't date guys who have a broken heart." It had been meant as a joke, but Nate's smile disappeared like she'd hurt him.

"Right," was all he said, and didn't say any more.

An uneasy tension settled between them and Flo just let it be. She wasn't in the mood to discuss things further.

It was better this way.

It was better not to get involved and not to dig any deeper.

CHAPTER NINE

NATE KEPT HIS distance from Flo for a week. Even though he shouldn't have been bothered by her *I don't date men who have a broken heart* comment, it had stung. It had been meant in jest and if it had been anyone else he might've got a chuckle out of it, but Flo had been the one to say it.

It shouldn't bother him, because it's not like he was going to do anything about Flo, but it did, because he was slowly realizing he cared about her and that was scary.

How was she getting past his walls? He didn't know, but he decided after the failed transplant retrieval for Kyle Francis that it was best he stay away from her. So after disappointing Kyle and having a long talk with him, Nate threw himself back into his work at night. During the day he avoided being in the office. He found little corners to work in and the clinic had a nice research library tucked away on another floor.

At night, he worked on his papers and spent a lot of time swimming, but even then Flo's presence was there, and every time he got out of the pool he expected to see her waiting for him.

He had to get a grip and remind himself that there was nothing between him and Flo, but he did miss her companionship. He missed their friendship. And that's why he was now standing outside her office, hesitating about whether to go in. Only he had to go in. There had been some whispers about whether or not their relationship had ended or perhaps was on the verge of ending, because it seemed the dream team was drifting apart.

Freya had noticed and Nate had just come out of a meeting with her, having assured her that the distance was nothing. He'd just been working and things between Flo and him were fine.

As fine as they could be for a fake relationship.

"The door is unlocked."

Nate turned to see Flo standing behind him, grinning at him, a sparkle in her eyes.

"You have a way of sneaking up on people, don't you?"

"I do." Flo moved past him and opened the door to her office. "You know this is your office, too, so you're allowed to come and go when you want."

"I know. I was thinking and you interrupted my train of thought." He walked into the office and Flo followed, shutting the door behind her. She took a seat behind her desk and put up her feet on it.

"Well, I'm sorry about interrupting your train of thought. You've been busy. I haven't seen you around much."

"I've been working on my research.

"What is your research about again?"

"Mostly working on ways of regenerating organs and also the possibility of robotic replacements."

She arched her eyebrows. "I'm impressed, Dr. King. I've thought along similar lines, too."

"I figured as much. You're just as passionate about transplant surgery as I am." He cleared his throat. "I just got out of a meeting with Freya and I think we need to talk."

Her smile faded. "I think I know. I had that talk with her, too."

Nate nodded. "Something happened after Kyle's failed retrieval."

"Yeah, I took it too hard. I'm sorry for acting that way." Only she didn't look him in the eye when she said that and he couldn't help but wonder if there was something else going on there. Something she wasn't telling him.

It's not your concern.

"Okay, and I do understand. It was hard on me, too. Hard to break the news to him," he said. "Freya wants us to make some public appearances together before the big gala fundraiser tomorrow night."

Flo sighed. "Oh. I forgot about that gala. I hate getting dressed up for those things."

"The investors we had that brief dinner with wanted to throw a gala to raise money for the Bright Hope Clinic and raise awareness for donating organs. We kind of have to be there."

Flo wrinkled her nose. "I know."

"So, before that gala, I think we should go out tonight. Make a few public appearances so the press will stop printing stuff about us drifting apart."

"Drifting?" A blush crept up Flo's cheeks. "Tonight. Sure. What did you have in mind?"

"Surfing."

Her eyes widened. "Are you serious?"

"Is that on your bucket list?"

"No, actually, but it could be. It sounds like fun."

"I took a look at our schedules. We're both off at three and I think we should take a drive out to Venice Beach, because it's nearby and I can show you a few things."

"You know how to surf?"

"I told you I'm a native Californian. Of course I know how to surf. I spent many summers on Venice Beach. Plus it's a pretty safe activity compared to tackling Everest or letting you drive again."

Flo chuckled. "I don't have a bathing suit here with me."

He frowned. "Well, I'm sure you can pick up something along Venice Beach. I don't have one with me, either."

She rolled her eyes but smiled. "Okay. It sounds good. I guess I can't really say no to that, but I didn't really have you pegged for the surfing type."

"Why?"

"You don't seem to take a lot of risks. Don't take it the wrong way, but when I talked about mountain climbing, you seemed pretty against any kind of risk-taking."

"I had a friend, she took a lot of risks. Maybe some risks she shouldn't have."

Flo tipped her head to one side. "What kind of risks?"

"Riding a motorcycle without a helmet, for one thing."

"I wouldn't do that one. I'm not that much of a risk-taker."

Nate grinned. "You want to climb Everest."

"Have you?"

"No." Only he didn't tell her that it had been on his list once. Back when he'd done foolish things, taken chances and lived life to the extreme. Of course that had been a long time ago. Now he was a surgeon and understood the kind of trauma that could be done to a body doing those things.

He shook those thoughts out of his head and decided to change the subject.

"Surfing isn't too bad, as long as you don't do too much of it at dusk when the sharks feed."

She sat up straighter, her eyes wide. "Sharks?"

"You'll be fine. I have to do a round because I promised James I would, but I'll see you at the front in an hour."

He chuckled to himself as he left her office and then stopped, because again she'd gotten through his walls. She made him forget that he didn't do things like surfing or rock climbing or even traveling hours out of town to drive around a drag strip.

That was the old him. Someone he'd buried years ago. Why couldn't he have suggested dinner or a movie?

That's not you, that's why.

But it was. It had been for a while now. Or at least he liked to think it was him.

Nate scrubbed a hand over his face, angry at himself for being so weak when it came to Flo. He was angry at himself for allowing the man he'd once been to come back, because that's not who he was now.

That man was long gone.

Flo walked through one of the shops at Venice Beach that sold bathing suits. Or rather pieces of thread that seemed to be woven together loosely. At least for women. It was bad enough that she'd forgotten herself for a moment and stripped down in front of him once. Something she never did, because she didn't want anyone to see her scar. If they saw the scar, they either knew what it was because they were a surgeon or they asked questions that she was not prepared to answer.

Which was why when the sales assistant kept bringing her bikinis, which were ridiculously skimpy, she turned them down.

"I want board shorts and a top that will cover my abdomen. I'm going surfing," Flo said.

The shop assistant frowned. "But this would look cute on you."

"Maybe, but, please, I just want board shorts and a top. It's only April. It's cold still."

The shop assistant sighed and went off to dig some out. Nate had disappeared next door into the store that catered to men and where he could rent a couple of surfboards for them. Hopefully he wasn't waiting for her.

"Oh, make sure it's not yellow. I heard that color attracts sharks."

"Oh, yeah," the shop assistant said, coming back with what looked like a one-piece wet suit. "Yum-yum yellow they call it on the Gold Coast in Australia. I learned that when I was studying over there."

Flo nodded. "Yeah, I definitely don't want to attract a shark."

"Well, this is a one-piece that is really popular with people who are looking for something more modest."

"I'll take it." Flo paid for it. "Can I wear it out?"

"Sure. The change rooms are in the back." The shop assistant handed her the bill. "Have fun."

"Thanks." Flo headed to the back of the store and quickly changed into the wetsuit. It was comfortable and most importantly it covered her scar. She packed her clothes in her bag and hurried outside to find Nate.

He was waiting beside his car, with two boards beside him and in a wetsuit, like her. Even though the wetsuit covered his gorgeous, muscular chest, it was tight in all the right places. He certainly filled it out well. Her cheeks heated and she tried not to think about the way he looked.

At least the scrubs at the hospital were loose on him. Shapeless.

Who was she kidding? He looked good in everything. It was almost criminal.

He smiled when she walked over to him. "Good choice, it's a bit chilly. It's only April after all."

"That's exactly why I picked it."

Liar.

She never really did think about the water being cold. Los Angeles was always warm and sometimes darned hot, but she didn't think about the water too much.

"You ready to go?" he asked.

"Just have to toss this in your trunk."

Nate opened the trunk and locked their stuff away, but pulled out a couple of towels.

"What're you going to do with your car keys?"

"My car is a classic. It was before computerized fobs." He pinned it to his wetsuit. "See no problem. Which board do you want?"

"As long as it's not yellow, I don't care."

Nate looked at her like she'd lost her mind. "You have an aversion to yellow?"

"Sharks like yellow."

"Who told you that?"

"I read something about it once. The shop assistant knew it, too."

Nate snorted and handed her a board that thankfully had no yellow on it. "Let's go then, you nut."

Flo stuck out her tongue and then jogged past him, the hot sand squishing through her toes as they headed toward the water. Thankfully there weren't many people out and about, so she wouldn't feel like such an idiot when she did a face plant or something.

She stood at the edge. The water was cold and lapped at her toes like it was taunting her. Nate set down his board and then knelt in front of her, his hands going around one of her ankles briefly.

"What're you doing?" she asked, startled.

"Proposing."

"What?"

"I'm adjusting your leash. The leg rope will keep your surfboard from being swept away if you fall, and you will fall."

"Thanks for the encouragement." She picked up her board.

"Have you ever surfed?" Nate asked as he wrapped the leash around his own ankle.

"No."

"Then you're going to fall. I haven't surfed in ages so I'll probably fall, too."

"I hope you do." And to prove her point she kicked some water at him.

"Hey!" He splashed her back, soaking her.

When she wiped the water from her eyes, he was already wading out into the water toward the swells.

What am I doing? What am I doing?

Yeah, she'd made a bucket list, but she hadn't done much about the bucket list. Though she had always had the intention of doing some of the stuff on it, her schooling and then her job had gotten in the way.

Maybe fear. Maybe Mom and Dad had been right. Maybe I shouldn't do this.

No. She wasn't going to chicken out. She'd spent her whole life being so protected and sheltered that she'd felt like she hadn't even really had a childhood. That's why she'd made the bucket list. She didn't know when her transplanted kidney might give up, but she had to *live*.

With determination she picked up her board and waded into the cold water after Nate, until she was beside him in waist-deep water.

"Glad you could join me." He smiled, that warm, charming smile that melted her heart.

"Let's do this. Show me how."

He nodded. "Okay, climb on your board. We're going to paddle out and then you're going to have to lift yourself up as fast as you can to ride the swell. Do you think you can do that?"

"I'll certainly give it a try." Flo took a deep breath and climbed on her surfboard, lying flat just like Nate.

She followed his lead, paddling out towards the swells. Thankfully they were small. She watched as Nate headed toward a larger one and, paddling faster, he leapt up with seeming ease and balanced as he rode the wave past her and toward the shore, before losing his balance and falling into the water.

Flo took a deep breath and aimed her sights on the next one. She did exactly what Nate had, paddling faster, and then tried to stand, only she couldn't. It felt like a ton of bricks was on her, and she got halfway up before the wave knocked her off her board into the water.

She surfaced, spitting water out of her mouth and rubbing it out of her eyes as she clung to her surfboard, which was now upside down.

Nate paddled toward her. "Good try. You almost got vertical there."

Flo groaned. "That was harder than I thought."

"I told you it's difficult. Do you want to stop?"

She grinned. "Not a chance."

They continued surfing until the sun began to set and she was absolutely exhausted, but that last time she stood on the board, albeit shakily, and rode the wave almost to shore, falling off in waist-deep water where Nate was waiting for her.

They picked up their boards and slowly carried them up the beach to where they'd left their towels. Flo sank down into the sand, using the towel to wipe the water from her face. Nate knelt down beside her, his blond hair plastered to his face, but it quickly began to curl in the warm breeze. He undid the leash on her leg.

"Thanks. My legs feel like Jell-O," Flo said. All she wanted to do was sink into the warm sand and sleep.

"You were awesome." He smiled up at her, making her heart skip a beat. "Better than Serena the first time I showed her."

Then his expression changed to something unreadable.

"Thanks." She could feel the blush creep up her neck. "Who was Serena?"

"A friend. She passed away."

"Was this the friend who was waiting for the organs?"

He nodded curtly. "Yeah, she's the one who lived dangerously, until she couldn't."

"Sounds like she lived life to the fullest."

"Yeah," he snorted. Something had changed. A moment ago he'd been relaxed and having fun with Flo, teaching her how to surf, and then something had changed when he'd started talking about Serena and her death. She couldn't help but wonder if Serena had been more than a friend, and that thought made her feel a bit jealous, when she really had no right to be jealous about who he had been with in the past.

If he'd even been with her.

Nate's past paramours, living or dead, weren't any of her business, as long as it didn't interfere with the facade that they were dating and had been dating for some time. That was the extent of her relationship with Nate, beyond a professional one, and she had to keep reminding herself of the fact. Though it was hard to when she found herself enjoying her time spent with him. She wanted to get to know him more.

"Well, thank you for taking me out there and teaching

me how to surf. Albeit badly. I really had fun," she said, trying to defuse the tension that had fallen between them.

"I'll take these back to the rental place and I'll be right back. Just wait here." He picked up his towel and dried off his face and hair, before picking up both boards with ease and walking back to the shop.

Flo let out a sigh of contentment and watched the sun set below the line of the ocean. The sky was full of brilliant oranges and reds. It was so nice out here and for one moment she forgot everything. She closed her eyes and listened to the waves lapping against the shore. It was calming. It made her think back to that one summer her family had spent on Whidbey Island and a particularly sunny day in the Pacific northwest. It had been one of the happiest moments of her life.

One stolen moment from her childhood that her family had had. They'd had fun and had forgotten that she'd been so sick. It was like they had just been a regular family. Not a family constantly going from the hospital to work, to home. She opened her eyes to see the sun had set completely. She hadn't realized how long they'd been surfing and her stomach growled in hunger.

"Bring your towel, Flo, and we'll rinse the salt water off."

Flo turned around and saw Nate. Her breath caught in her throat at the sight of him. He'd unzipped his wetsuit and bared his muscular chest, his wetsuit hanging around his slender waist. The afterglow of the sunset made his tanned skin glow like he was a bronzed god.

Think about something else. Quick.

Only she couldn't.

"Okay," she said, hoping there wasn't a tremble in her voice. She grabbed her towel and followed him to the showers against the surf shop where he'd rented the boards from. He pulled the cord and fresh water started raining down; she just watched him, mesmerized.

She shook off all the naughty thoughts that were going through her head and pulled the cord on the shower next to him, but nothing happened.

"It's not working?" he asked.

"Apparently not," she said, trying not to look at him. "I'll just wait until you're done."

"Don't be silly." And before she could say no he was pulling her under the water with him, their bodies close together. He ran his large strong hands over her, rinsing the sticky salt water from her body. Then he undid her ponytail, running his fingers through her hair, and she was frozen.

Her pulse roared through her body as he touched her.

No one had ever touched her like that.

No one else had run their fingers through her hair.

Then his hands came around and cupped her face, forcing her to look up at him. She realized how much he towered over her. His expression was unreadable but intense. It felt like time was standing still as she gazed up into his deep blue eyes. The water had shut off and the encroaching darkness caused the droplets of water in his hair to sparkle.

Kiss me.

Only she couldn't let him do that. It wouldn't be right, no matter how much she wanted another kiss, because she knew that kiss would lead to something more.

And she wanted that something more.

She wanted that night of passion.

Desperately. But it wouldn't be a smart move.

She broke the connection and stepped out of the shower, wringing her hair out. "That was great."

Nate cleared his throat. "Yeah, that was fun. I should take you home."

"That would be good." She picked up her towel and slipped on her flip-flops.

Nate did the same, wrapping the towel around his neck, but as they walked back to his car he took her hand. It sent a shiver of delight through her.

"What're you doing?" she asked.

"There's paparazzi here," he said in an undertone. "It's why I brought you into the shower with me."

And then she saw them out of the corner of her eye.

The shower had all been an act. The connection she'd thought they had hadn't existed. And even though it was for the best, it hurt all the same.

CHAPTER TEN

"Now, THERE'S THE hot doctor the whole entertainment world is talking about this morning!"

Nate shook his head as he walked into Kyle's room at The Hollywood Hills Clinic. Kyle was looking worse and the left ventricular assist device was starting to take its toll on him faster than Nate liked. Now Kyle sported a nose cannula and was on extra oxygen support twenty-four hours a day.

"I can't say that I'm flattered that you're calling me a hot doctor, Kyle."

Kyle snorted. "Please. As if. It's in the papers."

"What?"

Kyle tossed a trashy magazine at him and Nate picked it up to see pictures of him and Flo surfing. The caption said: *Kyle Francis's Doctors Get Hot and Heavy.*

And the caption wasn't wrong. He tried to tell himself that he'd pulled Flo under the same shower as him because he had seen paparazzi taking pictures of them. He'd done it as a stunt, but then, when she'd been so close to him, she'd aroused him.

She'd burned his very soul.

Before he'd known what he was doing, he'd been undoing her ponytail and running his fingers through her hair. He'd wanted to kiss her. Badly. But that would have been very bad, because if he'd acted on his impulse he wouldn't have been able to stop himself from making love to her right then and there.

He didn't like this loss of control. If he lost control, well, he didn't want to think about it. That carefree risk-taker he'd once been was long gone.

"She's really sexy," Kyle said, interrupting his thoughts. "You're a lucky guy. She's smart, too."

"Thanks," Nate muttered, suddenly feeling very jealous that a man like Kyle was calling Flo sexy.

So? She's not yours.

He shook those possessive thoughts away. "I came to check on how you're doing."

"How I'm doing?" Kyle asked. "Seriously?"

"Kyle, you've got to hang on. I know it's tiring…"

Kyle sighed loudly. "You know it's tiring? Do you? Have you ever waited for an organ?"

"Technically, yes. I've been waiting for yours for some time."

Kyle rolled his eyes and chuckled. "I guess you have. I'm trying my best, Doc. I'm trying."

Nate squeezed his shoulder. "I know you are."

"So what're you up to tonight?"

"Are you asking me on a date, Mr. Francis?" Nate teased.

"As if. Well, I guess sort of. You going to visit me tonight and keep me company?"

"I can't," Nate said. "Dr. Chiu and I are heading out to a gala tonight. I have to go rent a tux."

"Rent?" Kyle asked, horrified.

"Yes. I don't have my tuxedo with me. I wasn't prepared to attend any big parties out here."

"Pass me my cell, Doc."

Nate picked up the phone and handed it to Kyle. Kyle punched in a number.

"Hey, Martin. It's Kyle. Yeah, I'm good, man. Look, I need a favor. My doctor needs a tuxedo for tonight. He's about my size. I know I have something in my wardrobe. Can you bring a few of my choice ones from the last couple of award shows and we'll get him fitted. Great. Thanks, man." Kyle ended the call. "All taken care of, Doc."

"Who was that?"

"My personal assistant, Martin. Look, I never wear the same tuxedo to an award show or movie premiere twice. Usually at the end of the year I just donate them or give them to charitable auctions. They just sit there. I want you to have one."

"Thanks, Kyle. I really appreciate that."

"No problem. I'll have a nurse page you when Martin gets here and you can do a dying man one wish and show me which one you pick. Also, I would really like to see a picture of Dr. Chiu all dressed up."

"Yeah, that's never going happen, dude."

Nate turned to see Flo walk into the suite. She was smiling warmly at Kyle. "How are you today?"

"Dying apparently," Nate said.

Flo crossed her arms. "Kyle, we'll find you organs."

"I know, but can't I just milk that a little bit?" Then he flashed her that smile that melted the hearts of women everywhere. "Don't you have pity for me, Dr. Chiu? Just a bit?"

She rolled her eyes. "No one gets to milk anything around here. Haven't you heard the nurses refer to me as the difficult surgeon? I'm hard as nails."

"Somehow I don't believe that," Kyle said, grinning at the both of them.

Flo checked his vitals. "Well, Dr. King will see you

later and maybe if you're good I'll swing by in my dress. I'm getting ready here because the clinic is providing limos for everyone. So I'll take advantage of the free ride."

"Smart move." Kyle lay back down, looking exhausted.

"Get some sleep," Nate said. "I'll see you later."

He and Flo walked out of Kyle's suite and Nate shut the door.

"What do you think, Dr. King?"

"I think he needs organs sooner rather than later. He's not doing as well on the left ventricular assist device as I would've hoped."

She jammed her hands in the pocket of her lab coat. "I know. The LVAD gave his heart more time, but it's putting pressure on his lungs. They're deteriorating fast. I don't want to intubate him, his other organs wouldn't handle it for long. His chance for compartment syndrome and multi-system organ failure is high. Higher than I'd like."

Nate sighed.

Dammit.

Kyle was a nice guy. He may have been a world-famous superstar actor, but he was also a decent human being. He was in his mid-forties. That was too young to die all because he was on a waiting list.

Waiting.

Yet that's what had happened to Serena. Her injuries had been so extensive the only thing that might've saved her had been a new heart, but one hadn't become available, because she'd been so injured that the chances of her surviving a heart transplant had been low.

Then she'd gone into multi-system organ failure and she had gone before he'd even had time to process it all.

"You're thinking of your friend?" Flo asked gently.

"Why would you assume that?"

"Your expression. I may not have picked up my dad's flair for talking to a bunch of businesspeople, but I did pick up his knack for reading others."

Nate sighed. "You're right. I was thinking about her. Kyle's situation reminds me a bit of hers. I hate seeing Kyle suffer. I hate seeing him wait and slowly die when I know what the solution is. I could save him, but I'm missing two key ingredients."

"I know. Me, too. It's difficult waiting and feeling so helpless."

"Yes, helpless. I don't like that feeling very much."

"At least we can save one life tomorrow evening," Flo said.

"Eva?"

Flo nodded. "Everything is green lighted. It's time, and Ms. Martinez is ready and everything has been cross-checked. We're going to do the operation tomorrow night, because of Ms. Martinez's insurance."

"Okay. How is Eva doing?" he asked.

"She's good. She's scared and rightfully so, but I'm confident about this surgery. I did another MRI on Ms. Martinez, just to be on the safe side, and her kidneys are fine. I suggest you take the left kidney over the right."

"Sounds good."

Flo glanced at her watch. "I'd better run. Have some more rounding to do before the gala tonight. Shall we meet back up at Kyle's suite before we head down to the limo?"

"I thought you said to him, 'That's never going to happen, dude.' Changing your mind and wanting to impress the Hollywood actor?"

She laughed. "No, just letting him milk his situation a bit more."

Nate chuckled. "Okay. I'll see you here at four. That gives Kyle time to give us his best pointers for the gala."

She nodded as she walked backwards down the hall. "Right."

Nate ran his hand through his hair and headed back to the research library. He needed some time by himself, to collect himself before this gala. He was going to need all his wits about him to survive this and he certainly wasn't looking forward to wearing Kyle's tuxedo or trying on a bunch of tuxedos in front of him.

That wasn't his thing, but it was better than a rental.

At least now he didn't have to leave the hospital.

"I think that's the one, Martin. What do you think?"

Nate adjusted the cuff links and straightened the sleeve of the designer tuxedo Kyle had given him.

"I think so," Martin said. "It's the best fit. That's the one you wore last year."

Nate cocked an eyebrow. "Did you win an award in this one?"

"I did." Kyle chuckled and then waggled his eyebrows suggestively. "So it's a lucky tuxedo, too, if you catch my drift."

"I've been treating you for three years, Kyle. I *always* catch your drift." He glanced in the mirror in Kyle's luxurious private bathroom and straightened his bow tie.

Yeah, he could do this. He was uncomfortable, but it was just one night. He'd seen Flo dressed up before and this would be no different.

"Your date is here," Kyle called out.

Nate stepped out of the bathroom and then stopped in his tracks. He was not prepared for the visual assault to the senses that was waiting for him. He'd prepared himself to see Flo in a dress, but he hadn't quite prepared himself for this.

To have his breath completely and utterly taken away by her.

She looked a bit uncomfortable, standing in Kyle's suite. Her black hair swept up and off to the side, but it was the dress that caught his attention as his gaze hungrily devoured every inch of her.

Her dress was gray and flowing, with burn-out lace over top of it. The bodice was sheer with the lace strategically placed over her firm breasts. She spun around and her back was bare.

"What do you think, Doc?" Kyle asked.

Nate only briefly glanced at Kyle, who was grinning from ear to ear like a Cheshire cat. Normally Kyle's smugness about Flo would've bothered him, but he didn't care about Kyle or Martin or anyone else in the room.

He only had eyes for Flo.

And he knew at that moment he was a lost man.

Flo was shaking like a leaf; she only hoped that Nate didn't notice how nervous she was. She wasn't sure about the dress, but Freya had been the one to help her pick it out. She'd never worn anything so revealing before in her life.

She'd never gone to prom, so she'd never really dressed up.

Not that her parents would've approved if she had been asked by someone to go to prom. So this was her first real time getting dressed up to the nines.

Nate also made her nervous, because when he'd stepped out of that bathroom she hadn't been quite expecting a tuxedo or how *good* he looked. She'd seen him in a suit before, but there was just something about a designer tuxedo that made her heart beat a little bit faster.

"Well, what do you think?" she asked. "Is it too much for the event?"

"No. Not too much," Nate said. He walked over to her and took her hand in his, causing a shiver of anticipation to race through her. "It's perfect. You look...stunning." He brought her hand up to his lips, placing a kiss against her knuckles, which made her blood ignite in flames. She knew from that moment she was doomed.

"Thank you," she whispered, finally finding her voice.

Nate took her arm. "Shall we?"

"Okay," she answered, feeling like everything she was saying sounded dumb.

"Have fun, you two!" Kyle called after them. "If I wasn't laid up in this bed, Doc, you know I'd be stealing Dr. Chiu from you, so you'd better—"

Flo didn't know what Kyle was going to say as the door shut behind them. Nate was grinning and she couldn't help but laugh.

As they headed to the front, where a fleet of limos was waiting for those who were going to the gala, Flo caught sight of Freya, James and Mila standing there, waiting for Flo and Nate to arrive.

Freya covered her smile with her hand, her eyes gleaming with pride. She moved her hand and mouthed, "You look beautiful," to Flo. Even James was looking at her appreciatively.

Nate led Flo outside. They had their own private limo—the surgical dream team heading to the big gala that would raise money for the Bright Hope Clinic and many more transplant surgeries.

So it was only fitting that Flo and Nate arrived separately from the other people from The Hollywood Hills

and Bright Hope clinics, and that made Flo feel like a bit
like a Hollywood starlet.

The chauffeur opened the door and Nate helped Flo
climb into the back. She adjusted her skirt and Nate
climbed in beside her. The door shut and they were alone,
except for the chauffeur behind the privacy screen.

Nate reached down and picked up her hand, holding
it, his thumb circling the pulse point on her wrist, making her catch her breath just a bit.

"Kyle has good taste in tuxedos," she managed to say
finally.

Nate glanced down and ran his free hand over his lapels. "Yeah, well, this is designer and apparently this is
the tuxedo he won an award in last year."

Flo gasped. "You mean for *It's an Honest Truth*?"

"I guess so. I haven't seen that movie. Have you?"

"I have. It's a beautiful movie about the underground
railroad. It made me bawl like a baby."

"I'll have to watch that," Nate said.

"Maybe we can watch it together later."

He grinned. "Maybe another day. Tonight I don't
plan to watch much television. We do need to get a good
night's rest for Eva's surgery tomorrow."

Flo nodded. "You're right."

For one moment she thought he was suggesting
something else and she held her breath, but then again
why would he? This was all an act. He'd made that clear
the other night at the beach. But if he wanted to make
love to her, she wouldn't stop him.

Act or not, for once she wanted to taste that forbidden
passion. She wanted to know what it was like to take a
man in her arms and feel that moment of connection. She
wanted to experience what it was like to make love to a
man. And she hoped they'd still be able to have that after

she told him and everyone else how important transplant surgery was to her.

Nate had lost a loved one. He'd understand.

Flo couldn't hold it in any more. If she was going to give herself to Nate there would be no way to hide her scar. She had to be brave. She had to tell him that she was the recipient of a donor kidney. She'd almost died waiting and that was why she wanted to live life to the fullest.

It was time to be brave.

Nate was not Johnny.

She could do this. The bucket list was nothing if she continued to hide and not act boldly. Taking risks and doing some crazy things were one thing, but how could she be true to herself if she was terrified to keep hidden a part of her that she was proud of?

That was no way to live any more.

And Flo wanted to live. She wanted to feel.

And have a man make love to her. She couldn't think of a better person than Nate. She trusted him, she'd grown to like him, and even though nothing would ever come of their one night together, she could have that stolen time.

They didn't say much else to each other. The drive to the iconic Beverly Hills Hotel was brief. Soon the chauffeur was opening the door to a red carpet. There were flashes from cameras as Nate helped Flo out.

The investors and The Hollywood Hills Clinic had gone all out, making it a red-carpet event. The whole hotel had been rented for the night. Freya had told her that everyone would have a room, so no one would have to drink and drive.

Of course, that wouldn't be an issue for Flo. She didn't drink. She couldn't because of her transplant. Alcohol would be destructive for her kidneys and that was one thing she didn't mind missing. She had no desire to experience it.

Still, she might stay at the hotel, because when else would she be able to experience the opulence of old Hollywood by staying at a Los Angeles icon?

Nate placed his hand on the small of her back. This time, though, her back was bare and the brush of his hand on her skin made her gasp slightly. It burned even though it was hot out, but it burned in a different way. A way that made her body flush and tremble. He ushered her past the throng of press to the staging area, where couples were able to pose for their picture to be taken in front of a wall of sponsors' names.

Flo smiled as Nate put his arm around her and they posed for the camera. The surgical dream team. A force to be reckoned with.

Once their photo had been taken they were ushered into the hotel and led to the ballroom. When they entered it took Flo's breath away. On the ceiling there was a chandelier made of thousands of white flowers and twinkling lights.

There were flowers everywhere. White and sparkle lights filled up the ballroom. It was the most elegant thing she'd ever seen. They were shown to their table and took a seat with their investors.

The dinner was sumptuous, but all she could focus on was being in this amazing place with Nate by her side. He often took her hand. Champagne was poured, but she kept to water, even though there were a few curious glances. But she didn't care, because in a few moments she was going to get up there and ask a ballroom full of the rich and famous to give money to their charity and implore people to donate their organs, and she was going to tell them all why.

She was tired of hiding her kidney transplant. She never had before a man she'd loved had run from her because of it.

So Nate would soon know and she was okay with that. He was leaving anyway, but she couldn't hide it any more. He needed to know.

She wanted him to know, because maybe if then they connected in some way deeper than that moment she gave herself to him, it would mean so much more.

"Thank you all for coming here tonight," Freya said, getting the attention of everyone. "The Hollywood Hills Clinic is pleased to team up with the Bright Hope Clinic. It is our hope to continue to help this fantastic organization bring health care to those less fortunate."

There was a round of applause.

"Our first transplant operation with the Bright Hope Clinic is to help an underprivileged girl receive a new kidney, and to talk more about organ donation I am very pleased to introduce The Hollywood Hills' chief transplant surgeon, Dr. Florence Chiu."

Flo took a deep breath and stood up, making her way through the tables toward the stage. Freya stepped down and Flo was alone up there. The lights blinded her from those in the audience, but in the crowd she only saw one face. She focused on one person.

Nate.

"Hello, I'm Dr. Florence Chiu and I run the transplant surgery team at The Hollywood Hills Clinic. I'm also an organ recipient." Her breath was shaking and tears were threatening to spill down her cheeks, because it had been so long since she'd uttered those words without fear of retribution or even her own fear of admitting that her time was limited.

"I was born prematurely, and because of that I always

had health struggles. But when I was ten I collapsed and the doctors discovered my one functioning kidney was failing. I underwent years of dialysis as I sat on a waiting list. I had a couple of my own close calls, thinking that I was about to get a viable organ, only to find out that either the cross-match was negative or the organ wasn't viable.

"When I was fourteen, while I was lying in a hospital bed in Seattle, my time was almost up when my surgeon got a call from UNOS. A young man had died during a car accident, but he was an organ donor and his cross-match was almost perfect with me.

"Because of that young man filling out his donor card I'm here today, imploring you all to do the same. Because of him, I'm alive. I've been given a second chance and I chose to become a surgeon and help others like me. Like Eva. Medical professionals work hard to save lives, but you can save countless lives by donating your organs after your death. Also please think about donating financially to the Bright Hope Clinic and the amazing research that's being done in the name of transplant surgery. Hopefully one day donors won't be needed and lives can be spared while on the waiting list. Thank you for your time and enjoy your evening."

It was silent for only a moment, but then there was thunderous applause and a standing ovation, which made her cry, just for a moment.

She glanced over at Nate and he was standing, a smile on his face as he applauded her. There wasn't a sign of him feeling uncomfortable, or of him leaving because her future was so uncertain. He was still there and nodding his head in agreement.

He wasn't leaving and, best of all, he didn't look at her with pity.

There was no pity there.

She walked off the stage and shook hands with Freya, Mila and James, and then stood in front of Nate. He took her hand and kissed it again. Music started, because the dinner was over, and people began to drift out onto the dance floor.

Nate didn't say anything to her as he led her out to join them. People clapped as he spun her round and then pulled her close against him, his hand on her back.

Her knees were knocking together as she danced with him. So close to him. Her pulse raced and their gazes locked. The rest of the room was a blur to her, her only focus Nate.

All she saw was him. And she prayed her admission didn't drive him away.

"So that's why you don't drink."

She nodded. "That's why."

"Why didn't you say anything before?"

"Because I didn't want your pity."

"I don't pity you. There's only admiration here. I admire you," he whispered against her neck, making her body quiver with desire and relief. He was the first man who hadn't pitied her. Everyone pitied her.

Flo tried to swallow the lump in her throat, tears welling in her eyes. She didn't want to cry. Not now.

"Thank you," she said, finding her voice again.

"You make sense to me now," Nate said. "Before, you were so hard to figure out, but now... I get why you were so frustrated when Kyle's organs weren't viable. You've been there."

"I have."

He nodded. "You share my pain. Though it was a loved one I lost. I didn't almost lose my life."

"You still lost."

"I don't feel like I've lost at this moment," he whispered. "Being here with you, I feel...I feel like my old self again."

Her heart raced, adrenaline and desire coursing through her. If she didn't do this now, she might never do it. "I don't want to talk about that right now." And before he could say anything else she kissed him, but this was more than the featherlight butterfly kiss that she'd stolen from him when they'd been outside his hotel.

This was more.

This kiss was an invitation for him to take her, because what she wanted more than anything was to be with him. She wanted him to make her forget about her transplant, make her forget that she'd spent so many years sick and sitting on the sidelines.

Right now, she wanted to live.

He resisted at first, but only for a second, then his mouth opened against hers. His arms went around her, lifting her up on tiptoe as he deepened the kiss. His hands were hot on her bare back, holding her tight against him.

She'd never wanted someone as badly as she did Nate.

The kiss ended and she could barely catch her breath, her body quivering with desire. He rested his forehead against hers.

"Flo," he whispered.

"No, don't say anything." She took his hand and led him off the dance floor. No one was paying attention to them any more as people mingled, drank, danced and bid on the silent auction items. It was a perfect moment to lead him out of the ballroom to the elevators. She pulled the card she'd been given out of her wristlet and swiped it to summon the elevator.

Nate took her in his arms again and kissed her, pressing her against the wall next to the bank of elevators, grinding his hips against her, letting her know exactly just how much he wanted her. And the fact that he wanted her that much made her feel faint.

He wanted her, just as much as she wanted him. If they weren't wearing so many clothes, if they weren't in a public place, she would have had him right here and now, but she wanted this to be slow. She wanted to savor this time, because this wasn't permanent.

It couldn't be permanent because of her medical issue.

So she was going to enjoy this moment. They got on the elevator and her pulse was racing as they rode up to where her room was.

This was really going to happen.

The elevator dinged and she pulled him out into the hallway. She was nervous as she led the way to her room. She opened the door and flicked on the light, just one. The door shut behind them and she was suddenly very aware of him so close to her.

A tingle of anticipation ran through her.

"Florence," he whispered, using her full name.

"Nathaniel." And that was all she had to say and she was in his arms again. Kissing him. No words were needed, because she knew they both wanted the same thing. She stood in front of the bed and he was behind her, undoing the clasp on the back of her gown, the small piece of sheer fabric that held her dress up at her neck and the hook at her waist.

Once the dress was undone, he ran his hands slowly over her shoulders, pushing the dress down and off.

"So beautiful," he murmured, pressing a kiss on her shoulder. His hands skimmed over her again, and he drew the dress down over her hips so that she was standing in a pool of fabric, wearing only her slip and heels. She hadn't worn a bra because her dress had been sheer.

She was vulnerable to him and that would've scared her before, but suddenly it wasn't scary for her. It was all too real.

And she wanted it. She pulled off her slip.

He gently turned her around and her hands instinctively went to the scar on her lower abdomen, but he grabbed her wrists and held them, stopping her from covering up the scar, like she'd done before. Like she'd been used to doing. She'd thought it was so hideous, a blatant reminder to the world of her weakness. That she'd been sick, that she wasn't perfect. Then again, who was perfect?

"You don't need to hide it from me." He dropped to his knees and placed a kiss against the scar, catching her off guard. "This is part of you. This is what makes you strong."

And when he said those words a tear did escape her eye and roll down her face. No man had ever made her feel so beautiful, so wanted as Nate did right now. He stood back up and held her close in his arms. He brushed the tear from her face with his thumb.

"Don't cry."

"I usually don't, but I can't help myself around you."

"You're strong. Stronger than I thought."

He kissed her again. It was urgent against her lips as he drew her body tight against his. She began to undress him, because there was no turning back for her. First she peeled off his tuxedo jacket, then worked on the bow tie so she could get to his shirt buttons. She wanted them open so she could feel his skin and run her hands over his chest.

He took her hands and held them in his own and then kissed her again. A kiss that seared her down to her very soul. Their bodies pressed together and warmth spread through her veins, then his lips moved from her mouth down her body to her breasts.

She gasped in surprise at the sensation of his tongue on her nipple. Her body arched against his mouth and the pleasure it brought her. She'd never experienced anything like this before. Even though she was a virgin, she'd made out with a man before and it had never fired her senses so.

"I want you, so much," she said, and she was surprised that she'd said the words out loud, but it was the truth. She started to pull him toward the bed.

"Whoa, wait. I don't have protection," he whispered against her neck. "I didn't even think about it with you kissing me like that. I want you, Flo. I just never expected this."

Flo glanced at the jacket she had tossed away, cursing herself for not being prepared either, and then she saw foil from a strip of condoms sticking out from the breast pocket.

"What about those?"

Nate glanced over his shoulder and then shook his head. "Kyle. This is his tuxedo."

"I don't think he'll mind." Flo grinned.

"I don't care if he does. I wasn't going to ever ask him. I'm just going to take what I want." He scooped her up in his arms and carried her to the bed, laying her down and moving over her. She ran her hands over his partly exposed chest.

He sat up and whipped off his shirt. All that was between them now was his trousers and her underwear. Just scraps of fabric.

"There's something else I need to tell you," Flo whispered as he nibbled on her neck. "I'm a virgin."

He froze and she was worried that her virginity would be the deal-breaker. It wouldn't be the iffy future because

of the donated kidney, it would be because he didn't want
to deflower a thirty-something virgin.

"How can that be?" he asked in disbelief.

She blushed, embarrassed to tell him this, but she
hadn't wanted to spring it on him. He'd have found out
soon enough. "Do you want to leave?"

"No, I just don't understand how someone as beautiful and sexy as you still is a virgin."

"It takes a lot for me to trust anyone with my past. I'm
glad I shared it with you and that I waited."

He kissed her and she was lost, melting into him. "I'll
be gentle."

Flo sighed and he moved off the bed. She watched
him undress, her pulse racing as she drank in the sight
of him naked. This was finally going to happen and she
was more than ready.

Nate came back to her and slipped off her underwear
before holding her tight against him. She trembled and
he kissed her.

"Don't be nervous."

"I'm not."

He stroked her cheek and kissed her again, his hand
trailing down over her abdomen and then lower. Touching her intimately. Her body thrummed with desire. She
arched her body against his fingers, craving more. Wanting him. Nate moved his hand, pinning her to the bed as
he shifted his weight.

"Do you want me, Flo?" he asked some time later,
his voice hoarse.

"I do."

Their gazes locked as he entered her. She winced, but
the pain was brief compared to all the procedures she'd
gone through in her life.

"I'm sorry," he whispered.

"I'm not." She kissed him and he began to move gently. Slowly. He was taking his time. She wrapped her arms around him to hold him close as he made love to her. He kissed her again and then trailed his kisses down her neck to her collar bone. It made her body arch and she wanted more of him. She wanted him deeper and she wrapped her legs around his waist, begging him to stay close.

Her body felt alive. She had never thought a feeling like this would be possible. She had never thought that she would ever get to experience it. She'd hoped one day to, but the one man she had truly cared about had run from her when he'd found out about her past, and she wasn't the type of girl to hand over her first time to a random stranger.

Even though her relationship with Nate was not real and he'd leave once Kyle was gone, she was glad to have her first time with him. She trusted him.

Maybe love?

She shook that thought away. There was no room in her life for love.

There was just this moment.

She wanted to savor it. He quickened his pace and she came, crying out as the heady pleasure flooded through her veins. Nate soon followed and then rolled away, pulling her with him.

Flo rested her head against his chest, listening to his heart race.

Savoring her stolen moments.

CHAPTER ELEVEN

NATE FELL ASLEEP next to Flo. He hadn't intended to spend
the night. He hadn't spent the night with anyone since
Serena, and for one moment he had forgotten how *good*
it felt to be with someone again. To spend the night next
to someone, listening to them breathe.

Knowing that they were alive and not a ghost, haunting him.

He propped himself on one elbow to watch her sleep.
A little crack of sunlight peeked through the drapes and
a light warm breeze was blowing in through the sliding
glass doors, but she was oblivious to all of it.

She was so beautiful with her ebony hair fanned out
on the pillow, her plump lips pressed together in a pout
and her delicate hands folded together on top of her chest.
A strand of her silky hair curled around a pink nipple
and he had to tear his gaze away from her, because he
wanted her again.

It took all of his willpower not to wake her up and take
her in his arms again, but he couldn't do that. He'd had a
moment of weakness and that was all. There couldn't be
any more. No matter how much he wanted it. Memories
of being buried in her, wrapped in her arms, were still
fresh in his mind. The feel of her tender, soft lips against

his, her nails down his back and her legs around his waist as he'd thrust into her fired his blood more.

Flo stirred and then opened her eyes to look at him, a blush creeping into her cheeks. "Good morning."

"Good morning," he replied. "I hope I didn't wake you."

"No. You didn't. I forgot you were there for a while. I didn't know where I was at first."

He chuckled. "You've already put me from your mind, then?"

"No, I just haven't slept that well in a long time." She stretched and rolled over on her side, tucking her arms under her head. "What time is it?"

Nate glanced over at the alarm clock behind him. "Six a.m. Early."

"Well, we did skip out on the gala early." Flo laughed softly. "Yes. I'm sure we'll get an earful when we get back to the clinic."

"Right. We'll have to head there soon. Today is the big day. Eva's transplant surgery."

Flo nodded. "It is."

"How are you feeling about it?" Nate asked.

"I'm feeling good."

He nodded. Everything about Flo impressed him, but it had all made perfect sense to him when she'd told the audience why they should become organ donors, why she didn't drink and why she understood her patients so well.

And why she felt every loss, why she connected with her patients so deeply. Then it occurred to him that she had a bucket list and had made several references to fleeting time.

"This bucket list of yours," he said.

"What about this bucket list of mine?" she asked.

"Why do you have it? Is it just for fun or something serious?"

"It's serious. I spent all my childhood on the sidelines due to overprotective parents who thought I might shatter at any moment. So I started compiling a list of all the things I wanted to do when I became an adult. I haven't done much because of schooling and work, but life is short. Failure rates are high. Who knows how much longer I have left?" Flo rolled over and began to pull on her clothes.

Who knows how much longer I have left?

"Flo, you realize that as you had your transplant at fourteen, you know you're doing quite well. You've come so far."

"I know," she said offhandedly as she put her long hair back in a ponytail. "Still, I do want to *live* while I have the chance."

"What else is on this bucket list? I know driving was on there."

She glanced over her shoulder at him. "You seriously want to know?"

"Sure."

"Well, you know about the mountain climbing, like Everest or walking the Annapurna trail. I would like to ride a motorcycle through Africa. Or swim with sharks."

"Hold up, you were terrified of sharks when we were surfing."

She chuckled. "I know, but this would be in a cage."

Nate sat there listening to her talk about all these dangerous things she wanted to do. Things that he'd done himself, so he knew for a fact how risky they were, and he couldn't figure out why she wanted to do these things. She'd been given a second chance, why would she risk throwing it all away by doing something dangerous?

"I also want to do some rock climbing and tackle El Capitan in Yosemite."

That caught his attention and caused his stomach to clench as the memory of Serena slipping out of his grasp as she'd fallen from the halfway point of El Capitan all those years ago. It made him sweat, made him sick to his stomach to think about Flo up there.

She could fall. She could die. Just like Serena had. And then what would he do? And the fact she evoked this feeling in him, these emotions scared him. Made him retreat further behind the careful walls he'd built for himself.

Walls that were there so he wouldn't get hurt again, because he never wanted to feel that kind of pain again.

El Capitan was too dangerous. Risking her life for all these foolish bucket-list ideas was too dangerous. Why did she have to do these things?

It's not your concern.

She was throwing it all away, but he couldn't tell her that because it wasn't his business. They weren't anything to each other. This whole relationship had just been an act to protect The Hollywood Hills Clinic.

Once everything was done with Kyle and Eva he'd go back to New York. That's where he belonged.

Besides, a fling with a colleague was probably on Flo's bucket list, he just didn't want to know that. It was better it was left this way.

Is it? She did give her virginity to you.

She had to get rid of it some time. He was just the one she'd chosen. He should've refused. He shouldn't have let her kiss him. He should've been stronger.

"Sounds like your bucket list is pretty sorted." He rolled out of bed and started to get dressed; he could feel Flo's gaze boring into him.

"Are you okay?" she asked.

"I'm fine. I just want to have a shower and go over some stuff before tonight." He zipped up his pants. "Maybe catch a nap. I didn't sleep much last night."

She laughed and then pulled on her dress from the night before. She had a change of clothes but she wanted to feel the fabric on her skin and to relive the memory of everything that had happened for just a little longer. "Can you help me with the back?"

"Sure." He took a deep breath, trying not to forget that she was off-limits to him. So he quickly did up the clasps that he had been more than happy to undo the night before. Once they were done up he took a step back, because he knew that if he didn't put distance between the two of them he was liable to fall back into that sweet trap again.

She turned around and touched his face. "Thank you again for last night. I'm glad it was you."

"I'm glad, too."

Are you?

"I hope you know that I don't expect anything. I don't—"

"I know," he said, cutting her off. "I appreciate it."

She didn't look convinced, but he didn't want to spend the day talking about this with her. He didn't have time for that.

What's done was done and he could move on.

Can you?

Flo walked back into the hospital. She'd gone home from the hotel, had taken a shower, a power nap and drunk a whole lot of coffee to get her up to fighting standard for Eva's big surgery this evening.

She wasn't going to let Eva down.

Flo was going to do everything in her power to make sure that this kidney stuck. That it wasn't rejected. Not that she had any power over that. Rejection happened, but she was going to do her best to get Eva to fighting standard, as well.

As she walked to her office she caught sight of Nate, standing at a nursing station. He was typing something into one of the tablets and she could see a couple of the nurses eyeing him with admiration.

She couldn't blame them.

Just looking at him made her weak in the knees. Even more so now that she knew what was under those scrubs. She knew what he felt like and the memory of his lips on her skin, his body beneath her thighs, his hands in her hair made her blood heat and made her recall the pleasure he had made her feel.

Pleasure that she'd never thought was possible.

Her body responded to just the mere thought of him.

It scared her.

She was glad that Nate had been her first time. It's what she'd wanted and she kept telling herself that it was just a fling, nothing more. Yet the more she said it, the more ridiculous it sounded to her; the more she realized that being with him had probably been a huge mistake for her heart.

It was more than just a fling to her and that was terrifying.

Flo shook the little kernel of thought that there could be something more out of her head. They were just friends. Work colleagues. Both of them had always made that clear. There could never be any more.

If she tried to make it more than it was she'd get hurt. Hadn't she learned already that there was no room in her life for romance or any kind of emotional attachment beyond her immediate family?

Nate was all fine and dandy now with her kidney transplant, but he knew the facts. He knew that her time

was precarious. Eventually he'd leave for someone more
stable.

So, no, there couldn't ever be any more between them.

Even if she secretly wished there could be.

She tore her gaze away from him and tried to make it
to her office without being seen by anyone. She needed
a few moments alone to regroup and prepare for Eva's
surgery. There was a lot riding on it.

This was the first transplant surgery arranged between
The Hollywood Hills Clinic and the Bright Hope Clinic.
She knew there was some stuff from the past between
the Rothsbergs and Mila Brightman, something about a
wedding—Flo really didn't know. All she knew was she
had to be on her top game.

This surgery meant a lot and the world would be
watching.

She was well aware that the news of this surgery had
reached far beyond Los Angeles, because the email from
her father that morning and the countless text messages
from her mother had let her know exactly how far the
news had spread.

They weren't concerned about the surgery and whether
or not she could pull it off. They wanted to know who
Nate was and why she hadn't told them about her relationship with him. How could she lie to her parents?
She'd never lied to them before. There was nothing to
say about the relationship between her and Nate because
there was nothing there.

Really?

There was something there, at least on her end, but
she refused to admit it. She refused to give in to her emotions, because there was no place for them.

There was no place for love.

And putting a name to the emotions was out of the
question.

She got to her office and sat down. The light on her phone was flashing and she had no doubt some of those messages had to be from her parents. The rest would be from various newspapers and magazines, wanting updates on Kyle's condition and her relationship with Nate. Flo had no time to deal with any of that.

She didn't want to deal with that.

Not today.

"I was wondering what time you were going to come in," Nate said as he barged into the office.

"I had a nap. You said I should nap."

"So I did." He set down the tablet he'd been carrying and sat down on the couch. "Are you ready for tonight?"

She nodded. "I think so. You?"

"I am. I did a few laps in the pool this morning after I got back to my place. I needed to take the edge off. I've done kidney surgeries countless times, but today… I don't know what it is but I feel a bit on edge about it. Like I'm under pressure."

"Yeah, I understand. I'm feeling the same way." Flo leaned back in her chair. "There's a lot riding on this."

Nate nodded. "Look, about last night…"

She shook her head. "I don't want to talk about last night. Not right now. I just want to keep my focus on Eva."

"Fair enough. Nothing from UNOS?"

"You mean about Kyle? No, nothing." Flo scrubbed her hand over her face. "Have you been to see him?"

"I have his recent labs here." Nate handed her the tablet. "It's not good."

Flo glanced at the vitals and the labs from first thing this morning to only an hour ago. Kyle's condition was deteriorating rapidly.

Blast.

"He needs organs."

Nate nodded. "He needed them yesterday. If it continues to climb this way he's going to go into multi-system organ failure and then there's nothing we can do. He'll die."

"Yeah, and the world will say we're responsible." Flo groaned. "What're we going to do?"

"There's nothing we can do. We just have to wait. It's the hardest part. We'll continue to draw blood, monitor his situation and just hope for the best."

"Have faith?" she asked.

"Yeah, that, too." He smiled at her. It was a kind and tender smile. It made her swoon. There were so many things she adored about him.

Stop thinking like that. Get a grip on yourself.

"It's hard to have faith. It's hard to sit here and wait for someone else to die so that our patient can go on living." It was the one thing she hated about the job.

"I know." There was a change in Nate's demeanor, as if he'd pulled away. He could barely look her in the eye. She didn't like that.

At least he's not pitying you, like everyone else.

"How are we going to attack this surgery? We've talked about our plan before, but never really firmed up details."

Nate nodded. "I think that I should retrieve it and you should reattach it."

"Have them in the same OR?" Flo asked. "We have an OR that is large enough and has been put on hold for me indefinitely."

"I think that's wise. Less travel time for the kidney. Less chance of contamination, and it minimizes the cold ischemic time or for something else to happen. This kidney is Eva's best shot."

Flo smiled. "Is it? And you're the one who wanted to wait for a deceased donor kidney."

"I know. You were right."

She grinned and leaned back. "Say it again."

Nate laughed and rolled his eyes. "You. Were. Right."

"I know."

"So does that plan work for you?" Nate asked.

"Yes. I'll let the surgical team know." Flo stood up. "For what it's worth, I'm glad you're going to be with me tonight. It's going to make the surgery so much easier having such a skilled transplant surgeon working with me."

"My pleasure," Nate said quietly.

She nodded and left her office quickly. If she stayed she might say a few other things that she wanted to say. Things that she wasn't sure she wanted to even admit to herself.

Like the fact that she was very close to falling in love with Nate.

Something she'd promised herself she wouldn't do when she'd slept with him, but that was easier said than done.

CHAPTER TWELVE

FLO STOOD AT the door to Eva's suite. The nurses were milling about, taking care of last-minute preparations on Eva. Eva looked absolutely terrified. Flo knew exactly how she was feeling and seeing the terror on Eva's face brought it all back afresh to her. At The Hollywood Hills Clinic she did a lot of transplant surgery and consultation on transplants. She'd even done a lot of kidney transplants with both deceased donors and living donors. But they had all been adults.

She hadn't worked on a child since her days as a resident and even then she hadn't done a kidney transplant on a child ever as a lead surgeon and not an assist. There were a few technical differences. Eva was twelve so it would be similar to doing the procedure on an adult, but, like Flo, Eva had been a preemie. Her vessels could be smaller, which meant Flo would have to try a different approach. She wouldn't know until she got in there and that was the maddening thing about surgery and the practice of medicine.

At least it was maddening for her.

Skill-wise, the surgery was the same. Ms. Martinez's kidney would be of adult size and the donor kidney would be placed in the same location as Flo's had been, the cradle of the pelvis. Technically, everything would go easily. Of that Flo had no doubt, but emotionally this was harder than she had ever imagined.

You need to talk to her.

Flo took a deep breath and headed toward Eva. The nurses finished up and left the room, and Flo took a seat on the edge of the child's bed.

"It's okay to be scared," she said.

Eva looked at her. "It is?"

"Of course, but I will tell you it will be okay. You'll feel better."

Eva shrugged. "How do you know it will be okay?"

Flo lifted up her scrub shirt. "See this scar?"

"Yeah."

"When I was fourteen I was the one in a hospital bed, waiting for a kidney."

Eva's eyes widened. "You?"

Flo nodded. "Me. Only my mom and dad weren't a match. I had to wait a long time. I almost didn't make it while I waited for someone special to give me a second chance. You're very lucky. Your mom was a match."

"I don't want my mom to get hurt."

Flo squeezed her hand. "She'll hurt for a while. You will, too, but it would hurt your mom far worse if she didn't do this and something happened to you."

Tears rolled down Eva's face and Flo hugged her. "It will be okay. You'll both heal and this will be behind you. Then I want you to do something for me."

"What?" Eva asked, wiping her eyes.

"I want you to live. Make a difference."

She smiled. "How?"

Flo shrugged. "That's up to you. I became a surgeon who helps people like us. Your future is up to you now, because you *have* a future, thanks to your mom."

"Dr. Chiu, we're ready to take Eva down now," a porter said from the door.

Flo nodded and then stood. "I'll see you in a bit and I'll see you on the other side. Just think, no more dialysis. You'll be able to play sports within reason, learn to drive. Go to dances."

Eva smiled. "That's a good thing."

Flo chuckled and walked out of the room and headed toward the OR floor. There were always risks associated with organ transplants. Always. The graft could fail, Eva's body could reject her mother's organ, but she had a good feeling about this surgery.

The allograft survival rate was high for those who got a living kidney compared to people like her who had received their kidney from a deceased patient. She also completely trusted Nate, who was doing the retrieval.

Before she had really got to know him, when he'd first arrived, she had looked him up. Read his research papers and discovered that he was one of the surgeons who could do a live donor kidney retrieval laparoscopically. Flo knew what a technical challenge it was to do a retrieval that way, but Ms. Martinez's recovery time would be exponentially cut in half.

She'd only be in the hospital two to four days compared to the six to eight weeks if it was done via laparotomy. They hadn't even been sure that they could do it laparoscopically on Ms. Martinez until after Nate examined her and found her health in good order. She was the perfect candidate.

The large OR was big enough to allow Flo to work on Eva and allow Nate and the laparoscopic equipment to be on the other side of the room.

She headed into the scrub room and ran into Nate, who was scrubbing up. He glanced at her. "How is Eva doing?"

"She's scared. Unsurprisingly." Flo stepped on the foot pedal to start the water. "I told her it would be okay."

"Normally I wouldn't tell a patient that, given all the variables, but I have a good feeling about this one." Nate smiled at her. "Ms. Martinez is very determined."

Flo nodded. "You can't get in the way of a mama bear protecting her cub."

"Is that what it is?"

"Sure, of course." Flo chuckled. "My mom was a force to be reckoned with in the children's hospital where I had my surgery done."

"I can see that. You're sometimes a force to be reckoned with." Nate shook water off his hands and grabbed a paper towel. "I think this will be okay. I'm very skilled."

"I know you are," she teased, causing him to laugh.

"I meant at laparoscopic surgery."

"I know." Flo glanced through the window into the OR. She could see Ms. Martinez on the surgical table, mouthing words with her eyes closed. It took Flo a fraction of a second to realize she was praying.

"I'll see you in there," Nate said, disappearing through the sliding door into the OR.

Flo finished her scrubbing and sent out her own silent prayer. She needed this to work. She'd promised Eva. As she finished scrubbing, Eva was wheeled in to where she got to reach out and hold her mother's hand, just briefly, before being taken to the opposite side of the OR.

She herself walked into the OR, where a nurse helped her into a gown and gloved her. Flo headed over to Ms. Martinez, who was crying.

"Ms. Martinez, it's Flo."

Ms. Martinez glanced up at her. "I'm sorry for crying."

"Don't be sorry. Everything will be okay. It will be

fine. I'll take good care of Eva and Nate will take good care of you. She'll come through like I did."

"You?"

Flo nodded. "Me, and I was only two years older than Eva at the time."

Ms. Martinez nodded and Flo walked toward Eva. The scrub team was going over the safety precautions and Ms. Martinez was put under general anesthetic. Flo glanced back once to watch Nate as he went into action.

That part was in his hands now. He'd retrieve the kidney and Flo had to prepare Eva so that when the kidney was brought across the room, she could start implanting it.

"Flo?" Eva said questioningly through the oxygen mask.

"I'm here, Eva. Can you count back for me? It's time to sleep."

Eva nodded and started to drift.

Flo turned to the nurse. "Insert a catheter and then a bag of methylene blue and Ancef. I want to make sure I can see her bladder and not hit the peritoneum or bowel."

"Yes, Dr. Chiu."

Flo took a deep breath and waited for the dye and the catheter. All she could think about was the time she had been on the table in Eva's place. Eva had a better shot than she herself ever had.

You're here, though. You beat the odds.

Once she had successful confirmation that everything was a go, she got ready to work. All that mattered was making sure that Eva had the best shot at success. When that press conference took place tomorrow afternoon, she wanted to walk in there and tell them that the first transplant surgery between The Hollywood Hills Clinic and the Bright Hope Clinic had been a complete success and that mother and daughter would both make a complete recovery.

That was what Flo focused on as she worked and prepared the area.

As she readied the field where she would connect the kidney she heard, "Walking with the kidney."

She glanced up to see a surgical resident from the Bright Hope Clinic walking toward her with the kidney in a metal bowl full of ice. A perfect, healthy kidney, which had been taken from mother and was about to be implanted into the daughter.

Ms. Martinez had given Eva life. Twice.

It was a beautiful thing. It was a bit of joy.

The resident who was assisting her took the bowl from the other resident and prepped the kidney with solution, getting it ready for Flo to implant it in the intraperitoneum as Eva's external iliac vessels were too small. A slight change of plan, but one that Flo could easily handle.

"Walking with the kidney," her resident called as she carefully scooped up the kidney and handed it to Flo.

Flo cradled the kidney in her hand, marveling at it. Such an important organ. Just as important as any other organ and the most wonderful gift that she herself had been given. In time Eva would understand too what a gift she'd received.

A second chance at life.

Flo placed the kidney into the cavity and began the anastomosis. Eva's arteries and veins were delicate and her mother's donated kidney a little large, but she'd get it to work. Nate came over and stood on the other side.

"Can I assist you, Dr. Chiu?"

"Is Ms. Martinez okay?"

"She's on her way to Recovery. Everything is good and she came through beautifully."

Thank God.

"You can help," Flo said. "Her vessels are small and anatomizing to the aorta is a bit tricky. I was hoping she'd have larger vessels, being twelve, but her premature birth stunted some things."

Nate leaned over. "You're doing great and almost there." He continued to offer her words of encouragement as well as check on Eva's condition.

The blue dye allowed her to see the bladder when she attached the ureter.

And when she was done the kidney pinked up and a stream of urine shot out, letting her know that the kidney was functioning.

"Excellent job, Dr. Chiu!" Nate exclaimed as the surgical team applauded.

Tears stung Flo's eyes and she laughed when she saw that stream of urine. "Let's close her up."

Nate stepped in and they closed her up, making sure everything was where it was supposed to be. A pressure dressing was placed on the wound then Eva was rolled into the post-anesthesia recovery unit, where she would be extubated from her general anesthesia.

When that stream of urine had flowed, Flo had wanted to shout for joy, because the surgery had been a success so far, but there was still recovery and monitoring of Eva in the ICU to make sure that she didn't reject the organ or have stenosis or a clot. There were still so many risk factors for Eva, but so far she'd taken a step in the right direction.

There was still a long road to go, which was why Flo didn't want to give an update on Eva until tomorrow afternoon.

Right now she was exhausted.

She peeled off her surgical gown and mask, stuffing them into the appropriate receptacles, before scrubbing out.

Nate was beside her again.

"Good work, Dr. King," Flo said.

"Removing a donor kidney is easy—you had the hard job."

"Your job was just as technically challenging, Nate. Don't sell yourself short."

He smiled at her and toweled off. "How should we celebrate?"

"Celebrate?"

"We have to celebrate a bit."

"How about a pizza at my place? Usually I wouldn't have someone over to my place, but I'm wiped out and don't have the energy to bike home."

Nate laughed. "So that's why you're inviting me over. Sure. We can do that."

"Thank you." Flo dried her hands. "I'm going to check on them post-op and give my orders. Then pizza."

He nodded. "I'll meet you out front in an hour."

Nate watched Flo leave the scrub room.

What are you doing?

He really didn't know. After what had happened between the two of them last night and his absolute loss of control, he'd promised himself that would never happen again. For one moment, being with her now, he'd forgotten that he didn't do those kinds of things any more. They weren't a real couple.

He swore he wouldn't do things like surfing or racing or one-night stands again.

Nate strode toward the exit, mad at himself for letting

Flo in. It had been so easy for her to get past his defenses, under his armor. He couldn't let that happen tonight.

He'd celebrate with her because what they had just done together, saving Eva's life and completing a successful kidney transplant, was something worth celebrating. He could celebrate with Flo as her friend, because that's all it could be.

He had to remember to keep his distance after this.

He had to remind himself why he was here and that being in California was only temporary. His life was waiting for him in New York.

A lonely life.

A lonely life it may be, but it was what he deserved. He'd lived too recklessly as a young man and it had cost a life. Loneliness was the penance he gladly paid.

Or at least it had used to be.

CHAPTER THIRTEEN

"DID YOU CHECK on Ms. Martinez?" Flo asked as she rummaged around in her fridge.

"I did," Nate said as he took a seat at her island. Flo's apartment was small and her tiny table was covered with an assortment of medical journals and papers. At least the piles were neat. She seemed to thrive on orderly chaos, if that was possible. So they were having their pizza celebration dinner at her kitchen counter. Which was fine.

If he didn't get too comfortable he wouldn't have the impetus to stay or linger.

"How was she?" Flo asked.

"Relieved." Nate smiled to himself as he recalled telling Ms. Martinez how well the surgery had gone. How her daughter was strong and stable in the pediatric ICU and being monitored, and that so far there wasn't any sign of rejection.

The joy on her face made his job worthwhile.

Though both he and Flo had their phones out in front of them. Ready to jump at a moment's notice if a call came from the hospital that something was up with Eva or Ms. Martinez. Or if there were organs for Kyle again, because Kyle was not doing well.

His time was running out and that weighed heavily on Nate.

He'd been Kyle's physician for a long time and watching Kyle slowly die was taking its toll on him. He wanted so much for organs to be found, but his hopes were waning fast. He was losing patience. He wanted organs for Kyle so Kyle wouldn't die and so he could go home to New York. There were too many ghosts in California for his liking.

Los Angeles brought up too many bad memories. He also had to get away from Flo. Distance would be the best for them.

"How about grape soda? It's not wine, but I can't have wine."

"Sure," Nate said. "You know that it's okay for you to have alcohol every once in a while."

Flo shrugged. "I know. Two units a day, but really I don't want to risk it. Alcohol raises your blood pressure and I want to keep my kidneys for a long time."

She set down a tumbler and poured some grape soda into it.

"I feel like I'm ten years old during summer vacation." He took a sip and winced. "Just as I remember."

"It's not that bad." Flo then pulled a piece of paper out of her pocket and set it down in front of Nate.

"What's this?"

"It's part of my bucket list. It's what I want to do to celebrate Eva's successful surgery. I told her that she needed to go on living when she recovered."

A sense of dread filled Nate as he unfolded the paper and found himself staring at a picture of El Capitan in Yosemite. The sheer rock wall brought back the moment, which had been over a decade ago, flooding back to him, like it was fresh and new all over again.

"Hold on, Serena. Please hold on."

"I can't. I can't."

Nate crumpled the picture in his fist, trying to drown out the screams in his head.

"What're you doing?" Flo asked shocked.

"This is a bad idea," Nate said.

"Why?"

"El Capitan is the tallest vertical face. It's three thousand feet high from base to summit. Do you know how dangerous it is to climb?"

"I'm aware of how tall it is, but a lot of people climb it."

"Skilled climbers, and even then they die!" he shouted at her. Didn't she get it? She'd been given a second chance at life, yet she kept wanting to do these risky and strange things. Why was she trying to end her life? She'd been given a second chance when Serena hadn't. Flo was reckless.

You were reckless once, too.

"What has gotten into you? Why are you so angry?"

"Why are you throwing away your life?"

She took a step back from him, confused. "Throwing my life away?"

"Yes. You've been given a second chance so why are you risking your life, doing these dangerous things? Why do you even need a bucket list?"

"I need a bucket list because I don't know how much time I have left," she snapped.

Now it was his turn to be confused. "You said that before. What're you talking about? You had a kidney donation. Is your kidney failing?"

"No, but you know the failure rates. How long can a deceased organ really last? It may not last a lifetime. I've already surpassed fifteen years. I don't have many left."

"Do you hear yourself? You've passed fifteen years and aren't in renal failure. Why are you risking your health, wanting to do dangerous, stupid things? You avoid alcohol and I would say that's a lot safer than climbing El Capitan. You're throwing your life away."

It was like a slap to the face. She'd thought he would understand her passion to try new things. She'd told him how she'd spent her life on the sidelines, watching and never able to participate. Flo had thought he understood her.

She'd thought that he didn't pity her, but apparently she'd been wrong, because he was treating her like a fragile thing. Like she was about to shatter at any moment if she continued to try and live her life.

"I'm not throwing away my life. I'm living it until I can't any more."

"You still have years left, but if you continue down this trajectory, you won't. You'll get yourself killed and what kind of thanks would that be to your organ donor?"

He was stifling her. Just like her parents always tried to do. This was why love and romance wasn't for her. Fall in love and suddenly that other person tried to control your life. "How dare you? You don't know me."

"Don't I?" Nate rubbed his face.

"No. You don't. I'm making the most of my time. I'm not being ungrateful by putting my life at risk. I'm living my life to the fullest."

"No, you're not, because you don't understand the consequences."

"And you do?" Flo asked.

"I do." His expression changed from one of anger to one of sadness.

"I'm sorry you lost a friend while they waited on the list, but this isn't the same thing."

"Of course it is. They wouldn't have acted so recklessly."

"I'm not reckless. And what would you know about that? You're so rigid and guarded. You said you used to climb mountains, so why don't you any more? What happened?"

Nate sighed. "Before I entered medical school I lived like you. I took risks. In fact, the riskier the better as far as I was concerned, and my girlfriend Serena lived the same way. We were adrenaline junkies. We were also experienced rock climbers. We were always at the gym, practicing rappelling. We knew what we were doing until we didn't.

"Then, during a climb, halfway up El Capitan, Serena's rope slipped, the carabiner failed and she fell. She died in the hospital with multiple injuries, needing organs, but there were none to be had and she was far down the list because of her trauma. It was my fault she died. I don't remember if I checked everything as thoroughly as I should've. That's why doing these risky, foolish things is a waste, Flo. You're risking your life for a second of adrenaline. A minute of thrill. That's it. Life is not worth that."

Flo was saddened to hear his admission. He'd been carrying around guilt for so long that it had eaten away at him. She'd thought he was pitying her, trying to hold her back, like her parents did, because he didn't think she could physically do it, but it was something more.

He was afraid for her.

He was angry at her.

Nate claimed that she was wasting her life by doing such risky things, as if her time was up. And maybe he was right, but he was wasting his own life, letting the ghosts of the past hold him back. He was hiding behind walls of guilt and pain.

It was tragic Serena had died and that he blamed himself, but he was throwing away his own life by not living. Two people had died on that mountain, Serena and Nate.

"You have lots of time left, Flo. Don't risk that time by doing something stupid," Nate snapped.

"You're one to talk."

"What's that supposed to mean?"

"It means at least I'm out there, trying to live."

He snorted. "That's not living."

"And hiding behind guilt, letting guilt keep you back from ever having happiness again, is living? Maybe you're the one who needs to start living again. Maybe you need to take some risks."

Nate didn't say anything else to her. He just turned on his heel and left her apartment. The door slammed behind him.

Flo sighed. It had hurt, saying those things to him. She hadn't wanted to, but he'd said some hurtful things to her.

Only he's right.

She bent down and picked up the crumpled picture of El Capitan. Did she really want to do this?

No. Not really. She'd picked it because it had been the most advanced thing she could think of. Nate did have a point. Why was she so adamant on doing stuff she wasn't capable of doing? Maybe after some training she could tackle El Capitan.

Maybe Nate was right about it all.

Had she been so bent on proving to the world about what she could do, because for so long everyone she cared about had said she couldn't, that she was really risking this precious gift she'd been given? And in that pursuit she'd pushed away everyone, including the man she was in love with.

The realization hit her hard because even though she didn't want to fall in love with Nate, she was in love with him. And she had been so scared about him pitying her or keeping her from doing what she wanted that she'd pushed him away.

The tears began to flow down her face and there was no stopping them.

All these years she'd thought she'd been living her life, but she really hadn't been.

Flo didn't sleep well that night so instead she headed back over to the hospital and spent the night in the ICU next to Eva, watching her urine output and monitoring her vitals. There was no sign of Nate and it was better that way.

After what had happened between the two of them, Flo doubted she'd ever see him again outside work and the facade they had to put on. Even then, they seemed to have convinced the press a while ago that they were indeed dating, because the furor had died down.

There was no story to tell.

No scandal.

Everyone was just waiting for organs for Kyle Francis.

All she had to do was get through the press conference about Eva and, thankfully, she could present good news. She just hoped that she could hold it all together in front of Nate. Her heart was racing as she entered the press room. Freya and Mila were waiting for her and a smattering of press was assembled.

Flo shook their hands and smiled, silently letting the two of them know that the surgery had been a success. That she was here to deliver good news rather than bad. She glanced around, but Nate was nowhere to be seen.

And she was a bit disappointed.

What did you expect?

Flo took the podium and the din of chatter died down. "Thank you all for coming here today. Last night at ap-

proximately nineteen hundred hours Eva Martinez and
her mother were taken to the OR at The Hollywood
Hills Clinic where a successful live donor transplant
took place. Ms. Martinez went through a laparoscopic
left kidney retrieval performed by Dr. King and came
through her donation with flying colors. Her surgery
was minimal compared to an open dissection method."

As she said his name the door opened and he slid
in, standing at the back. His face was unreadable as he
leaned against the wall with his arms crossed.

Ignore him.

"I performed the anastomosis of Eva Martinez's kidney with implantation onto the aorta and IVC, intra-
peritoneal."

"Can you explain why you chose that method over
using the external iliac vessels?"

"I approached it this way because Eva's vessels were
too small given her age," Flo said. "Pediatric external
iliac vessels can be too small sometimes."

The reporter nodded and jotted down notes.

"Eva is doing well in the ICU and is expected to a
make a full recovery."

There was applause and that's when Nate began to
make his way to the front. Her heart sank. She prayed
it wasn't Eva.

"I'm sorry for interrupting," Nate said. "Dr. Chiu, can
I speak with you a moment?"

Flo stepped away from the microphone and Nate
leaned over, whispering in her ear, "There are organs
for Kyle across town."

Then, before she could say anything further, he moved
away from her, like he couldn't stand to be near her,
and left the press room. Everyone was watching her, the
room silent.

"I'm afraid I have to leave. Thank you, everyone." Flo

quickly turned on her heel and ran out of the press room, ignoring the rapid-fire questions of people asking if this was about Kyle. She'd let Freya and Mila deal with that mess. They were better at it.

Right now she had an important job to do.

Kyle didn't have much time left. He needed those organs.

Please, God. Let them be viable this time.

And since it was across town she'd get there in time to perform the examination of those organs herself this time.

Nate was waiting outside the press room.

"I'll prep Kyle. You go and get the organs," he said quickly. Then he handed her her cell phone. "You forgot this in your office. You almost missed the UNOS call."

"Sorry. Okay, and thanks."

He nodded, but he wouldn't look at her. "Call me when you have the organs. There's an ambulance waiting for you."

Before she had a chance to say anything else he turned his back on her and walked away, off to prep Kyle. Flo headed to where the ambulance was waiting for her. They had the equipment she needed and once she was in the back of the ambulance the paramedic shut the door and the siren blared. They took off across Los Angeles.

Flo's heart hurt, but, really, what had she expected?

She'd ruined her chances with Nate. After Kyle's surgery, he'd return to New York and she very much doubted she'd see him again.

It nearly killed Nate to see Flo. He'd planned to keep his distance from her today, but then he'd got the message from UNOS and had had to face her.

At least he had the excitement of telling Kyle about the organs to distract him.

It killed him to watch Kyle suffer. But now he had a real chance.

Kyle was conscious, but barely, as Nate walked into his room.

"Hey, Doc," Kyle whispered.

"Good news. We've found organs again. Dr. Chiu is on her way to retrieve them. This time they're not so far. Only across town. We need to get you prepped and into the OR."

Kyle smiled weakly. "That's great, but forgive me for not holding my breath. Also because I can't really. Bad lungs."

Nate chuckled. "Yes. Please, don't."

"So, you never did tell me how the tuxedo worked out."

"Didn't I?" Nate said, trying to ignore Kyle's questions. He didn't want to talk about Flo here. It was too raw.

"No. You didn't. Come on, what happened?"

"We went to the gala and raised money."

Kyle rolled his eyes. "Come on. There's been sexual tension between you two from day one. You're telling me nothing happened?"

Nate shook his head. "Really not going to talk about this with you."

Kyle grinned. "I knew it. How was it?"

"We have to draw some more blood from you before you go into the OR. I have your blood type ready and standing by for surgery."

"Come on," Kyle said. "Why don't you want to talk about your relationship with Dr. Chiu?"

"Because there is no relationship. It was a ruse. I kissed her accidentally on the rooftop once and then had to pretend I was in a relationship with her, but really there's nothing there."

Kyle's eyes narrowed. "You're such a bad liar, Doc. You care for her."

He's right.

Actually, it was more than caring for her. Nate loved Flo. He loved how strong she was. Even though she was a bit pessimistic about her own donor kidney, she still was out there, trying to live, and what had he been doing with his time? Hiding away behind guilt.

"I don't."

"I don't know why you're not admitting it when it's…" Kyle trailed off, his eyes rolling into the back of his head as he collapsed.

"Kyle?" Nate tore off his white lab coat. "Kyle?"

The monitors went nuts and Kyle flatlined.

"No, Kyle! No." Nate lunged forward and hit the code button. He lowered Kyle's bed and began CPR compressions. He couldn't shock the LVAD with an AED. As he fired off instructions for medicines, he continued his compressions.

Oh, God. Oh, God.

Kyle wasn't going to survive his own transplant surgery. No, he couldn't let his friend, his patient die. He just couldn't.

Come on. Come on.

The monitor picked up a heart rate, but every time Nate stopped compressions, Kyle crashed again.

Dammit.

His phone began to ring and a nurse picked it up.

"Dr. King, it's Dr. Chiu. She's got Mr. Francis's organs and they're viable. She said to get him into the OR."

Nate cursed under his breath and jumped onto Kyle's bed, not stopping his compressions. "Get us to the OR, stat."

The team moved quickly and Nate continued his chest

compressions on Kyle as they rolled them out of his suite and to the OR.

Nate hoped that Flo would get to them on time.

CHAPTER FOURTEEN

FLO HAD HEARD on the way back to The Hollywood Hills Clinic that Kyle had crashed. She moved as quickly as she could, yelling at people to get out of her way as she raced to the OR. When she got to there she learned that they had Kyle stabilized and Nate was performing his cardiectomy.

She scrubbed and then entered the OR. One of her younger surgeons was taking the organs and readying them for transplantation. A nurse helped Flo into her gown and she was gloved. She approached the surgical table and could see that Nate was about to remove the LVAD.

"The organs look good?" Nate asked, not looking up.

"They did. They're viable."

He nodded. "I will have the heart removed and then we can place it and work on the lungs. It will be a long haul."

"I know," Flo whispered. "Look, about—"

"I don't want to talk about it. Let's focus on Kyle, shall we?"

"Of course." Flo took her place as assist to Nate and she watched him work with bittersweet sadness, knowing that soon he would be going back to New York and she wouldn't see him again.

Even though she had resisted the idea of them pretending to be a couple to protect The Hollywood Hills Clinic, these last weeks had been the best time of her life. She'd had that bucket list for so long, but she had never really done anything about it.

Until she'd met Nate.

Not that he'd done anything risky with her, but he didn't treat her like she couldn't do things. He encouraged her, he treated her like she wasn't going to shatter at any moment, like her parents had always done.

She'd never minded being by herself. It was easier than risking her heart, as she had learned earlier on, but now that she'd had a taste of being with someone she cared about, someone she loved, she was going to miss Nate.

She was going to be lonely for a long time.

Focus.

Flo returned to the task at hand. They removed the left ventricular assist device and then went about removing Kyle's damaged heart. He was put on bypass and then they removed the lungs. The donor organs, which were in the icebox on a heart-lung machine, were brought forward. Flo took on the lungs while Nate worked on the heart.

No words were needed as they worked seamlessly together. It was like they'd been doing this kind of surgery together for years. Kyle lost a lot of blood, but blood was ready on standby for transfusion.

It was a grueling eight hours, but Flo didn't feel it. Adrenaline fueled her and when breaks were needed she took a shot of espresso, which was kept just outside the OR. Two transplant surgeries in a row and she was feeling exhausted.

"Remove the clamps," Nate said. "Let's take him off bypass."

Clamps were removed and the bypass machine was

shut down. Nate glanced at her and Flo nodded and sent up a silent prayer.

Come on.

As the machines started, Kyle's new donor heart pinked up and began to beat. His lungs moved as he took breaths. There was clapping and Flo laughed out loud.

Nate was grinning behind his surgical mask—she could tell by the way his eyes were crinkling. "Let's close him up, Dr. Chiu."

"Indeed, Dr. King."

They finished closing up Kyle, inserted drains and tubes and had him off to the post-anesthesia recovery unit. Later, if there were no problems, he would be moved up to the intensive care unit. Flo didn't plan on leaving the hospital at all. She was going to monitor Kyle all night. She peeled off her gown and disposed of it before scrubbing.

"I'll stay with Kyle tonight," Nate said. "He's my patient after all."

"Are you sure?" Flo asked. "I don't mind staying with him."

"He's not your patient. He's mine. I want to monitor him and when he's strong enough we'll take him back to New York. That's what he wants. He wants to go back to New York to recover. His parents are there."

Flo nodded and finished scrubbing. "We've managed to keep things quiet but we should speak to Freya and Kyle's people about giving a press conference about the surgery."

"You're not going to be there?"

"No."

Nate sighed. "For what it's worth, I'm glad you were in there with me."

Tears suddenly and unexpectedly stung Flo's eyes, but she wouldn't let them fall. "Me, too."

Nate left her alone and she leaned over the sink of the scrub room, letting the tears fall. Tears of regret, hurt and most of all relief.

She didn't want him to go, but she'd ruined that.

So it was best he went. Besides, how could she love a man who didn't want to be loved in return? A man who still clung to the past and punished himself for that?

The answer was that she couldn't.

Nate didn't bother changing or shaving. He just made sure his scrubs were clean. If the public wanted a press conference so badly after he had just finished an eight-hour surgery, then they could see him like this.

He walked into the press room, blinded a bit by the flashes, and took the spot at the podium.

"Thank you all for coming. As you are aware, a donor for Mr. Francis was found in a hospital about forty minutes away from The Hollywood Hills Clinic. Dr. Chiu retrieved the heart and lungs, which were found viable. After removing Mr. Francis's left ventricular assist device, Dr. Chiu and I successfully removed Mr. Francis's damaged heart and lungs and replaced them with the viable organs."

"How long did the surgery take?"

"Approximately eight hours. Mr. Francis will be in the intensive care unit for some time."

"How is his prognosis? Will he make his Broadway debut?"

"His prognosis at this moment is stable. The next forty-eight hours will give us a better picture," Nate said. "As for his Broadway debut, that will be on hold for some time. Mr. Francis's recovery will be long and he will be on anti-rejection drugs for the rest of his life."

"Where is Dr. Chiu?" someone shouted, and as Nate glanced at the man he saw Flo, in her street clothes, sneak into the back of the room. No one noticed she was there.

Seeing her made his pulse race.

Why had he had to ruin it? Why did she have to live so dangerously? The loss of control he felt around her was too much for him to bear. He had to put distance between them, even though he loved her.

"Dr. Chiu is monitoring our patient in the ICU."

"Once Mr. Francis is stable and returns to New York, what will become of your relationship with Dr. Chiu? Is this the end of the dream team?" There were a few chuckles.

"We'll see how a long-distance relationship goes." He glanced to where she was standing, but all he saw was Flo's back as she left the press room.

It killed him to hurt her.

Why did he have to hurt her?

Because you can't lose her, too.

And that was it. She was so determined to *live* her life and he wasn't. He was too scared to move forward. Too scared to lose someone he loved again that he was willing to damage his own heart.

"Now, if there are no more questions about Mr. Francis's surgery, I would really like to get back up to the ICU floor and monitor my patient." Nate excused himself, even though there was still a barrage of questions coming at him. He ran out of the press room to try and catch Flo.

There was no sign of her.

He cursed under his breath and made his way up to the ICU. When he got there, he checked on Kyle. He was still intubated, but his vitals were good. For someone who had just had a heart and lung transplant, he was doing well.

And Nate could recall the way his friend's heart had stopped under his hands. How he'd almost lost him.

"Serena, come back to me."

Only there had been no heartbeat under his hand when he'd held her. There had been nothing, just the sound of the doctor pronouncing her time of death.

When he held Flo in his arms, she was alive. She was here. Serena would want him to live on. She wouldn't have liked him living as he had been for the last decade.

Serena had been full of life.

She'd lived life to the fullest, just like Flo wanted to, and he'd never called Serena out on what she did. He'd never called her selfish for risking her life. Yet he did that with Flo.

Flo, who had fought so hard for her life.

She deserved to live it the way she wanted, and who was he to get in the way of that.

Because you don't want to lose Flo the way you lost Serena.

And that was the crux of it.

Only he didn't think he had much of a shot with Flo any more. Not after the way he'd been treating her, and he wasn't sure if he was brave enough to let Flo live the life she deserved to live. Maybe it was better for them both that he'd be leaving soon.

Flo hadn't seen Nate in three days. At first she'd thought he'd gone back to New York, but she learned from Freya that Nate was still in LA. He seemed to be working the opposite shift from her.

Which was probably for the best.

Maybe if she didn't see him again it would hurt less when he left for real.

Yet as she stood in her office, staring at the white lab coat neatly folded on the couch—his lab coat, with one of his scrub caps tucked inside—it hurt so much.

She'd thought she'd been in love before, but that wasn't true. The pain she'd felt after Johnny had left her had been nothing compared to this ache she was feeling.

I have to get out of this office.

She headed up to the ICU floor, where Kyle still was, although he would be moved back down to his suite soon if he kept doing as well as he was. Nate wasn't anywhere to be found, so Flo walked into Kyle's room.

Kyle opened his eyes and smiled, but winced just slightly. He was trying to show her that he wasn't in pain. She'd heard from one of the ICU nurses that he was trying to put on a brave face.

Flo couldn't help but chuckle. "How are you today, Mr. Francis?"

"I think I've told you to call me Kyle."

Flo nodded. "So you did. So how are you today, Kyle?"

"Sore," he whispered. "Tired. I don't think I've ever been this tired before in my life."

"Your body is healing and trying to get used to a new heart and lungs. That's a big deal."

"So I've heard." He rolled his head to one side. "How did it go, in your opinion?"

Flo sat down on the end of his bed. "It went as well as I expected. You're not showing any signs of rejection or any other post-op complications. I think that if you stay stable, tonight we can take you back to your private suite and in a month we'll have you back on that plane to New York."

"Oh," Kyle said, and he looked disappointed.

"I know you wanted to make your debut on Broadway but—"

"No, it's not that." Kyle swallowed hard. "I'm terrified, Dr. Chiu. I'm terrified at this gift I've been given."

A lump formed in Flo's throat. She understood what Kyle was feeling. There were so many times she felt that way, too. It was overwhelming.

"I understand. It's a gift that you can never send a thank-you note for. The greatest gift of all."

Kyle nodded. "That's it exactly. What if something happens...?"

"You can't live your life with the what-ifs. I lived like that for so many years." Flo sighed. "I had a kidney transplant at fourteen and I was grateful for my second chance and wanted to live, but I let my fear of life ending at any moment drive me. I felt that if I was going to die I was going to die on my own terms and not let an organ determine when that was going to happen."

"You've had a transplant?"

Flo nodded. "I know how you feel. The weight of having an organ from someone who died, it's a precious thing and I don't want you to squander it, Kyle. Live life, but live it to its proper fullest. Don't push away loved ones because of the off chance that your life might end. I mean, we never know how long our second chance at life will last, but living that second life alone...it's a life not worth living."

A tear ran down Kyle's cheek.

"That's it exactly. How long can this last?"

Flo shrugged. "I don't know. There are so many factors, but I think if you take care of yourself and the gift that you've been given, you can live a long while yet."

"Does this fear ever go away?" Kyle asked.

"No," Flo said. "It never goes away, but if you have

someone who loves you and you love them then it makes
it all worthwhile."

"Thanks, Dr. Chiu."

"Flo, remember?"

Kyle smiled. "Flo. Although I prefer to call you Florence, if you don't mind. I fell in love with a girl from
Florence. She was the love of my life."

"What happened to her?"

"I let her go. The worst mistake of my life, but maybe
Broadway will have to wait a little while yet. I think when
I get back on my feet I'll be heading back to Italy. I want
to see if I can track her down in Florence."

"I wish you all the best, Kyle." Flo got up and left
Kyle's suite before she started bawling. She wished she
hadn't pushed Nate away.

She wished she could have a second chance and tell
Nate how she felt, that she wanted him and that she
wouldn't risk her life in such a way any more.

For so long she'd lived her life saying that she wouldn't
let anyone control her, tell her what she could and couldn't
do, but really that didn't matter in the long run. What
mattered was love.

What mattered was not pushing away those who loved
you.

Life was not worth living without love.

Nate stood in the shadows and watched Flo walk away.
Her head hung low and her hands were jammed in her
pockets as she walked toward her office. When he'd first
met her she'd held her head high and run through these
halls with purpose, with drive.

This Flo was just as heartbroken as he was.

He'd come up to check on Kyle before he'd planned
on finding Flo. He'd wanted to say goodbye and thank

her again, but when he'd come to Kyle's room in the ICU he'd been shocked to hear her open up to Kyle.

To say the same things he felt about her.

He was scared. He'd been living a life of guilt and fear for so long, but that was no way to live. Flo lived a different fear, but she lived a fear nonetheless.

She just didn't let it stop her from living. Whereas he had.

He loved Flo and if she forgave him, he would spend the rest of his life making it up to her. So instead of making a stop to see Kyle he chased after Flo.

"Dr. Chiu," he called out.

She stopped and turned around, surprised to see him. "Dr. King? I thought you'd left for the evening."

"No, I was working in the research library. Can we talk?"

Flo nodded and he took her arm, leading her to her office. When they were both inside he shut the door.

"I'm sorry, Flo," he whispered.

"Sorry for what?" she asked.

"Sorry for trying to stop you from living your life."

"Nate," she sighed. "You didn't."

"I did. I just... When you said you wanted to climb El Capitan I became terrified. I couldn't lose you, Flo. Not after losing Serena. I couldn't bear it if I lost you."

She gasped. "What?"

"I love you, Florence Chiu. I think I loved you from the moment I first met you. I just wouldn't let myself."

"You could still lose me, though, Nate."

He shook his head. "I don't care. I know the risks, but I don't care what will happen. I doubt anything will happen to your donor kidney, but if something happens I will be right by your side. I'm not going anywhere. I'm here for the long haul. You breathed life into me again. You saved me."

"I thought I pushed you away. I've pushed away everyone. I thought I had so much to prove with that dumb bucket list, but I have nothing to prove. I let my fear rule my heart."

Nate took her in his arms and held her close. "I love you, Flo. I'm not going anywhere."

"I love you, too."

He tipped her chin and kissed her, holding her tight in his arms. She was alive. She was here and she was his.

A relationship that had started out as a facade, all because the person he used to be, the man he'd thought he'd buried a long time ago, had snuck out and kissed her. When he'd been told that he would have to pretend to be in a relationship with Flo he'd felt nervous, because he'd known that if he spent time with her he'd fall for her.

In her he saw who he used to be.

And he missed who he used to be.

With her, he could be so much more and he planned to never let her go.

Flo laid her head against his chest and sighed. "So what happens now? A long-distance relationship?"

"No, I think I'll be moving to LA. James offered me a job."

"Oh, he did?"

Nate nodded. "Also, I could really use a vacation."

"Vacation? I don't know the meaning of that word."

"I think you should learn. I think we both need a two-week vacation once Kyle is stabilized. I think we should accompany him to New York City, get him settled and my stuff dealt with, and then drive back out here. What do you think?"

"Drive across country?"

He nodded. "It was on your bucket list."

Flo groaned. "Don't even talk to me about that bucket list. It's done. It was for someone who thought she was dying. I have time."

"How about an anti-bucket list."

"What's an anti-bucket list?"

"A list of things we do while we *live.*"

Flo chuckled. "I like that idea much better. That's better than my bucket list. You're better than my bucket list."

And then she kissed him again and this time he didn't let her go.

EPILOGUE

One year later

FLO TOOK A deep breath and stood at the edge of Whistlers Mountain in Jasper National Park, staring eastward out at Canada. It wasn't Everest, but it was the highest mountain she'd ever been up, and the fact she was standing at the top, the air so cold and clear, was amazing. She could see for miles and miles. The sun was above them, but it was still morning and it was chilly. Which didn't surprise her as there was snow up at the summit of Whistlers.

Nate came up beside her and sighed, slinging his arm around her shoulder as he stood beside her on the top of the mountain, looking out at the small town of Jasper spread below their feet.

"It really is in the shape of the letter J." Flo pointed. "I didn't believe the hotel clerk when she told us."

Nate chuckled. "So untrusting."

"I trust people." She took a step away from him. "Although you have been acting mighty suspicious lately."

"I have not. See, you're totally untrusting."

"Well, you have been surprising me a lot lately. It's so unlike you." Flo grinned. "All this risk-taking."

"It's not really risk-taking, and are you telling me you don't like this surprise?"

Flo laughed and wrapped her arms around Nate. "I liked the surprise trip to Canada and I liked the surprise of climbing a mountain, even if we didn't really climb very far and it wasn't really that difficult."

"I thought taking a tram would be a nice foray into mountain climbing."

She raised an eyebrow. "The private cabin with the spring-fed hot tub is really nice, too, but it seems a bit posh. Did Kyle give you the idea?"

"He did. He knows the owners and managed to finagle a deal for us." Nate kissed the top of her head. "He wanted to do something to thank us for saving his life. He's doing a play on Broadway, but passed on the singing and dancing for now."

"That's good. I love Kyle, but he's not a singing and dancing type of actor," Flo said. "Don't tell him I said that though."

"I won't, or he'll be heartbroken. He still threatens to steal you away from me."

Flo snorted. "I'd like to see him try."

That earned her another kiss. She sighed and saw more people were taking the hour-long hike up to the summit of Whistlers. They moved off the path and headed out toward the glacier, trying to keep off to the side to enjoy their stolen moment of privacy.

Since Nate had started work at The Hollywood Hills Clinic and since their successful surgery on Kyle and the little girl Eva Martinez, people had been flocking to Los Angeles, wanting the dream team of surgeons to work on them.

Flo couldn't remember when she'd been so popular. Nate had also managed to get some more grant money for his research and he was starting a huge clinical trial at The Hollywood Hills Clinic. They hadn't had a proper vacation since they'd driven across the country together after saving Kyle's life.

They'd flown with Kyle to Manhattan and got him set up. They'd closed down Nate's practice in New York and moved him back out to Los Angeles. It had been a crazy road trip, and they'd stopped at a lot of touristy places on the two-week drive back to Los Angeles.

They had seen the Liberty Bell, had ridden on a river boat on the Mississippi. Had spent a night in the French Quarter in New Orleans, had seen Graceland and the Grand Canyon. They'd hit as many states as they could on their way back to Los Angeles. They'd even spent a night in Las Vegas before they'd meandered their way up to Seattle so that Nate could meet her parents and, of course, her *nainai*.

Surprisingly, her parents got along well with Nate. Usually both her mother and father disapproved of her dating anyone because of her health problems, but apparently that was all in the past because they wholeheartedly approved of Nate.

And Nate got along well with them.

After Seattle they'd taken a trip down to San Francisco, where Nate's parents now lived. Flo had been nervous, she'd never gone and met parents before, but they were delightful. When they'd returned to Los Angeles they'd found a bigger place near The Hollywood Hills Clinic so they could live together, and then they'd both thrown themselves into their work.

They hadn't killed each other yet.

It had been a great year.

Then last week Nate had surprised her by telling her he'd cleared her calendar. Their patients were all stable. No one was currently in dire need of organs and if they were, Nate had brought in one of his colleagues from New York to cover for them.

He'd booked two weeks off for them. They'd flown into Calgary, Alberta and then driven up to Jasper National Park, where a very private cabin had been waiting for them. The only connection they had to the outside world was a television that was hooked up to an old DVD player. The cabin had a large selection of old movies for them to watch if they got bored.

So far, Flo was not bored.

They had been hiking, they'd been to the Miette Hot Springs. They'd been white-water rafting and out to dinner. In fact, Flo was feeling a bit tired.

She was used to mountains, having grown up in Seattle, but she'd never been to the top of one. So even though she was exhausted from the supposedly relaxing, romantic vacation, she was glad to be standing at the top of this mountain, drinking in the sights around her.

Mountain climbing had been one of the things at the top of her bucket list and she knew this moment was hard for Nate, given his past. So even though they technically hadn't climbed Whistlers, other than an easy walk to the summit, the gesture was appreciated all the same.

"Thanks again for bringing me..." She trailed off when she saw that Nate had dropped to his knees. Her heart thundered in her ears. Maybe she was hallucinating. Maybe this was altitude sickness and she should get down off the mountain. "What're you doing?"

"Proposing."

She sighed in relief. "Oh, right, just like when we were surfing. Are we going to walk out on the glacier and you have to attach some kind of strap to me?"

He looked at her strangely. "No, this isn't like when we were surfing."

"What?" She began to shake. "Are you…what?"

He pulled out a box. "Flo, I'm actually proposing."

"Marriage?"

"Yes. Flo, I asked your dad's permission before we left. He was okay with it. He gave us his blessing, as did your mom. The question is, will you marry me?"

She couldn't answer him as she stared at the silvery diamond ring. She hadn't been expecting it. It was something she'd never thought twice about, because it was something she'd thought she'd never get to have, and now she was staring at it and she couldn't even find her voice.

All she could do was nod. Nate grinned and slipped the ring on her finger and then kissed her hand, followed by her lips.

"I'll take that as a yes, since you didn't fight to take the ring off."

Flo laughed and wrapped her arms around his neck, pulling him down to her so she could kiss him again. "Yes. That was most definitely a yes."

"I love you, Flo Chiu. You brought me back to life. You reminded me that life was worth living. I wanted to bring you up to the top of a mountain, in a place that was new to both of us, a halfway point for both of us, a place that would just be ours, and ask you to be my wife."

Now the tears fell down her cheeks. She'd been so guarded all her life, never showing her fear or any of her emotions. She hadn't wanted her parents to worry and she hadn't wanted to be looked at like she was weak, so she'd guarded her heart until the day that helicopter had landed on the top of The Hollywood Hills Clinic and changed her life forever.

Since then, it was hard for her to lock those emotions away.

She didn't want to lock that piece of her away.

She looked down at her ring, sparkling in the bright morning sunlight at the top of the world, or at least the highest she'd ever been, and she couldn't believe what a year it had been. Full of changes, full of opportunity, and even though her future was still a bit uncertain, she knew that she had the strongest man at her side. Her rock.

"Well, at least my suspicions about you were well founded."

"How's that?" Nate asked.

"I knew you were up to something. I just never expected this."

"Well," he said, pulling her tight against him, "it was risky. I mean, your dad did lecture me for a long time about wanting to marry his little girl. I also had to put up with your sister and brother. Thankfully your mother and *nainai* were easy on me."

"Yet you still took a chance on me."

He nodded. "You're a risk I'm willing to take, because you're the surest thing in my life and no matter what the future holds for us, I want us to be together forever."

"I feel the same. Though you might change your mind in a few months' time."

He frowned. "What're you talking about?"

"Wedding preparations. My mom told me horror stories about trying to plan her wedding with Dad. Do you really want to even attempt that? I mean, my grandmother in Atlanta is just as stubborn as my *nainai* and when you put the two of them together..." Flo shuddered. "Your mom is so nice. I think she might get eaten alive."

Nate laughed out loud. "How about neither?"

Flo was intrigued. "What are you proposing now?"

"A trip to Vegas after Jasper and eloping."

Flo laughed out loud. "I love it and I'm totally in.

Though you've probably just ruined your relationship with my parents and grandmothers."

"It was your *nainai*'s suggestion, actually."

Flo chuckled. "When do we leave for Vegas?"

"Tomorrow. I have it all arranged."

"You were so certain that I was going to say yes, then?" she teased.

"Yes, it was a risk I was willing to take."

* * * * *

Look out for the next great story in
THE HOLLYWOOD HILLS CLINIC
THE PRINCE AND THE MIDWIFE by Robin Gianna
Available June 2016.

And if you missed where it all started, check out

SEDUCED BY THE HEART SURGEON
by Carol Marinelli
FALLING FOR THE SINGLE DAD
by Emily Forbes
TEMPTED BY HOLLYWOOD'S TOP DOC
by Louisa George

All available now!

MILLS & BOON®

MEDICAL ROMANCE™

THE ULTIMATE IN ROMANTIC MEDICAL DRAMA

A sneak peek at next month's titles...

In stores from 19th May 2016:

- **The Prince and the Midwife** – Robin Gianna *and* **His Pregnant Sleeping Beauty** – Lynne Marshall

- **One Night, Twin Consequences** – Annie O'Neil *and* **Twin Surprise for the Single Doc** – Susanne Hampton

- **The Doctor's Forbidden Fling** – Karin Baine
- **The Army Doc's Secret Wife** – Charlotte Hawkes

MILLS & BOON®

Mills & Boon have been at the heart of romance since 1908... and while the fashions may have changed, one thing remains the same: from pulse-pounding passion to the gentlest caress, we're always known how to bring romance alive.

Now, we're delighted to present you with these irresistible illustrations, inspired by the vintage glamour of our covers. So indulge your wildest dreams and unleash your imagination as we present the most iconic Mills & Boon moments of the last century.

Visit **www.millsandboon.co.uk/ArtofRomance** to order yours!

0516_AOR